Black Music of Two Worlds

JOHN STORM ROBERTS

WILLIAM MORROW & COMPANY, INC.
NEW YORK • 1974

Copyright © 1972 by Praeger Publishers, Inc.

A Morrow Paperback Edition published by arrangement with
Praeger Publishers, Inc.

First Morrow Paperback Editions printing 1974.

All rights reserved. No part of this book may be reproduced or
utilized in any form or by any means, electronic or mechanical, including photocopying, recording or by any information storage and
retrieval system, without permission in writing from the Publisher.
Inquiries should be addressed to William Morrow and Company, Inc.,
105 Madison Ave., New York, N.Y. 10016.

Printed in the United States of America.

1 2 3 4 5   78 77 76 75 74

Library of Congress Catalog Card Number 74-6472

ISBN 0-688-05278-9 (pbk.)

CONTENTS

Part Three: The Music of Postcolonial Africa

PREFACE

In any book covering a field as wide as this one, a good deal must be left out, and a good deal must be touched on very rapidly. Above all, boundaries have to be set. I have not dealt with the "white" styles of U.S. music containing very important black elements, whether folk music, country-and-western, or rock. These are essentially black-influenced white styles, just as many of the styles I have described in this book are white-influenced black styles. In an area such as this, any definition can have holes picked in it. I have therefore deliberately used terms such as "black" or "Afro-American" in their broad, sometimes vague, but generally understood senses. The concept of black music is an imprecise and changing one. To be more precise is to be too precise. Black music, in this book, is music created *mainly* by people who call themselves black—or music containing significant elements derived from Africa, whoever plays it. At times I have probably strayed beyond these definitions. But the importance of considering the Afro-American musical area as a whole is so great that it seems to me worth the risk of some inconsistencies and even apparent self-contradictions.

It is worth mentioning what this book is *not*. It is not a straightforward history of Afro-American music. Too much is unknown about the black music of South America and the Caribbean for a history to be written about it; and there are already many histories of black musical forms of the United States. In view of this, I have had to tackle the different regions rather differently: I have included rather less straight description of styles in the United States than other countries. The facts about black U.S. music are pretty well known, but the question of Africanisms is still a much-argued one. The opposite is true of South America and the Caribbean.

The Afro-American musical area is one with a common background—the encounter of African and European music. The early chapters of this book deal with aspects of this encounter seen as a single phenomenon with effects that resembled or differed from each other for regional reasons. By the late nineteenth and early twentieth centuries, however, its component areas had developed very differently in many respects. The second part, therefore, looks at the music of the various regions separately.

Louis Armstrong is said to have remarked, when asked a question about folk music, "I ain't never heard no horse sing." Afro-American music includes folk music, urban popular music, and occasionally bubble-gum music. Too many books have been published condemning one or another style for reasons that boil down to the fact that the author has not liked them. I hope I have avoided this. On the other hand, criticism of individual pieces of music seems to me perfectly valid. I got involved in Afro-American and African music because I thought it marvelous —and I still do. If this has led me astray at any point, I can only quote Mary Frances, in Brumsic Brandon's cartoon strip *Luther:* "I got just as much right to be wrong as anybody else."

Errors of enthusiasm are one thing; errors of fact are another. If I have made many of the latter, I may perhaps comfort myself by remembering the obvious mistakes I have encountered in the works of famous authorities of all sorts. I hope the reader will therefore approach this modest effort in the same spirit as that shown by a Jamaican Revival Zion pastor who, interrupted once at length by a mentally afflicted member of his congregation, observed, "Wise people can learn from the words of foolish people."

ACKNOWLEDGMENTS

So many people have been so helpful in so many ways that it seems wrong to select—but I owe a special debt of gratitude to the following:

Mr. and Mrs. Eustace Brissett of Barton Court, Saint James Parish, Jamaica, for their warmth and hospitality;

Tony Cox, who suggested and produced the BBC African Service series that was the germ of it all;

Philip Harrington, for a great deal of technical help and general kindness;

David Lewiston, for more of the same;

Mrs. Stephanie Lloyd, Douglas, and Sandra, of Long Pond Estate, Jamaica, and Clem Lloyd of New York;

Alfred McLarty, who helped find singers and organize recordings in Maryland, Jamaica, as well as singing superbly himself;

Tomás Morel, of the Museo Folklórico Tomás Morel in Santiago de los Caballeros, Dominican Republic;

Jane Roberts, my wife, for typing, editing, proofreading, and assisting in the research, as well as for general exhortation;

Carey Robinson, of the Jamaica Broadcasting Corporation;

Dr. Manuel Rueda, Director of the Dominican Conservatory of Music, eminent folklorist, musician, poet, and dramatist;

Max Salazar of New York, whose unpublished study of Latin Jazz confirmed much of what I believed, and taught me more;

Dr. Aaron Segal, for introductions that proved very fruitful;

Bob Stack, for a great deal of help and for his loan of Latin records;

Mr. and Mrs. Bob Staples of Maryland, Jamaica, for warmth, hospitality, and help (as well as for employing, and introducing us to, Alfred McLarty);

His Excellency Dr. Adolph Thompson, Jamaican Ambassador to the Dominican Republic, and Mrs. Thompson, for their hospitality;

Bernard Vega, for putting us on the rightest of tracks in Santo Domingo;

Jeremy Verity of the BBC External Services, for sharing his Jamaican expertise and contacts;

The Walker family: Boysie and Jean in Philadelphia; Mas' Aaron, Mrs. Walker, and Valerie at Chatham, Saint James, Jamaica;

Mr. and Mrs. Tim Williams of Dover, Massachusetts, who came to the rescue so that we could do field research without our two children;

all the people in many record companies, from whom it would be wrong to single out individuals; and

most of all, all those who ever made the music that this book is about.

1 INTRODUCTION: AFRICA, EUROPE, AND ISLAM

The subject of this book is the meeting of two—and, as we shall see, possibly a third—musical traditions to create a fourth, and the development of this fourth tradition into a range of new styles of great richness and international impact. By the end of the last chapter, we shall have explored all these musical traditions in varying detail. But first it is worth taking a look at some of the main differences and similarities among African, European, and Arabic musical styles.

It is important to get away from the idea—a hangover from the old "Dark Continent" nonsense—that African music was for centuries cut off from the rest of the world; that it existed in some limbo or cultural Garden of Eden, unsullied by outside influences, until the colonial era, when it was raped by outside forces; and that it has never been the same since. In fact, Africa has always been in contact with other parts of the world. An ancient Greek wrote about the East African Coast in the *Periplus of the Erythrean Sea*, and ancient Greek musical instruments have been found near Khartoum. Chinese plates of the thirteenth century have been dug up in Mombasa. North Africa was an area of myriad musical influences. It had heard Phoenician, Greek, Roman, and Byzantine music before falling to invaders who brought an Arabic music containing elements of Coptic, Syrian, Egyptian, and Persian music—and even, some think, Indian. When the Arabs invaded Spain (with a Moor at their head), they founded European Islamic kingdoms the last of which was cast out seven hundred years later, in 1492, the year Columbus arrived in the New World. And there were always links between Muslim Spain and Muslim black Africa through North Africa. When the Arab dynasties in Spain were threatened, they called for help from the Almoravides, who came from the area that is now Niger. In fact, Arabic music—in its part-African Moorish form—is a highly important link between the musical worlds of Europe, West Africa, and parts of the New World.

Africa is a huge continent: It measures about 11,700,000 square miles (roughly four times the size of the United States). It has around 250 million inhabitants, forming at least 2,000 tribal groups, speaking between 800 and 2,400 tongues, depending on one's definition of what is a language and what is only a dialect. Every one of these units has its own customs, including its own music. Still, there is a certain unity underlying this bewildering diversity of peoples. Tribes and languages belong to a smaller number of groups or families: About 600 fall within the Bantu language family of Southern, East, and parts of Central Africa, for instance. And the larger regions of underlying similarity are reflected in the music, which can be divided into regional groupings in a number of ways. The most obvious division is into East, West, Central, and Southern Africa. But you can subdivide the major areas, so that in West Africa you have a wooded, coastal strip with one set of characteristics, and behind it the savanna lands with another (including a high degree of Muslim influence). Or you can differentiate those groups that sing in thirds from those which A. M. Jones calls the fourth-fifth-octave peoples.

Each of these regions, and even each tribe within each region, has its own musical styles. But certain elements transcend local differences, and it is they that are most significant for the music of the New World.

Speaking of the continent as a whole, the single most important form of musical accompaniment is probably handclapping; drums are found in most cultures, though their use varies a good deal in importance; there is a very wide range of other musical instruments, compared with most other musical cultures; the human voice is nevertheless of overriding importance; call-and-answer singing is by far the most common form of group vocal technique; African music is often built up by the use of relatively short musical phrases, often repeated, or of longer lines made up of phrases never repeated in just the same form; rhythm and, more generally, a percussive approach are fundamental; and above all, music is a communal functional expression to a far greater degree than in most other parts of the world.

African music differs from European music in that it is much more *functional*. Up to a point all music anywhere has a function: to please the gods, or to make work go better, or simply to give pleasure. Yet there is no doubt that in Africa it is more closely bound up with the details of daily living than in Europe. There is an immense amount of music for special purposes. All continents have lullabies for putting babies to sleep, of course, but in the Fon area of Dahomey there is a song children learn to sing on the loss of their first tooth. The Akan of Ghana have a song of derision aimed at habitual bed-wetters sung at a special ritual designed to cure enuresis. Punishment for wrongdoing frequently has its own music: The Akan also have special drums, which are played to accompany a petty thief while he is paraded through town with whatever he stole in his hands; and the Bamoun of Cameroun have some eerie and impressive music to be played when a court official is taken to be hanged. Examples of the social use of music are endless.

Another way in which music interconnects with everyday life is strikingly brought out in an anecdote told by the Ghanaian musicologist A. A. Mensah in an article in the *East Africa Journal:* He tells of a middle-aged woman trader who had just returned from a long journey and was telling members of her family about it. "As she came to the more exciting part of her narration, she burst into song, and her audience . . . joined in with a refrain."

This very close connection between music and every aspect of life goes much deeper than the existence of songs for special purposes. The Camerounian writer Francis Bebey has pointed out that, because of it, some groups—he mentions the Douala of Cameroun, but the same holds true for the Swahili language—have no indigenous word for music. They have words for musical forms, like "song" or "tune," but the idea of "music" itself has never been abstracted from the things to which it belongs. "The musical art is so much a part of man himself that he has seen no purpose in giving it a separate name," as Bebey puts it.

Music is very closely involved in religious practice. Whereas it is not essential to Christian rituals—however much it may add to their impressiveness—many African ceremonies simply could not take place at all without the appropriate music. To give just one example, the spirits are summoned by the drums in both Yoruba and Dahomeyan ceremonial, each by its own special rhythms. No drums, no spirits—and no ritual.

Another important aspect of African music is that it is only part of a greater artistic whole. Africans are beginning to feel that they should make no distinction, for instance, between music and dance, that they should avoid the European habit of separating the two and talking as if one *accompanied* the other. For them, the sound of music is only one element in a total experience, which may include the sight of costumes, the sensation of dancing, and so on. The Ghanaian J. K. Nketia says, "Music-making is an activity with a dramatic orientation." Performance attitudes, bodily movements, costumes, audience response, and so on are all a part of it.

Another deep-seated principle of African music is its relationship to speech. The word has been conceived as powerful in a fundamental way in many philosophies—not least in the Christian, as the opening of Saint John's Gospel makes clear. A Dogon legend tells that it was through the drum that God gave Man the gift of speech. Words are so powerful, even magical, that African songs tend to be oblique in reference and obscure in meaning, whereas European folk lyrics usually proceed in an orderly narrative fashion. It may seem paradoxical in a continent with such a variety of musical instruments, but virtually all African music is conceived vocally. In Uganda, for instance, there is a great body of xylophone music, and every piece has its lyrics, which are known by the musicians even though they are never sung.

Many instruments are in some way used to imitate the human voice. The most famous of the "talking" instruments are the talking drums of many West and Central African tribes, which send messages by imitating the inflections of the speaking voice, but there are many others. The Jabo of Liberia have talking xylophones, whose players sit in the market place and keep up a barrage of musical comment on the scene around them. The Nigerian Ibo use flutes and a trumpet-like instrument in the same way. Jean-Baptiste Obama observes that "the principal and essential traits of African music, its melodic, harmonic and rhythmic characteristics, are all linked to the making of the essentially 'speaking' instrument."

Though music is so closely related to religious and social activity, Africans do frequently sing to amuse each other (or themselves) or to pass away a quiet hour. The essential fact is that music—communal or private—is interwoven with every part of African life.

You might expect from this that every African is a musician. It is true that, growing up in a society where music—and rhythmic music at that—is so fundamental, most Africans display a considerable rhythmic sense. It is also true that in most African societies everybody takes part in certain sorts of music. But this does *not* mean that everybody or anybody can take over the lead drum in a major social dance, or any of the drums, for that matter. Ewe or Yoruba master drummers are highly skilled musicians, and they take years to learn their art. On the other hand, in most places the "general public" does not simply stand around and admire the "professionals." The music envisages roles for both the skilled musicians and the rest. The skilled musicians may drum and lead the singing, while the "general public" sings choral parts and adds to the general rhythmic effect by handclapping, dancing, and so on.

Besides the semiprofessional musicians—those whose musical skill determines their place in community functions—some African societies (especially Muslim groups and others influenced by them) have fully professional musicians. Generally called *griots,* they provide music for various occasions. Some are employed at princely courts. Others specialize in work music and praise music, often associated with a guild. The Hausa of northern Nigeria, for example, have *griots* who sing nothing but songs praising the products of certain butchers. There are *griots* who provide music to lighten the farmers' work and others who travel around to meet an indispensable need at weddings and other ceremonies.

The very close relationship between music and social religious life has had a number of effects on the music itself. The concept of music as a purely aesthetic experience is foreign to Africa. Africans get pleasure from their music, but the aesthetic element —the whole purpose of a Brahms symphony—is for them a by-product. Africans and Europeans judge music differently. In Africa, music is not so much "good" as "effective," that is, right for its purpose. Thus Francis Bebey says of singing: "African voices are . . . what the total nature of the music demands of them: clear to sing of the bride newly brought into the community, hushed to sing of something which one would have preferred to keep quiet, mocking in satire . . . harsh or soft, piercing or tender depending on the time and the place." A "beautiful voice" in the European sense is an accident, not the main point. The aim, in Bebey's words, is not to make agreeable sounds but to "live the actions of everyday life by means of sound." Singing, moreover, is everybody's art in a way that can never be true of musical instruments, which demand some technical ability. Anybody is a potential singer: A "fine voice" does not count, since the criteria for choosing a singer are social, not musical. He may be the priest, or he may be the oldest man in the age group.

The wide range of vocal tone in African music has partly to do with use and is partly regional or tribal. In Ghana, the Akan use an "open" voice quality, whereas the Frafra like a more intense tone. Other groups prefer a near- or true falsetto. Instrumental tone, for some reason, is less varied. There is a definite liking for a buzz tone, shown, for example, in the attachment of little bits of metal to the prongs of the hand-piano to give a slight rattling quality. (This deliberate choice of "dirty" tones is sig-

nificant in the consideration of New World black music.) Francis
Bebey associates the search for unusual, burred, "dirty" tone in
both vocal and instrumental music with a desire to bring music
as close as possible to natural sound, while creating musical
instruments that will supply melody and percussion at the same
time.

The similarities in African music extend to form as well as use
and practice. The stresses of the sung melody are generally
placed between the main beats of the percussion rhythm, though
sometimes the melody has a quite different rhythm from the accompaniment, in line with the African liking for cross-rhythms,
rhythmic interplay, and the use of differing meters in one piece.
Except in areas of Islamic influence, melodic lines on the whole
are rather short, particularly for certain musical instruments, like
xylophones (and drums, for that matter), which often build their
music out of the repetition of short melodic-rhythmic patterns
blending and contrasting with each other and perhaps with a
more complex, improvised lead-role instrument or singer.

By far the most common form of group singing in most parts of
Africa is the call-and-response style, in which a lead singer sings
a line, or a phrase, and a group answers it. This is quite different
from the common European form of a verse of several lines followed (or not) by a chorus. For one thing, the European verse
is complete in itself, while the African call by itself is only half of
the equation; it needs the response before it is complete. Moreover, though the lead singer is very important and has a good
deal of freedom to improvise, in many areas it is the chorus's
response that is considered the essential part of the tune.

Though the call-and-response at one time was probably more
common in Europe than now (some scholars see it as closely
linked to tribal and communal ways of living), by the time
African and European music met in the New World it had survived in European usage only in a few forms, such as church
litanies and ballad refrains. European folk music's most typical
feature, its division into regular "verses," comes from the equally
typical tendency of European poetry to be divided into regular
groups of lines, most often two, four, or eight. The musical form
tended to follow the poetic divisions, so that most songs—unlike

songs on a call-and-response pattern—are series of neat packages of four or six or eight or twelve lines, separated by pauses or joined by a bit of instrumental filling-in. This important link between European verse and music is maintained down to quite small details like connections between musical and verbal stress, and length of syllable and length of musical note. Take the accentuation of these lines from a British border ballad:

> Oh what's the blood that's on your sword, my son David,
>
> Oh son David?
>
> What's the blood that's on your sword,
>
> Oh son now tell me true?

Different singers may place the stress differently in some particulars, but it will never cut right across the verbal stress. That is to say, the words strongly affect the music, which is by no means the case all over the world, including much of Africa.

Despite the non-African's conception of African music in terms of drums, the African instruments most often used by the greatest number of people in the greatest variety of societies are the human voice and the human hands, used for clapping. Drums are essential to the music of some groups, especially in West and West Central Africa. They are highly important in many others. But some tribes never use drums, and many tribes use them only moderately. Besides drums, Africa has stringed instruments, wind instruments, rattles, gongs, xylophones—in fact, examples of almost every kind of instrument known to man.

Some instruments are very simple—a collection of stones that give musical notes, a xylophone made of a few logs laid across the knees. Many others are highly sophisticated. But, crude or intricate, they are always beautifully adapted to their purpose.

Though Africa is far more than a land of drums, there *is* something behind the general idea that African music is "percussive." But what is percussive is not just a dominant group of instruments. Alan Merriam stresses this:

It seems to be the totality of the musical concept which sees rhythm and percussive effect as the deep, basic organizational principle underlying African music. Drums and drumming, the use of idiophones, the forceful and dynamic vocal attack, and other characteristics reflect this principle; it is African music which is essentially rhythmic and percussive in effect, and the devices used simply reflect the principle.

Perhaps the most important formal element of rhythm in African music is that instead of having a single meter, either duple (two or four beats) or triple (three or six), a performance puts two or more different meters together, as if one drummer were playing in waltz-time and another in march time, for example. Rhythm is also based on contrasting recurrent beats with irregular patterns.

Rhythm as a musical fundamental cannot be overemphasized. Its use is highly sophisticated, and far from the old "savage drumming" stereotype. Meaningful sounds are the basis of African music, as they are of any other music, but there seems to be value not only in the sounds themselves but also, to use Nketia's words, "in their arrangement in orderly sequences or patterns of rhythm." In traditional music, at least in the "drumming tribes" of West Africa, such as the Yoruba and the Ewe, rhythm is basic to enjoyment. Pieces with almost no "tune" in a Western sense are enjoyed if there is sufficient rhythmic interest.

This rhythmic emphasis has led to the diehard cliché that African music is long on rhythm, short on melodic variety and harmony. Like any cliché, this is not totally untrue, but simply unhelpful, since it assumes European attitudes as a norm. The African approach to melody differs from the European, but only a rash or ignorant person would argue that it is more limited. As for harmony, that is a question of definitions. Sounding more than one note at a time in choral singing is certainly no less widespread in African music than in European folk music. In fact, choral singing as a whole is less common in European folk music than in African. If harmony means a theoretical structure of chords with a formal relationship basic to the structure of a piece of music, then it is not known in Africa, simply because Africa is not Europe. African choirs sing, on the whole (there are exceptions), by using parallel melodic lines a third, a fourth, a fifth, or an octave above or below the "basic" tune. But the whole concept of thirds, fifths, and so on is European. It is useful for description, but it has nothing to do with the way Africans themselves conceive of what they are doing when they sing.

The African approach to singing includes the use of a large number of ornamental devices, of which one of the most common is the slide up to the first note of a phrase, and the slide down off the last note. Notes are often "bent," and some songs are almost shouted rather than sung. Singing techniques vary from tribe to tribe, and the use of decoration in singing is connected with Arab-Berber influences in Islamic Africa. For the moment it is necessary to remember only that singing techniques are highly flexible and varied.

This is in sharp contrast to Europe, where—apart from conservatory standards of purity of tone—different regions have tended to adopt a single type of vocal tone and stick to it. Alan Lomax has divided singing styles in Europe into "Old European," "Modern European," and "Eurasian." The "Eurasian" style, high-pitched, strident, and harsh, is typical of Spain and Portugal and is suited to long, ornamented styles. It is probably an Arabism, though a similar sound is also found in parts of France and the British Isles. The other style relevant to our concerns is the "Modern European" which is found in most of France and England, the area of ballads and lyrical love songs. It tends to be associated with solo or unison singing; is harsh, strained, and usually less emotional than the "Eurasian" type; and shows a greater interest in the words than in the music.

North African Islamic music differs from the music of Arabia itself in a number of ways, some of which (especially a greater emphasis on rhythm instruments) may be the result of influence from black Africa. Because it influenced both Iberian music and much of the music of West and East Africa, partly through trade and neighborly contacts of various sorts, but mainly through the spread of Islam, it is important to the development of New World black music. The Muslim call to prayer is heard five times a day, seven days a week, wherever Islam is practiced. It has been heard for hundreds of years in many parts of Africa. Its relatively simple but long and highly decorated, very characteristic Arabic melodic approach found its way into much African music. That is perhaps the fundamental influence of Arabic music on African—the melodic. There are others, for similarities between North African and black African music, such as a liking for percussion and syncopation, made mutual influence easy. There has always been much travel between Arab and black Muslim areas. In the Middle Ages Timbuktu was a great university city, and there was as much moving about within the Arab Muslim world as there was in Medieval Europe.

There has tended to be argument—with an undertone of cultural and racial politics—about the extent to which Spanish music has been influenced by the eight centuries of Islamic rule. But there seems to be little doubt that in southern Spain the influence of Islam was immense. For eight hundred years Spain was culturally as well as spiritually divided in two: the so-called Mozarabic kingdoms, of which Seville was the musical capital, and the Christian area centered in Zaragoza. As a result, while some Spanish music, particularly in the north, is closely tied to France and Europe in general, the music of the south is still more or less heavily Arab. Some of the Arab characteristics of southern Spanish music include a rhythmic approach that is quite different from Northern Europe, a liking for recitative singing without obvious metric structure and with a great deal of ornament; a harsh, nasal singing tone; and a number of individual elements like the highly decorated syllable with which a singer may introduce a song (usually "ay-y-y-y-y" in Spain and "ah-ah-h-h-ah" in Arab music). Incidentally, a Moorish oboe called the *rhaita* is found among the Spaniards (where it is called a *gaita*) and the West Africans (the Hausa call it *alghaita*).

The picture is complicated by the fact that Spanish-Moorish music developed into a high form of its own during the eight centuries of Islam in Iberia and was taken back to North Africa when the Spanish Moors left Europe, where it proceeded to influence Moorish music and thus probably Islamic black African music. The Moorish element is also present in Portugal, which colonized Brazil, though to a lesser degree. Thus North Africa, parts of West Africa, and important parts of Spain and Portugal share certain common cultural traits, even though they have gone their own ways for five centuries. (In case you feel that the Arab influence in Spain must have died out in such a long time, it is worth remembering that songs written by Provençal troubadours eight hundred years ago are still sung by Catalonian peasants.) If we cannot trace exact Arabic survivals in Spain, this may be partly because Arab music was never written down, so we could never find an original with which to compare modern South Spanish music. Moreover, Spain, after having spent eight hundred years in the Arab world, has spent five in the European, so changes are bound to have occurred. Besides, musical evidence is not necessarily the best evidence of musical survival. We know enough from working on African and other non-European music to be highly suspicious of printed transcriptions. So much of the essence of all folk music gets left out in the writing. Better evidence of Arab influence in Spain lies in written accounts of the popularity of Moorish traveling singers and dancing girls or of the fisherman who at the siege of Calatanazor sang a complaint consisting of alternate Arabic and Spanish verses. Countless surviving accounts show a degree of social interpenetration so great that it is inconceivable that musical interpenetrations should *not* have taken place.

The debt of the whole of European music to Arabic influence is far greater than we usually realize. The surprisingly large range of musical instruments introduced from the Islamic world includes the guitar, the fiddle, and drums of all sorts. One clear link between North Africa and the Iberian Peninsula lies in rhythm. In Northern Europe, especially Britain and France, rhythm has tended to become relatively simple. Much folk music has gravitated toward the common meters such as 4/4, 2/4, 6/8, 3/4, whereas many old British and some French ballads used "free" rhythm, or rhythms that changed every bar or two.

But except for the old "free-meter" ballads, most North European folk music tends to have a basic beat and to stick to it, and any syncopation there may be takes a simple form, in which the melody places a weak beat against a strong beat of the underlying rhythm (as is quite common in Scots music). This is usually a passing effect, and it does not affect the underlying pulse. The relative rhythmic simplicity is also true of Northwest European dance music, in sharp contrast to Spanish and Portuguese dance music, which goes in for very complex rhythms (though not cross-rhythms like African music) and for the use of a number of different meters in succession, especially 3/4 and 6/8 (which are closely related in practice, even though the theory describes one as triple and the other as duple).

Another area of relative similarity between African and European music is the use of scales. European folk music uses a wide variety of scales: The "conservatory" scales of seven basic notes (diatonic scales) are by no means the only possibilities open to the musician. You can perfectly well have a song in a scale of only one note, and it needn't even be particularly dull. Melody is only part of what makes a song attractive. Rhythm and elements in the way it's presented—like vocal tone—are also important. Similarly, you can have songs using much smaller intervals than a semitone, which is the smallest note used in conservatory music. (Much Eastern music uses "microtones" far smaller even than a quarter-tone, and a scale of these microtones would have far more than seven notes.) Many European scales are what is called "pentatonic," having five notes. Others have six; yet others are diatonic. On the whole it is the older songs that used "gapped" scales—scales with fewer notes than the diatonic scale.

Although there has been much argument about the "African scale," most experts now feel that, in the words of the American musicologist Alan Merriam, it is "essentially a natural diatonic. At the same time, no brief is held for a universal African scale, for it is clear that intervals and their arrangement vary from culture to culture." Neither European nor African music makes much use of microtones, though neither Africans nor European folksingers necessarily use notes that are at "concert pitch."

Scales built from notes at European "concert pitch" are not the only scales possible, and "out of tune" has meaning only within a particular musical culture. A South African, John Ngcobo, once said on a BBC radio program: "When I first heard the Western scale . . . I thought it was terrible—quite out of pitch. And you can see small African schoolchildren today looking really hurt when they have to sing sharps and flats." But it should be clear by now that, though Europeans and Africans find each other's music strange at first, their musical cultures are not totally alien to each other. They are far closer together than either is to Chinese, or even Indian, music. And the similarities as well as the differences are important in the story of what happened when African and European music met in the New World.

PART ONE

Old
Cultures
in a
New
World

2 TRADITIONS PRESERVED: NEO-AFRICAN MUSIC

As LeRoi Jones remarked in *Blues People,* "Undoubtedly, none of the African prisoners broke out into 'St. James's Infirmary' the minute the first of them was herded off the ship." In fact, it took many years of mutual influence between the descendants of the African slaves and the descendants of the European pioneers whom they met in the New World. There are really two sorts of Afro-American music, though they shade into each other, the first being the neo-African music that this chapter is about, with elements still totally or very largely African. The origins of this music are fairly easy to establish by comparison with present-day Africa or, often, because its practitioners themselves still remember where it came from. The second sort, though it was developed either completely or largely by Afro-Americans, consists of various blends of European and African ingredients, all of which have been molded into a new and original music. The African origins of this music are more difficult to pinpoint, because even when we can still isolate African strands they are so changed as to have become truly "African" rather than Yoruba, Ashanti, Congo-Angolan, or whatever. We then have to try to find out what parts of Africa the slaves in a particular area came from.

The great majority were from three main cultural regions: (1) the coastal rain-forest area of West Africa, which includes the Yoruba, Ewe, Ashanti, Fon, Ibo, and other major Nigerian, Dahomeyan and Ghanaian tribes; (2) the savanna belt, which lies from the coast at Guinea across and to the north of the Sudanese rain-forest area and includes such largely Muslim groups as the Wolof of what used to be called Senegambia, the Malinke of Guinea, the Hausa and Fulani of Northern Nigeria and the parts around it, and the Mandingo, who cover a wide area including Senegambia and what is now Sierra Leone; and (3) the Congo-Angolan area, populated largely by people of another language and culture group, the Bantu.

These groups were brought in different proportions to different parts of the Americas at different times, partly reflecting political upheavals in Africa itself. For instance, in the mid-sixteenth century the old Jolof Empire was in the process of breaking up violently. As a result, a large number of Wolof were to be found in sixteenth-century America, though they were never again to form a significant part of the slave trade. During the nineteenth century, there was a great increase in the number of Yoruba enslaved because of the Yoruba wars, which lasted for much of the century, and for the first time a fairly large number of Hausa caught in the disorders on the edges of the Caliphate of Sokoto ended up in the New World.

African politics was not the only explanation for the ethnic makeup of the slave population. Different slaving powers had a greater presence in some parts of Africa than in others, even before the main colonial era. The Portuguese were politically active in parts of Congo-Angola from the sixteenth century on, for instance, and the British were powerful along the Gold Coast and the Bights of Benin and Biafra. So more Bantu were taken to Brazil and the Spanish areas, whereas British possessions in the West Indies and North America had many Fanti and Ashanti from what is now Ghana. In the sixteenth century, England drew more than 70 per cent of its slaves from the Gold Coast and Spain only 9 per cent. These factors partly explain why black music in different parts of the New World shows influences from different African regions. Besides the people brought directly from Africa, many slaves were taken first to one area, then eventually moved to another, which certainly had a significance in the development of the blended cultures of the New World.

In the very early days, as far as can be established, the various ethnic groups maintained their music fairly separate. Blending took place mainly during the last century. The Brazilian folklorist Oneida Alvarenga says that "only at the end of the 19th century did authentic Brazilian music begin to emerge." Nowhere else did the various elements ever produce a uniform "national" music, least of all in the United States. Meanwhile, differing African tribal musics blended in the New World to form neo-African musics that were almost entirely African-derived, and yet non-African, for they were not to be heard in Africa.

What African music did survive in the Americas, either in a pure form or in new amalgams? Perhaps the easiest survivals to recognize are the large numbers of musical instruments of African origin still found in the New World. Drums of various kinds play an important part in neo-African music, and many display African characteristics. "Peg drums" use an African method for attaching the skins to the body of the drum and for tuning, a system of pegs that stick out from the sides of the drum near the head to which cords from the drumhead are attached. The pegs are hammered in to tighten the drumhead.

I do not believe it is a coincidence that the drums in so much of the black music of the Caribbean and South America come in sets of two or of three, given that two or three is also the most common number for the "core group" of drums in most West African styles, including those of the Yoruba and the Ewe. In the "round drum" music of the coastal Barlovento region of Venezuela, three drums are used, the *pujao*, *cruzado*, and *corrido*. In the "big drum" dances of the same area, two are used, the *mina* and the *curveta*, or *curbata*. All these are single-ended drums, tall, usually held between the musician's legs. The *curveta* stands upright on three feet carved of one piece with the body, like some drums from the Congo. Playing styles show strong

African traits, too, including the use of a small stick in one hand while the drumhead is muted with the other hand, or with the drummer's heel if he is sitting on his instrument, to give a wider range of notes. Another Africanism, even more striking, is to have a second man beat a counter-rhythm on the side of the drum with a pair of small sticks. A tambo drummer whom I interviewed and recorded in the Jamaican village of Wakefield, Trelawney Parish, told me categorically that his music came from his Congolese grandmother. While the details of his family tradition had obviously become garbled, his style of drumming and singing seemed to contain definite Bantu elements, besides more generalized Africanisms such as muting his drum with his heel. His son used a pair of "catta 'ticks" to beat out a second rhythm on the tambo. Sticks are used to beat the side of the *bonko* drum in the Cuban Abakwá rhythm. The bomba dance of Puerto Rico uses two drums, the *burlador* and the *requinto*. A second man squats in front of the *burlador* and plays on its side with sticks. As I write this, I am looking at a photo of a Congolese drum played by two men in just the same way.

If the drum groups of so many areas are obviously based on African models, so are many features of the music they play. There is almost always a lead drum, which improvises, along with one or two others, which play repeated sequences. In the Puerto Rican bomba it is the *requinto* that improvises. Where there is only one drum, as in Jamaican tambo, it sounds rather thin without the support of subsidiary drums. This thinness, also characteristic of the Haitian virtuoso Ti-Roro, underlines the point that drum music is communal.

Old accounts often mention instruments of all sorts that have exact parallels in Africa. An architect named Latrobe, who visited New Orleans in 1819, provided a long description of a dance he happened upon, which is interesting despite the author's disapproving tone:

> The music consisted of two drums and a stringed instrument. An old man sat astride of a cylindrical drum about a foot in diameter, and beat it with incredible quickness with the edge of his hand and fingers. The other drum was an open staved thing held between the knees and beaten in the same manner. . . . The most curious in-

strument, however, was a stringed instrument which no doubt was imported from Africa. On top of the finger board was the rude figure of a man in sitting posture, and two pegs behind him to which the strings were fastened. The body was a calabash.

Further on, Latrobe described more instruments: "One, which from the color of the wood seemed new, consisted of a block cut into something of the form of a cricket bat with a long and deep mortice down the center. . . . In the same orchestra was a square drum, looking like a stool . . . also a calabash with a round hole in it, the hole studded with brass nails, which was beaten by a woman with two short sticks." The descriptions match the kind of slit-drum used by a large number of tribes from the West Coast and the Congo; another drum with its own feet (square drums are found in Ghana, and a twentieth-century author has seen them in Jamaica); and a calabash used as a percussion instrument. This last suggests a strong continuation of tradition; its brass studs and the fact that it was a woman's instrument are both features of calabashes played by the Hausa and other groups.

A less well-known reference to African instruments in the Western Hemisphere is a mention of the marimba, or xylophone, in *A True and Exact History of the Island of Barbadoes, written by Richard Ligon, Gent,* published in 1673. Ligon came across a slave called Macow, "sitting on the ground, and before him a piece of large timber, upon which he had laid cross, six billets, and having a handsaw by him, would cut the billets by little and little till he had brought them to the tunes, he would fit them to; I took the stick out of his hand, and tryed the sound, finding the six billets to have six distinct notes." Macow, in other words, was building himself a marimba of a very common six-tone variety.

African-derived instruments other than drums still exist in many parts of the New World (though not in the United States). The marimba is still found in Mexico and parts of South America, and most people probably think it is an Amerindian instrument. It used to be more widespread—it was found in Brazil until the nineteenth century, for instance. Where it is still found, the music played on it is often Indian, but a fine Nonesuch disc of black music recorded mainly in Colombia by David Lewiston presents marimbas combined with drums in fiery neo-African *currulaos* from the Colombian Pacific coast.

Two other instruments of purely African origin are the so-called mosquito drum, or earthbow, found in Haiti and the Dominican Republic (where it is called *gayumba*), and the stamping tubes known as *quitiplas* in Colombia and Venezuela and *ganbo* in Haiti. The earthbow is a stringed instrument built of a bent sapling, a cord, and a hole in the earth covered with animal hide, which acts as the resonator. Stamping tubes are differing lengths of hollow bamboo tapped on the ground in sequence by a group of men. Descendants of African wind instruments are found in the *vaccines* of Haiti, one-note bamboo trumpets, which the players blow in sequence to produce a highly rhythmic (and highly communal) music. Similar instruments are found in several African countries.

African-derived string instruments also have their place in the Americas. Sir Hans Sloan, writing of Jamaica in 1688, describes a gourd with a neck strung with horsehair, like one of the instruments Latrobe saw, and a "hollowed timber strung with parchment" (that is, a little drum) having a bow for its neck. Many African stringed instruments are made of gourds, and so were the early U.S. banjos, which were undoubtedly African-inspired at the outset but have changed a good deal since. The use of a little drum as a resonator for a stringed instrument, another feature of the banjo, is quite common in Africa too. The one- and two-stringed fiddles are frequently made the same way. Sloan's two-stringed instruments are no longer found in Jamaica, but in the 1920's Helen Roberts met some people who said they remembered them. She did find the *cumbe,* a small square drum on two legs rather like what Latrobe saw in New Orleans, as well as sheep's jawbones used as rattles or scrapers.

Another instrument whose background is African but whose function has changed in the New World is the hand- or thumb-piano, which many Bantu groups in Africa call marimba, just as they do the xylophone. It is a little box or board with metal prongs fastened to it, each of which sounds a different note when plucked. Small versions of them were seen in New Orleans and Trinidad in the nineteenth century and are still found in

Cuba, but much more common is a large version made of a packing case with four to eight metal keys. It is found in country districts of Haiti, Puerto Rico, Cuba, the Dominican Republic, Jamaica, and Trinidad. In the Spanish-speaking countries it is called the *marimbula* or *marimbola*. In Jamaica it is the rumba-box, and in Trinidad the *basse-en-boîte* (box-bass).

Besides the actual musical instruments from Africa (I could also have mentioned a wide range of maracca-like instruments, rhythm bells like the *agogó* of Cuba and Brazil, and countless others), many culture patterns relating to music are still strongly African. The role of the lead drummer in Africa includes giving directions to the dancers on sacred and secular occasions, a function widespread in the New World too. In the tamborito of Panama, the *repicador*, the smallest drum, summons the dancers and directs their movements. The Puerto Rican *bomba* drums were often given sexual attributes, as in Ghana, being called male and female, a relic of the African personalization of instruments.

The dances of black America have many more African characteristics than just the musical instruments and the way they are played. Many descriptions of neo-African dances show a close relationship between dance and music, in which neither is subsidiary. The daughter of a Puerto Rican bomba dancer says that her father would hold dances on Sundays, at which—just as in Africa—the spectators formed the chorus for call-and-response singing. The music was supplied by two drums, maraccas, and two sticks tapped on a bench (this was common in Cuba, and a Folkways recording of Liberian music includes a track in which a singer is accompanied by a man tapping on a chair). The rhythm was set not by the drummer but by the lead dancer. The whole form of the bomba was like many African dances, in which the voices open unaccompanied, then the drums come in with dramatic effect. In the bomba, the dancer would often integrate his action with the music still more by dancing up to the lead drum and beating out an improvised rhythm with his feet. The drummer would reply, and a competition would develop between dancer and drummer.

The bomba has many African elements: melodies of short

phrases repeated a great deal; varied, complicated rhythms; a collective dance form involving instruments, dancers and spectators in which nobody is passive; and simple, much-repeated lyrics (often of no importance, in many neo-African forms; a group I recorded near Santo Domingo used virtually the same words for four different numbers). All these qualities are true of a large number of Afro-Caribbean dances, such as the bamboula found in parts of the French- and English-speaking Caribbean and in the nineteenth century in Louisiana and Georgia; the juba; and one of the most widespread, the kalinda, which was also known in Louisiana. The kalinda is still sung in Trinidad, where it used to accompany the stick fighters at carnival time. Incidentally, the kalinda and the juba, or yuba, crop up in a group of Puerto Rican bomba dances.

Brazil was and is particularly rich in neo-African dances. The samba, also called batuque, had a large number of forms. Many were only part-African musically, but the *samba da roda* or ring dances were often African, including features like the umbrigada, a belly-bounce that is a sure sign of Africanism in New World dances (and that, incidentally, considerably upset white observers in the nineteenth century). The belly-bounce, quite widespread, turned up in Mexico in a group of songs and dances called the *chuchumbe*, which drew a denunciation from the Inquisition in 1766.

One type of samba described in Alvarenga's *Popular Music of Brazil* began much like the Puerto Rican bomba. A solo singer would open, improvising, then the chorus would come in. (The pattern of varied lead with set chorus extends to the tamboritos of Panama, the calypsos of Trinidad, and many others.) The drummer, playing the *bombo*—apparently a Portuguese, not an African name—would listen carefully until he heard that the singing was set, then would give a call-beat and launch into the rhythm of the song. On the call-beat the other drummers would enter and the dancing would begin. The lead drummer's main role was to direct the dancers. This is a common form of opening in many areas of Africa.

Besides the sambas or batuques, which became generalized and now belong to the whole country, Brazil has had many less renowned dances. There was the congada, a dance-drama with strong African ingredients. The Mozambique was a war dance using only percussion instruments. The cucumbí used to be danced at Christmas and carnivals. Because *cucumbí* was a local nickname for people of Congo origin, and because the songs had words of apparent African derivation, the dance is thought to have Bantu roots.

Most of these Brazilian dances could not be called "pure" African, but many seem to have had very few Portuguese elements, if any. It is possible that, like much Afro-American drumming, they represented a fusion of different African elements to arrive at a style that was "African" rather than Ewe, Yoruba, Fon, or whatever. It is also possible that some of them existed in Africa but simply disappeared there, where art forms are fairly fluid, to be preserved only in the Americas. (Far more of the melodies of British ballads, after all, have survived in the United States than in Britain.) There is still a great deal of work to be done on the relationship between African and Afro-American dances. In Brazil it is said that the word samba comes from an African word for the belly-bounce, *semba*, and that the word *batuque* is used in Congo-Angola in the same general sense, for a type of dance rather than an individual dance, as it is in Brazil. It is also said that Portuguese travelers in the past saw dances just like the batuque in Angola.

Music is used in both Africa and the New World to accompany formalized athletics. Wrestling to the accompaniment of drums and praise songs in support of one or another combatant is not uncommon in West Africa. Trinidad once had a sport called stick-fighting, which was always accompanied, until it was banned, by *kalinda* music, mainly praise songs to a percussion accompaniment. The Brazilian *capoeira*, a form of skilled fighting faintly reminiscent of judo, is accompanied by African-style lyres playing melodies of an African cast. The fighting is closely linked to the music, which, far from incidental, acts as a motivating force. Alvarenga states that *Capoeira de Angola* cannot take place without the lyres, called *berimbau*. The music consists of short rhythmo-melodic phrases much like those played on African stringed instruments. The constant repetition of short phrases, often with a slight increase in tempo, acts here as a physical energizer, just as, in the cults, it serves in attaining the desired state of possession. (Repetition of all kinds is a major positive feature of African-style singing, as a Panamanian woman affirmed: "The more you hear it the more harmony it has." A Jamaican interviewed by Helen Roberts remarked: "It don't make no matter how many time you sing it, you sing it till it get sour to your mouth." Those who use the word "monotonous" in criticism of black music are on the wrong cultural wave length.) *Capoeira* was the favorite sport of gangs of young blacks in Brazil in the nineteenth century. It got a bad name when they used it effectively against police harassment, but they also quelled a rebellion of European mercenary troops in 1828. The *capoeiragem* discovered something that has frequently been discovered since: If you are young, black, and poor, your activities are likely to strike the older, whiter, and richer power structure as subversive whatever they may be—*capoeira* in nineteenth-century Brazil, steel-band in 1940's Trinidad, or rocksteady and reggae in 1960's Jamaica.

Another neo-African form, in many cases, at least, is the work song. We shall be looking at the work songs of some areas in more detail later, but it is worth remembering that they were found in most places where people of African descent lived. Many work songs are highly African. In the Brazilian mining district of Minas Gerais, black diamond-miners sang songs with the Bantu-sounding name *vissungo*. An author long ago wrote: "At work, the blacks sang the whole day. They had special songs for the morning, midday and afternoon. As work began before sunrise they directed to the moon a song with an obviously religious theme." The texts of the *vissungo* mixed Portuguese words with others apparently from some corrupted African dialect. Like many African-derived or African-style songs, they were accompanied by sounds made with the working tools. In the mining area of Montijo, Panama, a black enclave in a largely Indian and white province, there was a song with the bitter line "Con los minerales vine, con los minerales voy [With the minerals I came, and with the minerals I am going]." Not all work songs are neo-African (Jamaican digging songs have strong English as well as

African elements), but on the whole the work songs of any country are among the more African styles of that country.

Neo-Africanisms, where they occur, are a clear and impressive demonstration of the connection between the New World and Africa. But there are some less striking elements that are more widespread, including many aspects of singing technique. As we shall see time and again through this book, African singing—African in its use of call-and-response, its varying vocal tone, its endless variation on the part of the lead singer, its use of falsetto —is common to all the black areas of the New World, whether it dominates or not.

Another component of African musical taste, the liking for impure buzzing or rattling tones, was noticed by Lafcadio Hearn during a stay in the French West Indies in the 1870's. He found drums across which had been stretched a string with thin strips of bamboo or cut feather stems to give the tones what he described as "a certain vibration."

Neo-African forms often exist in close connection with styles having strongly European ingredients. In some cases the neo-African survivals seem to result from a region's isolation, but not necessarily. The highly African *congos del Espiritu Santo* of Villa Mella in the Dominican Republic are a famous feature of a town only a dozen miles from Santo Domingo. Their music, associated with an Afro-Christian sect, is highly African in its characteristics. The *congos* themselves are two drums, *el mayor* and *el alcahuete*, the smaller, which plays the lead role. The rest of the accompaniment is carried by the *canoa*, a *claves*-like instrument (two sticks tapped together), and by maraccas. The most striking thing about the Villa Mella *congos* is the call-and-response singing, whose choral style could be taken for something Congo-Angolan. The dancing is strongly Spanish, with no recognizable Africanization. The music of the Villa Mella *congos* serves equally for sacred and secular purposes: I first heard it at a wake, which involved dancing around a shrine by a young adept in a state of semipossession, but when I recorded it a few days later, people were performing secular dances with no significance other than enjoyment.

The Dominican Republic is relatively isolated, which no doubt helps music like the *congos* of Villa Mella not only to survive but to thrive. But there are other possible reasons. One is the religious significance of the *palos*, as the African drums and their music are called there. Villa Mella has a legend involving the miraculous arrival of the drums in the village. If popular belief is correct, the Dominican *palos* are a legacy from the period of the 1820's to the 1840's, when Santo Domingo was governed by Haiti. This belief is held by many Dominican scholars, though the music of the *palos* appears to be rather different from Haitian music. If it is true, the fact that it arrived in the Dominican Republic relatively recently would explain its survival. On the other hand the historical hostility to Haitians, which is still strong, would surely have prevented anything introduced during what is still referred to as the Haitian invasion from becoming so widespread and lasting so long. On the whole the belief in the *palos'* Haitian origin seems mistaken.

Much of the neo-African music of the Dominican Republic is well established. In other countries it may exist in isolated pockets, as in the case of a number of strongly African survivals in Jamaica. Though Jamaican culture as a whole was always regarded as Ashanti, fairly strong Congolese elements were discovered about fifteen years ago. Most of them are to be found in Afro-Christian and neo-African sects, which preserve a number of Congolese words in their songs. A still more isolated example, already mentioned, is the Jamaican *tambo* drumming, which so far has been found only in the northern parish of Trelawney.

Similar examples continue to be discovered, and there is obviously much neo-African music known only to the people who make it. A few years ago, the first known survivals in Jamaica of Yoruba were discovered in the form of a number of songs sung in a garbled dialect, some of whose words were clearly Yoruba, by an old man in the parish of Westmoreland. Two of the songs have been issued on a long-playing record of the field recordings of Olive Lewin of the Jamaica School of Music, called *From the Grass Roots of Jamaica*.

How has so much that was African survived in a fairly pure

state? Largely because musical survivals have been associated with social survival. While many Africans escaped their fate in the New World by rebellion, flight into the interior, and suicide, others sought ways to organize themselves collectively in a strange and hostile environment. Some of the ways they chose helped to preserve African traditions of various sorts, for a while at least. Slaves often formed themselves into groupings that continued, either fairly exactly or in new forms, their old tribal ties. Slaves in the cities found themselves performing heavy labor, such as unloading ships or acting as porters of heavy loads. To do this, they formed into groups of half a dozen or so men, led by a "captain," all of the same tribe. In the early days before the slaves willy-nilly picked up English, French, Spanish, or Portuguese, their purpose was to be able to talk with each other. By working and living together, such groups preserved elements of their culture, including musical elements. A visitor to Rio de Janeiro in 1838 wrote that the porters there ran through the streets behind the leader of each group, who, to the sound of a gourd rattle, paced the others in a kind of trot. They all sang.

At a deeper level, the slaves in the Americas found a way to preserve old ties and come together for mutual support in new circumstances by forming ethnic clubs. These clubs, remarkably widespread, played a great part in the preservation of neo-African music. They were known as "nations" and, in the Spanish areas, "cabildos"—a *cabildo* being a city government in Spanish colonial administration. The "nations" and cabildos tended to preserve the names of African ethnic or regional groupings or to create new names to reflect new conditions in the Afro-American experience.

The "nations" were governed by a hierarchy and sometimes acted as intermediaries between their members and the slave-owners. In Colombia, the cabildos included the Mandingo, the Caravali (Kalabari), the Congo, and the Mina (after the Gold Coast slaving port of Elmina), each with its "kings" and "princes." There were apparently cabildos in Venezuela among free blacks as well as slaves. In Peru there were Angolas, Caravalis, Mozambiques, Congos, Chalas, and Tierra Nuevas. Old writers from virtually all the other Spanish colonies report similar groups. An eighteenth-century Nigerian former slave, Equiano, described in memoirs what he saw in Jamaica:

> When I came to Kingston I was surprised to see the number of Africans who were assembled together on Sundays, particularly at a large commodious place called Spring Bath. There each different nation of Africa meet and dance after the nature of their own country. They still retain most of their native customs: they bury their dead and put victuals, pipes and tobacco, and other things in the grave with the corpse in the same manner as in Africa.

The "nations" and cabildos suffered various fates. Some were banned, like those in Colombia, because enmity among the groups reached the fighting stage, or because they were seen as a threat to order, or because their dances did not suit the notions of "decency" or "civilization" of rulers and lawmakers. By contrast, Cuban slave-owners, finding that slaves grouped by tribe worked better, encouraged them. Other "nations" moved from a social to a spiritual role, either merging with or developing into religious groupings, which preserved the faiths of various regions of West and Central Africa. Sometimes the division into "nations" continued in new settings. In the Brazilian army, for example, the black soldiers formed four battalions, Minas, Ardras, Angola, and "Creoles." Some of them acted as mutual-aid societies. All, with the abolition of slavery, gradually ceased to be strictly ethnic organizations. That is to say, though they kept African ethnic names and customs, their members in fact came from various backgrounds, and not always African backgrounds. Harold Courlander tells of seeing six people initiated into the Abakwá cult of Cuba, all but one of them white. The French anthropologist Roger Bastide remarks that he knows "Daughters of the Saints" of French or Spanish origin who "are no doubt white of skin, but who are considered as Africans because they take part without any reservations in a culture brought from Africa."

Though the nations discontinued the ethnic divisions, they did preserve cultural elements of Africa, and very strong ones. Powerful and important cults kept African religions alive in the

New World, either in a relatively pure state or blended with non-African faiths. The neo-African cults, impressive in their own right, are among the main preservers of neo-African music in the Western Hemisphere, principally because the major role of music in *African* religions persists in *Afro-American* cults. The best known of them is probably the Haitian *vaudou,* or voodoo.

The reputation of voodoo has suffered from the sensationalistic nonsense perpetrated by whites prepared to believe anything of a religion belonging not just to blacks, but to *independent* blacks. In fact, like similar cults in other parts of the Americas, it is an extremely sophisticated system that accommodates and integrates various beliefs, philosophies, social conditions, and cultural and artistic elements. Haitian voodoo has turned the nations into "mysteries," or gods: Ibo, Bambara, Congo, Mayombe, Congo Mandragues, Mandragues Go-Roug, Mali, Badagri, Caplaou, and Conga. The Dahomeyan religion is dominant, and other African cultures have become subordinate to the Dahomeyan Fon culture. This is a common development and does not always signify the dominance of the majority-group culture; the sophisticated and integrated world-systems of the Yoruba and the Fon have almost always dominated the more diffuse Bantu beliefs, which end up adding new elements to a basically non-Bantu structure.

The religious music of the Afro-American cults is often almost indistinguishable from the music of the parent faiths in West Africa. The rhythms, the drum techniques and even specific patterns, and the over-all structures are basically the same. The main differences are a tendency to use longer melody lines divided into more European-style verses and, where the African scales are not similar to European scales, to adapt them.

The continuation of African music in the cults is not solely a result of religious music's universal tendency to conservatism. Music plays an absolutely essential role in the cults, just as it does in West African faiths. The spirits are summoned by specific drum rhythms, and if the rhythms are altered too much, the spirits will stay away. The drums are the voice of the god as well. Cult dancers in Guyana dance facing the drums for that reason.

The songs of the cults are ritual praises to the different spirits, hence the wording seems to be more important than the melody.

The basic style of the singing in the Yoruba cults of Brazil, the *candomblé,* is virtually that of Western Nigeria. Both incorporate the call-and-response form and the special group technique called heterophony, which is almost unison except that individuals slightly alter the main line from time to time. The result is a sound immediately recognizable and remote from European styles. Where the songs of the New World neo-African cults are solo, the melody line is fairly long and complex; the call-and-response phrases are repeated many times. Other pure African-isms include the practice whereby the soloist ends the song as well as beginning it, which would be quite unbalanced to European minds; a chorus replying with unvarying phrases to a leader's part that is improvised and hardly ever twice the same; the use of a hard tone in the women's voices and a frequent falsetto; polyrhythmic rather than polyphonic music, giving drums such importance that the vocal is an accompaniment to the percussion rather than the other way round; and the use of more than one meter at once, so that the vocals are often in triple time while the drumming is in duple time. Alan Merriam sums up the main African features of Brazilian cult music as "the metronome sense, dominance of percussion, the use of polymeter, the off-beat phrasing of melodic accents, and the overlapping call-and-response pattern." There is a Library of Congress record-ing of Afro-Brazilian cult music that gives fine examples of all these characteristics.

Others besides the big Brazilian and Cuban cults have pre-served strongly African music. Richard Waterman, who has studied the music of the Trinidadian Shango cult (named after the Yoruba god of thunder), points out that it too contains a bedrock feature of African music: "use of patterns of com-binations of duple with triple time which include simultaneous and coterminous duple and triple measures, duple accent applied to triple meter, and triple accent applied to duple meter."

Except in Haiti, where the Fon dominates, and in Cuba, where the multitude of cults includes some important Bantu ones, the Yoruba beliefs have tended to dominate neo-African religions. In Brazil and Cuba, at least, there have been Muslim cults as well, but most of them ended up joining the larger Yoruba groups. Most neo-Yoruba cults are like that of Cuba, where it is called Lucumi. The Lucumi worship a series of spirit-gods, or *orisha*, most of which are also found in Western Nigeria and Dahomey (the spirit-gods are called *loa* in the cults originating with the Fon of Dahomey). They include Ogun, god of the mountains; Obatala, god of iron and war; Yemaya, god of the sea; and many others. The songs of Lucumi worship are in a Yoruba pure enough to be mostly understood by Yoruba-speakers from Africa. The most important drums are called *batá*, and their players *olu-batá*, in both Africa and Cuba (in both places there are three of them, and they have a similar relation to each other). Much of the religious symbolism is preserved, including the association of the colors red and white with Shango.

In most places where they have been preserved, the African cults have been associated with the cult houses known as "saint's houses" (*ilé-ocha* in Yoruba). The priests and acolytes there undergo initiation and training that can last as long as a year in some cases and is clearly important in handing on African traditions. Of course, a great deal of change has occurred in the Afro-American cults, but the African cults are not static, either. In some instances, the American cults perpetuate traditions lost in Africa, just as Canadian French and American English preserve words and phrases forgotten in Europe. The Society of Hunters associated with the god Oshossi has been preserved in Bahia, Brazil, but is forgotten in the African town of its origin, Ketu.

One of the centers of Yoruba religion in the New World is the Bahia region of Brazil, which has so many saint's houses that its chief town, Santiago, was known as "the Rome of the Africans." Bahia has tended to preserve more pure African elements than other area. The anthropologist Melville Herskovits, on a 1941–42 visit there, heard a priestess give an impromptu speech in Yoruba, which demands a much better knowledge of the language than the recitation of set prayers. (How many Roman Catholic priests can give a good after-dinner speech in Latin these days?)

The neo-African cults are not simply museum pieces, as must be obvious. Like anything else that flourishes in new circumstances, they have survived by adaptation. There are groups that represent a blend of African and Roman Catholic belief (*ma-*

cumba) and African and Amerindian elements (*Guarani* and *Caboclo*). They reflect their mixed origins in their music. A good example is the first track of the Library of Congress record of Afro-Brazilian cult music, which I have mentioned, a *caboclo* song to Santo Juremeiro, who sounds like Saint Jerome but is also the spirit of the jurema tree. Herskovits, who recorded the album, points out the influence of Catholic liturgy in the invocation, but there is also an obvious Portuguese sound to the later solo singing, while the choral singing is call-and-response. The same record, incidentally, has a fine example of the use of the lead drum in a Ketu rite for the god Oshossi. First, it calls the god with the correct pattern and then, as the "voice of the god," signals the proper movements to the possessed initiates.

The underlying structure of the *candomblé* cults of Brazil, voodoo in Haiti, and *Abakwá, Lucumi, Arara,* and other cults in Cuba is African, though each has taken in Christian elements to a greater or lesser degree. In Haiti, for instance, voodoo altars are decorated with richly colored pictures of various saints and angels that have become associated with the *orisha* or *loa,* usually because of some detail of appearance or clothes. The god of iron and war, Ogun, for example, is often represented by a picture of the Archangel Michael, usually shown in armor with a sword. In Port-au-Prince, the capital of Haiti, worshipers at a voodoo ceremony often go on at dawn to early Mass. At the same time, Saint Soleil—"Saint Sun"—has also been welcomed into the voodoo pantheon.

The Bantu religiophilosophical outlook seems to have been especially prone to change. The Bantu cult groups consequently have often disappeared or altered beyond recognition. It was mostly Bantu cults that blended with Amerindian elements in the Brazilian *macumba, caboclo,* and so on. In Cuba, the Congo communities recently have tended to group and regroup. Similarly, according to the Cuban musicologist Argilliers Léon, Bantu musical instruments, instead of being preserved intact, have become prototypes for Afro-Cuban instruments. The conga drums, found in Latin American groups of all sorts, came from Bantu originals. Bantu drums are still known as *ngoma* in Cuba, just as they often are in Brazil (or by other Bantu forms of the same word, like *ingome*).

Of course, the differences between African and Afro-American cults are profound. The Yoruba cults closely follow family lines, which in the New World were broken by the anarchy of slavery. In Nigeria each cult is devoted to one *orisha,* whereas in Brazil and elsewhere, the cults lost their ethnic exclusiveness and, because numbers were smaller, brought devotees of various *orishas* together. As a result, in Africa usually only one worshiper is possessed, while in America many may be. Haitian voodoo is a particularly rich faith, although (or perhaps because) in some ways it has grown away from West Africa more than the Brazilian. Brazil maintained close contact with Africa: Heads of commercial houses in Salvador received honorary distinctions from the government of Dahomey, and rich Brazilian Negroes even imported soap from Africa. The continuing ties between Brazil and Africa include one reported by Roger Bastide that is quite modern. One Martiano de Bomfin went to Nigeria to be initiated, and on his return he introduced a new Yoruba element into his cult house, which he had learned in Africa.

In Cuba, ties with Africa were maintained in a more grim fashion by the continuance of slave-smuggling up to the end of the nineteenth century. Haiti, on the other hand, became independent in 1791–93, and when the Haitian Revolution brought an end to white rule it also cut Haiti off from Africa. Many in the country's mulatto middle class continued to take their fashions in music and other things from France. More paradoxically (since voodoo priests had played an important part in the independence struggle), the first three rulers of independent Haiti—Toussaint Louverture, Dessalines, and King Christophe—totally banned voodoo assemblies. Toussaint banned all sorts of African dancing as well. The result has been that Haitian voodoo has developed strongly non-African ingredients, though they are often African-*type* characteristics.

As the Haitian experience shows, the threat of the cults to slavery's "law and order" was real, hence they were much persecuted. In Jamaica the authorities banned *obeah,* a less highly structured form of neo-African worship that gets its name from the Ewe word for a spell or charm, *obia,* after the slave revolt of 1760. The leader of the revolt was a priest called Tacky, who is said to have been a Coromantee and a former chief in Guinea

("Guinea" was used rather vaguely by the ignorant slave-owners of the time). "Coromantee" refers to the port of Cormantin in Ghana; it is more likely that Tacky came from there, because the African elements in Jamaican culture are largely Fanti-Ashanti.

The political potential of the cults, which acted as a powerful unifying force, was not the only reason why they were attacked. Most whites of the New World were entirely uncomprehending about African culture, but they did at times distinguish between forms, and of course they objected most to non-Christian religious practices. A good example of the distinction between sacred and secular came out in a discussion held at the end of the eighteenth century, as reported by Gilberto Freyre. Talking to the Minister of State, Martinho de Mello e Castro, about black dances in Brazil,

> the Count of Pevolide, a former governor of a captaincy, was of the opinion that such dances should not be considered more indecent than the fandangos of Castile and the *fofas* of Portugal and the *lunduns* of the whites and mulattoes of that country. The Negroes dance in tribal groups and with the instruments typical of each, whirling like harlequins and with diverse movements of the body. From these acceptable dances those should be separated which are deserving of complete reprobation like those danced by the Senegalese Negroes in the secrecy of their homes or in clearings, with a black mistress of ceremonies, an altar to idols, adoring live buck goats and other fetishes of clay, anointing their bodies with oils and cocks' blood, eating cakes of cornmeal after pronouncing heathen blessings on them, making the countryfolk believe that those cakes so blessed bring good luck, working love spells on men and women, and the credulity of certain persons is so great, even those one would not think so ignorant, such as friars and priests, who have been taken prisoner in the ring I threw around such houses, and to unmask whom I had to make confess their deception in the presence of the blacks of the house, and then turn them over to their authorities so they could be punished as they deserved, and I had the Negroes severely flogged and ordered their masters to sell them far away.

The varying degrees of tolerance or hostility directed against neo-African cults had a direct effect on the black music of the New World. The African elements in U.S. music are far more transmuted than those of other parts, and there is no neo-African music such as is found in the Caribbean and parts of South America. One reason, no doubt, is that contact with Africa was broken earlier, and another is that—compared at least with some parts of the Caribbean—the black population is smaller. Moreover, it is probable that the main African influence on the United States was from a tradition that could blend well with white styles. But the banning of drums in many parts of the country was certainly a factor, especially in the disappearance of the cults. The prohibition of the drums, where successful, was bound to have a fundamental effect on the cults, since the role of the drums was so basic to them. When the drums were silent, the old gods came no more. Nevertheless, elements of African religion survived even where the cults themselves vanished. They included the central role of dancing as well as music, and possession states. Possession states came about when the gods were summoned and entered into certain members of the congregation, or "rode" them, as the cult members call it. These people then "became" the gods for a while, and each would dress and act like the god possessing him and dance under his impulsion.

It is not only the fully developed cults that have helped keep neo-African music alive, but also customs that are a memory of them. The Caribbean island of Carriacou, in the Grenadines, still preserves a "nation" dance that was originally Coromantee (Ashanti) but took in Ibo, Mending (Mandingo, Mende?), Arada, and Congo sections. African words are preserved in the dance, which is used in various rituals, including healing ceremonies. The name of Damballa, the Dahomeyan snake god, is preserved in the song "Caribo Damballa Bother Me." But survival is only part of the story, and neo-African music only a part of black music. While the slaves preserved a great deal of African culture, they were not musically conservative or unenterprising, and in the Americas they came in contact with the music of various European countries. When that happened, the next stage in the growth of black music in the New World began.

3 CULTURAL BLENDING: THE AFRO-AMERICAN STYLES

We have seen that the Africans, far from arriving in the New World without any cultural baggage, not only brought a great deal with them but planted it so well that it took root and grew profusely. But the Africans were not the only people who brought their culture with them. Nor, perhaps, did they alone cling to their culture as part of a memory of a lost home, though they suffered the worst loss by far, with the least compensation and the least choice in the matter, of all the new arrivals.

It has sometimes been suggested (in a natural revulsion to the old racist theory that black musicians, having nothing worth while of their own, created their superb music as if by magic entirely out of scraps taken from their white rulers and neighbors), that Africans in the New World fought against white musical influences, trying to keep the music of their past as pure as possible. But the evidence is against this theory. African musicians and those of African descent in the Americas preserved and developed their African heritage, but they also latched onto the new musical experiences they encountered, took from them whatever suited them, and made both what they took and what they already had into something their own. Their attitude, in other words, was entirely positive, as indeed one would expect from highly creative people. Francis Bebey quotes André Schaeffner to the effect that the African musician is "extremely gifted, sensitive to the smallest of influences, capable of assimilating them completely, always recognizable through what he has borrowed." John Ligon, "Gent," whom I quoted in Chapter 2, provides an excellent example of the inquiring nature of the dedicated musician. We heard from Ligon how he came across a slave called Macow making a six-note xylophone. Having got over his surprise that the thing worked, he wrote, "I then shewed him the difference between flats and sharps, which he presently apprehended, as between *Fa* and *Mi:* and he would have cut two more billets to those tunes, but I had then no time to see it done, and so left him to his own enquiries."

The point is that Macow took his chance to learn something new and to test its usefulness. Whether or not he decided that fa and mi suited his purpose after trying them out, he did not simply reject a new possibility as coming from a member of the slave-owning class, no doubt proffered with some condescension.

But granted that musically inclined slaves and free blacks— the manumitted slaves who began to form a growing minority quite early in South America and parts of the United States— might seize upon any chance to add to their musical range, how much chance did they have? Was there opportunity to hear European music, or were slaves kept too strictly out of contact with whites? The answer is that contact was usually plentiful, though the amount varied from area to area and from time to time. The evidence is that *musical* contact, too, was widespread and started early. In the Spanish and Portuguese colonies, in fact, it was organized. We have seen that the Portuguese and Spanish took a deep interest in the spiritual welfare of the slaves as they saw it, which entailed teaching them church music. In Brazil, the Jesuits by the early seventeenth century had set up a school for the musical instruction of slaves, which later became known as the Conservatorio dos Negros. Activity of that sort had to be confined to the towns, but there is evidence of some social and musical mixing even on the plantations.

Mixing seems to have been heaviest and come earliest in the Spanish areas, because the Spaniards did not subscribe to the apartheid notions common among the slave-owning classes of the Anglo-Saxon countries. The earliest written account of the bomba dance of Puerto Rico was published in 1798 by a French naturalist, André Pierre Ledru. Ledru refers to "a drum popularly called bomba by the workers of an estate, white, mulatto and black, as accompaniment to their dances." Elsewhere, describing a dance given at a country house for the birth of a child, he comments: "The amalgam of whites, mulattoes and Negroes formed a pleasing and agreeable group. . . . They danced in turn Negro and creole dances [creole here meant Spanish-Caribbean], to the sound of a guitar and of a drum commonly called the *bamboula*." Thus, Ledru mentions two of the most widespread Afro-Caribbean dances (more precisely, the drums from which they took their names), and both in connection with multiracial parties. In fact it seems as if the dances Ledru saw may have been re-Africanized later, so to speak, a common enough happening, as we shall see. Certainly the bomba dances came under heavy Haitian influence through slaves brought by French settlers after the Haitian rebellion. Their mixed ancestry is particularly relevant to their history in Puerto Rico, where the bomba did not become a national dance but remained part of the black heritage there, mostly in the area of the sugar plantations. Some bomba lyrics preserve a large number of words of African origin, like this one:

> Aya, bombe, quinombo!
> Ohe, ohe mano Migue!
> Ayaya, sahu, caru!
> Che, Che, quinombo!

The contact of blacks with white music did not stop with partying. The historian Gilberto Freyre says that in Brazil "there were also plantations that had their black choir boys, their musicians, their grand pianos. As early as the sixteenth century a rich planter of Bahia had his orchestra of Negroes directed by a Frenchman from Marseilles." He goes on to report the surprise of a nineteenth-century traveler (a missionary from the United States) when he visited a plantation and heard an operatic overture and the *Stabat Mater* performed by a full orchestra and choir, all black.

Contact between white and black Americans varied in its nature, of course, as well as in degree. By no means was it always strictly a master-servant relationship. Frederick Olmstead, visiting the Southern states shortly before the Civil War, remarked: "I am struck with the close co-habitation and association of black and white." LeRoi Jones, quoting Olmstead in *Blues People*, observes that, apart from a growth in the mulatto population, "certainly the most significant result was the rapid acculturation of the African in this country."

In the cities, there was a growing number of free blacks and also of artisan-slaves, who in many instances, as Henry Kmen describes them in eighteenth-century New Orleans, "lived as though they were free, reporting periodically to their owners for the purpose only of making a stipulated money payment from their earnings. . . . In short, New Orleans was full of slaves who, for part or most of their time, were not too distinguishable from their legally free brethren." In 1806 a number of slave-owners complained to the U.S. governor of New Orleans because the police did not prevent their slaves from frequenting bars run by free men of color. The slaves, the owners said, "passed most of their nights in dancing and drinking," and their work suffered next day.

Most slaves may not have had as much freedom as the blacks in New Orleans, and conditions on many plantations (especially in the British West Indies) were bestial, but there still was plenty of opportunity for Africans and creole blacks to hear and, more important, to learn whatever they found valuable in the music of white Americans. Even on the U.S. plantations, opportunities were not totally absent. Many slave-owners actively encouraged music-making (except for the dreaded music of the drums), especially the playing of white or white-oriented music, occasionally going so far as to supply fiddles and strings.

Of course—a fact too little emphasized—musical acculturation was a two-way process. Blacks and whites influenced *each other*.

Indeed, the Inquisition in the Spanish parts of the Western Hemisphere spent a large part of its time taking futile legal action against manifestations of black influence on its white charges. St. Hilaire, a French scientist who visited Brazil in the nineteenth century, reported rather disapprovingly on a governor's ball he had attended at which a mulatto girl had danced a fandango, with much shaking of her hips, in an intermission between the quadrilles. Again, there were complaints as early as 1691 in Puerto Rico that the dances for Noche Buena, which was celebrated in the cathedral, were becoming scandalous. Bishop Padilla wrote that mulattoes taking part "danced to the music of guitars; their movements were correct, but a voluptuous and sensual suppleness invaded the people watching."

It is no coincidence that the examples of contagion I have cited occurred in the Portuguese and Spanish areas. As I noted earlier, the Iberian Peninsula—especially the south, from which most of the emigrants to the New World came—had a musical culture, including dance, influenced by eight centuries of Arab-Islamic rule. Two of the three largest groups of Africans taken to the Americas, especially Brazil, had themselves come under second-degree Maghreb Arab musical influence. Where African and European music have the most in common, in fact, is in the Islam-influenced areas of both continents, and it is the black-Latin regions of the New World where a most truly national music has been synthesized from the two sources.

At all events, for different reasons and in different degrees, Africans and black creoles quickly became involved in the musical activities of their areas—as early as the seventeenth century even in Mexico, which was obviously less affected by the black experience than many other countries. In places where there were few whites willing to take up the relatively low-status music professions, the pattern that soon developed had blacks playing to entertain whites. Black musicians had to play music acceptable to whites, but when bending this music to match their enduring African or African-derived concepts of musicianship, they were also bound to Africanize white tastes.

In all the black regions of the New World, blacks made two contributions to the cultural pattern: the neo-African music they developed and maintained for their own private consumption, and the transformations they wrought in predominantly white music when they performed it. Black performance led to the creation of new black musical styles out of mixed elements, imparted African influences to "white" styles, and at the same time played a major part in the development of "Afro-European" national styles. The existence of both plantation slaves remote from white cultural influence and house and urban slaves who shared, and even influenced, a mainly white life was mirrored in a wide variation in the extent of black musical experience and effect from one place to another. The degree to which an "Afro-European" culture developed or a neo-African culture was retained depended on the relative geographical isolation of the areas involved and on their economic and social stagnation or development. Where the old single-crop plantations have survived—in much of Haiti, coastal Venezuela and Colombia, northeastern Brazil, and even parts of the U.S. South—change has been slow. It has always come fastest in any part of the world where different cultures have met and mingled most intimately.

Anthropologists have long recognized the differing degrees of African survival. Melville Herskovits devised a method of grading on a scale from A to E in the categories of technology, economic life, social organization, institutions, religion, magic, art, folklore, masks, and language. The village of Toco in Trinidad scored A for technology, while Port of Spain scored E. The Bush Negroes of Surinam rate consistently highly African, and Northern city blacks in the United States are consistently low. This sort of scale is a handy way to capsulize findings, but it can be dangerously misleading. It would be quite wrong to conclude that Northern U.S. blacks no longer retain any part of an African heritage. It has not been lost but is simply transmuted into a rich Afro-*American* culture. Besides, the question of quantity is vague and to some extent irrelevant. If one could measure it, would "5 per cent Africanism" be much or little? It might well be crucial in the development of a new culture. Raciocultural putdowns of any kind obscure the issue. The total impact of the various Afro-American cultures has been massive both in the New World and beyond it.

All these cultures have, in one way or another, preserved African characteristics, not just as decoration but as the major element distinguishing them from surrounding cultures. As we shall see, this is as true for the United States as for areas where far more overtly African music is preserved. Indeed, it may be more so: Where the neo-African music survives, the alternate music is often more a black-influenced national music than Afro-American music as such.

The mutual influences of different cultures in the New World were not all black-white, though they were dominant because of the numbers involved. I have already mentioned the Afro-Indian cults of Brazil. Another fascinating Afro-Indian mix is seen in the black Caribs of Honduras, the descendants of two shiploads of slaves who were wrecked on the coast of Saint Vincent in 1635. They were subjected by the Carib Indians among whom they fell to a gentle domestic form of slavery. Soon they, and other escaped slaves who had joined them, intermarried with Indian women and produced a people who look physically African and speak a Carib transmuted by African pronunciation. The black Caribs were deported to Honduras during one of the many Caribbean wars, and there they are to this day, part descended from Nigerian Efik and Ibo, and part Carib Indian.

As time went on, blacks who were excluded from all forms of political organization sometimes built up parallel structures, like the bodies in New Hampshire and Rhode Island set up to arrange carnival displays. Some were new organizations, others grew out of the neo-African nations. They often set up, in what appears to have been a *double-entendre,* structures of kings or governors, possibly to deride white institutions. In Haiti, communal work groups set up for harvesting and other farm work had a quite complicated mock military and governmental framework. Such organizations, wherever they grew up, ostensibly imitated white forms but also seem to have kept many Africanisms (of course, there were parallels between the African and European power structures to begin with, particularly relating to monarchy). They penetrated many levels of black life.

By far the most important Afro-American organizations were the black churches. In the United States, and to some extent in the British Caribbean, these took the loose form natural for adherents of certain Protestant denominations (mainly Methodist and Baptist). In the Roman Catholic areas the black churches, springing up around a Church that was much more rigidly hierarchical but also gave scope for far more kinds of official grouping, were more variegated but less fundamental. They were also more upsetting to the whites. In seventeenth-century Mexico, for example, there were complaints that Negroes were holding their own religious festivals, called Oratorios, simultaneously with the official festivals to "ridicule" them. The oratorios were first reported by the Inquisition in 1669. They continued for a considerable time despite the Inquisition's persecution. There was a mass trial of people who took part in a similar function, called an *escapulario*, in Mexico City in 1682.

It is debatable whether the black oratorios were in fact mocking white activities. In view of how extremely tenacious they were in the face of persecution, it seems more likely that the oratorios, *escapularios*, and similar happenings were attempts at a reinterpretation of Christian festivals to suit African and African-inherited attitudes toward worship. Such a reinterpretation is occurring in twentieth-century Africa, where a large number of indigenous churches have sprung up because European worship styles do not adequately express African devotion. The Spanish Catholic hierarchy of the time being both powerful and rigid in attitude, it is not surprising that black attempts at freedom of Christian worship met persecution in the Spanish Americas, when similar attempts in the United States met little worse than disapproval or condescending amusement.

The Mexican black Christians could not set up separate churches, but they did (in Guadalajara at least) have communities simulating the orders of Saint Dominic, Saint Francis, and others and held regular offices, services with sermons, and so on. In the Week of Our Lady of Sorrows, a Dominican Friar reported, these bodies held parades with trumpets and drums, "going round the wine shops," as he indignantly remarked.

As the Africans and their descendants moved toward the center of New World cultures, many of their customs also moved in the direction of Afro-Americanism. Thus, while preserving the neo-African cults, Afro-Americans developed all sorts of specifically Christian black traditions. In Venezuela, the feasts of San Juan and San Benito have their own music involving praise-songs in call-and-response style accompanied by drums. Afro-Christian traditions persist in a variety of burial customs found through most of the black Americas. Africans attach great importance to funerals, believing that a dead man's send-off will affect his status on the other side. Venezuelan blacks hold particularly splendid wakes for small children who have died, as do those of the Dominican Republic and Puerto Rico. The gaiety of such occasions seems to reflect an African attitude, though it is rationalized in various ways. The Puerto Ricans hold a *baquiné*, a cheerful sung ceremony, on the ground that a child dies without sin and becomes an *angelito*. The Jamaicans hold that nothing sad must happen at a wake—locally called a "dinky" or a "nine-night."

A much-discussed U.S. phenomenon is the ring shout, a religious dance of considerable Africanism. We shall return to it later, but for the moment it should be included in the category of religious adaptation, with its possession states and its features described by Courlander: "Postures and gestures, the manner of standing, the bent knees, the feet flat on the floor or ground, the way the arms are held out for balance or pressed against the sides, the movements of the shoulders, all are African in conception." Such traits are also frequent in Jamaican Revival Zion services, where a dipping and swaying of shoulders and a kind of marching on the spot are akin to dancing. Some originally religious music and dances became secularized, usually in connection with carnivals, like the Uruguayan *candombe*, a parade dance to devastating percussion only tenuously related to its ostensible origins in the "nations."

The Afro-American role in the growth of New World festivals and carnivals is significant. The carnival at Mardi Gras is an old European Roman Catholic habit. Indeed, in France and Spain—as to a lesser degree in Britain—Saints' Days have always been associated with jollity (and very often, to the distress of the authorities, "lewdness and offensiveness"). Anybody who has been in a small Spanish town on the local Saint's Day or on London's

Hampstead Heath at Easter knows this. European fiestas include dancing and parades but do not accentuate them (except for May pole dancing, a relic of pre-Christian ritual).

If anything sets the New World carnivals apart, it is their highly African mix of music (usually heavily Afro-American music), dancing, and parades, in which costume is a most important element. Most carnivals have focused on Mardi Gras, and most, from Brazil through Trinidad to New Orleans, are associated with Afro-American musical forms. We shall meet these forms in more detail later. For the moment their African content is worth noting. The history of the slaves' attempts to squeeze a little fun out of life in the face of the authorities is filled with accounts of black dances held in city squares. When they became loud and frequent enough to get on the nerves of white residents, they were either banned or confined to certain times and places. The celebrated dances in New Orleans's Congo Square are an example. Mexico City at the beginning of the seventeenth century allowed slaves to dance publicly only in the main square *on festival days*. Such actions may well have helped to bring about the Africanization of carnivals.

The process of Afro-Americanization is reflected, at a more functional level, in the appearance of a variety of Afro-American musical instruments that are clearly African in inspiration but cannot be called neo-African. The best known, of course, is the banjo. Another is the Cuban *quinto*, a rhomboid hollow box used as a rhythm instrument, developed from the African slit-drum. Harold Courlander surmises that the U.S. washtub bass was a descendant of the earthbow, an instrument found in Africa and also in Haiti and, occasionally, the Dominican Republic. He also mentions the use of frying pans tuned a fourth apart, found in the United States and Cuba, which is an obvious substitute for the two-tone bells or gongs found in many parts of West Africa. The Cubans also used a door, hit with the hand, as an instrument in some forms of the rumba (some experts claimed the music was not the same without a good doorline). The use of the washboard is quite well known. U.S. bands also used a jug, blown across the opening to produce a bass note. This too was used in Cuba: It can be heard on records by the Septeto Habanero, an old band that made many fine recordings of *sones*. Various other homemade instruments were contrived to make bass sounds. Old Jamaican *mento* bands sometimes used what was called a "wooden trumpet." I have one, which is really more like a bass recorder. It is a straight length cut from the trumpet-tree, which has hollow branches. The man who made it drilled two holes in the side near the end into which he blew and decorated it with faintly West African–looking doodles in red paint. It produces three lugubrious notes, rather reminiscent of jug-blowing. All these instruments, when used, sound much like African friction drums, and it seems possible that they were developed as substitutes.

The New World *marimbula* falls between the categories of neo-African and Afro-American. Though it is bigger, it is still similar to its African counterpart in principle. Its pitch and its function have changed. In Africa the hand piano normally supplies rhythmo-melodic counterpoint, usually to a singer; the Caribbean *marimbula* is used to provide a harmonic bass line. It still often shows African details in its construction (with most instruments of more than five notes, for example, the longest and deepest-sounding notes are in the middle, not at one end), but it usually plays the bass in popular dance music, which is itself a mixture of European and African ingredients.

It is relatively easy to spot instruments with a wholly or partly African background, but, as the case of the *marimbula* shows, one is on trickier ground when looking for the origins of playing techniques or the over-all role of certain instruments. Some techniques—that of the "catta 'ticks" or the use of a heel as a mute when drumming—are simple and obvious. But other possible elements are less so. Harold Courlander suggests that the use of a double-bass as a wholly rhythmic instrument, never bowed, is an Afro-Americanism. This seems plausible, but it is something one either believes or does not. It would be remarkable if African ideas of musical function, musical customs, and ideas of music's social role had *not* had an effect on Afro-American music, and we shall be seeing plenty of examples to show that they did. But many must remain a matter of belief. The Panamanian tamboritos appear to be exclusively a women's music, or at least to have been so in the past. Does this reflect the widespread African tendency to regard certain sorts of music (and even certain musical instruments) as being men's, and others as women's? I think so, but the idea is neither provable nor disprovable.

Of the strictly musical Africanisms that have endured to become fundamental Afro-Americanisms, one of the most obvious, though difficult to pin down, is an attitude to rhythm. In the words of Nestor Ortiz Oderigo, writing in the magazine *African Music*, "even in the countries where the melodic ground shows the impact of Occidental cultural patterns, the unmistakable Negro rhythm pulsates in full strength." The pervasiveness of neo-African rhythmic attitudes is hardly surprising, given the sophistication of African rhythmic techniques, but it is perhaps surprising that they persist even where the blacks themselves have either totally or largely disappeared, as in Chile and Argentina. Ortiz Oderigo reports that two of the most widespread Argentinian dances, the chacarera and the gato, make use of duple and triple rhythm played together, and that the *bombo* players beat alternately on the head and the rim of the drum, another Africanism. Naturally, the liking of Spanish music for triple and duple meter in the same piece of music, which is shared by many African groups, facilitated the adoption and retention of the African joint duple-triple polyrhythmic approach, but it is still a striking survival in what is known as White South America.

There has been a good deal of argument, apparently designed to downrate the African rhythmic contribution, about possible Spanish roots of various Caribbean and South American rhythms. There is an extremely widespread rhythmic pattern in the black music of the Americas, whose most usual form is this:

It is the basic rhythm of the Cuban habanera, the Argentinian tango, the Dominican merengue, and many Trinidadian calypsos. Alvarenga says it is widely used in Brazilian music. It is also the rhythm of the Puerto Rican danza, which was widespread in the Caribbean in the nineteenth century and is still popular in places. Those who point out that it is much the same rhythm as the tango andaluz of Spain have a case. But the case for an ultimate Spanish origin becomes much weaker when one considers how many songs from the "folk" stratum of the Southern United States use it—not, it is true, as the basic rhythm, but in melodic phrases that recur far too often for coincidence, and many which are stressed not *with* the verbal stress of the lyric but *against* it. When I turn to piano ragtime, I find that many rags consistently use the same rhythm in the right hand, set against a steady "oompah" in the left, and that, in the form known as the "cakewalk figure," it is a prominent ragtime ingredient. From ragtime it has passed into jazz, where it is a common phrasing in front-line solos (an example is Jimmy Archey's trombone solo in "Edna," on the RCA recording *King Oliver in New York*). I begin to find the tango andaluz rather a small root to bear this huge flowering all alone. I am prepared to accept a common rhythmic element in the Spanish and the Caribbean music, going back one way through the West Coast and the other through Iberia, meeting in the Muslim Maghreb. But when I see a widely differing European element and a common African element, in a field (rhythm) in which Africans excel, I see little reason to look further.

may not be an *African* rhythm in just that form, but it is derived from African rhythmic concepts. Alvarenga suggests that blacks may have systematized rather than originated it; the entry on Brazil in the Grove Dictionary of Music suggests that the Brazilian version

is a deformation of the Brazilian 6/8

accompanied by a drummed

Either way, it represents a common cultural element spread through the black New World from Brazil to the United States.

African melody seems not to have survived in a pure form. Very few actual African melodies can be found in the Americas, despite attempts to find a Zambian origin for "Swing Low, Sweet Chariot." On the other hand, African *attitudes* to music almost universally have parallels on the western side of the Atlantic, and so do certain techniques. One important instance is the universality of call-and-response singing in work songs. Not only the more neo-African work song forms are cast in the call-and-response mold, but also work songs that in other respects show a good deal of non-African influence. It is true of U.S. work songs. It is true of Jamaican work songs, which show strong elements of British folk and hymn harmonies. It is true of blended styles in Spanish-speaking areas too.

On the island of Margarita, Venezuela, two women were recorded pounding corn and singing like this:

> *c:* Ay ay ay ay
> *r:* viva el sol y viva la luna
> *c:* Ay ay ay ay
> *r:* viva limata 'e limon
> *c:* Ay ay ay ay
> *r:* Ay que vivan mis amores con el joven Asunción

This is a beautiful example of an Euro-African blend, its lyric and melody in a highly Spanish mode with the repeated "ay ay ay ay" (thought to come from the Arabic device of a highly ornamented, long-drawn-out "ah-ah-ah" before a line), but split up by the African influence so that it is call-and-response instead of solo. This work song comes from the largely black province of Barlovento, where the call-and-response form in melodies showing both Spanish and African content—usually accompanied by drums in a rhythm much like the ♫♫♪

I was talking about earlier—is quite common.

Of course, work songs are a natural form for call-and-response, and it might be said that the demands of communal work explain its widespread occurrence. But call-and-response is also found in music where its presence has no such logic. In the Cibao area of the Dominican Republic, for example, the most common forms of folk music are the religious *salve* and the secular *tonada*, sung unaccompanied, usually by groups of women. Both are of highly Spanish influence in music and words, and show absolutely no black characteristics, except that the *tonadas* are almost universally sung call-and-response. A large number of the *tonadas* use the old ten-line Spanish *décima* verse, and breaking into this tight form with single-line group responses is in the highest degree illogical. The practice is so ingrained that, when I asked one woman in a group I was recording for an example of a lullaby, the whole group came in massively with a "response." So there it is: *One* African feature in an otherwise totally un-African music—and a theoretically functionless (though in practice beautiful) feature, at that.

Given the importance of dance in African culture, it is not surprising that a wide range of Afro-American dances developed out of a twin Afro-European tradition. Both the African and the European dances that met in America tended to consist of a series of linked sections, each with its own music. Sometimes a fundamentally European dance became partly or largely Africanized, either taken over by blacks or "Afro-Americanized" by the infusion of creole elements, many of which were African-derived. One Africanized European dance, the contradanza, reached broad areas of the Caribbean and was popular as a salon dance in the nineteenth century. It is thought to have started as an English "country dance." During the nineteenth century it became a folk dance, especially in Cuba (where its descendant is the danzón) and Puerto Rico (where it is the danza). Its descendants are not black dances in any sense, but it seems unlikely that they could have become what they are—

and all—without the black experience. Venezuela has a dance that preserves the dual cultures quite neatly, the highly complex tamanungue, which has eight figures. The center four figures have pronounced black features, including a good deal of room for improvisation (unknown in European dancing of analogous kinds). The outer four stem from European dances, including the contradanza. The dance itself takes its name from the *tamanungo* drum, which is the core of its rhythm section.

Afro-American dances were extremely widespread in the Caribbean at least until the 1920's. Local forms of the polka, quadrille, and mazurka are still remembered with affection by older country people in Jamaica, for instance, as are waltzes and creolized forms, similar to the danza and the criollo. Such dances were played in a wide variety of styles: some were only lightly creolized, like quadrilles I recorded in Jamaica, which still preserved recognizable Scots tunes and rhythms. Others, like a quadrille I recorded among English-speaking settlers in the Dominican Republic, had equally recognizable British antecedents, but the hot drumming and fife-playing showed a high degree of Africanization of European material. Creolized waltzes are also found in the French-language black music of Louisiana, called *zydeco*. A highly syncopated "Lafayette Waltz" is played by the accordionist Clifton Chenier.

The black modification of dances extended beyond the folk stratum. One Afro-Brazilian dance, the lundú, moved from the streets to the bourgeois salons during the nineteenth century (purged of most of its hip movements), and thence traveled with a talented mulatto composer to Lisbon, where it became a rage. Allusions to a salon dance called the congo in Cuba and Louisiana and to hybrid dances like the congo-minuet indicate the same process.

It is remarkably easy to short-sell the surviving Africanisms in a sector where they are none too obvious. Marvin Harris, in a fascinating book entitled *Town and Country in Brazil*, states: "Throughout the area there are very few remnants of African culture patterns." Harris remarks (correctly) that what there are have moved out into the non-African population. But his state-

ment is true only of *neo-African* forms; he underestimates the
African contribution to national culture by saying that the samba
and allied forms are pan-Brazilian and ignoring their neo-African
source. He then goes on to recount a wedding custom that incorporates a samba containing the African *umbrigada*, or belly-
bounce. The point is, of course, not that Africanisms are rare but
that here, as in the New World as a whole, they have become a
fundamental part of everybody's inheritance. The New World
black culture is at the heart of the American experience.

Is there any logic in what died and what lived on? Was it hap-
penstance? Were the survivals no more than lucky, passive sur-
vivors of an onslaught, whether of physical oppression or of
cultural overlay? The anthropologist Ernest Bornemann some
years ago argued in *A Critic Looks at Jazz* that, from the start, all
the songs and dances that filled no function in the new master-
slave pattern died out; the surviving songs and dances were the
ones that fitted into the new cultural and economic patterns—work
songs, love songs, lullabies, play songs, and song games. Among
the songs that died out, he contended, were those related to African social structures, such as initiation songs, legend songs, and
genealogical songs. Now, there's no contesting this argument, if
it is strictly limited to the songs and dances that have obviously
survived unaltered or whose functions have not changed. But
legend songs most certainly survived. With changed circumstances came a change in the legends. Hero ballads, like "John
Henry"—and for the matter of that, badman ballads like "Stack-
olee" "and "Railroad Bill"—are legend songs. Further, if legend
songs are defined by function—giving the individual a sense of
cohesion with his group, elaborating the way in which the group
understands itself, and in general expressing the group's myths
about itself—then the blues fit that definition, too.

The crux of the matter lies in what one means by "survival."
Nothing, from an amoeba to a planet, can survive without adapt-
ing itself to new circumstances. Indeed, adaptation is a prime
sign of life. Some people saw the arrival of the electric guitar as
a sign that the blues were dead, when in fact it was a sign that
the blues were living. At one time anthropologists talked of survival and adaptation as if they were opposites. More to the point

is what the French scholar Roger Bastide called "adaptive survival."

In his book *Les Amériques Noires,* Bastide remarks that the African (or, as I have called them, neo-African) civilizations disappeared because the channels upward in the societies of the Americas demanded the acceptance of Christianity and Western values, and thus the rejection of African customs or beliefs. But, in fact, this rejection was never complete. And was it ever possible? Can any group of people deny itself? That is what wholesale rejection of its background (not to be equated with taking in new ideas and concepts) would mean. If I am to assimilate new ideas, my conception of them must be affected by my background, and thus by the old ideas that I am consciously rejecting. If I am to borrow some new religious or social structures, they are not going to provide the close web of direction for the myriad choices of attitude I have to make every day. For these I have to fall back on what I learned from infancy onward. The conscious adoption of a new culture, of course, is very different from acquiring new concepts by "infection," so to speak, by living cheek by jowl with new people in a new environment. This is not just possible but probably inevitable. Bastide remarks that a Brazilian black can participate in Brazilian political and economic life and at the same time be a member of an Afro-Brazilian cult without feeling any contradiction in this. There *is* no real contradiction, only an apparent contradiction in a set of categories set up by somebody else for his own academic convenience.

Perhaps the best statement ever made about the ultimate meaning of music in *any* people's life was made by LeRoi Jones in *Blues People:*

> The most expressive Negro music of any given period will be an exact reflection of what the Negro himself is. It will be a portrait of the Negro in America at that particular time. Who he thinks he is, what he thinks America or the world to be, given the circumstances, prejudices, and delights of that particular America. Negro music and Negro life in America were always the result of a reaction to, and an adaptation of, whatever American Negroes were given or could secure for themselves.

The question remains: What survived, adapted or not? And

further, given that there are many elements common to most African cultures, why did particular elements—Yoruba, Fanti-Ashanti, Congo-Angolan Bantu, Senegambian—dominate or die? Bastide answers with statistics showing that, in Brazil, in the seventeenth century the slave trade was mostly with Angola, and in the eighteenth and nineteenth centuries mainly with the area embracing the Yoruba, Fon, Ibo, and others. He points out that in the Bahia area the latter elements dominate over the Bantu and concludes that the African cultural traits brought over in the seventeenth and eighteenth centuries were evidently lost, and that Afro-American civilizations stem from the influences at the end of the slave trade. Unfortunately, the same logical deduction seems not to work for other areas. Paul Oliver, who discusses the question of Africanisms in the blues in *Savannah Syncopators*, argues convincingly that it was the Senegambian cultures (and allied cultures from the savanna belt) that provided the African ingredient in the blues. The point is that the Senegambian was the earliest ethnic group in the United States to dominate statistically, and after its early presence it never dominated again. This apparent anomaly is explainable, if one accepts that the early arrivals provided the basis for the enduring elements in many mainstream Afro-American forms, and the last arrivals the basis for the most African (least digested) forms.

Of course, it is easy to make mistakes in deciding whether Africanisms have survived. Some survivals belong to the category of items too small or intimate for people to give much thought to. An example is proverbs. "If snake bite you and you see lizard, you run" is a Jamaican version of a West African saying: "He whom a snake has bitten fears a slow-worm." Such apparently unimportant traces are apt to be ignored. The intimate category embraces a whole range of Africanisms in modern or recent Afro-American experience, from the naming of children after the day of the week on which they were born to ways of tying a headcloth, carrying a baby straddled on the hip, or plaiting hair into what the Haitians call a "garden" of little braids.

At the other end of the scale, one would look for any fundamental attitude or group of attitudes—whether inherent or due to early social training—shared by Afro-Americans as a whole, after allowing for individual differences, that might have some African background. The concept of "soul" certainly supposes that such an attitude exists. The Malawian Dunduza Chisiza, writing on the question of an "African personality" in the *Journal of Modern African Studies* in 1963, contended that there are common features found in most African communities. He noted that Africans are not inclined to meditativeness like Eastern peoples, nor "inquisitive searchers" like Europeans, but primarily "penetrating observers, relying more on intuition than on the process of reasoning," and excelling in personal relations. Chisiza also found them to be in pursuit of happiness rather than "truth" or "beauty." The ideal African way of life is communal, he wrote, based on strong and loving family relations shading into a general compassion (the Swahili expression for "my house" translates as "our house"). All activities, from hunting and harvesting to leisure pursuits, are communal. Generosity and forgiveness are encouraged, malice and revenge abhorred. Moreover, Africans are renowned for their sense of humor and dislike of melancholy. Now, this is obviously a highly favorable report, and it could be said to have its drawbacks as well as its merits. But in my experience it is both true and highly significant in outline, and this pattern of qualities seems to be both preserved in Afro-American life (where circumstances permit) and relevant to musical developments, though mostly in ways not easily described.

One other remark made by Chisiza is, paradoxically, relevant to what I described as a highly conservative field, religion. Chisiza holds that African cultures have "a habitual desire for change, even in religion." This interesting thought bears upon the rise of black Christianity and upon syncretism, the blending of traditions, in general. It has often been said that Africans have traditionally had a respect for their conquerors' gods. African theology tends to explain the universe as run according to a fate whose decrees can be changed by a supernatural being if one can, by sacrifice or propitiation, persuade such a being to help out. Defeat in war suggests that the enemy has been enlisting gods with greater power than one's own, in which case it is only logical to do the same, but without deserting one's old gods, who may also have their strong points.

Something of the sort seems to have happened in many parts of Afro-America. I think it is safe to say that *all* black religious groups—from the largely African-derived cults like *candomblé* or Shango to the Black Protestant churches of the United States— still contain major Africanisms of either belief or liturgy and worshiping practice, or both. (This is not to say, as some authors seem to, that there is little substantive difference between the worship of Shango and the services of the Baptist churches of the United States. Worship is a conscious act, and people who say they are worshiping the God of the Bible are worshiping the God of the Bible, not a lightly worked-over Obatala figure.) On the one hand, West African religions survived and flourished in the New World, taking in Christian elements that suited them. On the other, black converts to Christianity worshiped in ways that expressed their devotion adequately, whether with rhythm, dancing, or ecstatic possession. In countries that followed the relatively rigid Roman Catholic liturgies, West African faiths flourished, whereas in the Protestant areas they did not. One reason, surely, is that it was entirely possible for black Protestants to integrate into Christian worship healing, speaking in tongues, dancing, hand-clapping, a variety of musical styles, chanted sermons, possession by the Holy Ghost—features they knew from Africa, none of which was alien to Biblical Christianity. The Roman Catholic tradition, meanwhile, was less able to shed its European cast.

W. E. B. Dubois, speaking of possession and trances, commented that "many generations firmly believed that without this visible manifestation of the God there could be no true communion with the Invisible." Black Protestants saw no difficulty in integrating this central African belief with Christianity, because there *was* no difficulty. It already existed in the Christianity with which they had first come into contact. And in fact black Christians appear to have taken both African and white possession states and blended them. While it was and is a major functional happening in West African religions and, in an African form, in neo-African religions in the New World, possession was also common in the Methodist and Baptist "Great Revival," which spread from Britain to the United States and was responsible for the first large-scale conversions of slaves.

White possession states are different in many respects from African, as Dr. Erika Bourguignon pointed out in an essay in *Afro-American Anthropology* on the difference between possession states in Haiti and those on the island of Saint Vincent. She showed that the Vincentian pattern of jerks, rocks, trembles, and talking in tongues is close to early British Methodist possession states and that Haitian possession, which is much more specific to action, is African-based. Vincentians, unlike Haitians, do not interact with other people while in trance states.

The possession of states in black U.S. churches appear to result from a blend of African and English Methodist elements. I once witnessed a woman at a Jamaican Revival Zion meeting whose trance showed all the characteristics of the "English Methodist" forms—shudders, undirected swoops across the chapel, and "speaking in tongues" of a "white" variety. On the other hand, she played the tambourine and sang as part of the congregation, and her "speaking in tongues" was interrelated with another person: She shook my hand after the service and addressed me in glossolalia for about five minutes.

Dubois saw the conversion from African to Christian beliefs among slaves in the United States as a slow process, and there is no doubt that he was right. It was only in the early years of the nineteenth century that white Christians in any numbers showed much interest in ministering to the slaves, and these were mainly Baptists and Methodists, themselves hardly Establishment dignitaries. Dubois believed that the link between Africa and the new black churches was the Medicine Man or Priest: "He early appeared on the plantation and found his function as the healer of the sick, the interpreter of the Unknown, the comforter of the sorrowing, the supernatural avenger of wrong . . . thus, as bard, physician, judge and priest, rose the Negro preacher." He saw this the new black church as at first an "adaptation and mingling of heathen rites"—a *candomblé* or *vodun* (voodoo)—which moved toward Christianity through time, contact with whites, and missionary effort.

Bastide cites the case of Jamaica to suggest that the old faiths broke into two parts, one united with Christianity and surviving through reinterpretation according to Christian beliefs (water rites blending into baptism, and possession by the gods becoming possession by the Holy Spirit), and the other losing most of its theological qualities and becoming mere magic. (The Jamaican word *obeah,* is mostly used for witchcraft, though *obeah* seems to have retained some religious elements. It is, for one thing, connected like voodoo with the world of the spirits, though the sinister living dead, the *jumbis,* or the ghosts, the duppies, seem to play a more important part than do the zombies, whose role in Haitian folklore is rich but not very relevant to the basic concerns of voodoo.)

In many African religions, the dead play a part in the affairs of the living that may be benevolent or malicious. When religion degenerated to magic, the dead on the whole turned sour. The special importance of the dead in black Christianity is not easy to define, though it is easy to recognize from the emphasis given funeral rites, wakes, and similar ceremonies in all parts of Afro-America. Possibly it has moved from the realm of belief to the realm of custom. Sometimes one catches a glimpse of something deeper, such as the belief that you could send a message by the dying to the already dead:

> If you see my mother
> > Oh yes
> Won't you tell her for me
> > Oh yes
> I'm a-riding my horse in the battlefield
> I want to see my Jesus in the morning.

The lavishness of black U.S. funerals may reflect the African idea that the status of the shade in the other world is affected by the style of his going.

Magic, of course, is not necessarily sinister. It can involve healing, or it can involve smaller practical matters. In all cases, music is present. Sometimes the custom itself is not only African. Lydia

Parrish, in her *Slave Songs of the Georgia Sea Islands,* mentions that "when a field needs to be burned over, a sail is flapping idly, or rice is to be fanned, you may hear a Negro 'calling the wind.' 'Co'win'! Co'win'! Co!, Co'!' A prolonged whistle follows. . . . A gramophone record of a Togoland rain invocation is astonishingly similar." There is no reason why in fact such a small, intimate, and yet deeply important practice as wind-summoning should not preserve an African form among people of African descent, even though the practice is European also.

Other social functions besides worship have acted as "adaptive preservers" of Africanisms in music. Charles Keil, in *Urban Blues,* makes a persuasive case for the ritual function of much black U.S. entertainment. Many forms of black music have performed an important function as a catalyst of group identity. The soul syndrome, wherein a variety of social, cultural, musical, and even culinary elements are conceived as one clearly recognizable but hardly definable whole, is in itself reminiscent of the African fusion of aspects that Europeans perceive as separate. I have already said that the legend-role of African music, by no means lost in the Americas, is very much alive in the hero ballads and, in a less obvious but more pervasive way, in the blues and soul. What more *universal* manifesto has there been than Aretha Franklin's "Freedom" and songs like it? What is "Say It Loud, I'm Black and Proud"? Much more, certainly, than a political statement, and meaning more to more people on a more profound level.

And if the blues and soul (and, in a less obvious way, gospel music, more totally black in creation and audience than either) perform a group function, this reinforces the Africanisms in the music. Self-definition for any black group, at the mythopoeic level on which music works, must come about by contrast to an idea of "whiteness." As a result, what are perceived as "black" elements are re-emphasized. Perhaps this role has helped to reinforce continuously the Africanisms in a music that (like all American music) is in many respects deeply biracial. To quote Keil, black U.S. music "has become progressively more 'reactionary'—that is, more African in its essentials—primarily because the various blues and jazz styles are, at least in their initial phases, symbolic referents of in-group solidarity for the black masses and the more intellectual segments of the black bourgeoisie." Albert Murray makes a similar point in *The Omni-Americans:*

> When the Negro musician or dancer swings the blues . . . he is making an affirmative and hence exemplary and heroic response to that which André Malraux describes as *la condition humaine*. . . . The blues idiom become[s] survival technique, esthetic equipment for living, and a central element in the dynamics of U.S. Negro life style.

(Incidentally, notice that "or *dancer*.")

The social role of music in Africa is, as we have seen, all-embracing and paramount. And it is not much less all-embracing in the Americas. Take the mutual-help societies, which help to ease life and guard against trouble ("'societies to care for the sick and bury the dead'—and these societies grow and flourish," Dubois remarks). There is no inherent reason why such societies should be intimately connected with musical functions or social festivity. Yet they are. Just as African, Haitian, Trinidadian communal labor groups blended work and mutual help with a picnic atmosphere, music, and dance, so did the black lodges and societies of Southern U.S. cities like New Orleans give endless picnics and take part in endless parades—supporting an extraordinary number of black musicians in the bargain. The importance of musical parades is not new. Benjamin Latrobe, visiting New Orleans in 1819, was struck by the funeral parades, which he claimed were unique to the city, and described two, both black. In one, he said, there were more than two hundred people, mostly dressed in white (a probable Africanism). Militia band parades were popular among New Orleans whites, but they were standard European nineteenth-century activities anyway. What is important is the way they were adapted to communal social functions.

Musical parades, often associated with dancing (and often with carnivals), were and are a feature of most of the black New World. The *rara* bands of Haiti, the highly danceable *marchas* of Brazil, the New Orleans marching bands, and the Trinidadian calendar groups seem to be a part of a loose tradition associating dance, music, religion, social function, and royalty (real or as-

sumed), which I believe is to be traced to African origins in royal
and religious ceremonial in such old kingdoms as the Ashanti,
Yoruba, and Fon, and maintained right through the colonial
period. It is significant that parades and military-style para-
phernalia seem to strike a responsive note in Africa as trappings
of social dancing—as is evidenced by the Malawian *chiwoda* and
the Ghanaian *concomba*, both twentieth-century group dances
that show strong parade influences.

The carnival, parade, and society supply symbolic group identification—and indeed a physical haven—for people who might
otherwise be under threat, such as the nineteenth-century *capoeira*
fighters and the Trinidadian stickmen, whose art was already akin
to music and dancing. Parades and carnivals must have allowed a
larger amount of self-assertiveness with impunity and, indeed,
provided an opportunity for people rarely allowed to assert
themselves to do so in ways of their own choosing, the ways at
which they were best.

The total art form—music, dance, costume, and visual art combined—is by no means dead, of course. James Brown is adept at
it. So is Sun-Ra. LeRoi Jones described a Sun-Ra concert in
Black Music:

> Sun-Ra wants a music that will reflect a life-sense lost in the West,
> a music full of Africa. The band produces an environment, with
> their music most of all, but also with their dress (gold cloth of
> velvet, headbands and hats, shining tunics). The lights go out on
> some tunes, and the only lights are flashing off a band on Sun-Ra's
> head.

Quite often, conscious efforts to achieve an effect are less successful than the same effect achieved unconsciously, but the attempt
seems to reflect something basic and enduring in Afro-American
art.

The process of self-definition and group support in music has
had some more direct factors, of course. Music of overt protest
and resistance has not been common, but there are examples.
One is a Brazilian dance called the quilombo. The original
quilombos were independent hamlets of escaped slaves, the most
famous of which, at Palmares, lasted from 1630 to 1697. Qui-

lombo dances inspired by these are danced in the State of Alagoas at Christmas or local festivals. There are few things more African than dances in praise of group heroes.

Politics has often formed part of a more wide-ranging social-comment element. Perhaps the most famous example is Trinidadian calypso, which comments on anything and everything, as we shall be seeing. Paul Bowles, writing on calypso in *Modern Music* in 1940, argued, "There is no doubt that Calypso songs were used like our spirituals here, as a clandestine means of spreading illegal knowledge among the slaves." Bowles suggested that repression partly brought about by this function helped preserve Africanisms in calypso.

The question of the resistance spirituals is not so clear-cut. Perry Bradford says in his autobiography that "Steal Away to Jesus" meant "steal away from their bosses and beat it up north to the promised land." The choice of verb, which seems odd in a religious context, makes this plausible. On the other hand, there seems little justification for Janheinz Jahn's wholesale co-optation of the spirituals as disguised freedom songs. True, "Follow the Drinking Gourd"—the Big Dipper, which points to the North Star—appears to have been a sort of oral escape map, but it also seems to have been written by somebody who thought in European poetic terms ("When the sun comes back and the first quail calls . . . Left foot, peg foot, traveling on"), and Harold Courlander says that according to legend the slaves learned it from a peg-leg sailor who wandered around telling people how to escape. Many spirituals, obviously, could be taken in a number of different ways without departing from the religious connotations, but there seems no doubt that the religious context was the original one.

A common social use of music in Africa is to satirize people who have broken social rules. This function has carried over to the New World. Courlander says, in *Negro Music USA*, that in the coastal area of Georgia the banjo was often used to accompany songs of ridicule directed at members of the community who had got out of line, a procedure known as "putting on the banjo." I shall be looking more closely at the various social-comment uses of individual Afro-American styles. Fundamentally, they follow the charming description by the freed slave Equiano of his Nigerian society's songs:

> Each represents some interesting scene of real life, such as a great achievement, domestic employment, a pathetic story, some rural sport, and as the subject is generally founded on some recent event it is therefore ever new. This gives our dances a spirit and variety which I have scarcely seen elsewhere.

One of the most-quoted forms of Afro-American functional music is the work song, and it is true that work songs have retained many Africanisms. I have mentioned the quite remarkable similarity in sound between U.S. prison work songs and some African singing, even where some non-African harmonic strands are present. Work songs are particularly suitable for group manual labor, whether gang-hoeing in the fields, loading on the docks, tamping railroad track, or hauling up sails or anchors. All these and many more activities had a rich body of song associated with them. The communal work songs seem to have been dying out for a long time under the impact of new methods of farming and mechanization in general, but they were widespread until recently. An author writing in the 1940's reported group work songs in a call-and-response style much like the U.S. versions as having been sung in Trinidad "within the last decade." As in African work song practice and its U.S. equivalents, the lead singer was frequently employed full time to lead the work by singing. In the Dominican Republic, work songs called *plenas* seem to have been used mainly to relieve the monotony of work rather than to pace it. Some Dominican *plenas* adopted a more European form than the U.S. versions: They often used a rhyming four-line verse, and the chorus sang a brief, often wordless phrase after each line or two. On the other hand, many chopping songs from the southern Dominican Republic are almost wholly African.

Rice-thrashing songs, rowing songs, a Louisiana creole song for sweeping floors, and even songs to accompany ironing have been recorded in the United States—not to mention a song to wake laborers on the railroad:

> Wake up buddy and sit on the rock,
> It ain't quite day but it's four o'clock.
> *Ratatat* (stick on the door).

Whatever their form, the work songs followed the pattern of other Afro-American music: They endured as long as they fulfilled a social role, and not necessarily a practical role.

Even ritual songs of a highly African nature, like initiation songs, have endured until recently in various places—despite Ernest Bornemann's thesis quoted earlier. Edric Conor recorded examples of West Indian games for teaching rhythm and self-reliance; a mock-fight dance called "Mama Today Is Your Son's Funeral" (a calinda) with Yoruba-sounding singing and percussion like Yoruba *apala* drumming; and even a "Senegalese" dance song performed by girls at a puberty ceremony with the warning lyric: "I send you to school and you bring back a belly for me." Besides the patently initiatory songs, black U.S. taunting songs like "The Dozens" arguably fill an initiatory function—teaching adolescents to keep their cool.

Finally, black children's songs and games in most parts of the Western Hemisphere show a clear mixture of European and African elements. What seems to be consistent, and African in its source, is their turning of all play forms into dance, very often with the call-and-response form and lively or complex rhythmic patterns.

Function, then, has proved the key to Afro-American survival-adaptation in the New World as a whole, and it has provided forms and elements that are in some degree common to the whole area. But Afro-American styles, despite much common background, are highly individual. From now on we shall be looking at each of the main regions—South and Central America, the Caribbean, and the United States—separately.

PART TWO

Black Music of the Americas

4 SOUTH AND CENTRAL AMERICA

Though there is a good deal of overlapping among its various regions, South America can be roughly divided into three zones of cultural influence: black, white, and Indian. White South America consists of Argentina, Chile, and Uruguay. Indian South America comprises Bolivia, Paraguay, Peru, and vast inland areas of Brazil, Ecuador, Colombia, Venezuela, and the Guyanas. Black South America is a coastal strip running north from Uruguay and all the way around to Ecuador, the countries mostly concerned being Brazil, the Guyanas, Venezuela, Colombia, the northern part of coastal Ecuador, and Panama, which, though in Central America, has strong musical connections with Colombia and was part of the old Spanish colonial viceroyalty of New Granada, together with Venezuela, Colombia, and Ecuador. Only certain areas of these countries can be considered black South America. Brazil varies a great deal in the makeup of its population. In Bahia, Negroes and mulattoes constitute seven-tenths of the total population; in the southern part of Santa Catarina State, they represent only 5 per cent. In the south virtually the only blacks are in the cities. In the northeast and the east they are concentrated in the coastal areas, where the plantations used to be.

Uneven distribution holds true for the rest of South America. According to Roger Bastide, blacks represent just under .5 per cent of the Peruvian population, but on the coast they are almost 5 per cent. In Colombia and Ecuador there are blacks on the coast and in the valleys of the interior—as well as in the valleys of Bolivia—but none in the Andes. In Venezuela, the black population is again concentrated on the coast, the area of the old slave plantations. And in all these countries there are areas with an almost entirely black population. The term "black" itself, like any racial term, is vague. South American countries generally divide people into several categories: white, mulatto (mixed black and white), black, Indian, and mestizo (mixed Indian and white). But in Brazil, mulattos and mestizos are lumped together as *pardos*. This causes problems when one tries to establish cultural links between groups. Nevertheless, the main patterns are clear.

Though in some respects the Guyanas, and particularly Surinam, are more African, Brazil probably has the most impressive black music in South America. We have already met some of the blackest music of Brazil in an earlier chapter, but we have not exhausted it. Like most of the music of black America, Brazilian music grew out of a complicated intermingling of all sorts of musical styles, so that it is dangerous to be too dogmatic about who contributed what. Analysis is doubly hazardous in that all the main strains in Brazilian music—Iberian, West and Central African, and Amerindian—have a number of features in common. Characteristic elements of Brazilian Indian music were similar to basic elements in African styles: call-and-response singing, a wide variety of subject matter, a group of ritual dances, and the use of rattles in music. Nevertheless, it is thought that the Amerindian contribution to Brazilian music as a whole has been much smaller than the African contribution, largely because black and white were in constant contact with each other in wide areas of populated Brazil, whereas most Indians lived in areas isolated by forest.

The African contribution was certainly major. Oneyda Alvarenga, one of Brazil's leading musicologists, has described thirteen major Africanisms in Brazilian music. They include the frequency of six-note scales with a flatted seventh-note (usually held to be a hallmark of Afro-American music and a feature of the "blues scale" of the United States); the origin, or at least the standardization, of the rhythmic phrase ♪♪♪ (which, we have seen, is common in virtually all Afro-American regions); call-and-response singing involving a single solo line, often improvised, followed by a short, unvarying chorus; the breaking up of the neat melodic framework that European music tends to use; the *umbrigada*, or belly-bounce, in dancing; a large number of musical instruments, including the various drums known collectively as *atabaque;* the great importance of drums generally in Brazilian dances and their frequent function as organizers of the choreography; dramatic dances (which are not found as such in Portugal, though the Brazilian ones may have Portuguese components); and a certain rather nasal tone of singing, which may be a cross between the rather open African tone and the more harsh, high sound favored in Iberian music.

Alvarenga also suggests that the importance of wind instruments in Brazilian music reflects African practice, but it is more likely to be a result of two traditions supporting each other. Africa makes use of rather more wind instruments than Portugal, but the *gaita,* an oboe-like instrument descended from Morocco, is quite widespread in Portugal, and bagpipes and various forms of flute are also used. The popularity of bowed string instruments again seems more probably a joint than a solely African tradition. The fiddle, under its Arab-derived name of *rebeca* or *rabeca,* came from Portugal. However, the enthusiasm with which New World blacks took to the fiddle, not only in Brazil but in the United States and Cuba as well, is surely related to the occurrence of fiddle-type instruments in parts of Africa. Portugal supplied virtually all of the non-rhythm instruments of Brazil and the chordal basis for the plucked or strummed instruments, mainly guitars of various sorts. The harmonic base of Brazilian music as a whole is usually said to be European, but that is probably an oversimplification. Group singing in Brazil, when it is not in unison or the African form of near-unison called heterophony, most frequently uses parallel thirds, with one voice singing the same tune (or virtually the same tune) a third below the other. Parallel thirds are known in Portugal but in fact do not

constitute a major part of Portuguese folk music. They are also
rare in European art music. On the other hand, they are widely
used by certain African groups, including some that supplied
slaves to Portugal. So it looks very much as if *vocal* harmonies, at
least, owe a good deal to Africa, the Portuguese contribution
being a reinforcing element (a reinforcing element often determines which qualities become part of a permanent cultural
blend). All in all, Mario de Andrade's claim that "we shall find in
Portuguese music all that on which our own [Brazilian] music
is based," quoted in the *Grove Dictionary of Music,* looks like an
example of cultural bias, ascribing to one side what really results
from both.

The general quality of melodic lines in Brazilian music is
mainly Portuguese. Even the gayest Portuguese melodies are
found to have a certain underlying melancholy, and this applies
as well to Brazilian tunes. Much of the decided difference between Portuguese and Brazilian melodic styles seems to stem
from the Brazilian use of a frequently syncopated and more complex rhythmic approach with displaced accentuations and cross-
rhythms against the percussion, all features of West and Central
African technique.

The heavy Portuguese content in Brazilian melodies does not
mean there are many tunes originally from Portugal that are now
regarded as Brazilian. There must certainly be some, just as
there are surely some tunes in Spanish South America that came
from Spain. But on the whole Latin American melodies appear to
have developed in Latin America, either because people made
new tunes in European styles or because tunes originally brought
over were so changed as to be unrecognizable. A third possibility
—quite strong—is that at least some Latin American melodies are
in fact ancient Iberian tunes that are forgotten in Spain and
Portugal and preserved in Latin America (just as some British
border ballads were preserved in the United States after being
forgotten in Britain). Certainly some lyrics survived in extremely
Spanish forms in the New World. And even where lyrics did not
remain unchanged, subjects whose interest had long faded in
Europe sometimes endured. A Library of Congress record of folk
music from Venezuela contains a *galerón* about an incident in

the wars between the Moors and the Christians. On the same record is the "Corrido del Pajarillo," basically a famous fifteenth-century Spanish romance with an improvised beginning and end.

Portuguese is by far the most important European strand in Brazilian music, but not the only one. Others include Italian art music, which swept Spain and Portugal in the latter part of the eighteenth century and arrived in their colonies a little later, and children's songs from various countries, including that international favorite, "Sur le Pont d'Avignon." There is a fairly important Spanish admixture that arrived indirectly through the influence of various Spanish-American forms. The Argentinian *tango* and the Cuban *habanera*, both of which use forms of

were major components of the Brazilian maxixe, an urban popular dance that gained international popularity during World War I. Cuban urban popular music has had a recurring influence on Brazil and most other parts of Afro-America.

Earlier I mentioned the dramatic dances of Brazil, which have no counterpart in Portugal but do have many African counterparts, especially in the mime dances, which are extremely common. Some of the Brazilian dances, like the congos and congadas, offer ample reason, in addition to the African roots of their names, for supposing that they have connections with the Bantu Congo-Angola region. A salient feature of the congos and congadas is the "embassy," a mock emissary-to-a-royal-court episode, which is thought to be a purely African element. One of these dances involves two characters named Prince Suena and Reina (Queen) Ginga. Prince Suena is probably a corruption of Suana Mulopo, the title of the immediate heir of leading or royal families of the Lunda empire. Reina Ginga (also called Zinga Nbangi in some versions of the dance) was an Angolan princess, Anna Nzinga, who fought the Portuguese at various times during the early seventeenth century and notably led a mission to them in 1622 that resulted in a peace treaty favorable to the Angolans. The Brazilian congadas, therefore, fairly clearly commemorate a woman who must rank as a leading figure in African resistance to colonial rule in the early days, if only for her tenacity and resourcefulness. (Jan Vansina's *Kingdoms of the Savanna* has an account of her activities.)

Most of Brazil's dramatic dances are clearly African-derived, but some are of highly obscure origin, like the bumba meu boi. The dance drama involves the figure of an ox, which Brazilian authors seem to feel has some link with Africa. In this case I suspect the link is illusory. It is true that African mime dances quite often involve animal characters, but the ox is not an African animal. It seems more likely that the bumba meu boi goes back to some European ritual complex related to bullfighting, perhaps even to Mithraism, which was popular in Roman Iberia until Christianity replaced it. Other bull-mime dances are known elsewhere in Iberian America, including a seis del toro in Puerto Rico.

Of the nondramatic or "straight" dances, much the best known outside of Brazil is the samba. There are many different forms of samba, from neo-African to polite salon varieties. The best known groups are the Bahian, the carioca of Rio de Janeiro and those from São Paulo. In the slums of Rio, the samba still keeps its old, largely neo-African ring-dance it was, from which the urban Rio samba stemmed, and in turn the Rio samba which became internationally popular. The samba of the slums, music of devastating polyrhythmic drive, provided much of the aural impact of the film *Black Orpheus*, whose sound track gives some impression of the sheer power of Afro-American drumming and dancing.

A basic Africanism in the samba is the overriding importance of rhythm. Another, not striking in any individual case but important in the sum of its appearances all over the Afro-American world, is the common use of nonmusical instruments ("nonmusical" from a white point of view). In the 1930's, the samba writers of Rio used to meet in a certain cafe and sing each other their latest soon-to-be hits. None of them played instruments, except the matchbox, to the accompaniment of which they sang all their songs. The matchbox, according to Ortiz Oderigo, was often joined by the straw hat, and a dish beaten with a knife. Oderigo goes on to say, in an article in *African Music:*

Moreover, in the streets of São Paulo, the writer has heard Negro shoeshine boys making rhythms and singing to the accompaniment of their wooden boxes and brushes played as if they were drums with their tin cans of shoe polish played as *agogos* or *adjas,* both of them similar to African instruments of the Candombles of Ewe-Yoruba origin.

The Bahian samba, at least, and perhaps other variants stemmed from *candomblé* cult drumming. There is an example of a highly neo-African samba da roda on David Lewiston's Nonesuch recording *Black Music of South America.* It shows plainly—apart from the call-and-response singing typical of Bahian samba, led by a woman in the center of the circle—how a neo-African rhythm (skeletal in this case, since the instrumentation sounds like one drum and hand-clapping) gave rise to the characteristic samba beat. The singing shows the African trait of relatively unchanged choral responses to improvised (or at all events, embellished) lead phrases. The Bahian samba is not always accompanied by percussion alone. Alvarenga says its most typical instrumentation is a *pandeiro* (a form of tambourine), guitar, and rattle, sometimes with castanets and *berimbau.*

The transference from religious to secular music, incidentally, reflects a general tendency for forms to feed back and forth. Not only have ritual styles influenced the more neo-African sambas; they often filter into urban popular music—and not just as influences, but as actual melodies. There are two examples of transference in Folkways' *Songs and Dances of Brazil,* recorded on the island of Itaparica in the Bay of Salvador, Bahia. The group recorded is of a popular type consisting of a small four-stringed instrument like a guitar, a guitar proper, and a tambourine. It presents a "Brazilian" rather than a "neo-African" style, but two of its numbers come from cult music. One is the samba "Pena Verde," which was on the popular market at the time as "macumba" music (a category that in itself is an indication of transference). Although it was credited to a popular composer, J. B. de Carvalho, it was originally sung only in the Indo-African rite, *candomblé de caboclo.* Another samba, an instrumental, opens the second side of the record. Oneyda Alvarenga says in the liner notes to the album that she once heard it also at a *candomblé de caboclo*. (The *candomblé de caboclo* seems to be the least "pure" of the rites, and the most open to nonreligious influences).

Other black dances of Brazil included the jongo, described by Alvarenga as "a violent black dance" accompanied by drumming, which displays the repetitive and fragmentary lyrics typical of much neo-African music. The lundú, which we have met before, has a strange history apparently not uncommon for Afro-American dances of the nineteenth century. It began as a neo-African dance, and indeed some Brazilian musicologists claimed that it originated in Congo or Angola. It became entirely urbanized relatively early, turned into a bourgeois social dance, and in this form was taken to Portugal and Spain. One expert held that either the fandango or the bolero of Spain might be a descendant of the lundú. The lundú was the first African-derived music accepted by the Brazilian bourgeoisie, and it brought into middle-class musical customs both the flatted seventh and syncopation as a way of life.

One of the features of Brazilian music is a large variety of urban popular styles. In fact, though far from being an Africanism, this seems to be something of a feature of Afro-American music as well. Virtually all the urban *popular* music of the New World (as opposed to Tin Pan Alley music), from jazz through calypso to the sambas, is wholly or partly Afro-American, whereas most white American music is rural (as, of course, is a great deal of black music).

Town versions of the samba are the Brazilian urban music best known to the rest of the world, but many other forms grew up in the towns of Brazil before it, and had their influence on the world. Surprising as it might seem, Marvin Harris, in *Town and Country in Brazil*, argues that the Brazilians have in fact a largely urban mentality, however small the towns involved may be. Historically, the towns have been the centers of cultural communication, which was true of some other American countries, notably Puerto Rico and Cuba.

The first Brazilian urban form to grow up was perhaps the modinha, which developed as a salon music in the second half of the eighteenth century and was widely popular in both Brazil and Portugal. Forgotten in Portugal, in Brazil the modinha spread and became a popular dance by the latter part of the nineteenth century but was always a fairly European style: Popular modinhas had a melody line full of decorated phrases and made much use of arpeggios and wide jumps of interval. Originally it was accompanied by piano, but more recently by guitar, a frequent development for dances that moved out of the salons into the streets.

The Rio urban samba stems from the slum dwellers who live on the hills (*morros*) around Rio. It has produced two versions. One, still danced by the people of the *morros,* flourishes among the so-called samba schools, societies of dancers that arrange carnival parades, with a director who teaches and directs the singing and dancing. There is some argument about what is the "true" form of this sort of samba. One kind consists of a call-and-response technique in which the director sings a line which is repeated by the chorus. It often shows the highly African feature of an improvised, changing solo line and a more fixed choral line.

The other form involves a previously composed refrain sung by a well-drilled ensemble and a more improvised solo part. A characteristic of samba is a kind of back-to-front call-and-response (fairly common elsewhere in South America and parts of the Caribbean). Either there is a refrain first and then call-and-response passages, or a line-by-line call-and-response, but with the "chorus" providing the first part, or "call." Whether this is simply a variant on African call-and-response forms or comes from a blend of African and European elements, I do not know. The opening section often follows an introduction with guitar, *cavaquinho,* and tambourine, or a concertina and rhythm. The singing is backed by percussion only, consisting of two drums, a tambourine, and a friction drum.

The growth of the "downtown" samba is typical of the confused situation in which differing samba styles exert influence, and are influenced, in several different directions (popular music has this tendency, irritating to the tidy mind but very good for the music). Its style derives from the maxixe, which is itself a hybrid of Brazilian and non-Brazilian ingredients, and was one of the best-known urban dances before the city samba. In Alvarenga's words, the first stage in the maxixe's development was a habanera-ized lundú, which the Brazilians called a tango. The European polka gave the maxixe its movement, the Cuban habanera its rhythm, Afro-Brazilian music added its syncopation. It was rejected as indecent, or at all events over-sensual, by the bourgeoisie, and became acceptable only in a toned-down version. Even so, it met with great hostility, as did most dances that grew out of Afro-American forms.

Modern urban sambas cheerfully go on taking in influences from all over in true popular style, including jazz drumming licks, guitar phrases, and (when appropriate) piano stylings. The bossa nova seems to have remained a much less genuinely popular music. Sprung from an ultra-cool attitude to the samba and some rather tenuous connections with modern jazz, it has in fact developed into the "whitest" of styles, in which the rhythmic impetus and cross-rhythms of the samba have been schematized into a formula that (a giveaway, this) can pretty easily be handled by non-Brazilian musicians.

Another form connected with the samba and with even stronger carnival connections is the marcha, which has little to do with the military but is ideal for the dance-parade of carnival time. The marcha's main feature is a very lively rhythm, and it tends to be a sing-along music. Modern Brazilian pop composers often use the marcha form, sometimes to contrast with a slower and more romantic style. An example is "Voce Passa eu Acho Graca" (on an Odeon LP, MOFB 3549), which opens with a terrific carnival-style jam session for percussion including friction drum and chorus, then distills out into a skeletal rhythm for a beautiful balladlike solo song. The marcha has been open to all sorts of influences at various times, including the North American one-step.

Brazil also has a musical style vaguely reminiscent of jazz—not in the way it sounds, but in that it is instrumental and employs contrapuntal techniques somewhat as the early New Orleans jazz groups did. It is called the *choro,* which originally referred to the band itself but is now applied to the music it plays. The *choro* groups have a woodwind frontline: flute, clarinet, sax, and so on (without the brass typical of jazz, which of course is a major difference, apart from all the stylistic differences). The *choro*, which plays at both concerts and dances, goes back to the early nineteenth century, when military or semimilitary music (or at least groups vaguely based on the small German and French military orchestras that oompahed away in the parks of Europe and the Americas) were popular. *Choro* music used to be purely instrumental, but for the past twenty or thirty years it has been going over to vocal pieces with samba connections. The typical *choro* vocals used fluid and leaping vocal lines derived from the clarinet solo lines they displaced. *Choro* music in fact often used the samba form more or less completely, in hybrids known as *samba-choro*.

By now it should be clear that Brazilian music as a whole could exist neither without its African nor without its Portuguese components, and that in fact stereotypes about "European melody, African rhythm"—though they do, very inadequately, represent a very general musical tendency—are not the end of the matter. Even the question of rhythm in Portuguese music is not as simple as it might seem. We have seen that, in a very general way, the music of the Iberian Peninsula and the music of West Africa share a liking for brisk, pulsating, fairly dominant and complex rhythmic patterns.

The dominance of percussion in most popular Brazilian music is obviously related to African attitudes, but it should not simply be assumed to be totally African in its source. Many of the percussion instruments are of African origin, and the use of crossrhythms is African, but the rhythms of Portuguese music themselves seem to be a blend of Iberian and African. In fact, the presence in Brazilian *national* music of so much percussion must derive from the fact that Portuguese music also quite regularly uses drums, tambourines, and triangles—a legacy, along with some of the rhythms, of the Arab period. Indeed the Brazilian name for the bass drum, *bombo*, is also used in Spain and Portugal, as is the general Brazilian word for the drums that figure in ritual ceremonies, *atabaque*, though the names of the individual cult drums are usually African. Because the music of Portugal, especially southern Portugal, was influenced by the Arab domination (though not as fundamentally as southern Spain), and because at least one of the African regions represented in Brazil was also musically influenced from North Africa through Islam, the potential for a high degree of blending was plainly there. It seems that in secular, generalized dance music, particularly that of areas other than Bahia, the typical Brazilian rhythms are as often Portuguese rhythms treated in an African fashion, as African rhythms. The same reinforcement may have occurred in harmony, since like the music of many African groups the folk music of Alemtejo often used parallel thirds, but never three-voice harmonies.

Brazilian music and the music of Spanish South America sound quite different, because, despite an underlying connection, Spanish and Portuguese music differ considerably. Besides, the *national* musics of Spanish South America—even of the parts with the greatest African influence—seem to contain fewer Africanisms than Brazilian music. Within the Afro-Spanish area, similar general situations, together with regional variations, led to the growth of musical styles that were distinct but related and that modified each other mutually. The similarities were helped by the fact that the main Afro-Spanish countries, Venezuela, Colombia, Ecuador, and Panama, were cut off geographically from the rest of South America and were governed together for a good deal of their history.

The ties between Spanish music and the music of Spanish South America are, if anything, more obvious than those between Portuguese and Brazilian music, but this does not mean that South America has not developed highly original styles. Both Spanish and West and Central African music, in Bruno Nettl's words, "favored complicated driving rhythms with steady, pulsating patterns." This is true of the Spanish music best known to non-Spaniards, *flamenco,* and also much other Spanish folk music, especially that from the south. The similarity between Spanish and African approaches extended to the occurrence in much Spanish music of combinations of duple and triple rhythms, though not simultaneous. Many Spanish rhythmic patterns are quite near enough to African patterns for African techniques (cross-rhythms, the overlaying of triple on duple rhythm, and so on) to fit them perfectly. And the rhythmic improvisation, which is such a feature of some African drumming—the approach of the lead drummer in many areas—is not alien to the Spanish. A magnificent collection of Spanish folk music on the Spanish label Hispavox contains examples of very complex percussion, including a stunning display from a girl singing to the accompaniment of her own tambourine, which incorporates long passages of fiery rhythmic improvisation.

Even the cross-beats of African music were not totally foreign to Spanish music, one of whose Moorish-derived features was the use of handclapping (another important element in African music) to provide rhythms cutting across the main pulse. Drums themselves are not at all unusual in Spanish folk music of some regions, though unlike the tambourines they usually play a skeletal beat. All in all, therefore, conditions were good for a high degree of merging between the two traditions. One difference between Spanish and Latin American music is an apparent greater importance of musical instruments in America, which becomes more significant when we realize that the same appears to be true of U.S. black music and of the music of some parts of the Caribbean, and when we remember the number and importance of instruments in Africa, as compared with Europe.

Nevertheless, the Africanisms remain obvious in many cases, especially in the music of the coastal areas of the countries with most black inhabitants, Venezuela, Colombia, Ecuador, and Panama. Panama and Colombia, in fact, share a number of musical forms, including the cumbia. Colombia is the fourth largest South American country, with a population of 21 million, of which nearly one-third are of Spanish descent, one-half *mestizos*, and the rest blacks or Indians. Colombian music as a whole contains much that is African, but it is most noticeable in the coastal music. The main "national" forms are the *bambuco* and the pasillo. The *bambuco* is often described as heavily African, but in fact it is, as played, not strikingly so. (Various explanations link the name with an old kingdom in Mali.) The *bambuco*, it is true, mixes duple and triple beats, but not played together, for the most part, so this could just as well be a Spanish trait as

an African one. The fact that the *bambuco* tends to "European"
types of lyric, with narratively connected themes of unhappy love
(a topic of minor interest in Africa), social injustice, and the far-
away home, also suggests a heavy Spanish element.

The pasillo, a dance also found in Venezuela, seems to have
started as a salon dance and is connected with the waltz (which
has become fairly well acclimated in some parts of the New
World). In fact it is really a sort of syncopated waltz with heavy
first and last beats. Its main interest for us—apart from showing
what a mixture of Spanish and African techniques could do to a
highly European form—is that the Venezuelan pasillo rhythm is
an element in the Trinidadian calypso.

Truly Afro-Colombian music falls into two parts, that of the
Atlantic coast and that of the Pacific (divided by the southern
border of Panama). The Atlantic coast has the merengue, cumbia
and related cumbiamba, punto, porro, mejorana, and rumba. The
African and African-descended instruments found there include
the marimba, the *quitiplas* (stamping tubes), and the *merecure*
(a drum).

The merengue came originally from the Dominican Republic
and spread to most parts of the Spanish Americas. In Colombia,
it most often has lyrics of social or political comment rather along
the lines of the calypso, usually in a rhyming four-line verse:

> Si la justicia te encuentra
> Robando con los ladrones,
> Ay que yo le digo a la justicia:
> Que el que no roba no come.
>
> (If the law finds you
> Stealing with the robbers,
> Ay, what I say to the law:
> That whoever doesn't steal doesn't eat.)

Though African and Afro-American music makes great use of
social comment, on the whole this type of direct political statement sprang from a Spanish tradition.

The porro has been described as halfway between a cumbia

and a merengue, and in fact grew out of a section of the cumbia
that used a contrasting beat. The mejorana has two modes, one
sung and the other for dancing, and appears to have originated
in Panama, though this is disputed. It is played on a small five-
stringed guitar known as a *mejoranera*, with percussion. The
mejorana has one very African quality, a blend of two meters—
accompaniment in triple time and melody in duple—and frequently has a tune built up of short, much repeated phrases
reminiscent of a common African melodic technique.

But of all the Atlantic Colombian music, the cumbia is the
most strikingly African. Like many South American dances it has
a polite salon form, but it belongs in the streets. It opens with a
male dancer inviting a girl to dance by giving her a handful of
candles, which she holds while dancing in a circle round the
musicians and her partner, with much hip movement. Cumbias
are usually played in a driving style with a good deal of emphasis
on drum and rattle percussion, including variations from the
lead drummer, with a highly repetitive melodic line often played
by fiddle or accordion. The drumming in many examples makes
much use of cross-rhythms. It displays many Africanisms, and
even its obvious Spanish elements are heavily Africanized in
most cases. The cumbia has become a popular style with city
bands and is often given a Cuban sound. It is sometimes said to
descend from an African dance called the cumbe and has one
interesting feature that may well be an adaptation of an African
technique: a verse ending on a chord whose resolution comes
only during the first line of the next verse, so that the tune seems
to have no beginning or end. The African equivalent is a final
beat of a drum pattern acting as first beat in the melody line.
This is not at all the same as the frequent European technique
of launching again into the tune without a pause.

Perhaps the most characteristic Afro-Colombian music of the
Pacific coast of Colombia is the currulao, a fiery rhythm that is
both a dance form and a background for songs of praise (*alabao*)
for the festival of San Antonio. David Lewiston's record *Black
Music of South America* contains some examples of currulao from
Guapi, an extremely isolated black community on the Pacific
coast that has kept many Africanisms in its music, such as the

marimba xylophone, whose name is widespread in Africa. (Hugh Tracey, the African musicologist, theorizes that the marimba may actually have traveled to the New World from Mozambique, for the Shangaan people of Mozambique—a coastal group—call it *marimba,* and the first boatload of slaves was taken from the Shanga coast to South America as early as 1530.)

The currulao songs have many African traits, including call-and-response singing of very oblique and fragmented texts. Lewiston recorded one full of *double entendre* of a sort particularly enjoyed by West African audiences, who delight in songs that on one level are highly sexual and on another nonsexual, being sometimes instructional songs for children. The over-all style of the lyrics of many of these songs is reminiscent of African songs using apparently unrelated proverbs, references known only to a particular group, and so on, to build up a whole that, as it were, glances sideways at the main topic.

In the valleys away from the coast of Colombia, where the population is divided among Indians, blacks, and *mestizos,* there is a good deal of mixing of African and Indian elements. An example is a piece played at a cowherds' festival with pipe-playing that is mainly Indian combined with plenty of improvisation in the drumming. Colombian Indian music goes in a good deal for pipe-and-tabor styles (one of the popular types of Indian ensemble in the Cauca region is the *chirimia,* which contains many Indianisms but is named after a Spanish type of oboe).

As the existence of a large number of forms known collectively as *golpe* (beat) might suggest, Venezuelan music has a rhythmic basis heavily influenced by its more neo-African forms, as well as those neo-African forms themselves, and of course plenty of music whose background is largely Spanish. The *golpe* is originally a drumming pattern, stemming from the basic pattern of the *tambor redondo,* the purest neo-African mode, and the basic pattern of the *tambor grande* or *merecure.* We discussed the neo-African drum dances of the Barlovento region in Chapter 2, with their call-and-response patterns for drums; their polyrhythms, the extra beat provided by a second player drumming on the side of the drum with a pair of sticks; and the call-and-response singing, which proceeds independently of the drum rhythms, according to its own rhythmic structure, and thus provides another poly-rhythmic element. The *golpe*, in some forms, have become basic rhythms for a number of more generalized musical styles.

Black music in most Latin American countries shows a wealth of religious forms, often associated with elaborate wakes, an Africanism in the New World, as we have seen, and often accompanied by possession states similar to those in African and neo-African spirit cults. The wakes are religiosocial occasions, and much of what is played is whatever secular music may be popular at the time. The black areas of Venezuela, and many other countries, had an elaborate ceremony for the death of a child, the *mampulorio*, involving song-and-action rituals. The custom was dying out in the 1940's, having been outlawed, perhaps because the corpse of the baby, apparently, was often boiled.

Another religious ceremonial associated with black music in these countries, especially in Venezuela, is the *Velorio del Cruz*, celebrated in May. *Velorios* are celebrated in private houses, where an altar is set up with an image of the saint being honored. The music usually takes the form of praise songs, and in Barlovento it is broken up with competitive recitation of *décimas*, a basic Spanish poetic form, which died out in Europe but is still preserved in Spanish America. The *décimas* may be either religious or secular. The *velorios* are by no means exclusively a black phenomenon. In some parts of Venezuela the music is entirely Spanish in origin or often has strong Canary Islands influences. But the *fulias* sung at *velorios* in Barlovento show strong African qualities mixed with their fundamentally Spanish features, such as a long, highly decorated melody line. They are not always call-and-response, but when sung solo they may make use of a short refrain repeated after every line. The instrumentation for the *velorios* is usually *cuatro* (a small four-stringed guitar), six-stringed guitar, drums, and maraccas.

Black Venezuelan music is often associated with religious festivals, like various types of black music elsewhere. The Maracaibo neighborhood has a form of Christmas song called *gaita*, in call-and-response style, with a good deal of percussion, much of it improvised. The *gaitas* used to be religious but have tended to

develop into praise songs for the stores being serenaded in the
hope of handouts (the praise song aimed at earning gratuities is
a common phenomenon in many parts of West Africa, especially
those having professional *griot* musicians). There is also a dance
music in the Lake Maracaibo area associated with New Year's
Eve, which features improvised call-and-response songs accompanied by clarinet and drums.

The most "national" styles of Venezuela, the joropo and
galerón, are both dances of mixed ancestry, usually played by
string orchestras. Not particularly "black" music, they nonetheless
show clear African characteristics, such as the galerón's frequent
use of a call-and-response technique in the melody. The galerón
forms part of the *Velorios del Cruz* on the coast, but on the
plains it used to be danced. The old string-band dance form
traveled to Trinidad, in fact, where Venezuelan music was one
element in a highly complex mixture. The galerón does not use
much percussion, and the rhythmic techniques of the guitar,
cuatro, and mandolin seem to be largely Spanish and perhaps
Canary Islands–derived, though undoubtedly the existence of
black musical forms in Venezuela has influenced it, just as black
U.S. music has influenced most of the styles thought of as most
typical of white folk music.

"Joropo" is one of those words that, like "samba," mean all
kinds of things; indeed, it is often used simply to mean "dance,"
as in "Voy a un joropo esta noche." On the whole it is a popular
style, with composers who are known by name, but traditional
golpes are often called joropos, especially when their origin is
not known. In fact, the public will sometimes give the name
joropo to a piece of music called something quite different by its
composer.

Besides these examples, of course, Venezuela makes use of
styles that started elsewhere, such as the merengue and the
cumbia. Sometimes they may become naturalized and give rise
to a new form. This seems to have happened with the guasa,
a dance music that is said to be a development of the merengue.

Venezuela also has its share of dance-dramas, some of them
reminiscent of European mumming plays, with a cast including

a Doctor (or Sorcerer), a Snake who may represent the Devil, and various religious and magical symbolisms. These on the whole seem far less African than the Brazilian dance-dramas, though they have ritual elements that could well appeal to Indians and Africans and attract Indian and African musical traits. There is a Library of Congress recording of Venezuelan music that contains a "Snake-Killing Song" in this vein, and while much of it is in European-derived, acted mumming-play style, it contains songs with African elements of call-and-response, extreme repetition, and so on (and a tune in places remarkably like the old British West Indian song, "Hold 'Im Joe").

Panamanian music, though strongly connected with that of Colombia, has one notably African-derived form that is more or less exclusively Panamanian. This is the tamborito, essentially a women's music, accompanied by drums. I have already mentioned some of its African features, including the lead drum's role in guiding the choreography and the way in which musicians, dancers, and spectators each have a role in a musical whole. The lyrics of most tamboritos show strong Africanisms. They tend to be couplets rhyming in European style but endlessly repeated, and often highly cryptic, or proverbial, or simply in the general form of a proverb. Narcisco Garay, in his *Tradiciones y Cantares de Panama*, says of one tamborito: "It says nothing, in two lines: it is a mere pretext for singing and dancing." An example of the proverbial quality of many tamboritos is this one, with its suggestion of several layers of serious and ribald meaning:

> Mi mama me dió un consejo,
> No comer conejo viejo.
>
> (My mother advised me,
> Don't eat old rabbit.)

There is an old tradition of political tamboritos, going back at least to 1830. One of these, from the beginning of the century, was a response to the action of General Davis, president of the commission of the Panama Canal, in establishing separate postal facilities:

> Los gringos son los que mandan, Panameños en la yaya
> Los gringos no mandan nada en la Zona de Canal.

Another mixes business and pleasure:

> Con mi morena voy a bailar
> Lunes y martes de Carnaval
> Chiari sera, Chiari sera
> El Presidente de Panama.

> (With my girl I'm going to dance
> On Carnival Monday and Tuesday.
> Chiari will be, Chiari will be
> President of Panama.)

Some tamboritos show other Africanisms. "El Frijolar" has melody and words that in places do not coincide, in a fashion reminiscent of the music of the Ewe, who will frequently treat the last beat of a drummed pattern as the opening beat of the vocal part. It is intriguing that North African dance music (especially Algerian) is so played that it is often difficult to tell where the music starts and finishes, and that in North African music, too, the rhythm of the melody is independent of that of the accompaniment, as is the case in many tamboritos. An example of this "free rhythm" singing can be heard in a tamborito called "Hojita de Lemon," issued on the French Vogue record *Cumbias et Tamboritos de Panama*, where it is backed by 2/4 clapping and fast drummed triplets. This is a feature of some Spanish music, and of much more West African music, so there is an apparent continuum in which coincidence seems more improbable than influence, though of course which way the influence ran is not clear. In the New World the effect may be an Africanism, or a Spanishism, or more likely a phenomenon of mutual support.

Call-and-response is quite common in the tamborito, often with very short melodic phrases:

> Y mueve la colita
> *Tio Cayman*
> Como una señorita
> *Tio Cayman.*

In general the melody is quite African, with its two short phrases repeated many times. Together with the drumming, such repetition raises tension to a pitch at which musicians, dancers, and singers are whipped into a collective emotional and physical experience that provides a powerful sense of catharsis. The rhythmic build-up of constantly repeated phrases goes on until there is a sense almost of imminent explosion, when suddenly the lead drummer will signal a change from one rhythm to another, creating an extraordinary emotional discharge. As anyone who has danced to African or Afro-American drumming will know, this is not unlike hypnosis and is a highly refreshing phenomenon. As Garay describes it, the drummers, as the point of maximum tension approaches, appear "possessed by a strange mysticism; their glances, their contortions and the movements of their heads remind one extraordinarily of the gestures of the oriental fakirs." The accumulation of nervous tension is reflected in the singing, the dancing, and the women's handclapping; then, "when everybody seems about to reach a point of paroxysm, the sudden change of rhythm, the transition from *corriente* to *norte* or from *norte* to *corriente* opens like a safety valve." (*Norte* and *corriente* are common names for the two main drummed sections, one in 2/4 and the other in 6/8 time, though the names vary from region to region.)

The mejorana, which I mentioned in connection with Colombian music, is in Panama of obviously mixed ancestry, but one form—the mejorana-poncho—makes some use of duple and triple rhythm played together. Also, the small fiddle, a very common instrument in danced mejorana (a three-stringed instrument with the originally Arab name of *rabel*), often plays a melodic line of a quite different rhythm from the accompaniment.

The effect of African music on the music of the other countries of South America is somewhat more vague and open to argument one way or the other, all too often on grounds of cultural chauvinism. There is little doubt that the music of Chile and Argentina in "white" South America and of Bolivia and Paraguay in the mainly Indian sector has been affected by black music, whether through the former presence of slaves who left the country (as when Rosas gave freedom and a passport to many thousands of slaves in Argentina), became absorbed into the population as a whole, or formed small minorities of African descent in these countries, or through the influence of the music of other countries. Ortiz Oderigo claims that not only did the Amerindians adopt the African marimba, they also adopted African drumming techniques. In exchange, black musicians in some countries have borrowed the pre-Columbian *quena* flute. There are, too, a number of dances with names of apparent African origin, like the Argentinian milonga and malambo. (One can go too far in making these analogies, like Albert Friedenthal, who claimed that the Amerindian *yaravi* of Peru, Bolivia, and Ecuador was connected with the Arabic expression "Ya Rabi"—"Oh, Lord"!)

Some dances with African-style names presumably came from blacker neighbors, like the Argentinian zamba. Other influences in Argentina may have stemmed from the small coastal black population of Uruguay, though most of the musical currents flow the other way. On the other hand, there was at one time a definite neo-African culture in Argentina itself, since many authors have reported the presence in the eighteenth and early nineteenth centuries of "nation" groups and cults. Much of the African musical practice presumably just stayed behind when the majority of the slaves left, to become progressively absorbed into the mainly Spanish-influenced mainstream. Incidentally, that absorption would be the more complete in that Argentina is one of the few countries (with Chile) that preserved mostly northern Spanish traits—those that have least affinity with Islamic African music through North Africa.

5 THE CARIBBEAN

The music of the Caribbean is crucial to an understanding of how African and European gave birth to Afro-American music. The music of South America comes from African blending with European elements, Spanish and Portuguese, that had a certain amount in common with it to begin with. On the other hand, in the United States the blending process has gone so far that it is difficult to disentangle the strands involved. But the Caribbean contains music that embraces quite neo-African styles; styles that still preserve old European elements in a pure form; and every possible amalgam of European and African. Moreover, Caribbean forms on the European side were derived principally from three countries, Spain, Britain, and France. This is particularly helpful, because, if a given feature is found on several islands speaking all three languages, there is a strong possibility that it came from the African side. The European ingredients present (Spanish, British, French, and Dutch) are fairly different one from another. Hence, apparent Africanisms that are widespread are likely to have an African background, although extensive communication among various parts of the Caribbean carried certain elements of the music of one island to another. The interconnections were chiefly between islands speaking the same language, of course, but not entirely. Interisland migration, as well as the ebb and flow of pop styles, has made of the islands a network of influences. Besides, Trinidad has been affected by Venezuelan music, and Louisiana under French and Spanish rule was culturally part of the Caribbean, so that elements of Caribbean music have had their effect on the United States.

Of the whole Caribbean, Cuban music has perhaps had the most international influence, both within and outside the islands themselves, despite the fact that Cuba, along with Santo Domingo and Puerto Rico, was long a neglected backwater of the Spanish Empire. Until the middle of the eighteenth century there were very few settlers of any kind in Cuba, and slaves formed a small minority. It was not until the 1760's (about 250 years later than Brazil and Central America) that Cuba became involved fully in the so-called South Atlantic System and developed a plantation sector worked largely by African slaves. Puerto Rico did so even later.

Cuba was a Spanish colony longer than any other country in the Americas. Even as a republic it received a major Hispanic influx in the persons of 300,000 legal and several thousand officially "illegal" Spanish immigrants. Another important immigration was of Canary Islanders brought in to help develop the cigar industry. Canary Islands music is akin to, but not the same as, Spanish, and one of the differences is of relevance to blending with African styles. Whereas Spanish music tends to regular verse forms (though less rigidly than Northwestern Europe), some of the main Canary styles—especially the folia—go in for single lines separated from each other and building up a melodic pattern of phrases rather than verses. Cuba (like Puerto Rico and the Dominican Republic) acquired new European influences when it began to be included in the tours of traveling concert and opera groups. In 1842, a visit from an Italian opera company started a rage for opera, and the influence of romantic operetta on bolero singing in Cuba is still all too obvious. Among the famous musicians to visit the islands were the singer Adeline Patti and the U.S. pianist Louis Moreau Gottschalk, who almost alone saw the beauties of the local music and used it in his own compositions.

The course of Cuban popular music was affected by social developments, in particular by the desire of the Cuban elites just after independence to show that they were the equal of the "civilized" nations—equality in their minds meaning more opera houses and fewer Africanisms. In 1913, traditional carnivals were banned, and the African cults were intermittently persecuted for years, mostly at the whim of the local police.

Perhaps the best-known Cuban rhythm is the rumba, which in a much watered-down form was popular in North America and Europe in the 1920's and 1930's, and which in the 1950's and 1960's was of great importance in the development of one of the leading new African styles, Congo music. The rumba began life as a strongly neo-African secular festival dance of several movements. The original rumba music was percussive and showed the common African and neo-African feature of a lead drum (the *cajoncito de velas*) improvising over constant rhythmic patterns from the *cajón*. Incidentally, the player of the *cajoncito* is called a *quinteador*, just as the smaller drum in Panamanian tamborito music and the Venezuelan *tambor redondo* is a *requinto*. Besides these drums, the spoons play a part rather like metal percussive instruments in some West African ensembles, and the *claves* (two sticks tapped together) have a role extremely like that of the *gankogui* bell in Ewe music, its equivalents in much other West African music, or indeed the bottle tapped with a knife, which is quite common these days. It supplies an unvarying skeletal rhythmic pattern to which the other patterns are related and which acts as an unvarying base against which the rhythms of the other instruments are set off. The role of the *claves* is possibly the most striking parallel with a specifically *West* African basic instrumental practice. Another instrumental Africanism, taken over from Cuban Bantu ritual styles, is the use of rattles strapped to the *quinteador*'s wrists. The instrumentation of the rumba group was not highly standardized, of course; the *cajónes* could be replaced by barrel drums called a *tumbadora* and a *quinto*. Harold Courlander, in an article on Cuban musical instruments in the *Musical Quarterly*, mentioned a lineup consisting of a piano, two conga drums, *quinto*, maraccas, piano, and *claves*, which were also used as sticks on the side of one of the conga drums, in neo-African style.

The dance form of the rumba was a part of the festival as a

whole. Sometimes it was just one incident in the course of events, sometimes there would be several dances linked together under the general name of rumba. Like many Afro-American and African dances, the dance tended to open with solo song. In the *Rumbas de Tiempo'España,* two solo singers would sing a short passage, and the call-and-response would begin. The first soloist would also set the rhythm with the *claves,* to be picked up first by the big drum and then by the *quinto.* The pattern is very similar to that of a number of African and neo-African dances we have discussed, though here the soloist marked the beat with a percussion instrument, whereas in others the drummer picks it up from the vocal.

The dancing itself took the common African form of a couple (or solo) dance inside a ring of singer-watchers. In some rumba dances, like the yambú, there was—as in many African dances—a large element of mime, in the case of the yambú itself, imitating old age.

Another form of rumba, and the most influential in the long run, was the guaguancó. This began with a long solo vocal passage in narrative form, often with a topical or personal subject, which had a fairly fluid melody line with held notes and a rhythm faster than the yambú. The dance was essentially an attraction-repulsion courting dance. The guaguancó went into the popular theater and cabaret acts and was associated with costumes that originally had fiesta connotations. It is still popular with so-called Latin-jazz groups. Another common form of rumba dance, this one for a single person, was the columbia, which made references (usually joking or satirical) to the *lucumí* and *abakwá* rituals. The soloist often gets into a rhythmic "argument" with the lead drummer of a sort we have met elsewhere. All these types continue the strong song-dance-visual-aural-performer-spectator continuum that is fundamental to African aesthetic concepts.

A Cuban mode of great importance (and charm) is the *son.* To what extent the *son* came from black use of Spanish elements, or how much it was a general music with strong black content, is not clear. It sprang from an earlier and simpler form, the estribillo, which had been around since the eighteenth century, accompanied in the early days by the guitar and a small three-stringed guitar called a *tres*. At some time the bass came to be filled in by the *marimbula*, the big descendant of the African marimba hand piano, and the *botija*, a jug blown into to give a booming bass note (also used by many jook, spasm, and skiffle bands in the United States). The presence of these instruments, especially the *marimbula*, suggests a black origin for the *son*, which is not invalidated by the early use of the guitars, for there is evidence that black Cubans took to the guitar much earlier than blacks in North America (hardly surprising, since the guitar is fundamental to Spanish music, and not to white U.S. music). The bongos—the linked twin drums—and other small drums were used in *son* groups, and so from time to time were the *güiro* or the *maraccas*. The estribillo developed from the *décima*, the ten-line Spanish poetic form, but is said to have been adopted by black Cubans quite early.

The *son* came to town from the country in the early part of the twentieth century. Arrived in Havana, it developed a format of guitar, *tres*, *maraccas*, *claves*, bongo, and *marimbula*. Around that time, a trumpet was often added. The *son* then became a major urban popular form with recognized stars, some of whose records you can still buy today, reissued on LP. Among the best-known groups from the great days of the urban *son* were the Septeto Nacional, led by Ignacio Piñeiro; the Septeto Habanero; and the Quarteto Machin. Their groups played in a style still heavily influenced by Afro-American drumming and also (in some of the trumpet playing) by nineteenth-century Spanish military brass techniques. On the other hand, it was taking in influences from jazz both in the brass-playing and in some guitar work (the favorite jazz model in guitar was the French jazzman Django Reinhardt, whose style would blend with Cuban styles much better than most other jazz guitar). Numbers like the Septeto Nacional's "Echalo Salsita" already point the way forward with a B section in a style still played by groups in the Spanish-speaking Caribbean and by the Afro-Cuban groups in the United States.

The *son* form was firmly based on African concepts, though with guitar-playing in a strong Spanish vein. Most *sones* use call-and-response singing, and some show an African attitude by making the response the tune, "Para Que No Pago," for example, by the Quarteto Machin. During the B tune, this often drops the solo vocalist altogether, replacing him with improvised phrases first from the trumpet and then from the guitar. The *son* groups are the link between Cuban country folk music and the urban popular groups of today's Hispanic music world. They bridged the gap both in their instrumentation and in their growing complexity.

Other Cuban forms of some interest include the guaracha, which brought together Spanish and African vocal habits by using improvised solo quatrains answered by regular chorus refrains. It too was a strongly mime-oriented dance form. It began in the brothels in the nineteenth century and was taken over by the popular theater. It tends to have satirical lyrics somewhat along the same lines as the Trinidadian calypso. Some guarachas printed in the 1880's both began and ended with a solo verse, which is normally a strong African element. The habanera, whose tango-like rhythm, yet another version of ♪♪♪♪, developed from the danza, gained a certain amount of popularity in the United States, and occasionally crops up in jazz-related forms. The pianist Jimmy Yancey used it with very original effect. Another music that spread outside the island was the bolero, which was influenced by Mexican guitar techniques in the nineteenth century but whose present ultrasentimental nature seems to have come from fashions for would-be romantic—but mostly merely sentimental—music among the Cuban middle class in the nineteenth century.

A major feature of Cuban popular modes is the importance of instrumental music. This has tended to follow two lines of development: Afro-Cuban on the one hand, and more white-oriented on the other (though both, of course, fed each other). In modern terms, one might say, the first was represented by the mambo, and the second by the cha cha chá.

The Afro-Cuban strain grew out of various neo-African combinations—not only the rumba groups, but the *comparsa* Holy Week procession bands—using various combinations either of drums, rattles, and scrapers alone, or of drums, rattles, and scrapers with a guitar or two (or, in the case of the *comparsas,* trumpets) added. The more European form was represented by the *charanga francesa,* or "French orchestra," which also used guitars and rhythm but tended to feature flutes and violins. This style is by no means a thing of the past, nor should the distinction between the more "African" and the more "European" be taken too rigidly. The popular New York–based musician Johnny Pacheco's first group in the United States was called a charanga and featured lead flute and fiddle riffs that clearly went back to the old *charangas francesas* but were also related to the Afro-Cuban groups' trumpet and sax work. The interisland contacts today, and the islands' links with the United States, are typified by Pacheco, whose birthplace was the Dominican Republic, whose musical influences were Cuban, and who has made his name playing for Spanish-speaking audiences in the United States.

Apart from the *charangas francesas,* there were in the nineteenth century Cuban versions of the sort of small military band that used to give concerts in the parks of Europe. These would typically consist of two clarinets, cornet, valve trombone, double bass, *güiro,* and a couple of small drums, filled out perhaps with a pair of violins (probably tending toward the Cuban riff fiddle style after a while—at all events, the presence of the *güiro* suggests original elements in these groups). The playing of these groups is enshrined in the cornet work on many of the Septeto Nacional's discs.

In the twentieth century, Cuban instrumental music came under heavy jazz influence—as indeed Cuba as a whole came under too much U.S. influence, particularly economic. The *charanga francesa* at times became huge and bourgeois, as can be heard in the recordings of the Orquesta Antonio Ma. Romeu, which uses flute, florid piano, instruments that it would be coarse to call fiddles, and a suitably white-gloved rhythm section. Some of the Romeu orchestra's recorded pieces (which still sell briskly) show mainstream Cuban styles, but many take deep bows in the direction of Rudolf Friml and various other figures from overseas. The music most played by orchestras of this type was a development of the universal older contradanza, a creolized European form that was susceptible of a great width of treatment. We have met the contradanza in South America. In the Caribbean it was widespread, together with a number of middle-class dances of the nineteenth century. (Parts of the lancers, the quadrille, the mazurka, and even the waltz have become acclimated in many parts of the Caribbean, as we shall see.) The contradanza grew into a folk form (more correctly, a semifolk form) called the danzón, which is still popular, though there is rather a middle-class, "those-were-the-days" feel about it.

In the 1930's, more folk elements came back into Cuban popular music, and the influence of jazz began to be digested. Like most dance-band musicians, Cuban band members could and did play music of both types. As a result, such features as solo trumpet work with heavy jazz overtones and ensemble arrangements borrowing from big-band jazz became an integral part of a style that it would be artificial to call "black" or "white." The cha cha chá swept the island in the early 1940's, bringing back much of the *charanga francesa* style of flute and fiddles, which can be heard in old recordings of the Orquesta Aragón, one of the leading groups of the cha cha chá boom. This group, which was formed in Cienfuegos in 1939, was just another band until it turned to playing cha cha chás; it then had a number of hits, including "Cero Codazos, Cero Cabezazos" and "Pare Cochero," both of which are still available. The cross-fertilization between the more and less Afro-Cuban groups and styles continued, so that the cha cha chá is often played in an Afro-Cuban style as well as a charanga style, albeit a rather pallid one. In the last few years, there has been something of a return to the old *charanga francesa* style, with a flute like the one used in the danzón groups, fiddles, piano, and percussion, with various vocal combinations.

The general trend of Cuban popular music has been toward a rhythmic simplification. In particular, the complex structure of the old rumbas and *comparsas*, with layers of different rhythms on top of each other, was transformed into regular and simpler rhythmic patterns (though in any halfway decent group the main drummer still has a good deal of freedom). Alejo Carpentier argues that the simplification was a response to the demands of

the international market when the rumba became popular overseas. In fact, however, it seems mainly to have been the result of
urbanization and the shift of rumba and *comparsa* styles from a
purely black to a national music.

At the same time came an interest in rather more complex arrangements for the front-line instruments, especially U.S. techniques, which came in both in books with titles like *Arranging in
Five Easy Lessons* and with the many Cuban musicians who
went to work in the United States for a while. The new techniques contrasted with the old way of arranging by giving each
instrument a fairly simple riff pattern to stick to, which in a
sense provided a melodic equivalent of the drum patterns. Other
developments included the tendency for solo vocals to imitate
the more complicated lines of the trumpets, especially in some
sones. Later, especially in the mambo (which grew from the
rumba/*comparsa* Afro-Cuban styles), scat singing appeared, along
with the use of disconnected syllables and words. This indirectly
brought an African element, that of the cryptic vocal, back into
Cuban pop music. It also heavily accented the rhythmic side as
against the melodic. These elements had been present in other
forms, but their systematic use came with the mambo. Interestingly enough, the *canto de puyo,* which was of Congo-Bantu
origin, used this type of cryptic vocal with interspersed cries, and
the Cuban Bantu word for a song is *mambe* or *mambo.*

In its broad outlines Puerto Rican music is fairly similar to
Cuban, although it has fewer African-derived characteristics except in specifically black modes like the bomba. The strong Afro-
Cuban ingredients in modern Puerto Rican popular music are
mostly just that—elements taken from Cuban pop music, the
most obvious of which are a heavier percussion section than used
to be customary and a chanted call-and-response B section taken
over from the later *sones*.

Aside from the bomba, which appears to have vanished as a
purely folk dance but still goes strong as part of the repertoire of
Cuban-influenced city dance groups like Cortijo y Su Combo, the
Puerto Rican form of most relevance to us is perhaps the plena.
In its earliest form the plena seems to have been accompanied
by percussion alone, but it soon settled down to a grouping that

normally included the melodeon as a lead instrument, guitar, *cuatro, güiro,* and (from the 1930's onward) *maraccas.* The bongos, conga drums, and so forth, which are now used, are another example of Cuban influence. The vocal part of the plena consists of a four-line verse answered by a chorus, usually for two voices singing in parallel thirds, sixths, or unison with occasional octaves, a verse form a good deal more European than most of the Cuban styles. The lyrics tend to contain social comment or (often sharp) comment on girls and other subjects of general appeal. There is often a strong topical element:

> Cortaron a Elena
> Cortaron a Elena
> Cortaron a Elena
> Y la llevaron al hospital.

> (They wounded Elena
> And took her to the hospital.)

> Papeles son papeles
> Cartas son cartas
> Palabras de mujeres
> Todas son falsas.

> (Papers are papers
> Letters are letters
> Women's words
> Are all false.)

One of the earliest plenas still remembered, dating back to World War I, was called "German Submarine."

The over-all quality of the plenas is faintly melancholy, though they are usually up-tempo. The touch of sadness remains even in highly "Cubanized" plenas, such as those played by Cortijo. Of course, the changes in the plena have given rise to complaints from musical conservatives, but most of them are in line with inevitable musical evolution. (No doubt there was much complaint when the early plenas began to use melodeons.) Younger musicians have been apt to adopt the fast *güiro* pattern of the Dominican merengue, as well as Cuban drumming, and the harmonies are sometimes stretched to include flatted sevenths and other "untypical" chords. But the plenas are still instantly recognizable for what they are, quite distinct from Cuban music. Moreover, there is still a large body of plenas played with the old melodeon-led lineup, besides the groups using trumpet or sax. It is interesting that even the most Cubanized groups tend to use a large number of old plenas, like "Cortaron a Elena" or the beautiful and much-quoted "Santa Maria." The guaracha is also found in Puerto Rico, usually close to the plena, though it tends to have much simpler forms. It is, in fact, an earlier import from Cuba.

Puerto Rico also has a number of creolized nineteenth-century European dance forms, often played by the same groups as play the older style of plena. These also are often accompanied by melodeon, guitars, and *güiro* and are frequently nonvocal. The mazurca and polca (still found elsewhere, as we shall see) have died out; but there is a record available that contains several examples of the danza, a version which developed from the contradanza, and splendid creole examples of waltzes, including "The Anniversary Waltz" trimmed with Afro-Spanish rhythmic work. Another important form in Puerto Rican music is the seis, whose many types show African traits in their rhythms and their call-and-response techniques, but whose dominant content is Spanish.

As everywhere in the Spanish New World, religious festivals were important in black Puerto Rican music. *Aguinaldos* are a traditional equivalent of carols, sung just before Christmas. Bands of black Puerto Ricans going around with drum groups singing *aguinaldos* for alms were described by a visitor of the late eighteenth century, and the custom is still alive.

Puerto Rico's black citizens have their own musical styles, such as the bomba, but for the most part they have influenced national popular forms rather than creating a music of their own. This was largely because music presented a way of breaking out of the manual-labor bind (as it did in North America); but an earlier reason was that slave-owners were apt to regard African dances as bad for their slaves' morals (which generally did not so much bother Anglo-Saxon slave-owners) and encouraged their labor to learn European dances, which the blacks then tinged with their own techniques. The manner of development was thus similar to what happened in the United States, but—presumably because of Puerto Rico's size—no major black style grew out of this blending.

The Dominican Republic has produced one form that has had international influence, though, typically, this has happened indirectly, through Cuba. I refer to the merengue, which first became popular in Santo Domingo around 1850. Like so many popular styles in the Caribbean, the merengue is dance music. Its basic rhythm, as in so much Afro-American music, comprises various versions of ♫♫♩ . The modern merengue form was established around the end of World War I. It has three parts: a short introduction (often in practice left out), and two main sections, one of sixteen bars, which may have been the original form and whose length is likely to be a European influence, and another of a more African-derived type, which consists of two two-bar phrases repeated many times with variations. The effect somewhat resembles what happens in many Afro-Cuban numbers, such as the guaguancó, which has a fairly "melodic" first part, in the European sense, and a second part using more chopped-up phrasing during which the percussion goes to town. The latter section is often instrumental, but when it is vocal the singing becomes much more fragmented and rhythm-oriented, improvisation reigns, and everything cooks.

The instrumentation of the merengue varies, but in its country form it is normally melodeon (which virtually drove out the guitar during the nineteenth century), güiro, and a drum called a tambora; to these may be added a marimbula. You can still hear it played all over the Dominican Republic in a version that has many earmarks of the folk style unaffected by "art" or cabaret styles: a high, hard vocal tone that varies very little according to the subjects of the songs; a liking for repetition with slight variations; an absence of such musical effects as contrast; and a complete lack of such conscious stylistic tricks as holding certain notes to underline emotion or to dramatize, slowing up for the final notes of the song, and so on. Though the lead instrument in country merengues is the melodeon, there is also an urban sax style faintly reminiscent of some of the U.S. creole clarinetists, in particular Sidney Bechet—gay, repetitive, often slightly corny. Merengues played by Cuban groups at the time when the merengue was popular there used much the same format, but Cubanized, more "Afro" and less country-sounding. In return, the general popularity of Cuban music has inspired Dominican merengue styles that might just as easily have come out of Havana (as with all these styles, of course, there are also dreary tourist-nightclub versions concealing the real thing from the visitor).

The effect of Cuba on the other Spanish-speaking islands is only the most pervasive of a host of interisland influences. The merengue itself, which has a counterpart, the méringue, in the Haitian part of the island, supplanted a dance called the tumba, which in varying forms was popular in both the French and Spanish halves of the island and can still be heard occasionally in the mountains of the Dominican Republic. Just before the merengue became popular, there was a vogue for a dance called the upa, which had been introduced by Cuban regimental bands stationed in Puerto Rico. In Puerto Rico, the upa offended the authorities and was banned on moral grounds in 1848. As a result, new steps adapted from the contradanza were put to it, and the new dance was sometimes known as the merengue. Whether the dance went to Santo Domingo from there, or whether the one name was attached to different but similar dances, is not clear. One account of the first dancing of the merengue places it in 1844, during the war between Haiti and Santo Domingo. According to a Dominican writer, Rafael Vidal, a certain standard-bearer abandoned his post during a temporary setback, and the Dominicans, having finally won the battle, sang and danced a new song satirizing the deserter:

> Toma' juyó con la bandera,
> Toma' juyó con la bandera;
> Si juera yo, yo no juyera,
> Toma' juyó con la bandera.

(Tomas fled with the flag,
Tomas fled with the flag;
If it had been me, I should not have fled,
Tomas fled with the flag.)

Whether or not there is any merit in this story, the word merengue was being used in Dominican songs of the merengue form by about 1850.

The merengue, like most Caribbean music, seems to owe much of its characteristic rhythm to the black element in the Afro-Spanish equation, but it is not so basically neo-African as many Cuban forms. Still, one must not assume that the black contribution to the merengue is negligible. It is more likely one of those styles in which the African influence and the Spanish have blended over a long time and become largely indistinguishable in detail. There is a description written in 1810 by an English visitor, William Walton, which points to an Afro-American rather than neo-African music at an earlier stage of development:

> The lower order of the Spanish people of colour accompany their grotesque dances with yells and music created out of slips of hard-sounding wood, a furrowed calabash scraped gently with a thin bone, the banjo, rattles made by putting pebbles into a calabash, the teeth fixed in the jaw-bone of a horse, scraped with rapid motion, and the drum.

Walton's use of the phrase "Spanish people of colour" suggests that the players of this music were not slaves, nor were they the most African of the island's people, whom travelers of that time almost always described as African or Negro. "Of colour" normally implied people of mixed blood.

Merengues are almost all fast, and many are funny or satirical. The vocals are either call-and-response or solo, though some of the solo vocals have a form that suggests they may once have been call-and-response. The vocals in the final section, when there is one, are quite often call-and-response. A simpler version of the merengue, called the pambiche, consists of the last section only. A dance somewhat similar to the merengue is the mangulina, which comes from the south of the Dominican Republic.

Other dances show various blends of the Spanish and African-derived traditions. The sarandunga is very like the fast tap dance known in Spain as zapateado, but in the Dominican Republic it has acquired a far more African section during which only the percussion elements play, often the African-style drums known as *palos*. And instead of a tap dance for one couple, a whole group of dancers do a shuffle-step. It is usually accompanied by accordion, *güiro*, and *tambora* played with the hands only. Like Cuba with its rumbas and *comparsas* and Puerto Rico with its bomba, the Dominican Republic has, besides its black-influenced national dance, music that is more specifically black and uses neo-African drums in groups of two or three, the *palos* or *congos*.

The Dominican Republic illustrates the great richness and diversity of music in areas touched by the Afro-American experience. Within a country of 4 million people, the styles found range from the almost pure Africanism (language and musical implications aside) of some of the *palos* drum music and cantos de hacha (axe songs) of the black, sugar-producing south, to the almost pure, ancient Spanish salves and tonadas of the Cibao around Santiago de los Caballeros in the north of the island. And together with these extremes exist the rural dance forms, the merengue and mangulina and others, which have combined Euro-Dominican and Afro-Dominican elements into a music belonging to everybody.

The music of the *palos,* the cantos de hacha, and the other Afro-Dominican forms belonging to the black Dominicans contain Spanish elements, particularly in the solo "call" melodies; but the choral response, as well as the drumming (in the music of the *palos*) is extremely African in melodic and harmonic quality. So are a number of other features, including the unimportance of the lyrics in many cases. The *congos* of Villa Mella, whom I mentioned earlier, sang roughly the same set of lyrics to a criolla, a calunga, and two other songs. The tonadas and salves of the Cibao, on the other hand, display no Africanisms at all except for their call-and-response pattern. Their melodic qualities are very similar to ancient Castilian vocal forms, and many of their lyrics clearly came from Spain many years ago.

The example of the Dominican Republic illustrates that the

question of Afro-American or Euro-American culture is not necessarily one of skin color. While it is true that the southern
provinces have a high percentage of black inhabitants, the people in and around Santiago who sang old salves and tonadas to
us included black, brown, and Spanish-looking women in the
same groups. *On the whole,* the most African-inspired styles are
sung and played by black Dominicans, but the reverse is by no
means automatically true of the Spanish-derived styles, and these
extreme musical types are not the only music in which their per-
formers participate. Everybody shares the merengue, the mangulina, and similar dances.

The Spanish-speaking West Indies, then, form a relatively cohesive picture: three fairly large islands with a clear pattern of
similarities and differences. The English-speaking West Indies
are far more confusing. Jamaica and Trinidad are large enough
to contain a number of fair-sized towns and several different
types of rural areas. On the other hand, they are at opposite ends
of a long chain of islands, and Jamaica is further separated from
the other formerly British territories by Hispaniola and Puerto
Rico. The smaller islands are divided into the Leeward and
Windward Islands. Each of these small islands has some element
of geography or history to make it unique. Nevis and Saint Kitts,
which were originally settled by British convicts, have preserved
full versions of medieval mumming plays, such as St. George and
the Turkish Knight (which have become so much a part of their
heritage that settlers from these islands who migrated to the
Dominican Republic still perform "the mummies" in the streets
of San Pedro de Macoris). Barbados music, like its history, is
firmly connected with Britain. Saint Lucia and Grenada, on the
other hand, have folk styles that are largely Afro-French. The
Bahamas, though its political links have been with Britain, has
(like the Virgin Islands) come under heavy U.S. musical influence.

Undoubtedly the best-known music of the English-speaking
Caribbean is calypso. When you try to define calypso, the trouble
starts. The basic problem is whether it is a Trinidadian style that
spread to the other islands or an interisland style of which the
Trinidadian version is simply the best known. Other islands had

forms similar to calypso, some of them called calypso or something like it. But these styles were influenced by Trinidadian calypso, both because of the usual interaction of musical elements and because a certain businessman who had most of the Trinidad calypsonians under contract also owned a chain of record stores in many of the other islands, through which he pushed the Trinidadian records. Since the Trinidadian style of calypso was popular, the music of the other islands was sometimes played in a "calypsofied" way, and musicians from the other islands sang calypsos.

Though country calypso bands existed, the Trinidadian calypso itself is and seems always to have been essentially a town music. The calypso singer Atilla the Hun (Raymond Quevedo), who edited a collection of calypso lyrics in the 1940's, claimed that the earliest calypso was this "definitely captivating chant . . . sung in African":

> Ja ja romy aye
> Ja romy Shango
> Ja ja romy meta buri
> Ja romy Shango.

But this song bears no apparent relation to the calypso form as it grew up in the nineteenth and twentieth centuries. Quevedo suggested that its meaning was "I'm coming to the god's dance" and that Ja Ja was a god. Shango is the Yoruba god of thunder, and there is a flourishing Shango cult in Trinidad. It seems likely that the song quoted by Quevedo is connected with that cult.

Quevedo also asserted that the calypso was "undoubtedly African" and that the earliest version developed during *gayap,* a form of organized communal work that does in fact have African parallels. After the day's work was done, the work song leader, according to Quevedo, would improvise praise songs for his own team and songs of derision about the others. There certainly were songs of this type in Trinidad's past. In fact, work songs associated with *gayap* still exist there and on other islands where the same custom is maintained under various names. But it seems unlikely that satirical songs sung after work in the country can really be considered the first examples of a music that grew up almost entirely in the capital city of Port of Spain. It is much more probable they were only one of a number of styles that helped feed the calypso at various times.

Another possible source of the calypso is mentioned by Daniel Crowley in an article in *Ethnomusicology*. There is a legend that, during the French rule over the island, a certain Pierre Begorat appointed a slave called Gros Jean as "Mait' Caiso" on his Diego Martin estate. At that time, it is said, songs were usually improvised, with laudatory or satirical subjects, and frequently constituted wars of words between singers (a tradition that still lives, as we shall see).

The calypso was without a doubt fairly well known locally under its present name, or a version of it, in 1859. That was the year a luckless U.S. ornithologist, William Moore, was unwise enough to claim that calypso was nothing but variations on British ballads. Moore immediately experienced a full-blooded Africanism—the use of song for public and embarrassing rebuke —when a singer called Surisima, or Sirisima, the Carib turned up outside his hotel with a large, vociferous crowd and serenaded him in call-and-response fashion, the spectators in African style providing the responses:

> *Surisima:* Moore, you monkey from America,
> *Crowd:* Tell we what you know about we cariso!

Another Africanism, the dynamic use of repetition, also came into play, and a lengthy good time was had by all but one until the police finally broke up the party.

The early calypsos are said to have been sung in French patois. A singer called Norman (or, according to another version, Cedric) Le Blanc claimed in 1898 to have been the first to sing calypso in English. Whether this was true or not, by the 1870's calypsos were sung in English in something like their present form. Charles Espinet and Harry Pitts, in *Land of the Calypso*, claimed that the earliest known calypso *tune* was "Jour Ouvert," composed in 1876. (Jour Ouvert is the first day of carnival, and the peak of calypso in any year is the tent competitions during carnival time, when the king calypsonian is chosen.) But some *lyrics* survive from before that. A famous calypso singer of that time was a woman called Bodicea. Calypso at that period was very much a music of the Port of Spain underworld, and many of the singers and subjects of the songs, like many of the people responsible for the blues, were pimps, prostitutes, and obeahmen. The singers were "deeply involved in obeah, and most died violent deaths." Then as now, calypso throve on gossip, current events, and personalities. When Hannibal the Mulatto died in 1873, his grave robbed, and his head stolen for obeah, Bodicea was inspired. Tearing off her dress, she led a rowdy crowd around Port of Spain waving it as a flag and singing:

> Congo Jack steal Hannibal head
> You steal from the dead
> Look bacchanal.

(Congo Jack was another singer of the day. Bacchanal is still a Trinidadian word for any riotous occasion, from party on up.)

Another calypsonian, either because he was shocked or more probably because he was a friend of Congo Jack, was moved to reply to Bodicea in what is known as the "oration" form of calypso, which used fine phrases and a declamatory tune mostly on one note, an indication that calypso was fully developed by the 1870's:

> It was shocking, it was shameful and bad to see
> Carnival in the cemetery.
> It couldn't happen in Grenada,
> Saint Kitts, Martinique or Antigua.
> When such lawlessness can prevail,
> Tell me what's the use of the Royal Jail?
> Bodicea the jamette [prostitute] whom we all know
> Is a real disgrace to we cariso.
> I really can't understand
> Why she didn't take the training of the Englishman.

Cat and dog passing they mouth on she
Is better she die or lock up in jail,
She disgrace every woman in Port of Spain.

There is nothing obviously African about this lyric, except the
rebuking of social misbehavior, but call-and-response and other
elements are frequently present in calypso, to say nothing of the
whole concept of a satirical and topical "news sheet" music. The
original instruments which accompanied calypso included drums,
a scraper called a *vira*, rattles, and a bottle and spoon used like a
West African gong. Early calypsos often used short call-and-
response verses. When guitars, and the smaller guitars called
cuatro, began to be used, Venezuelan-derived dance tunes, particularly the pasillo and castillan, already played by the people
of Spanish and Venezuelan descent on the island, were adapted
to two- and four-line English lyrics. Espinet says the Venezuelan
influence is recent, though "Jour Ouvert" is clearly Spanish in
style, and suggests that there were two separate Spanish influences in calypso, one on the developing form, from the Spanish
rule in the island, and the other Venezuelan, from the radio and
other sources during this century.

Certainly calypso is a highly eclectic music. It has drawn heavily from various sources within Trinidad itself, including sources
of a higher African content than calypso itself. It also shows the
effect of Spanish, British, and French music. Some individual
calypsos have even taken elements from the East Indians, who
form the largest minority on the island. Similarly, though most
calypsonians were black and uneducated, Lord Executor had a
high-school education, Le Blanc was in fact white, Sirisima may
have been a Carib, Hannibal was a mulatto, and, to judge from
photographs and his name, Atilla the Hun was at least part
Portuguese or Spanish. At various times calypso backings have
favored Venezuelan music, jazz, Cuban touches, and rhythm and
blues. But like any strongly based and original music, it has
benefited from these rather than being swamped. Similarly, it has
been under fairly steady attack ever since at least the late 1930's
for having gone commercial. It seems that the latest but one
generation of calypsonians is always the last true one.

The music of calypso is impossible to pinpoint, because it is so varied. The rhythm is Afro-Spanish, at times more black and at others more Hispanic. Call-and-response is used quite often but is probably not the majority form. Perhaps the most striking Africanism lies in the nature and function of the lyrics. Like much folk and semifolk music, calypso tunes do not vary much. There is a floating pool of about fifty that are used and reused, altered and realtered, but the words must be fresh. Part of the nature of calypso is tied to its connection with carnival, whether it is in fact a carnival music or merely, as Espinet claimed, linked to carnival by a "marriage of convenience." The famous calypso tents have become a tourist attraction, but it is still there that the kings are crowned, in front of an expert audience. The calypsonians themselves possibly fulfill a group-identification ritual role. They were and are extremely dashing and must be surrounded by women and admiration. One calypsonian, who had taken a job in a fit of absent-mindedness, never appeared in the tent again. The flamboyant names—Lord Beginner, Atilla the Hun, the Mighty Sparrow, Edward the Confessor, the Lion—are part of this function. It is in part at least a stereotype, the idle rascal who contrives to live without actual criminality, one shared by the blues singer and, in many African societies, by the professional *griot* musicians. In the New World as in Africa, the cap may fit some individuals, but the image is often encouraged for professional reasons.

The social role of calypso is difficult to assess. It serves certainly as a vehicle of social and even political comment (and Sir Patrick Renison, a former Colonial Secretary of Trinidad, once stated that the government did in fact "take cognizance" of political calypsos). Sometimes calypsos would exhort the public to civic duty, like Sparrow's "You Got to Pay Tax." But much more common is the sort of current-affairs approach of Growler's comment on the 1943 meat shortage:

> I think I got to make a firm determination
> To stop eating beef in this meat depression.
> For we can't get cattle and we can't get hog
> And me mind only telling me I'm eating dog;

> Beef and pork was always me line,
> So them wolf-hound wouldn't eat out me intestine.

The twisting of words to make rhymes of excruciating ingenuity was a particular feature of the calypsos of the 1940's and 1950's. It was not simply a trick of prosody: It formed part of a battery of devices for producing a wide range of rhythmic effects in the vocal line. Another device was the use of lines of greatly varying length, which gave something of the effect of the drummer who enlivens a piece by contrasting patterns of few beats with bursts of many beats. The rhythmic effect often would be enhanced by the insertion of short phrases or cries between the lines of the verses themselves. Such a cry would produce a feeling of drive and gaiety, like the Spanish *olé,* but it also supplied offbeat rhythmic accents.

A popular aspect of the tent competitions were the wars of words, or *piccong,* an exercise in institutionalized abuse like the U.S. "Dozens." The *piccong,* or *mepri,* the only form of calypso in which much improvisation is used nowadays, preserves the calypso flavor in phrases that are often fairly standard:

> . . . why you standing there,
> You smelling like Pointe-à-Pierre.

(Pointe-à-Pierre is an oil refinery.)

Calypso has been used for social comment—and also, in its time, so rumor persistently has it, for blackmail. ("Pay me or I'll write a song about you.") The calypsonians' moral judgments are often subtle. One old lady who exposed a juicy sexual scandal was disconcerted to find not the sinners but herself the target for calypsonian outrage at the meddlings of the elderly. Perhaps the most common single subject for calypso is sex. Invader's "You Don't Need Glasses to See," Lord Kitchener's "Kitch," and Bedasse's "Night Food" all feature the naïve, uncomprehending male and the increasing ire of the woman scorned.

Though the calypso's melodic ancestry is mixed, it has a fairly high European admixture, including English, Spanish, and French. Basically the various forms of calypso corresponded to certain

root types. The so-called double-tone calypso had fairly long
melody lines. The single-tone calypso had a higher proportion of
elements of African or probable African origin: a shorter melody
line in call-and-response form, and generally more improvisation
and rhythmic interest. Another variant was the *leggo*, described
by Espinet as consisting of the choruses of the calypso, "stripped
of all the humor and other commentary trimmings." Paul Bowles,
in his article in *Modern Music*, stated that, besides greater simplicity, the percussive strain was more prominent in the *leggo*.
The opening procedures of the *leggo* as described by Bowles
suggest an African background:

> The soloist announces phrase number one, and then phrase number
> two, the chorus responds with phrase number one, which hence-
> forth is to be its private property uttered with unchanging uni-
> formity throughout the song. After two or three responses a police
> whistle is blown, the signal for the entrance of the battery of per-
> cussion.

Calypso is not the only Trinidadian music associated with
carnival. To judge from an indignant report in the *Port of Spain
Gazette* in the 1830's, some of the earlier modes were strongly
African:

> We will not dwell on the disgusting and indecent scenes that were
> enacted in our streets—we will not say how many we saw in a state
> so nearly approaching nudity as to outrage decency and shock
> modesty—we will not particularly describe the African custom of
> carrying a stuffed figure of a woman on a pole, which was followed
> by hundreds of Negroes yelling out a savage Guinea [song] . . .
> we regret to say that nine-tenths of those people were creoles.

The *Gazette*'s fulminations were not caused by culture shock
alone. The carnival had been a grand white affair during the
time of slavery but was taken over by the street people after
Emancipation, and like calypso it flourished on a mixture of fine
music and low life. One of the features of carnival in those days
was *canboulay* (*cannes brûlées*), a torchlight procession with
"stickmen" singing *kalindas* and performing stick fights. Otherwise known as *bois*, the stick fights may have derived from a
blend of African war-training dances and European single-stick

fighting. The sticks themselves were "mounted" with spells to help their owners. The *kalinda* was used to pace the game itself, like the Brazilian *capoeira* music, and was a music for drums and assorted percussion. A *chantwell* (solo singer) often accompanied the band to praise one fighter and deride his opponent in two-line songs in creole or English, with the band singing responses.

Besides the *kalinda* instruments, marchers used bamboo stamping sticks called tamboo bamboo, rather like the Haitian *ganbo* but longer, as percussion. They were dropped on the ground or beaten together. Unfortunately, they were also brought down on the heads of opponents and were eventually banned, along with *canboulay* and *kalinda* fights.

After the calypso, the Caribbean music best known overseas is the steel band. Most islands have their steel bands these days, but they began in Trinidad. Ironically, for a style that has been plugged to death by the tourist boards, it started out with as many strikes against it as any other Afro-American form. Daniel Crowley put it this way: "Here is a complex art form created by lower-class, ill-educated, underprivileged adolescents against the will of their parents, the ruling class, and the police." It is often claimed that steel band is in some way descended from African drumming. Handed-down Africanisms of rhythm and form added to a percussive instrument obviously offer some parallels, but in fact the steel drums have a range and sound rather nearer to African xylophones than to African drums. And even here, any parallels would be due to a generalized web of musical Africanisms rather than more specific "folk memories." The music, it is said, developed as a reaction to the banning of the tamboo bamboo. The basic instruments, called pans, are made out of large oil drums. The head of the drum is cut off, leaving six inches to a foot of the body. A series of bumps, each giving a musical note, is produced on the surface by heating and hammering. The pans range from instruments with many notes, to carry the melody, to bass pans of three or four notes. Their sound is resonant and rather sweet. Indeed, the trouble with steel-band music is that these days it is often too sweet and too eclectic. Steel-band musicians refuse to be daunted by anything and will play Tchaikovsky as enthusiastically as "Stone Cold Dead in the

Market." But the pans were best suited to Trinidadian music and to techniques like the call-and-response passage in the Trinidad All Stars' "Diana," where the call function is taken over by a pan with voices supplying the response (as Cuban musicians often do with trumpet and voices).

Besides these major styles, Trinidad has various forms that are less well known (as well as dances, like the limbo, that have had moments of fame) but often nearer to an African tradition. Some are directly associated with African sources. The congo is a *patois* song and dance form with a three-drum accompaniment, *chantwell,* and chorus. It is used by people of Congolese descent for weddings and baptisms. Similar is the yarraba, a dance music for people of Yoruba descent using three or four drums, sticks (*claves*), *chac-chac* (a West African term for rattles), *chantwell,* and chorus. I have already discussed the Shango cult music. Trinidad also has *rada* cult music, which is more important in Haiti. The *rada* cult hymns use three drums, sticks, an iron (like the West African gong), *chac-chac, chantwell,* and chorus.

The *bele* or *belaire,* which is found in Tobago, Grenada, and Carriacou as well as Trinidad, is a part religious (or magical) and part social form. In Tobago it can be both, and so too in Grenada, where it is connected with ancestor ceremonies and also can be a vehicle for songs of derision. All forms use drums and other percussion and call-and-response singing. The importance of the wake for the dead being as great in Trinidad and the neighboring islands as elsewhere in black America, there are a number of musical forms associated with it. For example, Trinidad and Tobago have the *bongo,* a mostly sung style often of social commentary, which in Tobago at least has the function of placating the spirits. "Sings," which punctuate storytelling, are found on all four islands and are basically a way of passing the time at wakes. "Pass play" songs have the same use and are also sung by children.

A dual function—or what in European terms would be a dual function—is reflected in many of the older musical forms of the islands. Often they reflect characteristically West African social or spiritual attitudes, in their function if not in their music. The Tobagan reel dance for solo singer, tambourines, and other percussion is a dance music, but at the same time it is used for the invocation of spirits before weddings and in cases of sickness. Its composite role suggests a reinterpretation of a healing dance. The small island of Carriacou has two dances with obvious African ancestry in both music and function. I have mentioned earlier the Big Drum Dance in connection with the "nations." It is music for a family or neighborhood ceremony to ensure the favor of the ancestors, accompanied by offerings of food. The *Reel Engagé* is a social dance music used for reels, quadrilles, and so forth at family dances, again connected with offerings for the ancestors. These musics contain Africanisms of performance as well as of instrumentation or form. A common one is the use of falsetto, as in Carriacou, when a singer will begin a dance song in falsetto and turn to normal voice when the drums come in.

Trinidad also has a minority population with strong links with Venezuela. In the past these people preserved Venezuelan customs, including the *Veiquoix* (*Velorio del Cruz*), which in Trinidad involved *piccong* (insult) competitions as well as the recited competitive *décimas* common in Venezuela. The instruments used in Trinidad as well as in Venezuela were *tiple, cuatro, bandol* (mandolin), guitar, and *chac-chac*. Unlike Venezuela, drums were not usually used. After the *Veiquoix* came the fandang, a dance at which a string band would play Venezuelan joropos, galerones, castillans, and so forth. The people who play this music live in a region called Grand Curucaye and are of Venezuelan descent. The *veiquoix* and the fandang groups nowadays are small, but in the past they were larger and grander. A fine recording of the Venezuelan string music of Trinidad was made by Beryl McBurnie years ago and issued in the U.S. on the Road Runner label. It contains joropos, galerones, a so-called parang, *veiquoix* music, and an *aguinaldo*. The parang and the *aguinaldo* are in fact much the same thing: Strictly speaking, *aguinaldos* were sung at parangs, though now English and German carols have crept in. A Tobagan parallel is the *quesh*, which involves the singing of French carols. These styles did not operate in total isolation from each other, of course, and the calypso also drew on many of them, at one time or another, until it became so codified that it could no longer easily take in folk influences.

A religious music of a different sort is that of the Spiritual Baptists of Trinidad, popularly known as Shouters. The Shouters practice a form of Christianity in which many African elements remain, reinterpreted to suit a new theology. Among them are the use of an inner priestly sanctum called a "sacred chamber," where certain rituals are carried out, and the division of priestly functions into a number of offices, some of which have no mainstream Christian equivalent: shepherd, prophet, healer, interpreter, pointer, diver, prover, nurse, and matron. Shouter ceremonies involve possession by the Holy Spirit, and sometimes by one or another of the Shango powers, with "tongues." Music is extremely important, but the drum is frowned on. The rhythmic base is provided by handclapping and foot-tapping, as it was in older black chapels in the United States. Baptism is important, of course, and pouring rites similar to ones used in the Shango cult sometimes take place. Worshipers occasionally dance; birds are sacrificed from time to time; and, more significant (having no sort of Biblical sanction), food is sometimes offered to the spirits. Shouter music is clearly European Christian in origin, and the sermons are similar to black U.S. sermons.

Calypso forms, as I said at the beginning of this section, are found in various other islands, whether they originated in Trinidad or developed separately. In the Virgin Islands there was the *careso* composed by the Queen of a bamboula dance in the nineteenth century. The *careso* was a two-line topical song. Saint Lucia has *caliso* topical songs resembling some old bamboula songs, but many of them seem to come from Trinidad. This is obviously the case with some calypsos recorded on the Colombian English-speaking island of San Andres and issued on the Folkways label.

Jamaica is the largest of the English-speaking West Indian territories. Despite 200 years of Spanish rule, it was not subject to the variety of influences that history brought to some of the others, especially Trinidad. But the broad sweep of Caribbean history affected Jamaica as it did the other islands.

A noticeable feature of Jamaican music is the high degree of British content that goes along with its plentiful Africanisms. Both are evident in this early praise song, sung by some black

Kingstonians to welcome a British captain who had fought off French ships in one of the numerous eighteenth-century wars in the Caribbean:

> Capy Crow da come again
> But em always fight and lost some mans.
> But we glad for see em now and then;
> Wit em hearty joyful gay,
> Wit em hearty joyful gay,
> Wit em tink, tink, tink, tink, tink, tinkara
> Wit em tink, tink, tink, tink, tink, tinkara.

This is clearly akin to eighteenth- and early nineteenth-century English songs (including many soldiers' songs, likely to have traveled to Jamaica with British garrisons) in that it begins with a couplet that changes from verse to verse, then goes into a non-sense formulation designed to express merriment—"With a two row, row, row, row, row, row," and so forth. The praise-song form itself is African. Ballads about the deeds of an individual did exist in the British music of the time, but they were far more narrative and tended to concentrate on official heroes of higher rank than captain, or else on folk heroes who more often than not were far out of favor with the Establishment. It is possible that the word "da" in the first line is Twi for "is," since the form "de" for "is" was common in Jamaica until recently. (It may, of course, be the equivalent of the North American black usage "done"; but "done," as in "my man done gone," may itself en-shrine a reinterpreted version of "da" or "de" attached to a pho-netically similar English word. It may also echo another African construction, found in the Swahili *amekwisha kwenda*—"he has finished going," that is, he has just gone.)

Neo-African music such as *tambo* drumming and the Yoruba songs recently found in the parish of Westmoreland still exists in Jamaica, though it is dying out (only a few elderly people main-tain it in a living form), partly because it is a century and a half since the last Africans came to Jamaica, and partly, perhaps, be-cause it has lost its original function. Where it has not, or where it has found new functions, as with the Congolese ingredients in the religious sects, it is stronger.

The most consistent body of mainly African survival in Jamaica is perhaps the Anancy stories. Significantly, the Anancy stories are highly eclectic. In Ghana, *anansi* is a spider, a rough equivalent of the Bantu hare who became Brer Rabbit in the United States. In Jamaica Anancy is no longer a spider. He has acquired cosmopolitan traits. The Anancy stories often preserve the old device (almost universal in Africa and occasionally found in Europe, as in "Rumpelstiltskin") of introducing a snatch of song at crucial moments. A detailed collection of Anancy stories and Jamaican music was made by Walter Jekyll at the turn of the century. Even allowing for the collector's probable tendency to reinterpret elements he did not understand in the direction of European models, it is still the best (and certainly the most thorough) collection there is. The eclecticism of Anancy is well illustrated by the names of three princesses in one of Jekyll's tales: Yung Cyum Pyung, which is the Ghanaian *Accompong;* Margaret-Powell-Alone, which looks like a reworking of Margaret-All-Alone; and Eggie-Law.

This eclecticism, a natural result of Jamaica's rich heritage, is furthered by the very nature of oral folk tales when they do not have a function—such as the perpetuation of oral history—that demands consistency. Storytellers weave their favorite features from other tales into whatever story they are telling. This was strikingly illustrated for me when I listened to two quite different Anancy stories, one told by a man in his seventies in a village near Kingston and the other by a girl of nineteen from the parish of Clarendon. Both included in their tales an incident in which Anancy makes one egg look like 100 by lifting it out of a barrel 100 times. Both tales showed the survival power even of vestigial Africanisms: Aubrey Davis used several words of African origin, such as *nyam* for "to eat," and Valerie Walker interspersed her story with snippets of song in African style (while adding something of her own generation to the tradition with the introduction of occasional recent slang expressions).

The musical themes of the Anancy stories are varied. One of

those in Jekyll's collection consists of a snatch of a very old ballad known in Britain as (among other titles) "The Bonny Broom" and in the southern Appalachians of the United States as "The Devil's Nine Questions." The Jamaican tune differs from these but is clearly a reworked border ballad. The riddle formula is almost identical, though all three versions have different refrains. The Jamaican version uses one of the questions (What is louder than a horn? What is deeper than the sea? What is meaner than womankind?—and so forth):

> The devil roguer than a womankind,
> The devil roguer than a womankind, oh
> Fair and gandelow steel.

There are several other examples of reworked bits and pieces from the English folk stock in Jekyll's collection: "Man Crow" is the tune of a widespread English children's game often called "A Finger and a Thumb Keep Moving"; another song uses the international children's tune whose original version is the French "Ah, que dirai-je vous maman?" but which has also gone into English infant lore; a line is taken from "The Three Little Pigs" ("I'll huff and I'll puff"); one song is very much like the Anglo-American "Paper of Pins," with a tune often associated with British ballads; and there are many other examples. But, prominent though the English influence is in the collection, there is plenty that is quite foreign to English practice. One example is a form of call-and-response (I have italicized the response element):

> None a we, none a we, *commando*.
> Sairey gone home, *commando*.
> Yahka yahky yak, *commando*.
> Suck your mother bone, *commando*.

The call-and-response form of this song is typical of what seems to be a particularly Jamaican style in that the response is a short semichant of two or three syllables, often on one note. Another version, from the Anancy canon, is:

> Timmolimmo, *man dere*
> Timmolimmo, *man dere*
> Come down make we battle, *man dere*.

In the case of "Commando," the rhythmic pattern of verse and refrain are the same, but in "Timmolimmo" the verse consists of eighth-notes and the refrain of two quarter-notes, which gives a definite total shape reminiscent of a drummed dance pattern common in Caribbean music, including some kalinda:

This contrast of long-note and short-note phrases is so widespread as to be a major feature of Jamaican folk music. It has rather the same effect as the Trinidadian custom of varying the rhythm with long and short verse lines. Not all the examples are like the ones I have quoted: "Matilda," a popular song that originated in the Anancy story "Devil's Honey-Dram," opens with two long-note phrases, "Wheel-o, wheel-o," and then comes the name Matilda in the shorter-note rhythm, which is maintained for the rest of the verse.

There is an obvious connection between this form of Anancy song and the digging songs that are an important part of Jamaican vocal music, as Jekyll's description makes clear:

> One man starts or "raises" the tune and the others come in with the "bobbin," the short refrain of one or two words which does duty for chorus. The chief singer is usually the wag of the party, and his improvised sallies are greeted with laughter and an occasional "hi," which begins on a falsetto note and slides downwards, expressing amusement and delight very plainly.

The call-and-response form; the singer chosen not for his singing but for his wit; the improvised lead and set chorus; the unscheduled "audience" participation by an audience that is also the chorus; the use of falsetto (in a "shout for joy," which is often used by much more modern Jamaican popular singers)—all are from Africa. The choice of a wit as leader is paralleled in Haiti, incidentally, where the song-leader of a *combite* communal work gang, who is called the *simidor* or *saniba*, provides allusively witty comment on the workers and the passing scene.

Jamaican digging songs (unlike the work songs recorded on U.S. prison farms, for obvious reasons) tend to be gay. They are attended by a good deal of merriment, with cries of "quartermaster" when the rum or water bottle is wanted, and so forth. For Jamaicans, communal work is a good opportunity for gaiety as well as mutual help. The communal nature was strongly underlined in the case of some digging songs I collected in the village of Maryland. They were preceded by a very slow, richly harmonized passage, which the diggers called a "bobbin" (they called Jekyll's "bobbin" a "chorus") and which they sang all standing together before work began, almost like an invocational hymn. Then the leader would break into the faster lead of the main body of the song itself, the picks would flash up, and work would begin.

Jekyll quotes digging songs with the typical short two- or three-note refrain. Here are just two:

> (1) Tell Mister Bell me go, *plant coco*
> Tell Mister Bell me go, *plant coco*
> Tell Mister Bell me go, *plant coco*
>
> Fuppence a quart for flour!
> Flour, flour, flour, flour,
> Fuppence a quart for flour.
>
> (2) Bad homan oh, bad homan oh, *nyam and cry*
> Me coco no ripe, *nyam and cry*
> Me hafoo no ripe, *nyam and cry*.

The repeated "flour, flour" in the first one is comparable to the opening phrases of "Matilda," except that it is a rising and not a falling call. The rhythmic effect is much the same. "Nyam and Cry" is about a lazy woman who does nothing but eat and complain. *Nyam*, to eat, is almost certainly related to the Twi *enam*, and perhaps to the Bantu form *nyama*.

Digging songs cover a wide range of topics. Some in Jekyll's anthology seem to have come from English sailors' songs, like "Miss Nancy Ray," which opens:

> Oh Miss Nancy Ray, *oh hurrah, boys.*
> Oh Miss Nancy Ray, *oh hurrah boys.*

The words and the tune of this are clearly picked up from contact with English sailors, perhaps by somebody working on the Kingston docks for a while, though by the end of the song they have become pretty thoroughly Jamaicanized. Some work songs offer personal comment faintly reminiscent of the blues: "The one shirt I have, ratta cut ahm." Others may be carried across from other sorts of music, like "Kisander," which I recorded in Maryland. This was obviously at one time a play-party song and may in the first instance have come from an Anancy story. The chorus "Kisander" is the name of a cat who appears in some old stories. The song itself sounds as though it began as a word game in which participants had to find new adjectives for the phrases:

> Show me your true name, *Kisander;*
> Come and show me your secret name, *Kisander;*
> Won't you tell me your first name, *Kisander;*
> Oh, tell me your funny name, *Kisander;*

and so on.

Digging songs in their turn may become dance tunes. Among those quoted by Jekyll is one that became famous much later, under the name of "Hold 'Im Joe." The old version starts: "Me donkey want water, rub him down Joe, rub him down Joe, rub him down Joe," and the long bobbin is repeated after a series of short phrases describing the donkey: "Me donkey like a peeny, Me donkey full of capers," and so forth. The modern versions are similar, and both forms allow for a great deal of improvised bawdry, as do other donkey songs, like "Donkey City," whose usual versions do not get onto commercial records.

In the past, digging songs were sometimes accompanied by instruments, including a fiddler whom Jekyll describes condescendingly but revealingly: "Holding it not up to the chin but resting it on the biceps, they rub a short bow backwards and forwards across the strings. If one of these is tuned it is considered quite satisfactory, and the rest make a sort of mild bagpipe accompaniment." This playing stance—Jekyll's amusement apart—is usual alike for players of the numerous African one- and two-string fiddles and for British folk fiddlers. In fact, the British fiddler often uses his lower strings as a drone, or what Jekyll terms a "mild bagpipe accompaniment," and some groups in West Africa use their fiddles to somewhat similar effect. This looks like an excellent example of two traditions coming together and reinforcing each other in the New World.

An important Jamaican form, widespread in the Americas and usually showing mixed Afro-European components, is the ring game, or ring play. It is just as popular among adults as among children and is still a flourishing part of Jamaican life, especially in the country. The games used to be played on all kinds of festive occasions, but these days they are most often found at set-ups and nine-nights, the beginning and end of a mourning period. Some ring plays, like "Sally Water" (also found in the United States), are of unmistakable English derivation:

> Little Sally Water, sprinkle in the saucer,
> Rise Sally rise, and wipe your weeping eyes.

Others have African words, repeated bobbins, and other national traits:

> Where me lover de? *See mya, see mya.*
> Me lover gonna sea? *See mya, see mya.*

De, we have seen, is an African word; *see mya* is "see him here."

But whether of English or African source or influence, Jamaican ring plays are truly Jamaican. And many, of course, were born on the island. One such is the very popular "Emmanuel Road," or "Mandeville Road," as it is sometimes called. This has been played as a band number, but it is basically a ring play. I saw it played after a digging session, when the men sat in a circle passing around stones that had been loosened by their picks. The object of the game is to pass the stones on rapidly without injury, or, as the song says, "finger mash no cry!"

Children's songs are in some ways more traditional but in others more volatile than adult music, and Jamaican children's songs are no exception. They include many games like "Emmanuel Road" and "Sally Water," but I also collected versions of "Humpty Dumpty" and other nursery rhymes sung in a style that owes a great deal to the local pop style called reggae and, through reggae, to rhythm and blues. Children also make up their own songs reflecting immediate concerns, including one with the immortal line: "ABC is a bloody botheration!"

Definite Africanisms are difficult to pin down in both ring games and children's songs, since even call-and-response is not uncommon in English children's games. The tendency of Jamaican ring games to turn into dances is a probable African trait. The freer and more complex rhythms of the songs or, in the case of English-derived songs, of their performance is another. Jekyll noticed this rhythmic approach in a song called "Ring-a-Diamond": "In many bars it is almost impossible to distinguish whether the tune is triple or duple." It is tempting to see this as a variation of the African use of duple *on* triple time.

Some Jamaican children's games are, as we have seen, reminiscent of African games designed to teach skills. I mentioned earlier the stick-fighting game collected in Jamaica in the 1940's. The fact that Jekyll also collected it at least forty years earlier is an indication of the strength of tradition.

Digging songs, traditional tales, ring plays, and to some extent children's games all tend to change slowly and to be remembered from generation to generation. Dance music naturally changes more quickly, but Jekyll's description of a country dance band is not so very different from what can still occasionally be found in remote areas today:

The music consists of three "flutes" [fifes], two tambourines and a big drum. This is the professional element, which is reinforced by amateurs. One brings a cassava-grater, looking like a bread-grater; this, rubbed with the handle of a spoon, makes a very efficient crackling accompaniment. Another produces the jawbone of a horse, the teeth of which rattle when it is shaken. A third has detached from its leather one of his stirrup-irons, and is hanging it on a string to do duty as a triangle. The top of the music is not always supplied by fifes. Sometimes there will be two fiddles, sometimes a concertina.

Besides its general similarity to groups found in most other parts of black America, the rhythm section described here corresponds closely to West African popular bands. There are the drums, including tambourines, which play something of the same role as the Ewe frame-drum. There are scrapers and rattles. And the stirrup is a successful substitute for the Ewe *gankogui*. The European or rural Jamaican instruments that augment the vocalists sit on top of a highly African rhythm section.

At the same time, the popular country dances played by these groups were creolized European, just as many were in the other islands. The main dances at the turn of the century were the waltz, the polka, the schottische, and quadrilles in five figures or six, of which the fifth was the most popular and tended to become separated from the rest. Jekyll reports that a version of the old Jamaican song "Linstead Market" was used as the fifth figure of a quadrille.

This type of country band has virtually disappeared from Jamaican life, killed off by Jamaica's equivalent of the juke box, the sound system. In some cases, death has come very recently. I was lucky enough to find a group that had given up the unequal struggle only a few years earlier, some of whose members reformed to record old mento numbers, quadrilles, and mazurka-polka. The group consisted of harmonica, grater, bass-trumpet, and various *ad hoc* instruments, such as bottles tapped together. Other groups still exist, like the Manchioneal Village Band in Portland, associated with a youth club with a strong sense of the need to preserve Jamaican traditions. Yet others remain only in the memories of older men, like our host in the village of Chatham, Saint James, who had played the guitar and mandolin for country dance groups until the mid-1920's and remembered with nostalgia the days when there were dances almost every night, and when every parish had its own way of dancing the Lancers and polkas. In Chatham and its environs, he told me, bands would often comprise a guitar, a flute, and an accordion, without graters. "I used to love dances, I used to love the quadrilles," he remarked wistfully.

The dance tunes came from a number of sources. Jekyll bewailed the tendency to depart from the "Jamaican type of melody" and to adopt, spread, and modify popular songs brought into port by sailors. But adoptions from English and other sources do not mean that Jamaican music was or is derivative, any more than any other Afro-American music. Songs borrowed from elsewhere were well and truly worked over, in line with the African approaches to music-making that we have seen to be strong everywhere in the Caribbean. The older examples are written down by the collector, and the mere act of writing them down strips them of most of their characteristic quality. In the hands of an amateur like Jekyll, with no knowledge of the background out of which Jamaican music sprang, the undoubted English element is likely to be overemphasized. Later examples, preserved on tape and occasionally on records, show what Jekyll left out. The Jamaican rhythms are faster and less flowing than Trinidadian calypso, perhaps because they had far less Spanish influence and retained the more foursquare quadrille sections. But some also have a percussive quality that suggests a higher proportion of African in the rhythmic mix. Others reflect British dance music, brisk and gay, though neither as rhythmically pulsating nor as complex as Spanish, let alone African.

Though the major ingredients in Jamaican music—apart from Jamaican talent—are African and British, other influences are also present. The Spanish streak that must undoubtedly be there (Jamaica was Spanish for 200 years, after all, even though rather precariously so) has hardly been studied, but then Spanish dominion ended a long time ago. A notable infusion that still continues comes from the United States. North American influence can be heard everywhere, especially in the newer folk music still being created by younger people. It is present in Jamaican religious music, including many of the Revival Zion "choruses," as well as the songs of the Pentecostal churches, which have been making many converts recently. The gospel influence on Jamaican religious singing, strangely enough, seems to be mainly white, principally because the recorded services of Billy Graham and Oral Roberts are popular. But U.S. influence is also present in many secular songs, including some of the newer play-party songs. They too are sometimes drawn from gospel tunes.

In the 1950's and 1960's, a new phenomenon hit Jamaica. A succession of styles, one leading directly to another, emerged: first ska, then rocksteady, and most recently reggae. Like calypso and steel-band music in their early days, they were the music of the disapproved young; the Rude Boys of Kingston, or Rudies as they called themselves, who in a number of rocksteady songs proclaimed: "Rudies is tough, boy, rudies is tough." Ska and its descendants have come under the usual heavy attack from all quarters: It encourages or, alternatively, is the product of delinquency; it is a feeble imitation of foreign styles; it uses electronic instruments; it is loud, uncouth, and generally obnoxious. But in fact it appears to be very much in a Jamaican tradition. For one thing the basic rhythms often differ little from earlier Jamaican dance meters. They sound different, because they are portioned out in a new way, between electric guitars and bass guitar, being influenced to some extent by rhythm-and-blues and soul bass-guitar techniques. What seems to have happened is that the youth of the streets got fed up with calypso, which was too popular among their elders. Black North America being somewhat of a fashion-setter, various artists cut records imitating such black ballad singers as Johnny Ace. But the results lacked the strong, dynamic rhythm of Jamaican music. Since people unconsciously tend to follow traditions they know, however consciously in revolt against them, the beats that came back in were essentially Jamaican, but sufficiently heavy, electrified, and generally ungenteel to upset older people quite satisfactorily.

Rocksteady and reggae have gone through a number of changes, and many of the stages of their development have been so chaotic that tracing trends is impossible. There was a fashion for sentimental strings, and another for effective but rather lugubrious slow trombone riffs over the mid- to up-tempo rhythm. There have been Jimmy Smith organs and James Brown vocals, but however many fads and enthusiasms rule the scene temporarily, the sound goes on being obstinately Jamaican.

Reggae has become a feature on the international pop scene, though only a minor one. Jamaican records have several times made the British hit parade. Popularity has resulted in a split in the music. On the one hand are the pop-oriented records of musicians like Byron Lee and Desmond Dekker, which are popular with the Jamaican middle class as well as with foreigners. Then there are the groups that record for the little record companies on Orange Street, Kingston; that rarely make it onto an LP; that record titles with Rastafari or, occasionally, Black Power messages; and whose numbers now and again are banned by the Jamaican Broadcasting Company. Many pop reggae numbers are excellent—Desmond Dekker's "A It Mek," for example, or Eric Donaldson's splendid single, "Cherry Oh Baby." But they can too often be tame. Rastafari, or Orange Street, or "underground" reggae, is often badly recorded, but it is always interesting, because it is a "people's music." Not coincidentally, it shows a high incidence of African-derived features, including a large degree of creative repetitiveness, an emphasis on rhythm, and a lack of interest in harmony. Reggae is not the exclusive preserve of the Rastafari, of course. It was also the music of the "Rude Boys," West Kingston's underprivileged teenagers, in and out of trouble with the law. Earlier reggae and rocksteady seemed to express unruly teenagers' feelings rather well, from the general joy in break-up of "Bangarang"—"Bangarang crash, everything smash!" —to the Heptones' "Be a Man," with its Black Power overtones. Clancy Eccles recorded a song called "Feel the Rhythm," which included large chunks of a much older calypso called "So Them Bad-Minded." "Limbo Girl" has a soul-style vocal.

The Rastafarians, a back-to-Africa sect with a large membership, especially in Kingston, have come into musical prominence recently. Rastafarian groups, such as Douglas Mack's Band, accompany Jamaican songs with drums, and many reggae titles reflect their influence. "Macabee Version" is on the theme of the Black Man's Bible (as opposed to the King James Version). A group called the Ethiopians (the Rastafari revere Emperor Haile Selassie of Ethiopia) recorded a number called "Selah," and the

Abyssinians made "Satta Amasa Gana," whose lyrics begin: "There is a land, far, far away, Where there's no night, there's only day." This appears to refer, with true African allusiveness, to Ethiopia and its "King of King and Lord of Lords," Haile Selassie. Much more explicit is Maxie and Glen's "Jordan River," which opens: "I saw Selassie I [a misunderstanding of the Roman numeral one] stretch forth his hand to take I across Jordan River." Its chorus goes, "Zion oh, Rastafari."

Reggae is in many ways a chaotic music, the product of a chaotic music business. Reggae records tend to come out with the same tune on both sides, one (called "version") instrumental; production methods are often eccentric and sometimes piratical. One large British company found to its embarrassment that a reggae record whose British rights it had bought owed its fine backing to the unrecompensed (and quite unconscious) cooperation of the world's highest-paid string orchestra. But out of this chaos has sprung a new and very vital music, almost certainly the Caribbean's only entirely new musical form in this century.

Trinidad and Jamaica have tended to dominate the other English-speaking islands in the popular field. Bahamian calypso singers, like Blind Blake, and most of the Caribbean's steel bands are pale versions of the originals, oriented principally toward a tourist market. For a different tradition, based on different sources and with a different development, one must turn to the French-speaking islands: Haiti, Martinique, and Guadeloupe.

Haiti, as we have seen, is one of the places that has kept the most Africanisms in its music. Not only is it rich in neo-African forms, but much of the Afro-American music of Haiti has a higher degree of Africanism than occurs elsewhere. Haitian secular music includes all the folk forms found in the other countries: work songs, play songs, story songs, songs of protest and ridicule, political songs, and secret society music. All of it springs from a principally or entirely African tradition. Besides folk music, Haiti has a number of carnival and dance styles, the best known being the méringue.

Work songs of the New World often preserve a large degree of

Africanism, and Haitian work songs are no exception. They are frequently associated with the *combite,* a communal field work party similar to those common in some parts of Africa and in other parts of the Caribbean. Whether the *combite* is a direct survival from Africa or developed because of Haitian conditions is sometimes argued. As with most New World Africanisms, the question is beside the point. For people faced with the suitable conditions to develop a communal approach to harvesting and other large farming jobs is natural. For people descended from Africans to organize a work pattern that is also something of a picnic—with a band and a vocalist to spur on the farmers and jeer at the idle, and a hierarchy of officers to perform various well-defined functions, from planning the work to hushing chatterers—and to do so quite independent of the fact that their ancestors took a similar highly individual approach to organizing work, is less likely than the idea that elements of traditions and attitudes were handed down among a people very conscious of tradition and revived when it seemed useful to do so.

Anyway, the work songs are there, and there is also work music, not identical to that played by Hausa *griots* to encourage the farmers of their locality, but having the same function and some of the same ingredients. Besides, many work songs are more directly functional in that they regulated the actual flow of work. An example recorded on a Folkways disc has two men pounding grain as they sing in French *patois* a song of humorous bragging, and the sound of the wooden pestles supplies the rhythm. This sort of song is common all over Africa. Hugh Tracey recorded women in Southern Africa whose pestles performed the same rhythmic role, and there is an Ocora record of women grinding grain with stones, which provides a subtle and complex accompaniment to their singing. In the Haitian example, the men sometimes use a falsetto voice in a way widely popular in Africa and Afro-America.

Songs of social criticism bulk large in Haitian folk music. Some make use of a proverb, like "Zamis Loin Moin," which suggests that friends nearby are a two-edged knife. A considerable degree of indirection and allusion is common. Reflections about a

Haitian President named Alexis Nord are put by the singer into the mouth of his wife, Cece, who praises him for nongovernmental virtues:

> Cece said Alexis Nord is a fine man all over!
>   [three times]
> Cece said he will quit whenever he sees fit.
> Cece said Uncle Nord is a fine man all over.

The indirect, multilevel praise-with-humor song is far from European tradition.

We have examined Haitian voodoo music. Another very important Africanism common to Haiti and all other Afro-American areas is the necessity of a good, indeed a splendid, funeral, and the holding of a social wake as part of a long series of death rituals. In Haiti as elsewhere, wakes mix religious and secular elements and are an occasion for games, storytelling, and songs. Many of the traditional tales told at Haitian country funerals contain songs, like the Jamaican Anancy stories and their African prototypes. Many of the playsongs come from these story cycles, and they become even more allusive when taken out of that context.

Carnival music is as much a part of Haitian life as it is of Brazilian or Trinidadian, though the scale of festivities is more modest. Carnival street dances include the rara and the mascaron. The rara is associated with the descendants of the single-note trumpets of Africa, called in Haiti *vaccines*. The music, a gay and highly skilled hooting, is underlined by the tapping of sticks on the sides of the bamboo *vaccine* trumpets (a variation on the African-derived tendency to use an instrument for two purposes at once). *Vaccine* orchestras of three or four instruments move through the villages of Haiti, followed by dancers, during Holy Week festivities. Rara music is often sung as well, providing an occasion for praising local officials and other popular figures. Not all rara bands are made up of *vaccines;* other groups use drums, trumpets, whistles, and so on.

Another form of festival song is the mayousse, which may be heard in Holy Week, on All Saints' Day, and on lesser occasions.

The marimba, Haiti's version of the African hand-piano, is quite popular for mayousse music.

Apart from the various traditional and folk styles, modern and often more urban popular dance music is found in Haiti. The leading Haitian dance form is the méringue, whose name is virtually the same as the merengue of the Dominican Republic, on the other side of the hills. The méringue's beginning is not entirely clear, but it certainly goes back to the first half of the nineteenth-century. Like so many Afro-American dances, the méringue developed into two forms, one for the salon and one for the streets.

The salon méringue was a piano music, often using violins also. There is a recording of this style, with Chopinesque moments and delicate decorations, by some members of a Haitian family famous for its classical musicians. Apart from its charm, it is extremely interesting because at certain moments this nineteenth-century, bourgeois, Afro-Parisian music is distinctly akin to U.S. ragtime piano and to certain Puerto Rican dances that make use of the same running patterns of syncopated triplets and of the telltale pattern 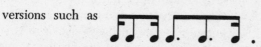 and ragtime-like

versions such as

The street méringue comes in various forms, all of which have met with complaints of foreign influence and general corruption. It is said, for example, that there is no Haitian guitar tradition and that love songs accompanied by guitar are foreign. Well, if you go far enough back, almost everybody's music, or much of it, came from somewhere else. The earlier style of rather sentimental, gentle solo méringues, such as "Nous Allons Dodo" on a Folkways record, certainly owes something to French music. So does most Haitian music, leaving out some of the most neo-African. What makes much of it so original is precisely the blend of the rather gentle and at the same time straightforward French

styles with African material common to much of the Caribbean.
The results are quite different from the music even of the other
part of Hispaniola, the Dominican Republic, with its Spanish
brio.

The band méringue style has come in for the heaviest fire.
Groups like the Jazz Majestic Orchestra of the early 1950's consisted of saxophone, guitar, banjo, drum kit, conga drum, and
iron percussion. Their music was patently related to other modern Caribbean forms and possibly had jazz touches, but it was
also unmistakably Haitian in its gentleness. The sax player used
a style whose origins would be well worth somebody's study. It
is similar to the Dominican merengue style, to the work of some
New Orleans creole reed players (especially Sidney Bechet), to
the Martiniquan biguine, and to music recorded in the dance
halls of French Guyana. Except for the Dominican Republic, all
these places had cultural links with France, and the French are
(or were in the nineteenth century) famous for their clarinet
technique, so this sax and clarinet style may well be part of the
French legacy.

The méringue is not the only modern Haitian dance form,
though it is the basic one. Mascarons and nineteenth-century
dances like the quadrille—especially in the form of the Lancers
—have been updated by such groups as the orchestra of Nemours
Jean-Baptiste, which some twenty years ago introduced changes
in the méringue style by using a more driving version of the
rhythm. Nemours's early records, reissued in the United States
on LP, include a number of contredanses complete with prom-
enade sections played by a group incorporating sax and accordion, backed by rhythm. Like most modern Caribbean popular
music, the méringues have recently been much influenced by
Cuban styles. On a later Nemours album issued by Cook Records, a guaguancó-style B section has been added to many of the
tracks. The accordion is still there, in a lineup including two
trumpets, alto and tenor sax, and a very light rhythm section of
bass and conga-type drum. The basic style is similar to that of
Nemours's older recordings, with gentle, "Frenchish" tunes, but
Nemours makes frequent use of unison trumpet shakes, which
sound as if they have been taken over from Cuban music and

modified to suit the group. The effect is not of a copy but of yet another set of influences taken over and in the process of absorption.

Another group, Super Jazz des Jeunes, shows a two-way set of tendencies. It added a piece of Haitian tradition, heavily reinterpreted, by incorporating *vaccines* into its rhythm section. At the same time, many of its tracks enthusiastically adopt a very superficial sentimentality that owes some debt to Cuban boleros, and perhaps even more to Parisian versions of Cuban boleros. Like Nemours, the Super Jazz des Jeunes plays a mixture of méringues and other dances like the mascaron and contredanse.

Martinique and Guadeloupe, two small islands that officially form part of France, might appear to have had little opportunity to develop music of their own. In fact, however, the Martinique biguine has achieved international success at various times—and as we shall see, was an early influence in modern Congolese dance music, with a faster rhythm than most méringues. A favorite lineup will include clarinet and trombone, both playing in a jazz-like polyphony. The effect, which can be raucous but is always fun, is a long way from "Begin the Beguine." Unfortunately, good biguines are hard to find on records.

Another popular music from these islands is the mazurca, yet another nineteenth-century dance that has been taken in and made over. Mazurcas tend to be slower and more staid than biguines, but not much. According to some, the Martinique mazurca is simply the European mazurka superimposed on a biguine beat. That may be so; mazurcas exist elsewhere in the Caribbean, but no one yet has seriously studied the various European dance forms and how they developed in the Caribbean.

A somewhat similar history lies behind the Guadeloupian waltz, which is basically similar to other creole waltzes. A certain tension is set up between the waltz rhythm and the beat of the *maraccas* or *güiro*, as they try to mold an alien rhythm onto a relatively rigid form. When the performance is good, the tension is not unlike that of African drummers superimposing different meters. Martinique's carnival music is the videe, a street march related to the styles found in Brazil, Trinidad, and beyond.

The Dutch islands of Aruba, Curaçao, and Bonaire also have

their own styles, though they are heavily affected from outside. One major influence is Venezuela, but there are contributions from all over the islands. A dance alleged to be native to the Dutch Antilles is the tumba, though whether it is really local or a descendant of the Haitian or the Dominican tumba is not certain. Curaçao also has a creolized waltz form, still extant though regarded as old-fashioned. An example on the Folkways record *Caribbean Dances* is the "Aura Waltz." This opens rather confusedly and after a while practically abandons the waltz beat.

Taken as a whole, then, the Caribbean is an unbelievably rich musical area. On any island one can find music that is essentially African and music both influenced by and influencing international show business. There is what must surely be the largest reservoir (with the exception of the European conservatory tradition) of living forms from a previous century to be played anywhere. Everywhere, both Europe and Africa have left their marks: in religious rites, in vocal and instrumental styles, in instruments themselves, and in the approaches to form, to material, and to function. But Africa has proved to be the catalyst, has molded and reworked European material until the music of the whole area, despite its several languages and myriad islands, is recognizably related—not one music, certainly, but one musical family.

6 NORTH AMERICAN STRAINS: FROM SPIRITUALS TO BLUES

In both South America and the Caribbean, the existence of Africanisms in the music of the black population is unarguable. A sizable body of music there is either untouched or only lightly touched by non-African influences. Just as important, much of the rest of the music there would not exist had it not been for the African side of the equation. The African elements did not simply work their effects long ago and then vanish. They are still present and important, and new developments are as likely to spring from currents traceable ultimately to Africa as from European strains. Besides, we have seen that, in at least some cases, not only the music of the black people of a particular region but also the national styles (in the sense of styles belonging to everybody) owe their existence to both Africa and Europe.

Is the same true of the United States? Certainly it used not to be thought so. Although what Herskovits called "the myth of the Negro past"—that is to say, the myth that New World Negroes did not have a past—is fairly well exploded now, people often are not too clear about what, if anything, is African in black U.S. music and what was taken from European sources. Nor are they certain what the white folk and popular styles owe to black music. In fact, as we shall find, the history of black music in the United States and the history of white music are inextricably intertwined. There is black music, and there is white music, but they are brothers, or perhaps cousins.

The place and time where one would expect to find the most African music in the United States is the countryside in the nineteenth century, and it is true that various sorts of music found in the countryside have a large number of obvious Africanisms. This is largely a matter of function, since the strongest elements of African music are retained when the music continues to serve the same sort of purpose as it did in Africa. One such purpose is to make work, especially communal work, go easier; hence, various work songs have preserved heavy African content in North America, just as they have in other parts of the hemisphere.

Naturally, work songs take on the qualities of the work they accompany. In Africa, for example, collective work songs are not all that common in the rain forest belt, which includes the Yoruba, Ewe, Ibo, and other tribes and corresponds roughly to the main drumming area. Forest crops generally need less communal labor than field crops. As a result, the more open savanna belt of West Africa has more group work songs than do the forests. But even in the savannas work songs often are supplied by professionals who play music to encourage, rather than direct, the labor. These musicians or singers do not take part in the work—or, rather, their part in the work is their music. Work songs sung by workers themselves tend to be fairly casual. There is an example on a Folkways record of music from Liberia, sung by men cutting back bush land preparatory to burning it off to take the new rice crop. They sing in an intermittent fashion, breaking off for conversation or a joke, their machetes providing percussion for their song.

Work songs in the United States do not share all the qualities of African work songs, but they unmistakably share enough to place them among the most Africanized of surviving forms. A fundamental Africanism is the very attitude that song is so necessary to work. Harold Courlander quotes a number of remarks made to him that underline this. An African told him, "Without a song the bush-knife is dull" (this is in fact a West African proverb), and an Alabama track-liner said: "Man, singing just naturally makes the work go easier. If you didn't have singing you wouldn't get hardly anything out of these men."

The heyday of the collective work song in the United States was the period of slavery, and not only because more people were nearer to their African background (though slaving went on illegally, albeit dwindling to a trickle, until 1859). Another reason was the nature of plantation work, which was frequently team work. Though it is not true, as LeRoi Jones claimed in *Blues People*, that all the different forms of labor common to Africans in Africa were reduced to plantation farming in the United States, it is true that various forms of labor on the plantation had parallels with certain forms of labor known in Africa, which supplied soil in which Africanisms could flourish.

Some types of work song in particular survived until quite recently—not, usually, in free society but in the Southern prison systems, which made use of a convict-lease system in many cases and preserved methods of manual labor long after mechanization had been introduced into free farming. The prison work songs that were recorded in large numbers in various parts of the South from the 1930's to the 1960's provide a great body of music that to some extent represents an older stratum in black styles. To some extent only, of course, because convicts are simply people who have been locked up, and thus bring musical developments from outside into the prison-song tradition. The body of prison work songs is so magnificent musically that there is a temptation to write about it at length. But its flavor—of superb musicality in most cases, but also of human bitterness, humor, and courage in adversity—can better be caught by listening to the recorded examples listed in the discography.

The degree of direct Africanism in the work songs is a matter for argument. Pete Seeger, in his introduction to a collection of prison work songs on Folkways, says that one song, "Long John," has been traced to a West African source. Remembering that one optimist once traced "Swing Low, Sweet Chariot" to a canoe-burial ceremony in the Victoria Falls region, one has to be careful about such attributions. On the other hand, many work songs,

like many other old black songs, may in fact have African antecedents. If "Stewball" can be traced with certainty to an eighteenth-century English source while African attributions are less
certain, this is because eighteenth-century songs in England were
written down and their African contemporaries were not. Even
if no existing U.S. tune could be matched with an African one,
this would not in itself disprove survival. Though African tunes
are longer-lived than African lyrics, they seem to be replaced by
new ones quite rapidly. Nor are work songs the most durable of
forms, having nothing like a religious sanction to enforce their
perpetuation.

Certainly nineteenth-century black work songs were of many
types. The British actress Fanny Kemble, in a much-quoted para-
graph, described in the nineteenth-century how she had changed
her earlier view that the black songs she heard were adaptations
of Scots and Irish airs. She wrote about a series of rowing songs
she had heard:

> I have been quite at a loss to discover any such foundation for
> many that I have heard lately, and which have appeared to me
> extraordinarily wild and unaccountable. The way in which the
> chorus strikes in with the burden, between each phrase of the
> melody chanted by a single voice, is very curious and effective,
> especially with the rhythm of the rowlocks for accompaniment.

The description gives one reason to wonder if she may not have
been listening to an African song like one (with the rhythm of
the oarlocks substituting for the swish of the paddles that accompanies the Nupe fishermen on the Niger River) that appears
on a striking record in the archives of the British Broadcasting
Corporation.

At times difficult to analyse, but unmistakable, is the link between the group singing of many U.S. work songs, especially the
earlier ones, and of examples from a wide range of tribes in West
and Central Africa. Some work songs use a form of near-unison
in which minute variations produce a distinct and unmistakable
sound very like the singing in Yoruba traditional music. Ulli
Beier, writing in *African Music*, described the effect this way:

"Yoruba singing knows no harmony in the European sense. Yet the singers are never in perfect unison either. Very small intervals between the different voices seem to give a kind of 'colour' or 'texture' to the sound." Other American work songs, using fourths, octaves, and occasional fifths, have harmonies almost identical to certain Congolese recordings.

A minor but significant Africanism, mentioned by Harold Courlander in *Negro Folk Music U.S.A.*, is a form of "dedication" in some work songs, which, like some African praise and chronicle songs, makes reference at the outset to all people of importance within earshot. Courlander quotes:

> I say I'm ringing in the bottom,
> I say I'm ringing for the captain,
> I say I'm ringing for the steerer,
> I believe we ring for everybody.

The formalities completed, the singer can proceed to another African favorite, the satirical song, with less fear of reprisal.

A large number of work songs have a structure that is definitely African, because it is common in African music and not used in Europe. They consist of a long litany with a group response after every line, often forming the second half of the "tune," in a version of call-and-response singing. The litany lines are often unrhymed; they achieve their aesthetic effect with striking imagery (balancing traditional formulations and fresh use of known images) and repetition, as does African poetry. "Hammer Ring," for example, is a series of single lines, each repeated and followed by the refrain "hammer ring." The key lines of the verse run:

> Won't you ring old hammer?   (Hammer ring.)
> Broke the handle in my hammer.   (Hammer ring.)
> Got to hammering in the Bible.   (Hammer ring.)
> Gotta talk about Norah [Noah].   (Hammer ring.)
> Well, God told Norah   (Hammer ring.)
> You is a-going in the timber   (Hammer ring.)

Noah here takes the role of a hero-figure who is invoked to inspire and encourage the listeners to emulate his deeds. The song, in fact, is not religious despite its use of a religious story.

The British blues expert Paul Oliver, in a book we shall be meeting again, suggests that much U.S. black music may in fact stem not from the rain forest areas, as is usually assumed, but from the music of the savannas. In this context, it is extremely interesting that many U.S. work songs use a form of call-and-response slightly different from the common improvised-call, fixed-response formula. The chorus picks up variations in the lead melody and, as it were, tosses them back, so that there is a constant variation in which a number of melodic themes are worked in. This is found in much savanna music, including most strikingly a long piece of ritual music recorded privately in northern Nigeria by Dr. Anthony King of the School of Oriental and African Studies, London. The woman lead singer is followed without a fault through a series of complex variations. Something similar is frequent in Yoruba *apala* music, which, although the Yoruba are of the rain forest drumming belt, actually shows considerable Muslim influence, especially perhaps in the vocal parts. "Long John," as sung on a Library of Congress record, is a fine example of this style.

Work songs cover a huge range of subjects. Perhaps the most recurrent, natural in the prison songs, are women, the length of the sentence, escape, and harsh jailers. A most chilling example was recorded in Texas in 1933 by John and Alan Lomax. Called "Ain't No More Cane on This Brazos," two of its verses run:

> You ought to come on the river in nineteen four
> You could find a dead man on ever' turn row.
>
> Little boy, what'd you do for to get so long?
> Said, "I killed my rider in the high sheriff's arms."

A feature of African music we have mentioned before is the indirect allusion, the use of oblique or cryptic references. Naturally, prison conditions encourage such a tendency, and "Long John" is an excellent illustration. It is about a legendary man who outran police, sheriff, deputies, and dogs on his way to freedom. The first verse is clearly about the escape:

> It's a long John,
> He's a long gone,
> Like a turkey through the corn,
> Through the long corn.

The nickname is oblique in itself; the image is vivid, but bound to a very humble, everyday country context (incidentally, animal similes of all sorts are extremely common in African song). The repetition of the word "long" is a highly poetic device that is closer to an African than to any of the European traditions likely to have affected the singer.

The next verse veers sideways, and John becomes the Evangelist:

> Well, my John said,
> In the ten chap ten [tenth chapter, tenth verse]
> "If a man die
> He will live again."
> Well, they crucified Jesus,
> And they nailed him to the cross;
> Sister Mary cried,
> My Child is lost!

The clear, though indirect, linking with the escaped convict of John the Evangelist and then, in an apparently irrelevant aside, of the crucified Jesus is evidence of major poetic talent. It is also typical of a tangential approach common in African music. Praise songs, for instance, may laud a man by mentioning all manner of revered figures and associations without ever drawing an analogy or otherwise connecting them to their subject. Similarly, the singer of this version of "Long John," known only as Lightning, makes no direct link between the Biblical characters and his protagonist, other than their appearing in the same song.

The allusive poetic style is not solely a matter of secrecy, though prison life naturally gives added force to the enduring

African feeling that, the world being the way it is, too much frankness is foolhardy. The use of poetic images without attribution is a general principle of African verse. The difference from European poetry emerges in a comparison of examples. Shelley, in "The Moon," creates a long and striking image for the moon, "like a dying lady lean and pale," but in the fifth line he names the subject: "The moon arose up in the murky east." "Old Hannah," on the other hand, is only named, never explained:

> Go down, old Hannah,
> Won't you rise no more?

and, in the next verse,

> Lord, if you rise,
> Bring judgment on.

From the context, the listener may be able to deduce that Old Hannah is the sun, but he is not told so, nor does he learn why the sun is called Old Hannah. Like African singers, Iron Head and Clear Rock are singing only for those who know or who feel.

Prison work songs represent perhaps the most cohesive body of labor music in the U.S. black experience. Naturally, not all songs are sung in the same way, even in the same prison. There was what Alan Lomax called the Mississippi style, "distinguished by the rough voice timbre used, the savagery of the singing, the overlapping of leader and chorus." The first and last of those qualities are very African, and it is undoubtedly significant that parts of Mississippi have traditionally had a very high majority of black residents, since on the whole Africanisms survive at their most obvious in such conditions.

Prison work songs endured longer than most others because conditions changed faster on the outside, and perhaps they reached a greater artistic peak because there was a good deal (to put it mildly) of the continuity essential to a group form. The prison songs are so superlative aesthetically that it is easy to forget the wide range of other work songs that were developed in the United States. Some were very simple, and some would seem at first sight to have little to do with Africa. The laying of railroad track, for example, was not a technique brought with the slaves, but the use of song for an extremely restricted purpose—instructing track-layers in what to do next—is indeed African. Europeans sing absent-mindedly, as it were, or as a pastime while working (with the two exceptions of obscure music like Sicilian mule songs and the possibly black-influenced sea-chanties). They do not pay heed to a man who stands by doing nothing but telling them in song, or in chant at least, how to unload and stack rails:

> Walk to the car, steady yourself.
> Head high!
> Throw it away!
> That's just right!
> Go back and get another one.
> You got the wrong one that time. . . .
> Walk humble and don't you stumble,
> And don't you hurt nobody.
> Walk to the car and steady yourself.

A highly specialized work song was the chant of the leadsman on the old sternwheelers of the Mississippi as he measured the depth of the river with a plumbline. Samuel Clemens took his pen name from one of these calls:

> Lord, I'm throwing lead line on the la'board side.
> Quarter less twain,
> Don't you change your mind.
> Heave it in the water just-a one more time.
> Eight feet and a half, Mr. Pilot, will you change
>   your mind?
> Run him on a slow bell. . . .
> Quarter less twain on the sta'board side. . . .
> Lord, lord,
> Quarter less twain. . . .
> I've gone low down, so mark twain,
> Mark twain.

This functionality is basic to African cultures. Indeed, the curious, ambiguous status of this sort of form defies European categorization. Is it a song? Not really. Is it a call, musicalized? In a sense.

John W. Work, in his *Negro Spirituals and Songs,* mentions a different category of work song:

> The men sang another type of song when they were not engaged in group efforts, but were working at individual tasks. This song was a solo affair whose melody had little significance. It was little more than intonation, though the two lines possessed a semi-cadence and cadence as well as a climax note. The song . . . was the singer's soliloquy on the trivialities of life as they directly affected him. Its verse was subjective, just as that of the blues, though probably not so poignant.

It was called the holler, a form of uncertain derivation for which much has been claimed, including parentage of the blues. Hollers consist usually of a long, wavering one- or two-line call, often using falsetto and in other respects suggesting African parallels. Lomax once wrote:

> The lonely Negro workers piling up dirt on the levees, plowing in the cotton fields, at work in the lonely mist of the riverbottoms . . . have poured their feelings into songs like these. The songs are addressed to the sun and the choking dust, to the stubborn mules, to the faithless woman of the night before, to the hard-driving captain; and they concern the essential loneliness of man on the earth. . . . The listener will notice the same use of falsetto stops, the same drop of the voice at the end of lines, that characterize the blues.

And characterize, as we have seen, much West African music also. Moreover, there is a powerful signaling element in the hollers. Harold Courlander speculates that early hollers, which he says, "undoubtedly were in African dialects, insofar as actual words were used," may have been used for signaling. This is done in Africa; when it is, the signaler often imitates not speech tones but the sound of a horn imitating speech tones.

Some hollers strongly convey a personal and almost ruminative note: "Mmmmmmmm. Boys, I've got a boychild in Texas, he ought to be 'bout grown." Others were still used for signaling

within living memory. Samuel Brooks, who recorded some hollers
for the Library of Congress in 1939, commented: "They usually
sing it on a plantation. . . . If one man starts, well, across
maybe another field close by, why they sing that same tune back
to him. . . .

> "Ooooooooooh,
> I won't be here long.
> Oooooooooooh,
> Oh, dark gonna catch me here,
> Dark gonna catch me here,
> Oooooooh."

Clearly, many hollers shade into short songs. Alan Lomax recorded a beautiful holler, "Wild Ox Moan" by Vera Hall, which
is quite remarkably like another intensely personal piece of
music from the Central African Republic—a lullaby sung by an
Isongo woman, available on an Ocora record. "Wild Ox Moan"
is slower, and the singer's voice less hard. But both pieces have
the same ruminative, sung-for-oneself quality. Most important,
the same entirely un-European use of falsetto or yodeled notes
as part of the main melody line occurs. (European yodeling, when
it is part of a song, is a separate entity, whether a chorus or
interpolated nonsense syllables. It does not happen on certain
notes of a word.) Vera Hall's "Wild Ox Moan" is still a holler,
not a song, insofar as the two can be differentiated. A much
longer version called "Black Woman," on the Folkways *Negro
Folk Music of Alabama*, is free-form but unmistakable blues.
The distinction is often subtle. But it would be nonsensical to
suggest, as some writers have, that the holler represented some
sort of inchoate welling-up of a new-formed musical sense. It
was a legacy from Africa of a particular kind.

The question of early black songs in the United States is complex. Quite early on, the slaves there, as elsewhere, began to
make use (as highly creative people, why would they do otherwise?) of the white styles they heard around them to supplement
the African forms they were continuing and transmuting. We saw
in the case of Jamaica that children's games did just that, and

before going on to more complex forms it is worth examining the same genre in the United States.

Not only did U.S. blacks take to English children's games like the Jamaicans, but in at least one case they adopted the same game. Here is part of an American version, as recorded by Harold Courlander:

> Li'l Sally Walker
> Sittin' in a saucer
> Cryin' for the old man
> To come for the dollar.

Naturally, Afro-Americans did not get the *idea* of children's games from the white population. African children's games are highly sophisticated aids to learning. When Afro-American children did adopt elements of the white kids' songs, they reinterpreted them in many of the ways that adults reinterpreted white song and dance forms. For one thing, in North America as in Jamaica, a large number of black children's games were really an excuse for dancing, so what mattered was individual dancing rather than the development of the story content.

Besides, white-originated games like "Sally's in the Skiff" had plenty of black counterparts with African features. This one is in call-and-response form and has a rhythm quite beyond most white children in their present state of musical culture:

> *c:* If I live
> *r:* Chool-dy, chool-dy
> *c:* To see next fall
> *r:* Chool-dy, chool-dy
> *c:* I ain' gon' raise
> *r:* Chool-dy, chool-dy
> *c:* No cabbage at all
> *r:* Chool-dy, chool-dy.

Children—black, white, brown, and yellow—sing out of not only their own but their parents' experiences, and even their grandparents'. The old English nursery rhyme "Ring a Ring of Roses" is a grim historical allusion to the pneumonic plague of 1665. The roses were a characteristic rash, posies the pathetic prophylactic of medicinal herbs carried in the pocket, and a-tishoo the pneumonic sneezing before we all fall down—dead. Alan Lomax recorded a group of children singing of a happier but just as traumatic a moment, emancipation, when the plantation bell fell silent:

> Ring, ring the big bell
> Ain' gonna ring no more;
> Fill me a pocket before I go,
> It ain' gonna ring no more.

The well-known "Shortening Bread" tells a truer and grimmer story in one version than is usually heard:

> Two little babies layin' in bed.
> One play sick and the other'n play dead.
> I do love shortening bread.

Harold Courlander tells of places in the starvation lands of Alabama where he was a guest at tables that never saw anything but shortening bread and molasses. This sort of staggering poverty, incidentally, is responsible for allusions that have tended to baffle blues enthusiasts. When Bessie Smith, in "Empty Bed Blues," used the phrase "he boiled my first cabbage" as a sexual metaphor, the effect seemed to outsiders less than ecstatic. But in the areas whose bitter experience produced "Shortening Bread," areas where greens were a luxury, the metaphor would naturally make more sense.

In the nineteenth-century frontier lands, play songs and games were not only for children, either white or black, and accounts of the period make it clear that black and white could learn from each other. A play-party song called "Rosey" shows very clearly one strain in the developing black styles that were to lead to the various forms of music we know today:

> Grab you a partner and promenade round
> Hah-a Rosey
> Pin my true love by my side
> Hah-a Rosey
> You do that now, you do that again,
> Hah-a Rosey.

This was clearly the kind of barn dance that had a caller telling the steps, in the old English and Scots tradition transported to the United States. But a call-and-response pattern had been added, and the chanting and response "swung" not in the extroverted, gay but relatively simple white fashion, but so that an apparent on-beat clapping accompaniment served as a base for a series of minutely displaced vocal accents by a singer using passing falsetto and semi-yodeling notes in the African style.

The evidence of early absorption of white music elements by black musicians is incontrovertible. The ways in which blacks learned white music and the types they learned were, of course, myriad. Henry Kmen's study of nineteenth-century New Orleans music reports the surprise of visitors to the city at hearing blacks in the street whistle operatic arias. Of course, not everywhere was there an opera house or a segregated gallery accessible to black citizens, and many influences came from quite different sources. Lydia Parrish, in her *Slave Songs of the Georgia Sea Islands*, reproduces a spiritual ("O the Robe") with a "Celtic lilt" and explains it by the presence of Irish hands imported to work alongside the local black labor, repairing the ricefield dikes of Glynn County and digging a canal between Brunswick and the Altamaha River in 1838–39 (Lydia Parrish did not attribute European origins to black music lightly; if anything, she rather strained after African explanations).

Because survival of Africanisms in the New World and the degree of adoption of new material depended partly on the strength of the traditions to be kept or acquired, it is not surprising that a whole field of black narrative song grew up with major white elements. Narrative song, in the form of both ballads and shorter numbers, is an important part of British folk music, whereas, except for historical epics (such as the Mali epic of

Sundiata), it was rarer in African culture. U.S. black singers did not take over white ballads whole. The process was complex and piecemeal. Sometimes they used whatever images out of British ballads appealed to them. Thus, Leadbelly suddenly interpolates into the Negro ballad "John Henry" lines almost identical to an old Scottish ballad:

> Tell me who's going to shoe your little foot,
> Tell me who's going to glove your hand.
> Tell me who's going to kiss your sweet little lips,
> And who's going to be your man.

The ballad "John Henry" itself and a host of other "epic" ballads—most but not all featuring badmen—show interesting developments. Their fuller versions are clearly modeled on British ballad forms in their narrative progression, sometimes in their verse form, and in their fondness of dialogue verses between two protagonists. But even on paper, leaving aside any consideration of performing technique, there are differences. Within the narrative frame, allusiveness creeps in. Who, for instance, are those women dressed in red who recur time and time again, sometimes mourning and sometimes joyful at death?

When a British ballad is taken over by black singers, it often comes out unrecognizable except for isolated motifs. Perhaps the most famous traveling song is "Saint James Infirmary," which went from Ireland to England probably in the eighteenth century; became a broadside ballad, "The Unfortunate Rake," about a man who dies of venereal disease; and split into myriad versions, all with certain common verses and much the same tune. Here is a version from Southern England containing verses that have cropped up in two American songs:

> And when I am dead to the churchyard they'll bear me,
> Six jolly fellows to carry me on,
> And in each of their hands a bunch of green laurel
> So they'll not smell me as they're walking along.
> So rattle your drums and play your fife over me,
> So rattle your drums as we march along.

Then return to your home and think on that young girl,
"Oh there goes a young girl cut down in her prime."

During the nineteenth century, some version of this song took
root in the seaport of Liverpool, became a seamen's song under
the name of "Saint James's Hospital," and set sail for the States.
There it split. The tune and many elements of the lyric, including the drum and fife and the laurel, changed to roses, became
the cowboy song "Streets of Laredo." The title, slightly changed,
and the image of the pallbearers, were taken over by black
singers. Their versions told of the plight of a gambler cut down
in his prime—it is sometimes called "Gambler's Blues"—and of
course it played hell with the rhythm:

When I die I want six crap shooters to be my pallbearers,
Three pretty women to sing a song;
Put a jazzband on my hearse wagon,
And raise hell as we ride along.

It would be a mistake to overemphasize the amount of British
balladry in black song of the nineteenth century, transmuted or
not. The amount preserved even in what is usually considered the
great ballad area, the Southern Appalachians, has been exaggerated. Whereas seventy-three British border ballads from the
massive Child collection were collected by five people in two
Northern states, Vermont and Maine, only sixty-nine were found
in the whole of the South by an army of collectors. What did
happen was the adoption of appropriate images and of the general ballad form, which was then altered and used for new
creations.

Besides the few songs that have been transformed wholesale,
British balladry seems to have influenced black forms and
imagery enduringly. The structure of the blues song "Two
White Horses," with its first line repeated three times (not two,
as in most of the blues), is quite common in both black and white
music of the South. Many of the images could be out of old
British ballads. At the same time, the direct question in the
third to last verse is most unlike British ballads, and very like

the person-to-person blues forms. The questions in verses three and four are rather different; they sound like "dialogue" verses in a song with other verses omitted (a favorite black way of creating a subtle, allusive form out of the European narrative songs). In addition, the singer in each verse lets his guitar carry some of what were originally lyrics, a device reportedly to be found in the savanna regions of Africa, as well as being widespread in the United States.

Now two white horses standing in a line,
Now two white horses standing in a (guitar)
Now two white horses standing in a (guitar)
Gonna take me to my burying ground.

Did you ever hear that coffin sound? (guitar)
Did you ever hear that coffin? (guitar)
Did you ever hear a coffin (guitar)
You know now poor boy's in the ground.

Please dig my grave with a silver spade
Please dig my grave with a silver (guitar)
Please dig my grave with a (guitar)
You can let me down with a golden chain.

It's one kind favor I'll ask of you
It's one kind favor I'll ask of (guitar)
It's one kind favor I'll ask of (guitar)
Take pains see my grave be kept clean.

Did you ever hear that church bell tone?
Did you ever hear that church bell (guitar)
Did you ever hear that church bell (guitar)
You know now poor boy's dead and gone.

Now two white horses standing in a line,
(continues as verse one)

> Did you ever hear a coffin sound?
> (continues as verse two)

The white horses might be an image from either tradition, though I suspect a thorough working over of an old ballad image. The silver spade and golden chain are originally British, in various forms. "Poor boy dead and gone" in different versions is a favorite wandering verse in the blues. The theme as a whole fits well with the inherited African concern for a rightful death and burial. The singing style and guitar are a country blues, as far as could be from British or Anglo-American singing.

In the black ballads and ballad-like forms, therefore, there is no simple imitation. There is acquisition and reworking for a new purpose. The result is at times something between a ballad without the verse form and the blues without the blues form.

Another difference between white and black treatments of the same subject stems fairly directly from the respective African and British traditions. A black ballad about the death of Railroad Bill records the historical though trivial fact that he died with a cracker and cheese in his hand. This fixing of a scene by an everyday detail is part of a mundaneness common in African and Afro-American music of many types. White ballads on the death of an evildoer almost invariably draw a moral. This tendency was the inheritance of the British broadside ballads rather than the old folk ballads, and it was exaggerated by market-minded songwriters. The Dixon Brothers' "Wreck on the Highway" is an extreme example of the tendency: "I saw the wreck on the highway, but I didn't hear nobody pray." It is true that "Frankie and Johnny" in some black versions has a payoff of a sort, but the tone is quite different:

> This story has no moral, this story has no end,
> This story only goes to show that there ain't no good in men.

Interestingly, when black singers point a moral they frequently show a far greater awareness of the Biblical injunctions about judging one's neighbor. Olive Woolley Burts, in her *American Murder Ballads*, tells of collecting a song on the Lindbergh kid-

napping virtually as it was being improvised in a free, archaic
blues-ballad form:

> Oh who would steal a baby out from his little bed?
> The world is full of trouble, trouble,
> Oh Lord have mercy on us folks!

The sanctimonious finger-pointing of many white ballads is missing altogether from this lament for original sin.

We have seen that the sources of black song are widely varied.
The creole music of Louisiana had strong affinities with the
French *patois* songs of the Caribbean and almost none with the
rest of black music, except for Zydeco, the music of the blacks in
the bayou regions settled by the Cajuns, descendants of French
Canadian refugees. The very form of these French-influenced
songs set them apart. Call-and-response passages come out more
like the bobbin of Jamaican song, as in "Zamours Marianne,"
which uses an interpolated "Michie'-la" or "Marianne" rather
than the longer response phrases of the rest of the Southern
states.

But the Caribbean influence on Louisiana creole music (which
is significant for the development of certain elements in jazz)
is most striking in the dances. Louisiana knew the universal
Caribbean dance, the kalinda. In Louisiana, according to Mina
Monroe's *Bayou Ballads,* it took the form of a stick-fight dance,
as in Trinidad and elsewhere, with the added complication that
the opponents had to balance a full bottle of water on their
heads, and the first to spill a drop was the loser. A white Cajun
version, the Colinda, can be heard on an Arhoolie recording of
Cajun music. The kalinda was said to be the dance observed in
New Orleans's Congo Square by early witnesses. Of the other
dances described in New Orleans, most were Caribbean also: the
juba, the bamboula, the babouille (baboule in Haiti), and others.
We noted the juba earlier. The words taken down in various
U.S. locations make it clear that it was essentially a called reel:

> Juba jump, Juba sing,
> Juba cut that pigeon wing.

A version from the Sea Islands is reported by Lydia Parrish. It appears to have been known in Georgia and the Carolinas, as well as Louisiana, and to have become a children's game song:

> Juba this and juba that,
> And Juba kill the yellow cat.

The Buzzard Lope, highly African in inspiration, had a very common animal-mimicry basis. One dancer lies down in the center of a ring and plays a dead cow, while the other moves around him impersonating a buzzard. Its accompaniment seems originally to have been patted and clapped.

We have described the neo-African dances of the Congo Square, and there is every reason to suppose that their equivalents could be found wherever there were enough Africans to preserve them and hand them down. But the neo-African dances soon existed alongside music that made use of European instruments. As early as 1799, fifes and fiddles were used in Congo Square, and banjos, triangles, jews' harps, and tambourines also appeared. It seems significant to me that all these European instruments were counterparts of African types—especially, as Paul Oliver pointed out in *Savannah Syncopators*, from the savanna regions. Hausa *griots*, among others, frequently played in groups consisting of *kukuma* or *goge* fiddles with drums or frame drums and some sort of metallic percussion instrument. As Oliver put it: "The skills of the players of *kukuma* or *goge* would soon have been adapted to the European fiddle under active encouragement. And encouragement was certainly there."

It certainly was. Though the drums (which could be used to signal revolt and by all indications were so used, not only in Haiti and Jamaica but at times in the United States) were banned in many states, many slave-owners took the view that after hours their property could make as much racket as it liked—at a suitable distance from the house. Some, whether out of kindness or enlightened self-interest, not only permitted music but even bought fiddles and other instruments for their more musical slaves and encouraged Saturday night dances. The newspapers of the Southern states during slavery days were full of advertisements that explode two stereotypes at once: the happy slave and the African who rejects all he can of white culture. Paper after paper announced the flight of some slave "very skilled on the French horn" or one who "took with him his fiddle." There can be no doubt at all that the two black instruments of the nineteenth century were the banjo and the fiddle. One was African, the other European, but each represented a more complex version of an instrument known in Africa.

The blending of African and European styles was encouraged by contact between the races. As LeRoi Jones points out, it was after Emancipation that, with bitter irony, "Negroes became actually isolated from the mainstream of American society. . . . The newly activated Jim Crow laws (Virginia's were not passed until 1901) and other social repressions served to separate the Negro more effectively from his former master than ever before."

The isolation was not actually complete. The father of Mance Lipscomb, the Texas songster, was a full-time fiddler who after Emancipation played for dances in the Scots-Irish, Bohemian, and Negro settlements of the Brazos bottoms in Texas. For each he must have produced the appropriate music, and it is inconceivable that he did not retain elements of all—music simply does not work that way.

Jones's thesis that, during the more repressive post-Reconstruction period, black music lost many of the more superficial forms it had borrowed from the white man might be rephrased: Black musicians were then in the process of integrating what had been, on the one hand, definitely African survivals and, on the other, relatively undigested borrowings. The synthesis was being completed. A music that was truly Afro-American, in which African-derived musical techniques and concepts fundamentally made over such elements as had been taken from white America, was coming to maturity. The white elements endured, of course, even in the blues, alleged to be the blackest of black music (not with total justification, perhaps). The blues of Sonny Terry, for instance, still shows signs of the old reels and jigs that went into country breakdown music. And breakdown music itself is a paradigm for the new black music that was slowly growing throughout the nineteenth century but was caused to explode when Emancipation caused profound social and economic changes. As LeRoi Jones noted: "The entrance of Negroes into the more complicated social situation of self-reliance posed multitudes of social and cultural problems that they never had to deal with as slaves. The music of the Negro began to reflect these social and cultural complexities and change."

Meanwhile, country music of all kinds continued. The small dance groups, using whatever instruments came to hand, fiddles, mouth harps, and guitars, but also washtub basses, kazoos, and various improvised percussion instruments. Having in the early days drawn much of their inspiration from Africanized white styles—reels and the like—they now moved on farther toward the newer musical styles. *Ad hoc* music took all sorts of forms. A nineteenth-century visitor to New Orleans made it clear that even brushing a customer in a barber's shop became a rhythmic art:

> With what facility he moves his supple wrist and makes the down-driving broom play over your back the most complicated tunes . . . beating time the while with his foot. . . . How often does the double and triple and common time put you in mind of the castanets of the Castillian maid, and rub-a-dub-dub of the drummer at tattoo or reveille!

The author of this passage could hardly be expected to know the real sources of this rhythmic genius, but his observations were sound enough. There is a track on an Arhoolie record in which a barber stropping a razor provides the accompaniment for a guitarist.

So far we have been discussing what might be described as folk forms. However, during the slave period and, at a quickening pace, after Emancipation, major music was brewing, music that went far beyond the folkloric. Simply for analytical convenience, I am going to divide this into the mainly vocal and the mainly instrumental. In both cases the word "mainly" is important. It must be understood that all styles fed each other, just as they were fed by, and in turn fed, the folk music.

The first black music to catch the serious attention of white America was religious. Negro spirituals began to filter into the general American consciousness just before Emancipation, and its progress was highlighted by a spectacularly successful U.S. and European tour of the Fisk Jubilee Singers in the early 1870's. The Fisk Jubilee Singers undoubtedly presented something of the richness of what must surely be one of the world's greatest complexes of religious styles. Their music, though novel to white America, was not in fact new. Moreover, they appear not to have presented black religious music as it really was. That was not the aim of George L. White, the musical director of the original Fisk Jubilee Singers, as a contemporary described it: "Finish, precision and sincerity were demanded by this leader. While the program featured the spirituals, variety was given it by the use of numbers of classical standard."

Something of the style of the Fisk Jubilee Singers can be heard on recordings of later versions of the group, like the one on the RB record *An Introduction to Gospel Song*. The sound of these, together with the description of White's aims, make it obvious that the group's repertoire represented an art re-creation in a line that continued through the Eurocentric concert performances of Paul Robeson and Marion Anderson—music that had little to do with the worship of the black Christians who originated the spirituals.

The early history of the spirituals is uncertain. The Reverend Samuel Davies, in 1750, calculated that only 1,000 Negroes out of 120,000 in Virginia had been converted and baptized, and presumably that approximated the average for the colonies. In the mid-eighteenth century, therefore, slave religion was presumably African. Even in the absence of evidence, analogy with both the importance of religion in African life and what happened in other parts of the New World makes this a fair assumption. By the late eighteenth century some clergymen were quite active in pastoral work among the slaves. The Reverend John Davies of Virginia, in a letter to John Wesley, told of giving some of his converts copies of Watt's popular hymnal:

> The Negroes, above all of the human species I ever knew, have the nicest ear for music. They have a kind of ecstatic delight in psalmody; nor are there any books they so soon learn, or take so much pleasure in, as those used in that heavenly part of divine

worship. . . . Sundry of them lodged all night in my kitchen; and sometimes when I have awaked at two or three in the morning, a torrent of sacred psalmody has poured into my chamber.

"An ecstatic delight in psalmody" might still serve as the best description for the superlative religious music of U.S. blacks.

In the early nineteenth century, Fanny Kemble heard her boatmen singing what she called "an extremely spirited war-song, beginning, 'the trumpets blow, the bugles blow—Oh, stand your ground.'" This was almost certainly a spiritual; military metaphor is common enough in Christian music, as witness "Onward, Christian Soldiers" and "I'm a Soldier in the Army of the Lord."

The term "spiritual" has come to cover a wide range of religious music. In fact, black religious songs include staid versions of white Protestant hymns; shouting songs that accompany the nearest thing possible to African dancing in a church that regards dancing as sinful; so-called long-meter songs, very highly decorated, which can be traced back to early white American religious styles (made over, of course, into something distinctive) and past them to seventeenth-century Britain; duet prayer song and solo street-evangelists' songs that musically are virtually blues; and chanted, almost sung, sermons.

Professor John W. Work has divided spirituals into three groups: the call-and-response chant; the slow, sustained, long-phrase melody; and the syncopated, segmented melody, the tempo of which is usually fast and "stimulates bodily movement." The form of pre-Emancipation spiritual that caught visitors' attention most often was the so-called shout. The shout—whose name the black linguist Lorenzo Turner traced back to a Wolof word, *saut*, "to dance before the tabernacle"—was the most obviously African of the religious forms of the black United States. It was a call-and-response form and, besides, a religious dance, fundamental to African worship, but—except for certain parts of the Spanish Roman Catholic Church—unknown in Christianity.

There are several descriptions of shouts, or ring-shouts, as they were also called, in magazines of the 1860's. Essentially, they consisted of a circle of people moving single file around its center to singing, accompanied by stamping and heel-clicking. According to Lydia Parrish, the people of one Sea Island parish used broom

handles to beat on the floor, a version of the Dahomeyan
dikgambo, the Haitian *ganbo,* the Trinidadian *tamboo bamboo,*
and versions found in Jamaica and elsewhere. The tempo of a
ring-shout may build up gradually. The excitement certainly does,
until possession by the Holy Spirit takes place (or, where possession is not formalized, possession-like states). James Weldon Johnson described the moment:

> The music, starting perhaps with a Spiritual, becomes a wild,
> monotonous chant. The same musical phrase is repeated over and
> over one, two, three, four, five hours. The words become a repeti-
> tion of an incoherent cry. The very monotony of sound and motion
> produces an ecstatic state. Women, screaming, drop out of the
> shout. But the ring closes up and moves around and around.

Johnson says that the shout was, in his experience, "looked
upon as a very questionable form of worship. . . . The more
educated ministers and members, as fast as they were able to
brave the primitive element in the churches, placed a ban on the
'ring shout.'" He also makes the point that the shout was not, as
far as he could discover, geographically universal.

The shout was clearly an attempt at preserving traditional
forms of worship in a new context. The ban on dancing was
circumvented, because the participants in a ring-shout never
crossed their feet. Physical action, dance as well as music, was an
integral, basic feature of African worship, brought in with the
slaves and kept alive. And in the United States, wherever ring-
shouts were not practiced, marching round the church often was
—not in a European processional, but as a semidancing march to
an intensely rhythmic spiritual. This was reported by John Work
as late as 1940, and various forms of dancing are part of worship
in churches in many parts of the United States today, not only
in the Southern countryside, but also, and perhaps even more, in
the ghettos of big cities like New York, Chicago, and Detroit.

The ring-shout was by no means the only way in which black
Christians managed to reinterpret the use of dance in worship.
A mid-nineteenth-century visitor to New Orleans described a
service there:

> The congregation sang; I think everyone joined, even the children, and the collective sound was wonderful. The voices of one or two women rose above the rest, and one of these soon began to introduce variations. . . . Many of the singers kept time with their feet, balancing themselves on each alternately and swinging their bodies accordingly.

Soon the preacher "raised his own voice above all, clapped his hands, and commenced to dance." The implication of this testimony is that dancing was at one time more common in black churches than today. Beyond that, the mention of a "swinging" rhythm is interesting in the light of John Work's remark that, "in all authentic American Negro music, the rhythms may be divided roughly into two classes—rhythms based on the swinging of head and body and rhythms based on the patting of hands and feet. Again, speaking roughly, the rhythms of the Spirituals fall in the first class, and the rhythms of secular music in the second class."

This may well have been true of the early performance of many of the spirituals, though other styles of black religious music are based on patting, not swinging. Other qualities in the old spirituals, as described by those who heard them, are of obvious African derivation (most are precisely the elements European notation cannot express, which is why writing down spirituals, or any black music, is a travesty). Work tells how a black musician plays around with the fundamental beat, a reinterpretation of West African rhythmic attitudes, applied to European or European-influenced measured time:

> He will, as it were, take the fundamental beat and pound it out with his left hand, almost monotonously; while with his right hand he juggles it. . . . Even in the swaying of head and body the head marks the surge off in shorter waves than does the body. . . . It is often tantalizing and even exciting to watch a minute fraction of a beat balancing for a slight instant on the bar between two measures, and, when it seems almost too late, drop back into its own proper compartment.

Work, like so many other writers, mentions the "turns and quavers and the intentional striking of certain notes just off-key." The use of sliding up to and down from a note is common in

African singing and we have noted too that the "tempered" scale, in fact, belongs only to European art music.

Gilbert Chase's *America's Music* describes the distinctive choral sound of black congregations in much the same terms as Ulli Beier used of Yoruba music: "The manner of Negro singing cannot be accurately described in terms either of 'unison' or 'harmony.' It is more complex than that. . . . A clue to the style is contained in Emily Hallowell's remark that the 'harmonies seem to arise from each singer holding to their own version of the melodies.' " The concert-solo approach to the old spirituals has tended to obscure the fact that many of them were in call-and-response form. Here are two, both fairly well known:

> They crucified my Lord,
> And He never said a mumbling word.
> They crucified my Lord,
> And He never said a mumbling word.
> Not a word, not a word, not a word.

> I know moon-rise, I know star-rise,
> I lay this body down.
> I walk in the moonlight, I walk in the starlight,
> To lay this body down.

At one time, some scholars tried to show that the Negro spirituals were simply copies of white forms. And, more generally, the theory has been raised that it was natural for black Christianity to follow white models more closely than black secular music. Actually, however, much the same complex of influences seems to have operated in religious and secular music alike. It has been shown beyond a doubt that many Negro spirituals were adapted from white hymns. But music is not simply markings on a page, and black music is far more than that.

It is certain that black and white Christians worshiped together in the Great Awakening of the early nineteenth century, and trustworthy accounts written at the time attest that slave converts were most taken with the psalm books of white Baptist and

Methodist preachers. The reasons for the great preponderance of Baptists among black Christians have been repeated many times: The Baptist preachers were willing not just to preach to the slaves but also to sit down and eat with them; the importance of water ceremonies in many West African religions, including water initiation ceremonies, found a parallel in the Baptist emphasis on immersion; and the organization of the Baptist churches was democratic, giving each church considerable antonomy and allowing it to supply the black man with something he could seldom find elsewhere. To cite Phyl Garland, in a reference to the modern Baptist and independent churches: "It was the sole arena where a chauffeur or a handyman, reduced to facelessness and namelessness by his employers and often mute within his own home, might speak with some seldom exercised authority as a deacon of the congregation." Equally important, though perhaps not at the conscious level, the Baptist insistence on personal experience of Christ, combined with fervent expressions of conviction regarding personal salvation, offered a rough parallel with the African custom of possession by the gods. In simpler terms, the Baptist tradition allowed Africans and their descendants to behave in what to them were the proper ways of expressing worship.

Many aspects that tend to be considered exclusively part of black religion were once shared by black and white. The phrase "to get happy," describing a powerful emotional conversion experience that sometimes borders on possession states, as in the lines, "I went to the valley and I didn't go to pray,/But my soul got happy, and I stayed all day," has been regarded by both blacks and whites as a purely black expression, implicitly of a black experience. Actually, the expression was common in camp meetings. McCurry's collection of revival hymns, *Social Harp*, has a version of a popular hymn, "Jesus, My All, to Heaven Is Gone," with the refrain "Happy, oh happy" added:

> We'll cross the river of Jordan,
> Happy, oh happy,
> We'll cross the river of Jordan,
> Happy in the Lord.

And an even more obvious white example occurs in a camp-meeting chorus:

> I want to get happy as I well can be,
> Lord, send salvation down.

The word "spiritual" itself is usually used to mean black religious music, but it seems to have originated in English evangelical circles as "spiritual songs" (in *America's Music,* Gilbert Chase in fact accepts this derivation as definite).

There is, however, room for doubt that either term was adopted outright from white religion. There is no such doubt in the case of the slow, ornamented "surge" style. The "happy, oh happy" chorus quoted above may well have served originally as the answer in a call-and-response formula. Since it is known that black Christians attended camp meetings in large numbers and that in fact black preachers at times preached to white and black together, it is perfectly plausible that the addition was actually an Africanization adopted by black and white alike. Again, one must emphasize that this was not a case of some untutored enthusiasts latching onto something totally alien and imitating it, like the well-worn stereotype of the Japanese distiller of "Scotch." The "surge" style of Mahalia Jackson, Cleophus Robinson, and many others is undoubtedly seventeenth-century British in its broad conception and even, to some extent, in detail. If you copied down the notes of the Caravans' version of "Jesus Saves," you would find it very similar to the old white version quoted by Chase. Some Jamaican hymn-singing occupies a position halfway between the British and black U.S. styles. However, a host of differences are there all the same: vocal tone, fractions of timing, backing—a whole developing tradition. Also, some African singing, especially Muslim prayer songs such as the Guinean "La Illah Ila Allah," available on Vogue Esoteric, makes equally striking use of long, highly decorated notes. (Another example can be found in the recording of a Dan woman's lament for her husband on Barenreiter, BM 30 L 2301.) In other words, the surge style is probably another instance of a feature taken over because it corresponded with something already familiar.

By no means were all Negro spirituals reworkings of white hymns or based on them. Chase cites Richard Waterman's report on an unpublished study by M. Kolinski showing that:

1. Thirty-six spirituals are either identical or closely related in scale and mode to West African songs. One, "Cyan Ride," is almost exactly the same as a Nigerian song, and "No More Auction Block" echoes an Ashanti song.

2. A wide range of technical musical elements are shared—too many for coincidence.

3. The opening rhythms of thirty-four spirituals are almost exactly like those of several Ghanaian and Dahomeyan songs.

4. The overlapping of call-and-response patterns produced identical polyphonic patterns in many spirituals and African songs. Fifty spirituals were found to have the same formal structure as some West African songs.

Kolinski concluded that many spirituals, though patterned after European models, were either bent to conform to West African musical practice or chosen because they suited it.

All in all, when early black Christian music used existing white material, this material was immediately subjected to a molding process, bringing it in line with established musical practices developed from African sources: call-and-response, increased rhythmic flexibility, the use of handclapping for percussion (which can lay claim to being the *major* African percussive practice, and which was reported in black U.S. religious music by the eighteenth century), and the emphasis on possession states as a form of worship and a sign that the spirit was present. The African provenance of possession states has been disputed on the grounds that religious possession affected both blacks and whites at the camp meetings and had been known in Europe. But European possession was passive and never expressed itself in dancing (at least not in areas which could have affected the United States), and the white manifestations either died out after a few years or remained only in isolated cases. Possession is a *major* feature of many different types of black church in all types of community.

Possession seems to be associated largely with certain kinds of music, or at any rate such music greatly increases its likelihood. On the subject of Africa, M. J. Field writes in an essay in *Spirit Possession in Africa:*

> Drumming, singing, clapping and the rhythmic beating of gong-gongs and rattles, alone or all together, are the commonest inducers of possession. The drumming is exciting, the clanging iron is a harsh monotony from which consciousness readily recoils. More possessed people are likely to be seen at a well-orchestrated dance than on any other occasion.

Many of the elements described here are present in black church services, if one substitutes for the judgmental word "monotony" the more accurate concept of repetition. The ring-shouts, as we have seen, could continue for up to five hours; the singing in churches today—the congregational singing, not the music of the small, trained gospel groups—swells on and on in great waves whose result, conscious or not, is exactly that of the repetitive drumming of the cults of Africa, Brazil, or Trinidad.

A lesser similarity is the fact that the trances are in some cases controllable. Field says: "Most possessed persons appear to have some control over the duration of their trances and to come out of them conveniently at dinner-time or just before the passenger-lorry departs. This has been wrongly taken as evidence of faked possession, but it merely adds another similarity between trance and sleep." It does not always happen of course, but it is a feature in black U.S. Christian rituals as well as in Africa. A change from song to sermon or sermon to song will often suffice to end a trance. On a recording by Herbert Pepper of services in two Harlem churches, a woman who had been emitting frequent possession cries can be heard to tail off within minutes, at most, after a change of tempo in the service.

A tendency of the postulant on whom the hand of God has descended to go off and roam at night in the bush or the country-side is amply documented in Africa and referred to in a line from a spiritual: "My head was wet with the midnight dew." Whether the tendency of new converts in U.S. rural areas to go off into the woods was an unconscious reflection of the period of seclusion at initiation in African and neo-African cults or the "mourning" period in such sects as Revival Zion in Jamaica and the Spiritual Baptists in Trinidad is, for the present, a matter of conjecture.

The fact that many spirituals were written down early has created the impression that they were a fixed form. Nothing could be farther from the truth. James Weldon Johnson makes the point that the creators of religious songs were rarer than those who could recall and lead them. Ma White, one of the latter, made it her task to "sing down" a long-winded or uninteresting speaker, or even to cut too long a prayer short. "Singing" Johnson, on the other hand, made his own songs, traveling from church to church and teaching new songs to the congregations.

The spirituals were essentially the congregational singing of the churches of the nineteenth century, and in that sense they still exist. Certain spirituals became codified simply because outsiders put them on paper. "Swing Low, Sweet Chariot" was a well-known spiritual in call-and-response form. Everybody knows it today, but only in one version that a collector happened to pin down. Lydia Parrish collected a radically different version:

> Oh swing low, oh swing low,
> Oh swing low sweet chariot, swing low.
> Oh swing low, oh swing low,
> Oh swing low sweet chariot, swing low.
> It must be Jesus passing by;
> Oh swing low sweet chariot, swing low.
> Swing low in the east,
> Swing low.
> Swing low in the east,
> Swing low.
> Swing low in the east,
> Swing low.
> Swing low sweet chariot, swing low.

We have no record of how this was sung, but its call-and-response form and its repetition of exhortatory formulations such as are basic to the success of West African rituals reflect something much nearer to Africa than to Europe or Euro-America.

A form of religious music quite common from at least the 1920's (and presumably in fact much earlier) was that of the wandering street evangelist. Singing solo or in twos or threes, usually accompanied by guitar, their music often had strong connections with the blues, though most would have hotly resented the association with "sinful" music. Many of these singers were recorded, but the records of most are now rare. Blind Willie Johnson was perhaps the greatest of those who have survived on disc. Johnson accompanied himself on guitar singing songs with religious themes in a deep, deliberately gravelly voice that has been said to resemble the possession voices of priests in some African cults. Whether there is a direct link is unsure, but the adoption of strained and "unnatural" voices is known in Africa. An example occurs on a recording of the first Festival of Negro Art in Senegal, in a Serer song by a singer called Sombel.

Other street gospel singers, like the Gospel Keys, used guitar and tambourine and a two-voice style that continued into the 1940's with the excellent gospel singers Sister Rosetta Tharpe and Marie Knight. It is still sometimes heard today: A recent recording of "Sweet Home" features Brother Cleophus Robinson and Sister Josephine James in a magnificent example.

This brings out an important point about black religious music: Its many styles may perhaps be arranged chronologically according to which began first, but all are still sung today and are widely popular. "Gospel music," said to have gotten its name from the former blues singer Georgia Tom Dorsey, who was converted and turned to religious music (he wrote the famous "Precious Lord"), dates from the 1920's. Dorsey's conversion is said to have taken place at the National Baptist Convention of 1921, though he was certainly playing secular music after that. Gospel music has been defined as music "addressed to the people as an expression of personal testimony. Its purpose is to direct the mind inward to one's own experience and needs; to warn each of us of the consequences of sin and give the promise of spiritual release. The gospel song is light in character and expresses a spirit of reverence." Ordinarily, gospel music is presented by a trained group. Some, like the Dixie Hummingbirds and the Original Five Blind Boys, are based on the old barber shop close-harmony technique, but with a soaring, improvised lead vocalist. It is tempting, and I believe valid, to see this style as a logical extension of call-and-response singing. As we have seen, African singing styles often increasingly overlap the lead and the response. Many black religious songs consist essentially of "response" phrases from the group, with the leader improvising above them as if the overlapping had become complete.

Another black religious style that grew up early and is still powerful today is what has been called the "surge" style, in which the slower spirituals were probably sung. This is highly decorated, majestic, of soaring power. Most gospel singers use it from time to time. Perhaps the exponent most famous outside the black community was Mahalia Jackson, whose early records were superb examples. It is typical of the complex story of American music that the surge technique is the one that can be most surely traced back to white origins. It is, in fact, a preservation of the very old British long-meter folk psalmody popular in the seventeenth century, which became equally popular in eighteenth-century America (to the disgust of the "trained" musicians in both lands) and became the patrimony of black and white Christians alike through such joint religious occasions as the camp meetings of the Great Awakening.

White versions of this decorated style can still be heard on recordings of southern white folk singers, but it is rarer in white religious music. The white style is a rustic survival, but black Christians took the old Anglo-American form and really developed it. The white-derived decorations (something almost totally alien to African music, with the exception of strongly Arab-influenced styles) were made richer by the subtle displacement of rhythmic accents and by the addition of a clapped or patted rhythm, which simplified but retained something of the cross-rhythms of African music. To this was added a variation and contrast of vocal tone, which European singers mostly avoided in favor of a high, deadpan delivery. Black singers had made use of the dual heritage to create something essentially new.

Gospel music is varied and constantly changing. Early descriptions of church services make it clear that very rough tone was used in congregational singing in the nineteenth century, usually by the leader, but not always. This rough tone survives, often intensified, employed by Marion Williams with the Clara Ward Singers in "How Many Miles?" and by the Mighty Clouds of Joy in richly rhythmic numbers—their use of electric guitars and bass reflecting rhythm-and-blues—that are descendants of ring-shout singing, a rare example of which is preserved on the Library of Congress recording "Run, Old Jeremiah."

There has always been a close relationship between black U.S. religious and secular music. Even allowing for a proreligious bias in the earliest, usually abolitionist collectors, it does seem that a large proportion of nineteenth-century black song used religious themes. A report on a tobacco factory in Richmond, Virginia, quotes its manager, commenting on the workers' singing: "Their tunes are all psalm tunes, and the words are from hymn books; their taste is exclusively for sacred music; they will sing nothing else." Even songs of protest seem usually to have been adapted spirituals (which may account for the notion that spirituals as a class were disguised songs of protest). An example, which makes a direct reference to Emancipation, is:

> Done with driver's driving [three times],
> Roll, Jordan, roll.

The obvious modern example of the close relationship between sacred and secular music is soul-singing. Not only is it rooted largely in the churches, but most of its best singers began in choirs or gospel groups. But the connection between the two is much older than that, and has always been two-way. Rosetta Tharpe was a former blues singer, and her guitar-playing owes much to secular hoedown styles. Thomas Dorsey's gospel songs, as well as those of Blind Willie Johnson, are "bluesy" in nature. There has never been a clear-cut division between "sacred" and "secular" musical instruments, either. Though the guitar was regarded by W. C. Handy's father as the "devil's box" (a role earlier reserved for the fiddle), it has backed many hundreds of sacred verses. During the period (still continuing, in some measure) when piano and organ were the favorite instruments to support gospel singers, the barrelhouse blues qualities in the piano style were often quite plain. (Trombones were common at one time, and Elder Beck of Buffalo played swinging vibes.) None of this is surprising. Junior Parker once claimed that the blues singers' stories of church background were often exaggerated, but there is no doubt that many blues and jazz musicians ended in the churches as singers, musicians, or preachers.

The stylistic elements of black religious music are, as can be seen, quite mixed. Many, but not by any means all, of the oldest spirituals came from white sources. A recording trip in Alabama, Louisiana, and Mississippi found many older people still singing hymns from "Doctor Watts," which had an American edition in 1820. But just as clearly, the music was much changed. Later songs were composed by blacks in the various Afro-American or "re-Africanized" styles, using handclapping, falsetto singing, and a wide range of vocal tone, call-and-response, rhythmic complexity, and cross-rhythms through vocal syncopation and contrasting hand and feet rhythms, all of African descent, though sometimes considerably transmuted in the New World.

The very importance of song in black worship is an Africanism hard to overestimate. Possession by the Holy Spirit is the outward sign of worship and faith, and in Africa "the spirit will not descend without song." But the ubiquity of song is not the end of it. Religion is bound into everyday life in a way that ought to be true of all Christians but is not. Besides, God, Jesus, and other Biblical figures are extremely close to black Christians, just as African spirits and gods are felt to be very close. I do not believe it is a coincidence that the oldest spirituals did what only intellectual liturgy-experimenters do in the white churches: express Biblical stories and even the words of Jesus in what really was the singers' own languages. Courlander quotes two fine instances:

> Old Job said, good Lord,
> Whilst I'm feeling bad, good Lord,
> I can't sleep at night, good Lord,
> I can't eat a bite, good Lord,
> And the woman I love, good Lord,
> Don't treat me right, good Lord.

The second example comes from an account of Jesus's encounter with the Samaritan woman at the well:

> He said woman, where is your husband?
> She said that I don't have one.
> He said woman you done had five,
> And the one you got now ain't yours.

In *America's Music*, Gilbert Chase analyses the song "Michael Row the Boat Ashore" and brings out a similar point: the bending of religious themes to suit the mundane activities at hand, in this case rowing.

Themes and subjects of religious songs vary immensely, of course. Some seem to belong to certain periods and not others. It has been claimed that the doings of Old Testament prophets, which featured very prominently in slavery spirituals, have not been popular since. But as old songs are still used alongside very new ones, this suggestion should be treated with some caution. Some themes are simply modernized. A Sea Island spiritual used the image of a horse as the way to salvation:

> Loose horse in the valley.
> Aye.
> Who's going to ride him?

More recently, the analogy of the train became very well known, with a great range of versions. One of the most famous is:

> This train is bound for glory,
> If you ride it you got to be holy.

Similarly, in both songs and sermons there are extended metaphors involving the "Christian automobile," which runs on the word of God, and Courlander reports songs that update the theme by using an airplane.

Like the blues, black religious music covers the whole range of human experience, and the whole range of artistic expression, including bathos. And even the bathetic sometimes is expressive. John Work was scornful of the improvised couplet:

> Wait till I get upon the mountain top,
> Goin' make my wings go flippety flop.

But it seems to me fairly expressive of the clumsiness an apprentice Saint might expect to experience.

There is a tendency to say that modern gospel songs are exclusively concerned with personal testimony of salvation and exhortation; but though many are, like Sister Rosetta Tharpe's and Marie Knight's superlative "Up Above my Head, I Hear Music in the Air," others may tell a Biblical story, like the same singers' "Two Little Fishes and Five Loaves of Bread," or may have a strong theological content, like the "salvation through works" theme of the Consolers' "May the Work I've Done Speak for Me."

Gospel singers have lately tended to assume a more consciously social role, as have churches in general. In a concert in June, 1970, Marion Williams sang the song for which she is perhaps best known—"He's Got the Whole World in His Hand"—and improvised verses about peace in Vietnam, Cambodia, and the United States. And Dorothy Love Coates of the Birmingham group the Gospel Harmonettes said in an interview: "I know who I'm singing to. Men who can't get jobs, deserted mothers, boys heading to the army. My people need a message."

The sermon is an important component of black religious services. While of course many black clergymen preach in styles indistinguishable from "mainstream" white sermons, the improvised or part-improvised "spiritual" sermon is regarded by most blacks themselves as a distinctive contribution to the service of the Word. The "spiritual" sermon normally begins in a conversational tone, differentiated from white sermons only by the responses of the congregation, reminiscent of the old African belief that it is discourteous to listen dumbly, without response, or of the interjections made during the *griot*'s telling of traditional tales. Gradually, the preacher's manner becomes more rhythmic. Soon he is chanting. Preacher and congregation begin to build up a complex pattern of call-and-response, not in song but in chant; very often certain preachers will begin to use the "holy laugh," a sharp exhaled "Hah!" between lines, which acts as an extra rhythmic element and is similar in sound (though not in usage) to the hoarse, rasping, rhythmic breathing that is part of Jamaican Revival Zion music. The congregation cries back, in agreement, in sympathy. The piano, organ, or whatever instruments are available may play a part. The tension rises until a point of maximum effect when the preacher, or sometimes the choir, will transform the chant into a song.

The origins of this style are not certain. White preachers in the South use a version of it, but a more hysterical and less integrated form. As Francis Bebey points out in *Musique de L'Afrique*, there are African parallels. I have heard recorded sermons in Yoruba, from the Nigerian Church of the Cherubim and Seraphim, of almost exactly the same character. The emotional sermons of the Great Awakening are patently one point of origin. But, though it can never be proved, the presence in the chanted sermons (black and white) of certain Africanisms and the fact that the white style is vestigial and limited, whereas black chanting preachers may be rural or urban, peasant or middle-class (added to the presence of similar techniques in Africa itself), suggest that the transference was from black to white.

The mode in Africa is not confined to indigenous Christian denominations. Recordings of non-Christian rites sometimes give examples of something similar, and I myself attended a healing dance on the East African coast that involved an element of sermon-like exhortation. There, too, the officiant (in this case an *mganga*) built up to a strained-voice, rhythmic style culminating in full-scale music. The chanted sermons are not simply a Southern rural or impoverished urban proletarian phenomenon in the United States. Nor do all sermons present the same sort of free-association evocation of Biblical and salvation motifs. Many show profound theological insight, the relation of topical subjects to religious interpretations of universal currents, and moral teaching of considerable sophistication. The notion of the "hellfire" preacher, as applied to these pastors, is a grossly false stereotype. Their sermons are a major aesthetic experience. They are certainly, taking their range as a whole, quite as pastorally and theologically excellent as the written and read homilies of the "mainstream."

How much of African belief, as opposed to practice, was carried over into black religion in the United States has been the subject of argument. First, it is obvious that, just as blacks come of all sorts of American backgrounds, so they hold to all sorts of styles of churchmanship and belief. But apart from old beliefs near enough to the new to be rationalized easily, certain elements of African religions have been preserved. One, missed by most early commentators but discussed fully by Melville Herskovits, was the attitude to Satan revealed in many black Christian songs, whereby he resembles the trickster god of the Yoruba more closely than the mighty potentate of Christian belief. One should not go as far as Janheinz Jahn in *Neo-African Literature*, who at times makes it seem as if black Christianity were the thinnest veneer for the old African faiths. However, Jahn's observations that African religion is not contemplative but evocative, and that in Africa, as well as in the Negro spiritual, faith is expressed through invocation, whereas in white Christianity it is expressed by adoration, contain some truth (though again he somewhat over-sharply divides what is in reality not easily separable).

Jahn also points out that the role of the spirituals as invocation is closer to African practice than to the European, where hymns almost always state theological truths (in fact serving as a major school of theology for the ordinary man). On the other hand, many gospel songs are declarations of faith, not invocations. If they have an African content, it is in the use of specific social comment:

> I got a home where the gambler can't go,
> I got a home where the gambler can't go.
> Oh, Jesus lord have mercy.
> I got a home where the gambler can't go.

To take "Jesus lord have mercy" as an African invocation, because it is sung, would entail the Africanization of the *kyrie eleison*, which is pushing matters altogether too far.

An especially interesting kind of survival—though one that does not receive much attention—is the continuation of belief in evil spirits, which exist in the Bible but seem to be insisted on by black members of some sects to a degree that suggests a link with West African belief. This insistence is not confined to obscure parts of the countryside. On Radio WADO in New York on February 21, 1971, I heard a preacher remark: "Yes, these evil spirits must go!"

Gospel music's variety, I think, indicates one reason for its popularity. Along with its relevance to a living and widespread faith, it provides a complete religious substitute for sinful secular music—fast, dance-like tunes, ballads, blues, barrelhouse piano, guitar, rhythm-and-blues, and even FM rock. In black gospel music, of all religious music, the Devil does not have all the best tunes.

But if the Devil does not have all the best black tunes, by the reckoning of the more devout he has most of the best-known ones. The blues was—and to many people still is—"sinful" music. Yet, as much as the spirituals or gospel music, it sprang from deep within a people's experiences to become one of the world's great musics.

Nobody knows when the blues began, partly because few people can agree exactly where other forms—the holler, in particular—end, and the blues begins. When a worker on the levee sang,

> O-o-o-o-ah,
> Going down the river before long,

he was hollering. But when he developed the musical line a little and sang,

> Going down the river before long,
> Going down the river before long,
> Going down the river before long,

was this a complex holler or the birth of the blues? Does it matter? The man who sang those verses was singing in a tradition still full of African elements—allusive lyrics, presumably (given the lack of development of the words) interest in the music, and repetition as both a musical and a poetic form.

He didn't call it the blues. The word, applied to music, began creeping into use around the first decade of the twentieth century. It seems to have been about that time that the music began to be codified into a number of forms, of which the most common was the twelve-bar blues, its verse consisting of a couplet with the first line repeated. But this form seems to have developed when blues began to be played by more than one man. A musician singing to the accompaniment of his own guitar or without any instrument at all can please himself whether he allows a verse twelve bars, eight, or eleven and a half, and many early blues songs were in fact that flexible. A good example on record is "Poor Boy Blues" by an obscure Texas singer called Rambling Thomas. His verses are irregular, and the whole piece is plainly close to the field holler, extended and with guitar accompaniment.

Of course, blues singers did not sit down at a table and form a Committee on the Standardization of the Blues. Most blues numbers, once the style was developed, were twelve-bar. But the great woman blues singer Bessie Smith probably sang more songs that were not twelve-bar than ones that were. What is true is that the blues *tends* toward a twelve-bar or an eight-bar form (a couplet without repetition of the first line).

The blues has a very complex history spanning seventy or eighty years, and our concern here is not to try to condense it, but to learn what we can about where the blues came from. At first blush, there does not seem to be the same African quality in blues forms as there clearly is in much Caribbean music. The blues is sung in English, accompanied usually by guitar (with or without rhythm section) or, at various times, by small jazz groups. It has, in its mature twentieth-century form, a harmonic structure apparently based on European theory. It also follows a rhyming verse structure.

One misleading factor is that the extensive recording of the blues began in the 1920's, by which time the form (as it was played in and around towns, at any rate) had become fairly structured. People are apt to base their impression of blues on the commercial records, and most of the earliest blues records were made by women singers in Chicago, accompanied by piano and sometimes small jazz groups. These women—of whom Bessie Smith was undoubtedly the greatest, along with Ida Cox and the slightly older Ma Rainey—were professional entertainers. They had roots deep in the country, some of them, but nevertheless were affected by the conditions of both the city and their own sector of show business. A great many of their songs were not blues but vaudeville songs, though by sheer artistry they made blues of them.

Still, the basic structure of the blues sung by the "classic" singers was rooted in the folk blues, and for good reason. Blues was an improvised music in which singers created either their own songs or new versions of old songs by impromptu imagination, free association, and the use of what the folklorists call "floating" verses (lines that crop up time and again in a wide variety of songs), for example: "I'm a poor boy, long ways from home," "Laughing just to keep from crying," and "I got a woman, she's six foot tall / Sleeps in the kitchen with her head in the hall." Other verses or phrases are borrowed because they are so expressive. In the 1940's, Hot Lips Page, in "Uncle Sam's Blues," sang:

Uncle Sam ain't no woman, but he sure can get your man.

The same line turns up in Snooks Eaglin's "I Got My Questionnaire" in the 1950's. But it may well have originated long before Page put it on record.

Borrowings may be direct quotes or more allusive, as when B. B. King picks up from "Make Me a Pallet on the Floor" in his own "Country Girl," with a reference to a "pallet laying on the floor."

Improvisation is a complex creative procedure, and an improvising musician—or poet—is greatly helped if he can use a framework that is both simple and flexible. The blues, whether of eight or twelve bars, supplies just that. Besides, the blues is not as neat as descriptions of the twelve-bar pattern might suggest, and many of the apparent raggednesses turn out on inspection to be not incompetence within a European frame but Africanisms. In folk blues, for example, the last syllable of a line often coincides with the first beat of what is thought of as a separate section, the four-bar instrumental "answer." Significantly, call-and-response in earlier black American forms tends toward overlapping, and this is also a frequent trait in African choral singing. Even more relevant to the source of certain relationships between voice and instrument in the blues, in voice-and-percussion music the last beat of the vocal rhythmic pattern may often fall on the first beat of a drum pattern—exactly what happens in the blues, as well as in quite a lot of non-U.S. black music too. The principle was clearly important enough in African and African-derived music to be preserved in U.S. vocal forms and then reapplied to the relationship between voice and instrument when the opportunity arose.

The question of call-and-response in the blues raises a basic problem of interpretation. Just as there have been scholars who have violated all sense in an attempt to prove the essential whiteness of black music, so there have been others who have too hastily ascribed an African origin to virtually all its features. One dictum is that the twelve-bar pattern—two-bar vocal, two-bar instrumental, two-bar vocal (first line repeated), two-bar instrumental, third line of vocal, two-bar instrumental—is a call-and-response pattern and thus a major Africanism. Now there are good reasons for accepting this in principle, but not without recognizing the considerable differences between classic African vocal call-and-response and this blues pattern. The first difference is that the response in Africa is indeed vocal, not instrumental. The second is that, on the whole, African tunes are defined by the *response*. I think it would take a fanatic to claim that "Saint Louis Blues" was defined by Armstrong's obligatos, not Bessie Smith's singing of the vocal! The third difference is that, while the solo lead, or call, in much West African singing is improvised, the response tends to be fixed; if it is not fixed, it reproduces the call line.

The mere device of filling in gaps in a vocal form is obviously not African in itself, of course. European and Anglo-American folk music sometimes has instrumental bridges between the verses. It must be said that this is rare, however, and most Anglo-

American singing was unaccompanied until so late that a black influence could be postulated. Church and conservatory music, of course, has always used instruments to bridge gaps between vocal passages.

This said, I believe that the case for the blues as a development of a call-and-response form—or at least as profoundly influenced by it—is overwhelming, provided one accepts that cultural survival is not the antonym of change but depends on it, and provided one does not assume all blues accompaniments take the call-and-response form. Many blues singers, especially country blues singer-guitarists from certain parts of the South, made little use of the call-and-response pattern. But for most, the two-bar instrumental sections were *clearly* used not as a bridge to lead to the next vocal line, as a European musician might use them, but as an answer to the previous one. The examples are endless. Some keep the form of solo/chorus, as when Ma Rainey in her magnificent "Stormy Sea Blues" is answered by Kid Henderson on cornet and Lucien Brown on alto. Others are duetlike, but still with an instrumental answer to a vocal statement, as in Armstrong's replies to Bessie Smith in "Reckless Blues," which bring the instrumental role onto an equal footing with the vocal so that it is part of a discussion rather than a chorus of assent. The call-and-response pattern has become as varied as the blues itself, but the twelve-bar blues structure is as if designed for it, with its equal segments allotted for the instrumental replies, so that in formal terms the instrument has as great a role as the voice.

What else is African in the blues? In much country blues, the guitar is used in ways reminiscent of the music of the West African savanna belt. A notable feature of West African stringed-instrument technique is its relationship with singing. Francis Bebey remarks: "The single-string bow-harp is often magnificently used not only for accompaniment . . . but at the same time as a percussion instrument, the musician plucking the string and knocking alternately on the resonator." This particular technique is not common in the blues, but the joint "accompanying" and percussive function of the guitar in much country blues is so powerful that the concepts "rhythm" and "melody" can hardly be disentangled (as they never can in African music, in quite the same sense as in European). Another vocal-instrumental relationship common in African accompanying techniques is the repetition of a short phrase by the instrument or instruments (usually varied, though not greatly) while the singer uses a longer melody, also repeated with improvised variations. This is also a frequent means for accompanying fairly fast blues on the guitar, as witness Robert Johnson in "Dust my Broom" or Elmore James's version of the same bass in tracks like "Held My Baby." In fact, it is the foundation of most blues piano of the style that became known as barrelhouse, especially in the specialized form called boogie-woogie. A third accompanying style for guitar does not exactly *answer* the vocal line but performs the function given to stringed instruments in Ghana, which "*fill in the breaks* with accompanying figures."

The parallels between African musical custom and blues techniques, many still used by modern blues singers like B. B. King and by the joint blues-and-gospel-formed soul singers, are considerable. So endless, in fact, that one has to be careful not to fall into the trap of forgetting that the blues has strong European strands also, and calling it an "African music," as one or two people have done recently. LeRoi Jones, in *Black Music*, brought out a fundamental Africanism almost in passing, when he remarked: "Even beautiful R & B blues, or the uses made of these forms by our contemporary mainstream, are repetitious, though not necessarily boringly so—this music accepts repetition as an already accepted fact of life." In fact, African and Afro-American dance music do not merely *accept* repetition. Repetition is a major functional element—in ritual as an aid to possession, in social situations as an aid to dancing without fatigue. And we must not forget, as people too often do, that the blues, like most black music, is closely linked to the dance. Mack McCormick, describing first-generation blues singers like Mance Lipscomb, made this point:

> These men did not think of themselves as blues singers. They were singers whose employment was often to provide music for dancers and thus they thought of its rhythms, not its poetic structure. Thus, to Mance, the ballad "Ella Speed" is a breakdown; the work song

"Alabama Bound" is a cakewalk; the bawdy "Bout a Spoonful" is a slow drag. For the most part he thinks of "blues" as a particular slow-tempoed dance that became fashionable around World War I.

A most interesting subdivision of country blues is the music of the country blues bands, which tends to shade into the instrumental dance music we shall be discussing in the next chapter. The typical lineup of many Caribbean and South American dance groups, with their iron gongs, scrapers, drums, and voices, corresponds to the West African rain forest's characteristic ensemble. The early blues bands, by contrast, consisted very often of fiddle, guitars, and sometimes homemade percussion, which would easily accommodate techniques learned in the savanna groups with their bowed *goge,* lutes, and rattles. Paul Oliver draws attention to parallels with African savanna music: "To the ear attuned to the blues it is the manner of playing that impresses, with the moaned and wailing notes of the bowed instruments, the rapid fingering of the lutes and harps, and the combined interweaving of the melodic-rhythmic lines when two or more musicians play together."

The analogy is especially striking when one listens to records with a strong Muslim element, such as the Ocora disc *Niger: La Musique des Griots,* in which, according to Alan Merriam, "the vocal line tends to be more straightforward than that of the bowed lute, which elaborates and ornaments the melody fairly extensively, though the two are obviously the same basic line. . . . Other outstanding items include the long, cascading, downward-moving, ornamented, arhythmic Arabic melodic lines."

Oliver points out that "the blues uses stringed instruments in a melodic-rhythmic manner with a fairly complex finger-picking" and associates this with earlier black instrumental techniques: "The sliding notes and glissandi of the fiddle were matched upon the guitar strings. . . . The percussive 'thrump and strum' of the banjo was carried on the bass strings."

The parallels between African savanna-belt string-playing and the techniques of many blues guitarists are remarkable. The big *kora* of Senegal and Guinea are played in a rhythmic-melodic style that uses constantly changing rhythms, often providing a ground bass overlaid with complex treble patterns, while the vocal supplies a third rhythmic layer. Similar techniques can be found in hundreds of blues records. In parts of "Let's Go To Town," Memphis Minnie McCoy sets up a complex pattern with the use of arpeggios whose rhythms cross with those of a fast dance beat. Fred McDowell's version of the Sleepy John Estes song "Drop Down Mama" uses very complex strummed guitar rhythms, far advanced from the basic "common time" four-to-the-bar stereotype of the blues. In a different vein, Robert Johnson's "Come On in My Kitchen" uses guitar in unison with his voice, a technique not unknown in European folk music but common also in West Africa, a case, perhaps, of twin-culture reinforcement. Rambling Thomas's "Poor Boy" is another instance of the same technique.

The rhythmic sources of the blues, as of black U.S. music in general, present more problems than the rhythmic elements of other parts of the black world. Certain specific ingredients can be isolated. One is "playing around the beat" or "singing around the beat," the displacement of accents so as to set up cross-rhythms—not between drums and various forms of percussion, as in Africa, but between voice and instrument in the guitar blues. Another fundamental feature of West African music-making, also widespread in Afro-America, is again present in the blues and in jazz. This is the tendency to use triple and duple rhythms at the same time, which is arguably the reason for the extensive use of triplets in both blues and jazz. Blues are usually said to be in duple time, but the young rock-blues musician Al Wilson, of Canned Heat, expressed the reality of blues rhythms far more accurately in an interview with Pete Welding in *Rolling Stone:* "There's really not a rhythmic definition because nothing in blues rhythm is anywhere near ubiquitous. Really, totally modally organized blues conforming to the basic model appears in even duple meter, in more or less metronomic triple patterns . . . and in loosened-up, jazz-influenced triplet patterns." The use of triplets against a basically 4/4 beat to create the duple-triple tension so fundamental to wide areas of African music, though perhaps more common in jazz, is frequent in music stretching from the Blind Lemon Jefferson recordings of the 1920's through the up-tempo "New Orleans" rhythm-and-blues style of people like Fats

Domino, right up to the generation of Bobby Bland and beyond. (It is also a major feature of the piano accompaniment to much gospel music.) A good blues example is the opening to Howling Wolf's "How Many More Years."

Satisfaction with rhythmic interest and subtlety as sufficient in themselves, which has been emphasized as an aspect of African attitudes to music by Dr. Kwabena Nketia and others, is less obvious and more intermittent in the United States, but it is a recurring phenomenon in the blues and similar musics. Perhaps the clearest example among recent styles is James Brown's progressive moves toward a music of "pure rhythm." Besides stressing the interplay of bass and drums, Brown's cries and the jabbing sax interpolations build up a polyrhythmic structure that, however modified by contact with European measured time and the use of European instruments, owes its existence principally to Africa.

The rhythm of blues verses themselves—though they have tended to become more regular as time went on—operates according to a metric system different from the European. In essence it is like, though less extreme than, the calypso verses, which allow for great rhythmic subtlety by using irregular numbers of syllables in between the main verbal or poetic stresses; the result is often a series of cross-rhythms over the (normally) more steady beat of the accompanying instrument. The importance of this factor is obscured somewhat by the overpowering early position of the "classic" women blues singers who dominated the first year or two of the blues recording industry. A large number of the songs these women sang were not blues in form, though they used blues vocal techniques in singing them. In fact, some of the classic blues singers constituted a separate subform with sometimes tenuous relationships with country blues on one side and jazz on the other, especially in the matter of rhythm. Sippie Wallace's "Jack o' Diamonds," Chippie Hill's "Pratt City Blues," and even Bessie Smith's "Reckless Blues" simply do not swing in the jazz sense. Nor do they have what Oliver calls the "'slow and easy' slow drag of the country blues band." But if some examples do plod, hampered by leaden tubas, others have a "sway," a reminder of Weldon Johnson's remark quoted earlier about the swaying and the patting rhythm. The classic blues often ceased to be dance music. When country techniques came to town, introducing various complex guitar- and piano-based rhythms, they revolutionized city blues in more ways than are always recognized. Incidentally, the use of a wide range of different *types* of beat-complex (not simply of time-signatures) is typical of African but not (except in Spain) of European music.

This range of rhythmic complexity can be traced right through the blues and allied forms, through rhythm-and-blues, and into soul, where the "Big Beat" concept still exists and yet singers like Martha and the Vandellas, in "Dancing in the Street," employ as rhythmically sophisticated a complex of displaced beats as do any of their more solemnly studied elders.

The African-derived approach to rhythm, of course, has long since been built into black music, and any change in it is as likely to involve an increase as a decrease. The search for new sounds in recent black music does not necessarily mean an adoption of Euro-American Tin Pan Alley methods. When the unfortunate but at times interesting group Sly and the Family Stone began to work away from the gospel call-and-response techniques, they in fact developed a greater rhythmic subtlety with complicated scat and sung dialogues and a general breaking up of what was left of the European-style formal structure of their choruses.

One of the oldest battlegrounds for the wars between jazzologists and bluesologists is the existence or nonexistence of a blues scale. Those who do not deny its existence say it consists basically of a diatonic scale but with certain "blue notes," that is, with the third note flatted irregularly (in the key of C a blues pianist may use an E natural, an E flat, or, indeed, both together, and a singer or player of an instrument capable of it may render something between the two), and a flatted seventh note. It has been claimed that, since the development of bop in the 1940's, the flatted fifth has also become a blue note, but Gunther Schuller asserts that flatted fifths have been used since the 1920's.

The question of scale is more complex than the existence (or not) of a "blues scale." Courlander was once told by an Alabama blues singer that he "played with the notes" just as he "played with the beats," which suggests not vagueness about pitch, which some authors have attributed to black singers, but a high degree of tonal sophistication. An extremely interesting contribution to the argument about tone and scale was made by Al Wilson. Of the relation between speech and song in the blues, which is so much nearer to African than European usage, Wilson said: "This is the thing about words, why they are important in singing the blues melodies using those four or five notes in the standard blues mode. . . . You pattern the words to rise and fall in a way similar to the way that you would speak them, and construct the words not just any way but so they flow naturally with the flow of the melody."

We have seen the intimate connection between speech and melody in African music, which arises partly from the fact that so many African languages are tonal. The existence of a similar rapport in the blues is not coincidental. (Much work needs to be done on the tonal values of black U.S. speech, incidentally. Does it actually preserve West African intonations, as does, for instance, the Haitian French *patois?*) The possibility of a connection between speech tone and blues scales has not yet received enough attention.

Much of the dispute about the so-called blues scale seems to be a matter of definition. The basic question has not been whether "blue notes" exist (which is obvious), nor whether all or most of the blues use pentatonic scales consisting of either the top or the bottom half of the diatonic blues scale. The point of the bickering has been whether, if these things exist, they indicate an African ancestry for the blues. Alas, the blues scale is perhaps the least satisfactory of all areas for disputes about Africanisms. It is true that a certain vagueness around the third and seventh exists in some West African music. However, the English musicologist A. L. Lloyd points out in his book *Folk Song in England* that the vagueness about thirds is a prominent feature of English folk songs and, indeed, seems to be a major feature of the music of wide areas of the world. Moreover, pentatonic scales and some form of diatonic scale are now generally accepted as characteristics that African and European music have in common. The provenance of the blues scale seems likely to remain a topic for late-night argument, but little more.

It is fair to say that, while an ambiguous third is common to the music of all three continents, the flatted seventh seems more common in Africa, including at least one region that supplied cultural traits to the United States. Kwabena Nketia, in *African Music in Ghana*, says, "The flatted seventh is frequent and well-established in Akan vocal music."

Al Wilson suggests that both the blues and soul music use basically five-note scales, but different ones. He allots the scale C, D, E, G, A, C to gospel music and soul, and C, E-flat, F, G, B-flat, C to the blues. If Wilson were right, it would certainly help to explain why the blues element in much soul music, though there, is far less obvious than the gospel.

A large number of vocal and instrumental techniques are found both in some parts of Africa and in some blues. An example is the frequent tendency of a singer to drop the last word or two of a line and leave the guitar playing solo. Harold Courlander once asked a singer who had just done this whether he was tired or had forgotten the lyrics. The singer replied: "No, I just step aside and let the guitar say it." One instance occurs in the lyric "Two White Horses," quoted earlier in this chapter. Fred Mc-Dowell's "Baby, Please Don't Go" on his Capitol album and Lightning Hopkins's "Black Cat" on Kent are other examples. Big Bill Broonzy does the same thing to great effect in a version of "John Henry":

> Well, he died with his hammer in his—
> Yes, he died with his hammer in his hand.

Behind this musical technique lie vestiges of two widespread aspects of musical instruments in Africa: (1) a "talking" function that goes far beyond the well-known use of talking drums, or even talking flutes, xylophones, and so forth, and (2) the semi-personification of instruments, which are considered to have some form of soul. Musical instruments figure prominently in many African creation myths, of course, and certain drums used in worship are treated as sacred, but personification goes far deeper than that. Francis Bebey tells of offering to buy a drum from a man, who coldly remarked that he came to market to play music, not to sell slaves.

A somewhat similar technique among country blues singers, incidentally, is to sing only a few words at the beginning of a line and then to hum, or even fall silent, so that the guitar carries not just the end of the line but the main burden. Many singers have used this style, from the gospel blues singer Blind Gary Davis and the urban blues singer and pianist of the 1930's Leroy Carr to John Lee Hooker and Howling Wolf. It is also common in some forms of African vocal-and-string music, and in both cases it indicates an attitude to the relationship between instrument and voice that is common to Africa and black America but alien to Europe.

In general, the great range of vocal tone used by blues singers —not just the differences between singers, but the contrasts of tone used by the same individual—appears to be part of the African legacy of the blues. The President of Senegal, Léopold Senghor, a noted poet, once wrote of African singers: "Negro voices, because they have not been domesticated by training, follow every shade of feeling or imagination; drawing freely from the infinite dictionary of nature, they borrow its tonal expressions, from the light songs of the birds to the solemn roll of the thunder." A striking example of vocal intensity, harshness, and rough tone is to be found on an Ocora record of music from Upper Volta, in a track recorded by three Bousance praise-singers. Though the rough tone in African music is mostly associated with a fairly high-pitched voice, rather than the deeper tone of blues singers like Bukka White, deeper voices are not unknown in Africa either, as a track on the Folkways album *Africa South of the Sahara* shows. This presents a Bakwiri singer with a deep voice, a fast vibrato, and a thick tone. Blues voices range from the highest of near-falsetto to the deep, gravelly quality of Blind Willie Johnson or Bukka White. The use of falsetto and the use of a passing yodel in the middle of a sentence seem to some extent to fluctuate according to fashion. The yodel in midline was popular in the urban blues of musicians like Scrapper Blackwell in the mid-1930's. A memorable instance was Casey Bill Weldon's

"WPA Blues," though Robert Johnson also used it in "Walking Blues." It also occurs in a more rural setting, most strikingly in John Dudley's "Cool Water Blues," recorded by Alan Lomax on a field trip in 1959, and in "Lonesome Katy Blues" on the Arhoolie album *Mississippi Blues*.

The falsetto is an extremely common technique in African and Afro-American music. We have met it in more folkloric settings in the Caribbean and South America. As individual notes (but not quite a yodel), it is an effective part of Red Nelson's "Sweetest Thing Ever Born"; Robert Johnson uses it in "Kindhearted Woman Blues"; so does Aretha Franklin in "The Thrill is Gone." In fact, if anything it has come back with renewed force in the soul styles, which draw part of their inspiration from the falsetto lead singers, as well as the tearing, growling tones, that are an essential part of the style in the churches. Examples of falsetto singing from Africa are to be found on the Folkways *Music of the Cameroons* in a song about a sanitary inspector and a funeral song, among others.

Blues vocal styles did not all stem from African models, of course. The shouting Kansas City style, of which Joe Turner and Jimmy Rushing were perhaps the most famous early exponents, was born, in part at least, of the need to dominate noisy bars and large bands. But the intensity and the tearing quality in many blues singers' voices have many counterparts in Africa and none either in Europe or in white American styles, and the same holds for the great variety of tone heard within one blues song. Euro-American folk music tends strongly toward a high, harsh, deadpan tone.

Charles Keil sets forth in *Urban Blues* a certain formula that he feels is at the heart of modern black music; he says it can be described in several different ways:

"Constant repetition coupled with small but striking deviations"; "similar wails and cries linked to various tumbling strains and descending figures"; or simply "statements and counterstatements"— all of which equal "soul." It is a pattern that a Negro child in the rural South or the urban ghetto learns by heart, normally in a church context, and it is as old as the oral traditions and call-response patterns of West African poetry and music.

In strictly musical terms, this supplies quite a good definition of some of the major factors—generalized from a number of varying but in some respects interrelated African patterns—that go into Afro-American music, including blues of all sorts and church music, as well as the music that derives much of its manner from both sources—soul.

With soul music, the infusion of gospel elements into a popular music that until then had been developing from the blues on one side and white pop ballad styles on the other became so strong that most of the best soul and other gospel-tinged singers came from the churches—Aretha Franklin, Ray Charles, Wilson Pickett, Nina Simone, O. V. Wright, and many others—like the many before them who went into the fields of jazz, the blues, and popular music. Of course, all the black styles, whether blues, country music, gospel, jazz, soul, or rhythm-and-blues, have drawn from each other continuously—though more at some times than others. Like any popular music, the blues has been subject to rapid change, and the Africanisms favored have changed along with everything else. "Dirty" tone, which was strong in the Chicago Blues of John Lee Hooker and Muddy Waters, has been rejected by some blues fans in favor of the lighter style of B. B. King. One interviewee told Charles Keil, "B. B.'s cleaned up the blues; they've refined it, so it's smooth and easy—no harps, moaning, or shit like that. Those guys have brought the blues up to date." This is a reaction less against Africanisms in the blues than against the emphasis of some of them to the point almost of self-parody. African music itself is, however complex, "smooth and easy."

We have seen that many Afro-American songs continue the African use of song as a vehicle of social comment of all sorts, including praise songs and songs of derision. The blues maintains this tradition strongly, though with less emphasis on current affairs than, say, calypso. Only recently have socially conscious musicians like Leon Thomas used the blues to express sentiments like this:

New York City without rent control would be like a thief
stealing from the blind.

> These leases and those rent increases would drive a *poor*
>   man out of his mind.
> So welcome to New York, brother, it's a city full of fun,
> They got plenty of rats and roaches, welfare for everyone.

Juke Boy Bonner's "I'm going back to the country where they don't burn the buildings down" is in the same spirit.

A feature of blues themes that is most un-African is the large number of songs concerned with love. But even here, non-European attitudes to the use of song creep in. Some, but very few, blues songs express love for somebody and are addressed to that somebody. Most are in other categories, such as the boasting songs (an important African category with overtones of sympathetic magic):

> If your man ain't treating you right,
> Come up and see your Dan.
> I rock 'em, roll 'em, all night long,
> I'm a sixty minute man.

The blues appears to lack any counterpart to the African praise song. As we have seen, of course, in a hostile or indifferent society the hero and the bad man change places. The opposite of the praise song, the putdown, or song of derision, is certainly present in the blues, especially in the form of the "The Dozens." And a kind of sexual praise song, at least, does occur—for what else is that old favorite, "My Daddy Rocks Me with One Steady Roll"?

7 JAZZ: "PEOPLE" MUSIC BECOMES "CLASSICAL"

Jazz is the best-known U.S. black instrumental music (and perhaps the most important music of the twentieth century). But before jazz came many other Afro-American styles born of the African encounter with the music of white America. Early reports make it clear that black Americans were using European instruments, as well as European tunes, early in the nineteenth century. The most common black instruments of that century were fiddle and banjo, together with percussion of various sorts. Henry Kmen's book *Music in New Orleans: The Formative Years* quotes various pieces of evidence as to what black musicians were playing in that city, mostly culled from court reports and newspaper accounts of police action. In one raid, three slaves were arrested and charged with playing the violin and dancing with white persons; banjos are mentioned in a report of another raid. A reporter gave details of a somewhat grander affair, which was broken up at 2:30 A.M. one Sunday:

In one part of the room a cotillion was going on, and in a corner a fellow was giving a regular old Virginia "breakdown." . . . The music consisted of a clarionet, three fiddles, two tambourines, and a bass drum. The dances played were galopades, cotillions, and others heard also at white balls. In the refreshment room an old man was playing "Jim Along Josey" on a banjo.

A later description, quoted by Gilbert Chase from Lafcadio Hearn's "Levee Life," gives a vivid account of a working-class dance of the late nineteenth century, which seems to have been in itself a short lesson on the re-Africanization of part-European music and dance:

A well-dressed, neatly-built mulatto picked the banjo, and a somewhat lighter colored musician led the music with a fiddle, which he played remarkably well and with great spirit. A short, stout negress, illy dressed . . . played the bass viol, and that with no inexperienced hand. . . .

Then the music changed to an old Virginia reel, and the dancing changing likewise, presented the most grotesque spectacle imaginable. The dancing became wild; men patted juba and shouted, the negro women danced with the most fantastic grace, their bodies describing almost incredible curves forward and backward; limbs intertwined rapidly in a wrestle with each other and with the music; the room presented a tide of swaying bodies and tossing arms, and flying hair. The white female dancers seemed heavy, cumbersome, ungainly by contrast with their dark companions; the spirit of the music was not upon them; they were abnormal to the life about them.

Once more the music changed—to some popular Negro air, with the chorus—

> Don't get weary,
> I'm going home.

The musicians began to sing; the dancers joined in; and the dance terminated with a roar of song, stamping of foot, "patting juba," shouting, laughing, reeling. Even the curious spectators involuntarily kept time with their feet; it was the very drunkenness of music, the intoxication of the dance.

This happened to be an urban dance, but it could have been a country dance up to at least the 1930's, and—with a change in instrumentation—it could have taken place last week. Well into the twentieth century, and to some extent until today, fiddles were used with guitar, which took over from the banjo; mouth-harp or harmonica, and various forms of home-made instrument such as kazoo (a version of an instrument widely found in Africa), washboard, washtub bass, and whatever else was available to play for country dances in the "jook" and "skiffle" bands. The origins of this music lay partly in the cotillions. In the country, much of it was probably picked up from Scots and other white neighbors (though instrumentally most of the influence was the other way). But it soon moved away from its origins in ways that have to do with the African sources of black musical concepts. The relationship between blues practices and practices common in such savanna areas of Africa as northern Nigeria, where fiddle-type instruments are used with plucked strings and percussion, holds equally true for black American country breakdown dance music, with its "alley" fiddle style, as much rhythmic as melodic, its loose and constantly changing rhythms, and its persistent repetition. An Arhoolie record of music by Blind James Campbell's Nashville Street Band contains very good examples of this feature in the fiddle playing by Beauford Clay. Clay's breakdown is particularly fine.

Specific Africanisms in this music are similar to those found in the blues: variation of tone on fiddle or mouth-harp and long, blending and swooping notes similar to the Islam-influenced styles of much of West Africa. In early forms, an absence of harmony in the European sense is also common. In black country dance music, as in the blues, a more African technique was employed. It still can be heard in the way in which Alec Stewart on guitar backs up Sonny Terry's harmonica in a number of his Washboard Band recordings, for example. Rather than going through a harmonically conceived structural pattern of chords, Stewart will shift his chord at the end of a verse, thus using chord change without harmonic intention, but as a lute pattern will change under an African vocal to produce the effect of slight change in an apparently repetitive over-all form. The result is not as formally integrated as much African music but creates a progression based on similar musical concepts. Of course, this is not the only formal structure used in country breakdown and rags, and in fact European-based three-chord progressions are more common. But one-chord accompaniment and chord changes that do not correspond to melodic changes but supply a second layer of musical interest under them are characteristic of the style.

The rhythmic complexity of West African music is also present in music of the jook and jug bands, in the especially African form of an interplay of rhythms from different instruments, no one of which is necessarily complex in itself. A role rather similar to that of the lead drum in rain-forest music is sometimes taken by the guitar or, especially, the banjo, whose melodic function is often little more than that of an African tension drum. The basic musical procedure is the use of short, rhythmo-melodic phrases to provide a pattern or series of patterns. Sometimes the American banjoist will stick to an ostinato role, like many African xylophone or lute parts; sometimes he will improvise more freely, like a lead drummer. Sometimes, of course, he will carry a melody in a fairly European style, but even then the melody is almost always bent in the direction of African-derived techniques and is usually selected in the first place for its amenability to such techniques (like the European hymns used as a basis for spirituals). Examples of most of these elements can be heard on tracks from the Blues Classic album *The Jug, Jook and Washboard Bands*. The jug bands, especially, often used the kazoo as a melodic-rhythmic instrument, repeating rhythmic patterns whose over-all contribution was quite African and akin to the riff technique of the later jazz bands.

Like their descendants, black country dance modes were informal, largely improvised, and "people's" rather than "specialist's" music. But at the end of the nineteenth century a style of black music that was quite the opposite developed: ragtime. Ragtime in its "classic" form was a composed piano music, written down and intended (as one of the great ragtime composers, Scott Joplin, writer of "Maple Leaf Rag" and of many other famous tunes, insisted) to be played as written.

Some authors have described piano ragtime as the music in which African components were weakest and most etiolated, and others have treated it as a straight transfer of "African" plantation banjo patterns to the piano. Neither characterization is correct. Ragtime in its original form was the work of musicians who were well aware of "European" musical features and used them, just as early black dancers danced, among other things, the cotillion. Most true rags have a form comprising several contrasting strains based on the march form (which, as we have seen, has been an influence in both Brazilian and Cuban music, and which was an important ingredient in jazz). In fact, many early rags were called marches, like Scott Joplin's "Combination March." It is no coincidence that ragtime developed in the Midwest, where, as Gunther Schuller points out in *Early Jazz*, march bands have always been popular. The formal structure of piano rags, therefore, was extremely European and quite un-African, which allied them indirectly with such nineteenth-century Caribbean manifestations as the danzas and other dances taken over from European models and "Africanized," first rhythmically and then by gradually dropping the formal divisions into different strains. Indeed, the same thing happened to ragtime as time went on.

But ragtime also had strong connections with other black music. In particular, the dance called the cakewalk, which began as a slaves' parody of white "society" ways, became an important part of minstrel music and was popular during the growth of ragtime (which, remember, was a product of parts of the United States where blacks and whites mingled, if not on equal terms, at least a great deal). Many minstrel tunes, including "Old Zip Coon" and "Old Dan Tucker," use a syncopated figure that became a standard cakewalk figure; it is the first part of a pattern we have met before: ♪♪ ♩ . The novelist Rupert Hughes, in 1899, made a connection between more popular dance styles and formal ragtime when he wrote in the Boston *Musical Record:* "Negroes call their clog dancing 'ragging' and the dance a 'rag,' a dance largely shuffling. . . . Banjo figuration is very noticeable in ragtime music and division of one of the beats into two short notes is traceable to the hand clapping."

One of the most common types of right-hand pattern in piano ragtime was the same one we have met from Brazil, right through the Caribbean, and into the blues. Scott Joplin wrote a series of ragtime exercises that presented basics of the true style, of which he was a pioneer. The first two bars of one of these exercises look like this, rhythmically: ♩ 𝅘𝅥 𝅘𝅥𝅘𝅥 𝅘𝅥 | ♩. 𝅘𝅥 𝅘𝅥𝅘𝅥𝅘𝅥 . Of course, this was an exercise, not a full-blown composition; but it was designed to teach a fundamental rhythmic element in ragtime.

There can be no doubt that ragtime's right-hand syncopation, which uses rhythmic patterns basic to black music from virtually every part of the New World, came from the banjo rhythms of less sophisticated musicians (less sophisticated in the European sense, that is). The history of ragtime repeated a standard pattern in Afro-American music, the blending of African and European ingredients. Like so much else, it loosened up and became more subtle as it went along. From the beginning it supplied crossed rhythms, right hand against left. But even in the hands of fine players, early ragtime was a little stiff. Moreover, the march-derived four-strain form, with its codified formal repetitions, seems to have militated against improvisation. Guy Waterman remarked in an essay in Martin Williams' *The Art of Jazz*, "In ragtime there are four equal themes; each is as important as the others. Such a structure is not suitable for improvisation. Which melody shall be used as the base-point?" As a result, one theme tended to dominate.

Scott Joplin insisted that his music be played as written, but actually ragtime became infinitely more subtle in rhythm when men who knew what they were doing were able to give free rein to their complex rhythmic sense. Jelly Roll Morton above all demonstrated this: Compare his recording of "Frog-i-More Rag" with the way it looks on paper, or his version of "Maple Leaf Rag" with Scott Joplin's own rendition, which has been put onto a record from a piano roll. Even allowing for the inflexibility of pianolas, whose rolls are the only examples we have of Joplin's playing, Morton's and Joplin's are clearly products of a different attitude to music. (This is no criticism of Joplin's interpretations, of course; but ragtime was not a wholly suitable vehicle for African-derived musical Afro-Americanisms.)

Even in its heyday, ragtime was not as purely European as those who know little about African music may think. Besides the basic rhythmic element, another African feature—not as fully developed in early ragtime as in later piano forms—was the construction of melody from short, repeated rhythmic phrases, or repetition with variations. Almost all rags by black composers show this characteristic, though it is to some degree disguised by the use of European-style chord changes. For all its beauty and complexity, the strict piano ragtime, black America's first non-folk music, did not give black musicians the freedom they sought. Even in band ragtime the formal elements limited the musicians considerably, as is evident in a delightful ragtime-style version of "The Entertainer" by Bunk Johnson, on Columbia's collection *Jazz in New Orleans*. Consequently, the early concept was soon modified. On one hand it was taken over by white America, where a simple version of ragtime held sway until a simple version of jazz took over from it. In its piano form, ragtime developed until it merged into piano forms of jazz. How this happened, both at the piano and orchestrally, is illustrated by the music of Jelly Roll Morton.

Morton's style was firmly rooted in ragtime, as many of his compositions and solos in band recordings show. But he was also one of the last jazz pianists to take ragtime's use of contrasting sections seriously (just as, on recordings at least, King Oliver's Creole Jazz Band was the last ensemble to do so with any consistency). Morton developed a left-hand technique that was freed from the oompah bass and, by using syncopation, held notes, and misplaced accents, created a much more complex polyrhythmic structure. Morton, then, was a bridge figure in piano, but it would be a mistake to think that he alone created piano jazz out of piano ragtime. Jazz was already in the air, and Morton was a jazz pianist with strong ragtime links. His approach to freeing the left hand was based on a jazz element. As his biographer, Alan Lomax, has brought out, many of his bass lines stem from trombone techniques (Morton's father was a trombonist). Besides, the greatest ragtime composers were themselves aware of the limitations of the straight march beat. Scott Joplin's later rags began to take on a more melodic cast and to seek more flexibility generally. Pianists like Morton were roaming the country and introducing new ideas, however, by the time "Rose Leaf Rag" appeared (1907), so Joplin's new flexibility may have been a jazz influence rather than an internal ragtime development.

Sedalia, where Joplin worked, was perhaps the birthplace, but Saint Louis was the center for piano ragtime. Other cities witnessed significant moments in the growth of "rag" bands, basically small outfits of the brass-band type that played ensemble versions of rags. These groups were widespread, and their existence was an important source of early jazz. New Orleans was important in ragtime, as well as in the growth of jazz proper, because it offered so many employment opportunities for small groups and because ragtime pianists (not jazz groups, as legend had it) were in demand in the brothels of the red light district, Storyville.

It is important to remember the existence of small brass-and-wind groups playing ragtime in many parts of the country. The postulate that jazz was born exclusively in New Orleans has recently come under powerful attacks, but much of what is now held up as early non–New Orleans jazz was probably in fact ragtime, an element in jazz, but not jazz itself, which is a music of many elements. Similarly, claims about Northeastern jazz piano styles at the end of the nineteenth century seem to refer to late ragtime, in which even the initiators were loosening up their left-hand rhythms. Ragtime did not go only into jazz. It also became an ingredient in country breakdown music. There is a fine example of a guitar rag, in fact, in *Country Rag*, played by Smith Casey in a Texas prison camp in 1939 and recorded for the Library of Congress.

By the time of World War I, two widely differing types of black piano-playing had grown up. One, with strong ragtime derivations, is represented by the "stride" piano of musicians like James P. Johnson, Lucky Roberts, Eubie Blake, and Willie the Lion Smith. This tended to be a Northern style, and many of its practitioners had some "conservatory" musical training, like James P. Johnson, born in New Brunswick, New Jersey, whose mother taught him piano. Fats Waller was perhaps the most famous inheritor of the "stride piano" legacy. It developed into a complex of styles that embraced those of musicians as disparate as Earl Hines and Art Tatum. The rather vague term "jazz piano" probably covers as well as any other the varying styles of this type, which drew not only from ragtime but from blues, band jazz, and you name it but were nonetheless products of a broadly similar attitude to the piano. Like ragtime, the African-sprung factors in jazz piano were not immediately obvious but were fundamental. The most striking were perhaps the constant crossing rhythms between the two hands and the tendency to build triplets against duple time, which I have suggested is a reinterpretation of West African polymeter techniques.

Piano blues was another matter. Various styles have been distinguished, but basically barrelhouse blues—whether used as a solo style or to back the pianist's own vocal—contained a high degree of Africanism in its general concepts. This is most clearly shown by the type of barrelhouse blues called boogie-woogie, a dance music whose basis is the repetition of short, rhythmic phrases by both hands that continually cross each other rhythmically. Boogie-woogie must surely represent the purest example of how various African strands in a culturally mixed music can come together to produce music that, though nonexistent in Africa, is non-African only in that it is played on a piano and usually makes a nod in the direction of three-chord harmonies.

There used to be a theory that the growth of boogie was due to lack of pianistic skill on the part of self-taught musicians, who were compelled to keep their left hand in one position and to repeat the same figure constantly. This is a classic example of the absurdities that can be advanced in the attempt to avoid looking Africa in the eye. Boogie is only one form of barrelhouse piano, and the other forms do not in fact use such "restricted" basses. Certainly barrelhouse pianists did not have a very wide range by Eurocentric standards, but Eurocentric standards are irrelevant here. They acquired the technique needed to do what they wanted to do. Paul Oliver tentatively points out the remarkable similarities between barrelhouse piano and West African xylophone techniques, where short, rhythmic, contrasting patterns are set off against each other, patterns that use a restricted number of pitches and that it would be meaningless to try to categorize as "melodic" or "rhythmic." In fact, the analogy with xylophone music, though it must surely be indirect, is extraordinarily close. Hugh Tracey has recorded a Congolese piece with a xylophone introduction that is exactly the same as a fairly common boogie left-hand figure! Though such coincidences are not central, they do illustrate that the basic techniques of boogie are very close to specific African examples.

William Russell has suggested that the piano enabled Americans to approximate the patterns of the drum orchestra. Indeed, barrelhouse piano *is* percussive; so, for that matter, is all African instrumental music, and boogie-woogie's melodic range on the whole is nearer to that of the xylophones than the drums. True, the left hand could be seen as substituting for the underlying drum patterns and the right as in some way duplicating the master-drum role. But that would be too simplistic. The point about boogie-woogie is that for a brief spell it brought together a number of Africanisms, all of which had been present in the United States in more diffused forms, and thus produced an eerie *doppelgänger* of African music. Barrelhouse piano as a whole, and boogie especially, use the short, ostinato rhythmic phrases; cross-rhythms; lack of "melody" in a European sense; repetition with gradual development; and, in the very heavy use of right-hand triplets, the three-on-two rhythms of African music in a startlingly pure form. A perfect example is Meade Lux Lewis's "Honky Tonk Train Blues," in the second and third choruses, where triplets and eight-to-the-bar patterns are breathtakingly crossed. "Six-Wheel Chaser," by the same pianist, has virtually no "melody" at all. Its interest lies, as Nketia said of Ghanaian music, in the relationship of rhythmic patterns.

Boogie-woogie is a special case, though not so much of a freak as some writers have made out. In most barrelhouse piano, the right hand plays a part that approximates a missing vocal line. Barrelhouse also tends to a looser left hand, in which walking basses and other figures—in boogie repeated with a remorseless build-up of tension—are mingled with passing melodic phrases and generally varied in a way that strongly reflects certain styles of blues guitar accompaniment. Blues piano and one version of "country ragtime" met, incidentally, in a piano style sometimes called Western rag, a rough and ready, heavily blues-tinged ragtime typified by Will Ezell's "West Coast Rag" and Dink Johnson's "Las Vegas Stomp."

Barrelhouse piano and boogie-woogie, both strongly formulaic musics, nonetheless do not restrict the development of individual styles. From Lewis's powerhouse approach, through Pinetop Smith's delicate drive, to Jimmy Yancey's lyricism, blues piano—like the blues as a whole—shows the value of a simple but fairly flexible framework for the improvising musician.

The African legacy is an essential part—either "major" or "minor"—of all styles produced by black Americans. But detailed analysis of Africanisms in some modes is made difficult by the fact that many individual features are the result of musical reinforcement by compatible elements in both European and African music. The situation as regards band jazz is especially complicated. For one thing, the word "jazz" covers many different periods and styles, from Freddy Keppard to Sun-Ra. For another, jazz and Tin Pan Alley—not to mention commercial dance music—often shade into each other. Would Ella Fitzgerald be a jazz singer while performing "Singing in the Rain"? If Dinah Shore sang "Beale Street Blues," would she become a jazz or blues singer? What about Peggy Lee?

The first apparent stumbling block for those who hold jazz to be African is its almost universal two-four or four-four beat. Early jazz came from a number of sources, including march band music, ragtime, and the blues, with perhaps lesser contributions from spirituals and other sources—and *all* of these have a seemingly solid duple time rhythm. The only exception among the elements that went into jazz was the creole tinge inherited from New Orleans's past position as an honorary Caribbean outpost. Attempts have been made to rationalize the apparently entirely European content of the basic jazz beat by analogies with African drum corps, polyrhythms, polymeter, and so forth. But listening to a wide range of early jazz will show that the *rhythm section* of virtually all the early groups was far removed from the superimposed rhythms of different time-signatures characteristic of the only African music the jazz writers seem to be aware of: that of the drum-oriented rain forest area.

Phyl Garland, in *The Sound of Soul*, quotes the musician Noble Sissle as follows: "Who created this beat? The answer is, the American Negro, because none of the other immigrants brought it with them." Yet actually the basic *beat* of jazz, in the sense of the basic time, was indeed European in origin, stemming from march music, Protestant hymns, and a number of other minor sources. But this is not to say that the rhythm was European. What *did* stem from Africa, not necessarily linked with the drum-corps music of a restricted region, was an attitude to various musical elements shared in differing degrees by most of the African groups that came to the United States. This African-sprung attitude was crucial: Without *either* the European-derived common-time beat, *or* the African-derived rhythmic approach that transformed it, jazz would not exist. This is hard to prove from purely internal evidence. If anybody chooses to doubt that jazz drum phrasing springs from an Africanization of European march band drumming, nothing within jazz can convince him. It was particularly exciting for me to find corroboration in a non-U.S. music: the drumming that accompanies a black version of a medieval British mumming play preserved by Nevis immigrants in the Dominican Republic. The black drummers turned the medieval-*cum*-military British origins of their music into something full of jazz-style phrasing.

One of the fundamental facts about jazz is that it "swings." Anybody with a feel for jazz knows what this means, but to define it is a very different matter. Barry Ulanov, in his *History of Jazz in America*, quotes the attempts of a number of musicians to define the concept of swing. The results were enlightening in their lack of enlightenment. The three best definitions of swing were from Frankie Froeba, Louis Armstrong, and Ella Fitzgerald, in the following order:

"A steady tempo, causing lightness and relaxation and a feeling of floating."

"My idea of how a tune should go."

"Why, er—swing is—well, you sort of feel—uh—uh—I don't know—you just swing!"

Gunther Schuller, in a chapter of *Early Jazz* that makes a considerable contribution on the question of the relationship between jazz and African music (though he leans far too heavily on the work of one man), suggests that jazz has two elements that do not normally occur in conservatory music. One is a certain sort of accentuation and inflection, and the other is the way in which notes are linked in what he ponderously calls a "forward-propelling directionality."

Jazz is commonly described as "syncopated," meaning that what would "normally" be weak beats are accentuated. But among the least swinging of bands are precisely those Dixieland groups whose drummer consistently wallops the second and fourth beats, a technique used by many bands of the 1920's and 1930's for a special effect, particularly to ride out a final chorus when nobody had any better ideas. It can be an exciting effect, but only when used sparingly. What jazz musicians in fact do with the basic two-four or four-four beat is much more subtle, and more in line with African practices: They *play around* it, anticipating it, laying back on it, creating a sort of reverse syncopation by cutting across a rocking rhythm with a series of notes of exactly equal value. Basically, the good jazz musician plays melodic-rhythmic patterns that intermarry (to this extent there is a resemblance with the drum corps, but only insofar as the drum corps is a special application of a more general principle). The effect of syncopation is caused by the use in jazz of an African-descended technique in a context that contains European material—measured meter, bars, and so forth. (A fine piece of polyrhythmic play between a lead instrument and the rhythm section is Henry "Red" Allen's solo in "Stingaree Blues," with King Oliver.)

Paul Oliver has pointed out that the drum groups of the Ewe or the Yoruba do not swing in the jazz sense, that their procedures are built upon quite different principles. But this is not the whole story. Though Yoruba drumming does not use syncopation, the total effect of the music is similar to certain types of jazz's rhythmic effects. Moreover, what is true of the Yoruba and

Ewe is not true of all the musical styles that influenced Afro-America. There is much music of the Congo-Angola region, especially music for groups including drums and xylophones, that does, in fact, swing like crazy. The failure of theories about the sources of "swing" to transcend a too-narrow range of African styles may invalidate the theories, but it does not invalidate the tie between jazz and African music. Many problems have been caused by attempts to draw close parallels.

Many of the African elements found in the New World, including North America, are also present in jazz, either in a pure form or, more often, as modifying or modified by European elements. The highly sophisticated "syncopation" jazz musicians use is a workable compromise of the desire for crossed rhythms with the European monometric framework. Baby Dodds's work in the second and third choruses of "Ain't Misbehavin'" with Sidney Bechet, on the RCA Vintage series *Blue Bechet* album, is a direct example. Dodds cuts loose from the basic, easy swing of the four-four beat and produces a series of patterns, vaguely reminiscent of brass-band drumming, that are effective cross-rhythms and also rhythmo-melodic patterns analogous to the sort of drum tune used by African drummers. Examples of the way in which jazz musicians employ polyrhythms in what is ostensibly a monorhythmic context are legion. The music of Charlie Christian, the guitarist who influenced the bop musicians of the early 1940's, was full of what Al Avakian and Bob Prince have called "metric denials." Bop rhythm sections made a conscious effort to go back to a more polyrhythmic style after the swing period's solid four-four, epitomized by Count Basie's rock-firm four to the bar.

Yet even the swing bands did not really abandon polyrhythmic approaches. Most good swing bands (and even more the small groups of the 1930's drawn from the ranks of the big bands) used the steady four-to-the-bar rhythm section as a floor off which to bounce a complex of front-line cross-rhythms and conflicting accents. Not always, of course: From the start, jazz has been a music of many different movements, and at times certain individuals or groups would opt for an on-the-beat approach in order to explore some other aspect of their style. But these other aspects in their turn were likely to prove to contain the same subtle indices of African-derived attitudes to music-making. I have mentioned before that I believe the consistent use of triplets over a basically duple beat to be a reinterpretation of the three-on-two metrical phenomenon of West African music. An example of a reinterpreted binary-tertiary consonance comes in Lionel Hampton's recording of "Short of Breath" on Showcase SSH-102-7, in the band breaks and also in a break in the middle of the piano solo, which makes use of the theme usually called "Snag 'Em."

Much of the misapprehension about polyrhythmicality in jazz stems from a tendency to concentrate on the rhythm section rather than to consider the rhythmic interplay of the group as a whole, and from a tendency to forget that jazz musicians vary greatly in stature. For example, Ross Russell writes, in an article on bop:

> One must listen carefully to the best records of Armstrong or Roy Eldridge, of Bechet or Hawkins, to find rhythmic accents as rich as those in Dizzy Gillespie's line on "Congo Blues" or Parker's on "Koko." Baby Dodds and Jo Jones are two of the greatest drummers of jazz, but the patterns of Menny Clarke and Max Roach are more complex, and swing as freely.

Quite true—but then, one would expect only the best musicians to measure up to the best musicians. An interesting point might be made about the drumming: Certainly the role of New Orleans drummers seems to have been less subtle than that of more modern musicians, though there is a good deal of conflicting evidence on this point. But rhythm is not the exclusive prerogative of drummers, nor are polyrhythms. Besides, early jazz *was* early. It is significant that, as jazz musicians became more at ease in their music, they re-Africanized it.

Talking of bop drummers, it is interesting that Kenny Clarke is on record as saying that his style owed nothing to African music (he meant directly), but that he felt he had ended up close to the African style. Naturally enough, given the strong African content in all black music, this is not too rare a phenomenon. It happened especially with boogie-woogie, when a concentration on certain African-sprung factors in Afro-American music "coincidentally" produced a highly African (or, more accurately, neo-African) effect. Of course, the results may be a long way from Africa even when the procedures are similar, as in the case of the pianist Cecil Taylor. Archie Shepp said of Taylor, in an interview with LeRoi Jones reprinted in *Black Music*, "Cecil plays the piano like a drum, he gets rhythms out of it like a drum, rhythm and melody. . . . In a way it's more of a throwback rather than a projection into some weird future. A throwback in the direction of the African influences on the music." Apart from the customary obsession with the drum, and the fact that "throwbacks" have been happening all the time, this is a fairly good assessment.

One last point about rhythm, jazz, and Africanisms. Jazz, like virtually all Afro-American music, has been a dance music for most of its existence. Like most Afro-American music, the rapport among dancer, spectator, and band is similar to the African totality. Here is Malcolm X, on the Roseland Ballroom in Boston:

> "Showtime!" people would start hollering about the last hour of the dance. Then a couple of dozen really wild couples would stay on the floor, the girls changing to low white sneakers. The band now would be really blasting, and all the other dancers would form a clapping, shouting circle to watch that wild competition as it began, covering only a quarter or so of the ballroom floor.

What was true of Roseland was equally true of the Savoy Ballroom in the time of the Lindy Hoppers, of the bomba dances, or of social dances anywhere in Africa or Afro-America.

Structurally, the most obvious link between jazz and African music—descended through the music of the nineteenth century and the blues—is the call-and-response technique, instrumentalized. This was at its most obvious in big-band music like Count Basie's, where it was a favorite arranger's trick to have an ensemble riff answer a couple of bars of solo, or the brass section answer the sax section, or any number of similar possibilities. Perhaps nobody made more subtle and continued use of it than Duke Ellington. Instrumental call-and-response existed in a number of forms before the big-band era. Sometimes it was a repetition of a phrase, the obvious example being opening bars of "Basin Street Blues," where the first line is first played by a solo instrument and then repeated by the full band. Another version occurs in many renderings of "Memphis Blues" and in Clarence Williams's "Milk Cow Blues," in which the call is the first half of the melodic phrase (often taken by trombone), and the answer the second half, taken by the ensemble. Sometimes there will be longish calls and answers, and sometimes very short, as when Victoria Spivey's "moans" in "Moaning the Blues" are answered by the band. The call-and-response effect between soloist and ensemble is too common to need more comment.

An important development of call-and-response, which we touched on while discussing gospel music, is the riff (representing the response) over which is played a free solo. Count Basie's "John's Idea" is an excellent example, but the style was already common fifteen years earlier in the so-called stomp pattern. This was a very highly rhythmic and repetitive tune, longer than a riff (which is a phrase, whereas a stomp pattern is more like a line of melody), over which a solo was also often played. King Oliver's Creole Jazz Band made extensive use of this pattern, notably in "Canal Street Blues," under Johnny Dodds's clarinet solo. I have already said that I consider this style an extension of call-and-response arising partly from the demands for greater liberty posed by an instrument with wide melodic possibilities and partly from the common overlapping of call-and-response found in both Africa and Afro-America.

The call-and-response structure of the riff gave rise to another melodic form that was extremely, though rather indirectly, African. The riff alone, used repeatedly to build a tune (Charlie Christian was an adept at this), is quite like the technique of short-phrase tunes used in Africa. Another jazz phenomenon that may descend from call-and-response, in this case evolving into the form of a dialogue, is the "fours," in which two or more musicians will trade passages of four bars apiece to construct a single, logical solo line.

It has been claimed that the alternation of solo and chorus in jazz is an Africanism. Such a claim, however, is part of the Africa-or-bust syndrome. If anything, African music uses this pattern less than most. Besides, to term a thirty-two-bar chorus a "call" seems extreme; the practice is actually much nearer to a European verse-and-chorus style. The next step would be to hunt down the African origins of the concerto form.

There is, however, another way in which the chorus pattern of jazz does reflect African practice, and this has been pointed out (as far as I know, for the first time) by Gunther Schuller. He reminds us that the series of "choruses" conceived of as variants within accepted limits of the preceding choruses is the basic structure of at least the music of the Ewe studied by the Reverend A. M. Jones. Each of seven dances analyzed by Jones comprises a certain number of "master patterns." Within each pattern some variation may occur. But more important, each "master pattern" is conceived as a variant of the previous pattern. Allowing for syncretism with European forms, this is very much what happens in jazz structure: The chorus is not simply repeated, as in simple dance styles in Europe; nor is the form one of contrasting sections, as in more developed European music, especially dance music. When European-style tunes are played, jazz tends progressively to drop all but what is perceived as the main chorus. This is not universally true: The older jazz forms stick to the march form when playing numbers that originated as marches. But for the most part the chorus as a series of master patterns repeated with variants dominates, unless a composer's hand is at work or the jazz is in such an archaic state that the European contributions in it have not been re-Africanized. The recourse to the West African master-pattern formula is, of course, reinforced by the fact that it makes improvisation easier. The bands that were supposed to be miracles of collective improvisation working their way through complex contrasting sections— notably King Oliver's Creole Jazz Band—have been shown, on the contrary, to have rehearsed very tightly, at least for recording.

We have already looked at the question of the blues scale. Whatever its origin, the "blue tonality" permeates jazz. So does something else, which would tend to support Paul Oliver's positing of a savanna-land basis for many of the Africanisms in U.S. music. I refer to the frequent bending of notes, reminiscent of Islamic African music, but occurring among the coastal peoples (except under Islamic influence) mainly in the form of rising to the first note of a phrase and falling from the last. The bending of notes is, as we have seen, of major importance in vocal blues, producing quarter-tones especially at the third and fifth and seventh of the scale. It has continued throughout jazz history, principally as a carryover from the blues. (It is present in jazz descended from ragtime and march music, but less frequent.) It has been most common, of course, among singers. Billie Holiday used it with the greatest variety perhaps, not only in the blues but in popular songs as well. As sung by her, a note may (in the words of Glenn Coutter) begin "slightly under pitch, absolutely without vibrato, and gradually be forced up to dead center from where the vibrato shakes free, or it may trail off mournfully; or at final cadences, the note is a whole step above the written one and must be pressed slowly down to where it belongs." Coincidence or not, all these features are found in Islamic African music and hardly at all in other styles.

A most fundamental feature of jazz style is the use of a variety of tonal or timbre techniques instead of the "pure" tone of the European classical ideal. The use of a wide range of tonal qualities—sharp, smooth, and piercing—of varied vibratos, and of special effects like growls, shakes, and dirty notes of all sorts is a noticeable part of jazz, to which the use of mutes with brass instruments for special effects is related. Legend has it that the New Orleans trumpeter Mutt Carey was the originator of the varied muted style of which King Oliver made such use. Trumpet-muting reached an apogee with the growl trumpet of Duke Ellington's trumpeters, Bubber Miley and his successors, and was never again employed to such an extent. But it was jazz that created the array of cup mutes, wa-was, and so on from which a brass-player can now select. Gone are the days when the trumpeter's only choice was a sort of metal pear.

The special effects, the growls and spitting tones, were only a part, usually a small part, of a wider concept of instrumental tone that is much more common in jazz than in Africa. As Nketia points out, the use of tone *contrasts* in African musical instruments is unusual, though tonguing and trilling are sometimes featured. More to the point is the type of tone chosen. African musicians in most areas have a great liking for burred or buzzing tones. There is no doubt at all that this is a matter of choice, not accident. In the Folkways record *Africa South of the Sahara,* there is a recording of a Hororo flute player using a burred tone, who very firmly said that this tone was "to my will." I myself have a Ugandan hand-piano carefully fitted out with little coils from a cut-up tin can, which rattle as the instrument is played. I have cited plenty of other examples from various African styles. The fondness for a burred tone is equally present in jazz, though as a music of mixed origins jazz takes the opportunity to use it in contrast with "purer" tone. Here, too, the possibility that accident or incompetence has contributed can be ruled out. For one thing, a reasonably smooth tone is not difficult to acquire when learning a wind instrument: easier in fact than a growl. For another, examples abound of burred or rough tones used by musicians of the very highest skill, as well as the stylists of an earlier generation who sometimes come under attack from technically Eurocentric critics. Ben Webster, for instance, was unquestionably one of the five or six greatest tenor sax players. In "Jive at Six," he uses a heavily burred tone (not blurred—in fact it has a sharp edge). Sandy Williams, a fine trombonist of the 1930's small-band swing vintage, specialized in a tone so hoarse that one note could identify him. Ellington, a composer of recognized genius, for many years incorporated growl techniques in his greatest works, and not simply because of Bubber Miley's specialty. Jabbo Smith sat in for Miley on one cutting of "Black and Tan Fantasy," and the main concern when Cootie Williams took over Miley's chair was: Would he be able to learn the growling plunger-mute techniques?

Less outstanding examples of the varied tonal quality can be cited by the hundred. However, like the contrasts, they are merely manifestations of a fundamental principle: The styles of playing instruments in jazz are based on the human voice, and an instrumental solo bears a singularly close relationship not only to song but even to speech. We have looked at the extremely intimate relationship of speech, song, and instrumental music in Africa. Some of the rationale behind it has been lost in the United States, but it remains operative in remarkable detail at times. Most African languages are tonal; that is, the pitch of a syllable can determine its meaning, so that a spoken sentence in some languages is sung on two, three, or four notes. Actually, there is no single middle note from which the ups go up and the downs down: Different languages tend to have different over-all sentence shapes (like a rising or falling melody), and the ups and downs are relative to those varying tone centers.

One of the most striking things about jazz instrumentalists of whatever style is their highly individual "tones of voice." I once had a Nigerian friend who, unlike most Africans, really knew jazz, historically and stylistically. He possessed the most remarkable gift for recognizing musicians after a few bars—not just soloists, but the bassist on some obscure and ill-recorded old disc. I asked him how he managed it. "Well," he answered, surprised, "you can recognize your friends' voices, can't you?"

The components of a jazzman's instrumental tone of voice may vary, but it is always highly expressive and highly personal. Louis Armstrong, in his heyday, played the trumpet just as he sang, uncannily so. Other musicians simply let instruments talk for them. Listen to the incredibly varied voices of Charlie Parker, Lester Young, Sidney Bechet, and Rex Stewart's solo in "Finesse," or the bluffness of Jim Robinson's trombone. Every time a movement in jazz turns away from the instrument as human voice, there is a turn back again. Leon Thomas recently said what Jelly Roll Morton had said another way forty years before: "The most proficient horns are those which do not play the regular phrases and come close to the human voice and screeching and crying and shouting." Morton was not a man for screeching and crying and shouting, but Thomas is saying what every black Christian touched by the spirit, every good blues singer, has always known and proved. And my mention of Christianity is not random. Marshall Stearns tells how Dizzie Gillespie explained vibes player Milt Jackson's sense of rhythm (a vital element in powerful song and speech): "Why, man, he's sanctified!"

It is significant, by the way, that the role of the individual in jazz has been of such overriding importance. Virtually all the major changes in jazz have been associated with a few individuals (though clearly they could not have wrought the changes single-handed): Buddy Bolden, who appears to have provided a bridge between band marches and ragtime and band jazz; Jelly Roll Morton, in somewhat the same position; Armstrong, who introduced the era of jazz as a music for soloists; Coleman Hawkins and Lester Young, who helped turn jazz from a trumpeter's to a saxist's music; Charlie Parker and Dizzie Gillespie; Ornette Coleman and Cecil Taylor; and perhaps Archie Shepp.

If the African musician is, as we are told, usually a communal craftsman; if the idea of the "personality" has come to Africa only recently, under European impact; and if the intense individuality of jazz speaking/singing/playing tone is not European, where does it come from? I think the answer is both simple and unprovable. African musicians spoke as secure members of a secure society. Black American musicians speak for a people whose major group experience has been a denial not so much of humanity as of individuality. For all their presence at the heart of the American experience, for all the plausibility of Albert Murray's claim that black Americans are *the* Americans, the Omni-Americans, black Americans have constantly suffered the indignity of being "they." Are the jazzmen not, each in his individual tone, saying "I am I!"? Certainly, just as black America is not Africa, black American music is not going to resemble black African music at every dot of a quarter-note. And the individuality of tone of voice does stem naturally from what *is* an Africanism, the speech/song/instrument continuum.

The same can be said of improvisation, another major element of jazz. There are differences between the contexts in which improvisation occurs in the U.S. and in Africa. African musical groups do not go in for "collective improvisation." They employ differing mixtures of improvisation within defined limits—usually, in the rain forest area, specific drum patterns over which the master drummer improvises more freely but also with limitations. And what happens in jazz, or, at any event, what did happen until the advent of Ornette Coleman and his followers? Exactly the same improvisation within limits—limits of a melody, limits of a chorus pattern, limits of a chord progression. In King Oliver's "Canal Street Blues," for instance, all the instruments but the clarinet are either playing head-arranged or written parts during

Dodds's solo or improvising within the strict limits of a quite intricate stomp tune. This is precisely what happens not only in the drum corps but also in much other African instrumental music. And besides, when improvisation *was* collective, each instrument had a clear function within the whole. Incidentally, it is sometimes pointed out that improvisation is also found in Europe. But even so, this can only refute an argument that improvisation in jazz was *solely* African-descended. If there is (much restricted) improvisation in Europe, its existence no doubt acted as a reinforcement to the improvisatory techniques in jazz, which plainly spring indirectly both from African patterns of improvisation and from other African-derived practices that have helped to define the terms in which improvisation is expressed.

Harmony in jazz is undoubtedly a strongly European influence. Harmony, in fact, is a European concept. But the European harmony in jazz has always been crossed with African attitudes. In *Early Jazz,* Gunther Schuller puts the problem of jazz and European harmony neatly:

> It would . . . be easy to conclude, as most studies of jazz have, that the harmony of jazz derives exclusively from European practices. In one basic sense, this is true, but this conclusion seems to be another one of those over-simplifications in which historians indulge so readily when documentation is scanty. For in another sense . . . the *particular* harmonic choices Negroes made, once they adopted the European harmonic frame of reference, were dictated entirely by their African musical heritage.

This is perhaps putting it a bit too strongly. It might, on the evidence, be safer to say that *many* of the harmonic choices in jazz, and also many of the occasions on which jazzmen saw no necessity of a choice, were dictated by musical attitudes that originated in Africa. Clearly, on many other occasions jazz musicians elected to make use of European harmony, or at least to accord an un-African attention to harmonic implications. The bop era is a case in point. But there are certainly parallels between jazz and African music here, too. The interweaving roles of the front-line instruments in New Orleans jazz was like much Western Bantu heterophonic singing. An example is Bunk Johnson's "Alexander's Ragtime Band," a fine record by a group first overrated and later underrated. Even more interesting are recordings made by Frederic Ramsey of brass bands in the Southern countryside, issued on Folkways. Listening to these recordings is an almost hallucinatory experience, for the approach of the accompanying instruments, indeed the over-all sound, is like nothing so much as the groups of trumps and shawms found in many parts of West Africa—in Islamic Hausaland, but also among the forest Bantu peoples—in which horns, each producing one or two notes, are played together to make a wind-instrument music more rhythmic than melodic. The Haitian *vaccines* work on the same principle. In view of Haiti's intensely African culture, this should not be surprising, but to hear the Lapsey Band's euphonium playing a repeated phrase of two blaring notes extraordinarily like the Hausa *kakaki* notes is staggering. Such a close parallel is no coincidence. And if it exists in brass-and-drum ensembles (albeit reinterpreted, and with a wide African catchment area), one must wonder what other discoveries are still to be made.

The Lapsey band represents a very early stage. But even in much later jazz, European notions of harmony have often been ignored. Schuller analyzes a riff pattern that is in full agreement with the underlying chords in only two out of six bars, which he finds in a "developed" form of jazz that had been heavily affected by white show-business music!

Incidentally, the idea that the "arrangement" is a "decidedly 'white' influence," as Schuller put it, is inaccurate as far as African music is concerned. African music is organized, and usually the roles of the participants are mapped out beforehand by an "arranger"—in the case of the Ewe music on which Schuller leans so heavily, usually the master drummer. Indeed, some African groups compose major orchestral forms. The Chopi of Mozambique play xylophone and choral dance symphonies (if I may use the expression) that comprise several contrasting and linked movements. The same is true of the Ewe themselves, as attested by the very quotations from Jones used by Schuller when he is talking of form. If this is not "arrangement," what is?

Jazz, then, is rich in African elements, which have fused with its European content to produce a new and major music. Craig

McGregor with justice has called it "the black man's classical music." Henry Kmen amply documents the European end of the events that turned New Orleans into a catalyst, combining into one rich style the ragtime, jazzlike marches, and blues that were being played elsewhere. March music was an important ingredient in the blend. Just before the birth of jazz, as many as a dozen black brass bands took part in the funeral procession for President Garfield in 1881. Even before that, residents complained that bands were "going about the city early on Sunday mornings, squeaking and rattle-te-banging away . . . and waking everybody." New Orleans became brass-crazy in the 1830's, when rival theaters presented famous virtuosi of the trumpet and trombone running concurrently in an attempt to outdraw each other. The trumpeters were Alessandro Gambati and John T. Norton, who had already engaged in contests in New York. The trombonist was Felippe Cioffi, and a famous clarinetist, James Kendall, was also featured.

New Orleans also was accustomed early to the notion of bands that could serve as both march and dance groups, as was common in the early jazz days. In 1840, the Neptune Band advertised that it was available for quadrilles and also as a military band, if required. So, whatever the merits of the dispute over New Orleans's claim to be the founder-city of jazz (which depends largely on how one defines ragtime, brass-band music, and jazz), it certainly had a very rich mix ready to pour into the new black music at the turn of the century. Adding to it, New Orleans at times had as many as three opera houses going at once before the Civil War, and this in a town with a population of 60,000, of whom only 25,000 were white. The blacks, including slaves, formed an essential part of the public of these opera houses.

While on the subject of European influence and the history of jazz, we ought to remind ourselves that jazz was never a music entirely by or for blacks, despite black musicians' overwhelming dominance both in sheer numbers and as leaders in most jazz developments. Nor were white musicians always mere imitators. Some were, as LeRoi Jones said of Bix Beiderbecke, innovators. Some minor white figures influenced important black musicians: Frankie Trumbauer influenced Coleman Hawkins, and for a while Harlem saxophone styling took on features of Guy Lombardo's sax section. From Beiderbecke to Steve Cropper, virtually all forms of black music except gospel music have been shared by whites, though rarely if ever as leaders, and usually as junior partners.

After a period of emphasis on the "European" technical elements absent from early jazz, there have been successive waves of movement away from European factors. The bop movement was one, though its new treatment of harmonic concepts in fact relied heavily on the European element of harmony. More recently, John Coltrane tried to abandon the song, as Phyl Garland reported, "as a necessary point of departure, and opened up the music, enabling it to move in all directions." But always there has been a clear continuity in jazz. Coltrane himself worked with Eddie "Cleanhead" Vinson, Gillespie, Earl Bostic, and Johnny Hodges. Similarly there was a clear line of development among trumpeters from King Oliver to Armstrong, then to Roy Eldridge, and finally to Dizzie Gillespie. Archie Shepp's father was a banjoist in a small group, and Shepp himself played in blues bands. Even musical anecdotes have a sort of continuity. Once, when Coltrane announced a number, one of his musicians said, "Man, I've never heard *that* before." Coltrane answered: "Well, you'll be hearing it now." In the 1920's the pianist Lil Armstrong auditioned with King Oliver. "Hit it," they said. "What key?" "Never mind about keys," they said, "just hit it." Jazzmen's procedures have not changed much since—or is it their sense of humor?

One thing has changed. Jazz for the first forty or fifty years of its life was a people's music and a dance music. Now, in Craig McGregor's words, it has become a "classical" music. The change is reflected in the attitude of many musicians. Miles Davis put it bluntly in a 1970 *Newsweek* interview: "We don't play to be seen. I'm addicted to music, not audiences." According to Alice Coltrane, John Coltrane felt much the same: "One point he made above all others, and that was 'Don't ever play *down* to anyone. Play just what you feel yourself.' He didn't believe in playing what people might want to hear." Whether as a cause or as an effect, one important factor in the progress of jazz from a black popular to an avant-garde music was the increasing exposure of jazz musicians in the last twenty years or so to European conservatory music. To take only one example, Coltrane himself studied at Granoff Studios and the Ornstein School of Music, besides serving a more traditional apprenticeship in the bands led by Gillespie, Vinson, and Hodges. Attacking the absurd tendency of journalists to write of the younger jazz musicians as "unlettered geniuses" (he was thinking particularly of Ornette Coleman), Nat Kofsky wrote in *Jazz and Pop* for November, 1970: "By 1960 . . . the typical young black jazz musician was likely to be at the very minimum a high school graduate with extensive private musical study; many, like the iconoclastic pianist Cecil Taylor, had conservatory training or the equivalent."

The new attitude to jazz on the part of some of its players has undoubtedly been influenced by contact with the solemnity of too many "classical" musicians. Not that this attitude is altogether new, nor is it entirely conservatory-spawned. According to the jazz critic Barry Ulanov, the pianist Art Tatum once stood up and asked a buzzing audience, "Do I have to perform a major operation in here to get quiet?"

This attitude contributed as much as anything else to the split in the 1940's between band blues and band jazz. Louis Jordan, for instance, began as a jazzman in the Eckstine and Earl Hines groups of the early 1940's, which contained such outstanding innovators as Gillespie, Charlie Parker, and Art Blakey. Jordan decided, as he said, that "those guys . . . really wanted to play mostly for themselves, and I still wanted to play for the people. I just like to sing my blues and swing."

There, perhaps, we have it. Jazz has, like many a major music before it, become an "art" music, no longer a "people" music. In this, it has left behind the greatest Africanism of all, for African music, with few exceptions, is (as well as a gods' music) a "people" music. (This is not to make value judgments. There is not merely room for both but a desperate need for both.) "The people"—the black people, that is, since the other "people" have hardly heard of it—respect avant-garde jazz; people usually do respect integrity. But the heroes, the folk myth-makers, are not in the jazz world any longer. They are in the world of blues and soul, they are the descendants of Louis Jordan, not of Charlie Parker. And in a culture with so much left that is African, the reason may well be partly functional: Now jazz is no longer a dance music, and dance music is central to African culture everywhere.

Yet if jazz for the moment has ceased to be a black majority music, bluesmen, soul arrangers, singers, gospel shouters, and jazzmen all learn from each other. As Phyl Garland remarks, much of the increasing complexity of soul arrangements is indirectly owed to jazz. Black styles were never totally separate, and they are not now. Of course, jazz is as subject to pendulums of taste as any other art form. In the mid-1960's LeRoi Jones, in an article reprinted in *Black Music*, remarked that "funk (groove, soul) has become as formal and clichéd as cool or swing, and opportunities for imaginative expression within that form have dwindled almost to nothing." This was true enough of its time, but by 1971 many musicians were tiring of the evident failure of most free-form jazz to communicate or even to express anything that struck the man in the street as relevant to him. The inevitable result was expressed in the title number of Freddie Hubbard's album *Backlash*, which makes use of a soul beat and feeling. Perhaps a swing of the pendulum will bring jazz nearer to the people again. Certainly the big-business Motown music machine is devouring music as efficiently as any of its white predecessors and processing it into bright, marketable little plastic soul-bubbles; so something else is about due to come along and confound the Jeremiahs. There are new sounds in the air, and there is a drawing together of new strands, some from farther afield than before.

8 FUSIONS: JAZZ, LATIN AMERICA, AND AFRICA

From its earliest days, the Afro-American music of some parts of the United States has had connections with the very different styles of the Caribbean. We have seen how Louisiana, which at various times was under Spanish and (much more significantly) French rule, was musically closer to the French islands to the south than to the rest of the U.S. mainland. Not only were New Orleans creole songs sung in French *patois*, but their tune-types and their rhythms were Caribbean. These Caribbean qualities spread out, though much reduced in degree, into other parts of the South. The juba, the neo-African dance popular in Haiti, Martinique, Guadeloupe, and other French-influenced islands, was found not only in New Orleans but also in Georgia and the Carolinas.

Creole music became part of the heritage of New Orleans and passed as one element into jazz, to which the "creole" musicians, especially the clarinetists, brought a French touch. The "creole" tone, inherited from French reed technique, instantly distinguished clarinetists like Albert Nicholas, Sidney Bechet, or Alphonse Picou from the much bluer and more African-derived sound of black New Orleans musicians. Creoles like Nicholas, Picou, Paul Barbarin, Danny Barker (also of the Barbarin fam-

ily), Jelly Roll Morton, and Kid Ory brought to jazz a degree of
"legitimate" musicianship, which allowed it to broaden its base
without swamping the more earthy elements. There were also a
few creole songs in the jazz repertoire. The most famous, perhaps, is "Eh Là Bas," which Kid Ory made popular during the
New Orleans revival of the 1940's. Something of the Caribbean-
creole touch remained in these tunes, but not as a major ingredient. A band would rather uneasily play one chorus with a
"Caribbean" creole beat and then launch with relief into four-
four. The result was nothing very fundamental. What might
have happened if the creole songs had been present in New
Orleans jazz in larger numbers and if the rhythm had been preserved can be heard on a recording of "Eh Là Bas" in which the
creole beat is maintained throughout, and in which Danny
Barker plays a fine, and a very "West Indian" banjo solo.

The Caribbean touch continued in jazz as a minor but enduring streak. Jelly Roll Morton, a creole himself, called it the
Spanish tinge and used it—effectively but rather as a sauce—in
the Red Hot Peppers' version of "Jelly Roll Blues." (His piano
solo "The Grave" made a more basic use of a habanera
rhythm.) But despite the creole element in jazz, the "Spanish
tinge" in its various forms seems mostly to have resulted from
the fact that during most of the history of jazz the United
States has gone through one Latin fad or another. In 1914 it was
the tango, and W. C. Handy (a musician whose attitude to jazz
and other vulgar music changed rapidly one night when he saw
that there was money in it) composed a number with a tangana
rhythm, related to the tango, in one section and called it "Saint
Louis Blues." In the 1920's it was the rumba, in the 1930's the
conga, and in the 1940's the samba. The habanera rhythm and
various other Afro-Spanish rhythmic devices were in fact a permanent minor element, sometimes simply taken over or adapted
from "Latin" music and sometimes developed separately. We
have seen how one particular rhythmic pattern,

was basic to most Afro-American styles. The ragtime musician
Eubie Blake tells of a piano number called "The Dream," played
by one Jessie Pickett around 1898, whose bass was essentially
this same pattern. In the 1930's, the boogie-woogie pianist Jimmy
Yancey often used versions of the same figure in his left hand,
especially on slow numbers like "Five O'Clock Blues." Writers
on jazz have referred to this as the use of a tango or a habanera
rhythm. Given how widespread it has always been in Afro-
American music (including the right-hand patterns of ragtime
and the melodies of many old blues and spirituals), however, this
attribution seems too hasty. In fact, it is a fundamental rhythmic
element in all Afro-American music, *including* jazz, though of
course habanera or other fads may at times have reinforced it.

Louisiana creole contributions and passing fashions aside, the
first major impact of Caribbean music on jazz during the twentieth century took place in the mid- to late 1940's when, once
the bop revolution had established itself, a wave of experimenta-
tion with joint forms got under way. One factor that made this
possible was a steady influx of large numbers of Cubans, Dominicans, and Puerto Ricans into the United States, so that even
by the 1930's there was a large market for Spanish-Caribbean
music in the country. During the Depression, a group led by
Noro Morales played authentic Cuban music in a club in Harlem.
The big "gringo-Latino" bands, which produced rum-and-water
versions of Cuban music for the U.S. trade (Xavier Cugat is perhaps the daddy of them all) imported first-rate Cuban musicians,
who would at some point leave and set up for themselves. Some
continued to cater to the *gringos*, but others played for the Hispano audience.

Thus, by the 1940's there were really two major Afro-American
styles of dance music in the United States, or at least in certain
big cities. One was jazz, and the other was basically Cuban,
of which the most famous representative at the time was probably Machito's orchestra. About 1946, the two began to come
together. The leader of this trend from the jazz side is commonly
assumed to have been Dizzie Gillespie, but the white bandleader
Stan Kenton preceded him. In the winter of 1947, Gillespie be-

gan playing with an immigrant who had been a drummer with the Cuban *lucumi* sect, Chano Pozo. Pozo burst upon an unsuspecting world at a concert in New York's Town Hall, soloing with the Gillespie band, an event frequently taken as the start of the Afro-Cuban period of jazz. But in fact, Kenton had begun to use Latin rhythms seriously in 1946. Not all of them were Cuban: in July, 1946, he recorded a number called "Ecuador." But in the spring of 1947 he recorded "Machito," using a couple of the percussionists from Machito's band. In September, 1947, Kenton had a new band that included the Brazilian guitarist Laurindo Almeida, who was later to be involved with Stan Getz in another jazz-Latin fusion, the U.S. version of the bossa nova.

Kenton is apt to be dismissed these days as variously a pretentious and an insignificant bandleader, but he did play a leading part in the "Afro-Cuban" period of jazz. His arrangement of "Peanut Vendor," made in 1947, was possibly his best-known number. In the words of his discographer, Anthony Cox, "hackneyed though it may be now, it was a brilliant piece of arranging for its day, and the avant garde boys could learn from it today." I remember traveling to Mannheim to hear the Kenton band, which included Lee Konitz and Zoot Sims, among others. At that time I would not have given a nickel for the Kenton group: I was there for the soloists. I sat through most of the evening hating the ensemble work as I had expected; but then the brass opened up with what I did not then realize was essentially a polyrhythm of Afro-Cuban percussion patterns, and I was electrified. The number was "23° N, 82° W," which, as I was not to know for another fifteen years, is the grid reference for Havana. This experience did not convert me to big bands or to Kenton in general, but it taught me not to be too sure of my aesthetic judgments.

Kenton was first (if one allows for a few individual exceptions, like Cab Calloway's series of "Conga" recordings, Ellington's "Caravan," and others in the 1930's, or Woody Herman's jazz rumba "Bijou" in 1945). But the leading bop musicians—especially Gillespie, with "Manteca," "Cubana Be," and "Cubana

Bop," and Parker with "Night in Tunisia"—soon followed. And because they were greater musicians, they soon dominated. Nevertheless, Kenton was showing control of Afro-Cuban material when Gillespie's big band was still feeling for its feet, as can be heard by a track reissued on the RCA Victor vintage album *Dizzie Gillespie*. "Woody'n You" was recorded at just about the time—December, 1947—that Chano Pozo joined the group. Neither the jazzmen nor Pozo were yet accustomed to each other, with the result that the band lifts only in four-four passages, during which Pozo sounds stilted. By December, 1948, Gillespie's band was more at home in the idiom, as is shown by "Guarachi Guaro" on the same Victor album. (Chano Pozo was not on this, but another Cuban drummer, Sabu Martinez, was.) "Guarachi Guaro" is a much more integrated piece of music, even though "Woody'n You" has some fine moments.

As a matter of hindsight, it is clear that more credit was due to Chano Pozo and the other Cubans involved in the movement than they have received. A number of jazz musicians made good or acceptable Cuban-flavored numbers. Some of the most successful musically, though not the best known by a long chalk— "Lady Bird," "Jahbero," and "Symphonette"—were made with Chano Pozo by Fats Navarro, a fine trumpeter who died young. Navarro had some background in Caribbean sounds: Part Cuban, part Negro, and part Chinese, he came from Key West, Florida, a very Hispanic city. But the jazzmen on the whole were really only the cherry on the Afro-Cuban sundae, a fact demonstrated, I think, by one of the best of all recordings of the time, "Cubop City." This contained excellent solos by Howard McGhee on trumpet and Brew Moore on tenor, but it was Machito's band that made the record what it was. Even more significant, hundreds of recordings in the same style have since been made by obscure groups with no jazz "names" present.

The Afro-Cuban phase in jazz, which started in 1946–47, was more or less over by 1953. Since then there have been other outcroppings of Latinism in jazz, like the bossa nova craze (which was not really very Afro-American, since it united a very "white" Brazilian style with mostly white jazzmen) and groups like that of Herbie Mann. But these have been isolated or minor developments. More important things have been going on, as we shall see later, in the underground.

The off-and-on relationship between jazz and Caribbean music has been paralleled by a relationship between jazz and African music. This arose in the 1920's out of the general white perception of jazz as "jungle rhythms." Though the stereotype was a white product, many jazz musicians, being businessmen, played up to it. Duke Ellington in particular, when he had the resident band at the Cotton Club, provided "jungle" music (one of his records from the period is entitled "Jungle Fantasy") for the floor shows. The audiences of the time were hardly likely to know the difference between Bubber Miley's plunger-mute growls and African music. No doubt they were put vaguely in mind of lions, and the fact that lions do not live in jungles was not allowed to spoil their fun.

Serious interest in African music among jazz musicians began to develop just after, and to some extent in connection with, the decline of the Afro-Cuban phase. In London, Kenny Baker's Afro-Cubists actually used two African drummers, Ginger Johnson and Guy Warren. By the late 1950's there were quite a number of African musicians in the United States. Meanwhile, the black consciousness movement was turning people's minds toward Africa as a source of pride. The two elements fused. In particular, American drummers began to learn from their encounters with drummers of other traditions. Kenny Clarke had played alongside Chano Pozo for a while in the 1947 Gillespie big band. Later, Max Roach went to Haiti to study neo-African drumming styles, and like many other jazz musicians began to listen to the available recordings of African drumming. Roach, Art Blakey, and other drummers have been making a serious attempt to relate African drumming to their own tradition. Other jazz players have consciously turned to Africa for inspiration. Art Farmer made a disc in the mid-1950's called "Uam Uam," which is Mau Mau backward. Somewhat later, Coltrane recorded "Africa." There have been a number of jazz recordings of the Hispano musician Mongo Santamaria's "Afro-Blue"; and, of course, Ellington's *Liberian Suite* is a prime instance.

The degree of African-ness in these examples varied, of course. Sometimes it showed in little more than a name. But, whether through listening to records, or through the influence of the South African Miriam Makeba, who introduced Johannesburg pop styles to the United States, or merely through a feeling of mystical rapport, African music—or the idea of it—became important to the jazz scene in the mid-1960's.

Some jazz players have studied African music with great care, but the new African elements that have come through into jazz are relatively minor. Somehow, when black American musicians apply African music to their own music it becomes Afro-*American*. This appears to be because they are re-creating what produced Afro-American music in the first place: the fusion of African musical procedures and European (or largely European) concepts of measured time. The same has happened in Africa itself, where the encounter of Western and African music has produced new forms of Afro-American music—Afro-Afro-American, if you like. There is perhaps no way of blending these two very different basic theories of music, or at least no way that has yet been discovered, other than what has happened naturally over the last four hundred years. This is not a criticism of individual pieces that these experiments have produced. Like any music, they vary. In fact, it is worth looking at a few examples to see what has worked and what has not.

Art Blakey made a number of records in the mid-1960's that combined African and American components. One was a two-album set called *Holiday for Skins*, which combined U.S. musicians with Hispano musicians working in the United States. The session (except for a couple of numbers) was put together in the studio, and the sides were cut between 11:00 P.M. and 5:00 the next morning. As Blakey described the philosophy: "You just get good men together, and tell them to play. It works out." Alas, it did not, and the reasons are complex. One is that the two musical streams represented never really coalesced. Blakey's entries into the not always inspired but always well-integrated Hispano rhythm section tended to have a disruptive effect, and his cross-rhythms did not jell. This may be partly because he was playing a jazz drum kit with sticks and using cymbals too much, and partly, for sure, because Afro-Spanish rhythm sections are already highly functional, each man having his part, as in the African drum choirs. There is no doubt that their functions can be expanded, but for a drummer of another tradition, even the most brilliant (and Blakey is one of the best), simply to come along and play does not work. Another element in these tracks that reveals much about the failure so far to use African music meaningfully in a jazz context is the intermittent singing, such as Philly Joe Jones's vocal on "The Feast." Here, part of the problem is a failure to understand that the sort of slow African (or Cuban-African) chanted tune of this type is specifically part of a polyrhythmic music involving faster, highly complex drum accompaniment. "The Feast" puts the chanting first, and the drumming follows.

A later Blakey experiment was *The African Beat*, by Art Blakey and the Afro-Drum Ensemble. Here the numbers were all African or composed by Africans, and many of the musicians were African. The album contains some fine things (although again Blakey tends to be the odd man out; one might suppose that the drum kit is the problem, were it not for the fact that many modern African dance groups combine drum kit and conga drums). The numbers composed by Africans are all in the modern African styles, which we shall be discussing in the next chapter and which themselves contain Afro-American elements. Thus, a degree of common ground existed. Moreover, the presence of Africans in considerable force helped, especially that of the Nigerian Solomon G. Ilori, who did the singing. The embarrassing vocals of *Holiday for Skins* were absent from this record. The jazzman Yusuf Lateef showed a genius for gap-bridging. He was at his best in the highlife track "Ayiko Ayiko," to which his tenor playing made a major contribution, but even when he provided little more than a musical joke, as on his hand-piano solos, the joke was good. In fact, the only real drawback of *The African Beat* was the failure of Blakey's style to blend with the rest.

The jazzmen's interest in Africa is in an early stage. Ultimately, it makes musical sense. It is a logical part of the continuous long-term process of which the Afro-Cuban movement in the 1940's was an earlier manifestation. Moreover, though what has been done already is by no means African, much of it is good music. Big Black's *Elements of Now*, for instance, is a fine record bringing together strands of the Afro-*American* scene—big-band jazz, country-blues techniques, and so on. Big Black plays what is imprecisely termed an "African kongo drum," and the one "African"-titled number, "Burundi Pose," is as American as the rest. But such facts do not really matter. Ultimately it is the quality of the music that counts, not the label it wears.

The same applies to *Home Lost and Found*, by Wali and the Afro-Caravan. This owes a good deal to Cuba. Mongo Santamaria's "Afro-Blue" is one of the tracks, another is called "Guaguanco Stroll," and the drumming is basically a rather gentle Cuban-style. One track, "Journey to Mecca," which bears no resemblance whatsoever to Arab music, is agreeable enough, if a little camp. The over-all sound of the disc is somewhat reminiscent of Herbie Mann. One thing it is not, is African. In fact the only objectionable feature about the record is the liner notes, where a claim that the sound is "all African" forms part of a musico-mystagogic spiel that would be more obnoxious if it were not so naïve.

A more cynical-seeming exploitation of African music is found in *Accent on Africa*, by the Cannonball Adderley Quintet. The sleeve notes make no claim that Adderley is playing African music, but suggest that the album is meant to "show the influence." It contains every absurdity, from Hollywood-style strings to pseudo-knowledgeable titles, at least one of which is nonsense. "Gunjah" is explained as "the name of a Swahili intoxicant, similar to hashish or marijuana. It has a creeping quality, and seems to develop slowly in intensity." The Swahili for hash is *bangi* or *bengi*, from *bhang*. There is no *gunjah* in Swahili, though there is *ganja*, which means "the palm of the hand." *Ganja* meaning pot is a Jamaican word. This type of recording represents little more than an attempt to cash in on interest in Africa. Nevertheless, the experiments go on, not only in jazz but also in pop crazes like the Watusi. And behind the majority faddism, identity-seeking, and uncomplicated enjoyment of a passing novelty, there are smaller groups on both sides of the ocean that are deepening their knowledge of the two musics. A key role is

played by African musicians in the United States, men like
Ilori and the South African Hugh Masekela, with his group, the
Union of South Africa.

Meanwhile, another fusion has been going on in North America, almost without drawing any comment, to produce the music
known on the Spanish-language radio stations as "latin jazz." It
is a version of the "Afro-Cuban jazz" of the 1940's, but in reverse,
so to speak. There is a wide range of latin jazz styles, but the
most basic starts from the Cuban (later Spanish Caribbean) two-
part *son*-rumba format. The first part, containing what Euro-
America would recognize as "the tune," moves toward jazz simply in that the melody line and its phrasing show more jazz (or
anyway, North American) influence. The second section, improvised and more percussive, often called the *montuno,* allows for
even more overt mingling in the form of jazz solos, usually of a
boppish tinge. Latin jazz is, inevitably, a country without fron-
tiers. Cuban music has been using jazz material ever since the
days of the Septeto Nacional, whose trumpet work was definitely
jazz-influenced, as opposed to some of the earlier work of the
Septeto Habanero, which enshrined something of the nineteenth-
century military band cornet solo approach. But on the whole,
the Hispano-Caribbean groups that either moved to the United
States or were formed there, in any event those catering to the
young Hispano-Americans of the big U.S. cities—Los Angeles,
Miami, and particularly, perhaps, "el barrio del Bronx"—have
moved toward, and in fact mostly achieved, a blend very near
what the Kentons and Gillespies were aiming at. Indeed, the two
movements approached the same goal—whether a conscious or
an unconscious goal—from opposite directions. The goal, of
course, was the reuniting of the two major strains of Afro-
American music: the Caribo–South American, whose regional
differences do not hide an over-all stylistic unity; and the U.S.
jazz-blues-gospel syndrome.

Leaving aside the big *gringo-latino* groups, such as the Cugat
and (after its earliest days) Perez Prado orchestras, which do not
represent much of anything, one group that bridges the gap most
clearly is that of Mongo Santamaria. Santamaria's group has followed a career pattern common to many others in all fields of

Afro-American music: It has never again been so good as when its first discs hit the public. Nevertheless, Santamaria at his best shows some skill in interweaving the two strands. Many of his compositions have been picked up by jazz musicians, notably "Afro-Blue," which has been recorded by at least seventeen other ensembles, including Wali and the Afro-Caravan and John Coltrane (who has been credited with the composition on at least one occasion, as too often happens in the music world). "Para Ti" is another Santamaria number that has been popular among both Afro-Hispanic and jazz musicians.

Some of Santamaria's better tracks show quite plainly the continuing fusion of jazz and what I am going from now on to call Cuban elements. He uses jazz solos much more freely than the more orthodox Cuban groups. While the latter stick to the traditional trumpet, Santamaria makes frequent use of saxes. His "Para Ti" is an example of what musicians with a foot in both traditions, in this case the Cuban tenorist and violinist José "Chombo" Silua, can do. Santamaria's use of jazz-style trumpets is illustrated on "Pito Pito," and there is very good sax work on the old Afro-Cuban standby, "Manteca" (for the strengths and weaknesses of Santamaria's group, it's worth listening to this together with the Gillespie version). He himself lived in the Jesus Maria district of Havana (which preserves many African customs) until he was twenty, and he is a drummer. He followed the path of many Hispano-American musicians, having played with Perez Prado, Tito Puente, and Cal Tjader in the United States before setting out on his own. Since his national success with "Watermelon Man," Santamaria has shown signs of going increasingly *gringo-latino*. It may simply be that the inner flame of the Cuban styles vanishes with too much success. His "Mazacote" is a piece for percussion lasting more than ten minutes, played in a reasonably authentic manner (there is a little muttering from piano and front-line instruments, but it is largely incidental). Somehow, the number never catches. Back in the old days in Jesus Maria, the plaster would have been raining down off the ceiling at the end.

Johnny Pacheco's band also represents the fairly Cuban-orthodox end of latin jazz. I have already discussed Pacheco's early,

charanga-francesa-style discs. Even these showed latin jazz tendencies in places, including really superlative alley-fiddle touches.
Pacheco's group was in fact responsible for a new rhythm, a New
York–born Latin beat that had its moment of glory and even was
picked up by a few African bands. It was called the pachanga, a
name Bronx teen-agers are said to have formed as an acronym
from *Pach*eco char*anga*. Later he dropped the fiddles-and-flute
charanga formula and turned to the vocal, trumpet, piano, and
percussion lineup of the Afro-Cuban *conjunto* (as in the album
La Perfecta Combinacion and the later *Compadres*).

Pacheco's later music aligns him with a wide array of U.S.
Cuban groups, going back to the mambo bands of the 1940's, of
which the most famous was probably Machito. These ensembles
(which now play mostly various forms of rumba, especially
guaguancónes) have a style combining plenty of percussion,
chanted rhythmic and highly repetitive vocals (often consisting of
just one or two lines in call-and-response form), and a mixture of
trumpet ensemble riffs and jazz-type solos. Call-and-response
often will be set up between the solo voice and trumpet ensemble or between solo trumpet and group vocals. Interestingly, to a
large extent these numbers, especially in their *montuno* section,
are defined, like their African counterparts, by the choral response. But the most common form (except in the guaguancó,
which usually has a solo vocal in the first section) consists of a
chorus of one line repeated, then a two- or four-line solo "verse"
repeated ad lib until the onset of the *montuno*.

Jazz influences in latin jazz are various. Some of Mongo Santamaria's tracks contain baritone sax work reminiscent of Leo
Parker. Willie Rodrigues and other trumpeters favor a style
rather like Conto Candoli's but show a lot of Gillespie at times.
Both trumpeters worked in an Afro-Cuban vein in the past, and
perhaps were early personal influences. But Latin musicians are
individuals like any others, when they are not forced into playing
stereotypes by an ignorant public. You are just as likely to hear a
saxist who has been listening to Coltrane as to Hodges or
Hawkins.

Latin jazz is a formulaic style, of course, and (like any music)
it "sounds all the same" until one's ears are attuned to it. But in

fact it fulfills the important role of a framework for improvisation and variation, and it is no more "all the same" than the twelve-bar blues, the New Orleans jazz ensemble pattern, or the later jazz head-arrangement-with-string-of-solos formula. Within the latin jazz mode there is a good deal of variety. Rodrigues, a good trumpeter, includes more solos of higher quality than many others. The Allegre All Stars used a free-wheeling approach with a lot of solo work. The group of Kent Gomez, a young pianist, is rather consciously hip and incorporates a high percentage of Americanisms, especially from the rhythm-and-blues/rock field. Gomez is also capable at times of a development of the all-percussion build-up over several minutes, using piano and percussion.

The piano, actually, has a past in Cuban music. It used to improvise what were called "floreos" in the old charanga francesa. When the "*estilo* feeling" was the rage among the middle class, the piano supplied sub-Chopin, sub-Debussy touches. In U.S. Latin groups of the early 1950's the piano was brought pretty much to the fore, but its role was not well defined, and it tended to supply a heavy *gringo-latino* element. Then bands like Pacheco's and Gomez's hit on giving the piano a function in the ensemble similar to that held by the guitar in the early *son* groups: playing rhythmic patterns analogous to a barrelhouse piano left hand. The takeover of a guitar role was not an overnight phenomenon, any more than it was in the blues. It was important, because it freed the piano from its somewhat romantic earlier contribution and allowed it to play a variety of parts extending to percussive and chordal, while continuing the old "floreos" tradition where appropriate.

Gomez, in particular, used jazz and blues elements in his piano style, just as he sings English phrases along with the Spanish. The significance of this, as of the whole U.S. latin jazz movement, is quite different from that of earlier U.S. influences in Cuba and elsewhere. Those were foreign influences, naturalized as they may have become. But Hispano-Americans born in the United States are beginning to make up a larger proportion of the Latin musicians playing there, and they use blues, rock, and Cuban elements together because they are all part of their own heritage.

When Joe Cuba's group played numbers like "Bang Bang," the result may not have been sensational, but it was logical enough—a Latin rock, rather than a rocked Latin. Earlier, on the West Coast, Richie Valens had produced a Chicano-rock style that spoke to young Hispano-Americans of a Mexican background. The evidence of this new, joint music is widespread. The most recent, and on the whole a highly successful, example was Santana, with its FM rock/latin jazz blends. But the U.S. Latin/rock blends so far have been peripheral. Much more characteristic is a style unified out of Cuban and jazz ingredients: big-band brass, very heavy, if a little inflexible, with plenty of rhythm, from a band with a lineup of four brass, piano, bass, and percussion.

It seems likely that the existence of a huge, young, increasingly group-conscious public of both Spanish-Caribbean and North American culture may help bring about major new directions in Afro-American music. Temporarily, at least, each of the various current Afro-American styles has to some extent painted itself into a corner. Jazz enthusiasts, like the devotees of most "classical" musics, are a small minority. Soul has become the most commercial of the black musics, though there are still musicians of a caliber to rise above it (even Aretha Franklin, in her best album for years, *Spirit in the Dark,* has begun to repeat herself, which is a bad sign). The blues, though still very much alive, may be gently passing away.

Latin jazz until now has been too specialized to appeal outside its own market except as a novelty, or in a very watered-down form. But the Latin musicians have been engaged in bridging the *musical* gap between the Northern and Southern Afro-American concepts, just as—rather tentatively so far—the jazz musicians have been trying to bring together jazz and African music. There has been a gradual drawing together of musical threads in the Americas over the last thirty years, and more especially over the last ten. But the key lies in Africa, and what has been happening in Africa in recent years is as significant as anything on the western side of the Atlantic.

PART THREE

The Music of Post- colonial Africa

9 THE MODERN
URBAN POPULAR
STYLES

New World music was born of the encounter between African and European concepts of music, which intermingled, interwove, and fought their way into a relationship that produced two major new contributions to the world. There was, however, another area in which Western and African music came into contact and produced a series of new styles. And that was Africa itself.

As we have seen, Africa has never been isolated from the rest of the world. Its music has taken in aspects of other traditions as the circumstances have dictated, sometimes extensively, sometimes in small degrees. The foremost outside influence was Arabic, or at all events Islamic, but others may have preceded it. One school of thought, in fact, holds that the xylophone came to Africa via two large-scale immigrations of peoples from Oceania a couple of thousand years B.C., and that other musical and nonmusical cultural elements widespread in certain parts of Africa started in the Pacific. There is also a theory stating that, on the contrary, Oceania has been influenced from Africa. Either way, the arguments for contact between the two areas are impressive.

The influence with which this chapter is concerned, however, is much more recent. It began with the contact between Europeans and Africans either before or during the colonial era and has resulted in the development in this century—particularly in the last thirty years—of a number of what I shall call modern urban popular styles. Music in these styles is played on Western or a mixture of African and Western instruments and contains material from both cultures. The styles exist in most parts of Africa, but the best known and most highly developed are the highlife of English-speaking West Africa, Congolese dance music, and the styles of South Africa. These last are perhaps best known in the United States because of the work of Miriam Makeba and Hugh Masekela, though in different ways both present music slightly different from the straight township pop forms.

There has always been popular music in Africa, of course, and there are types of African music showing no European influence, or almost none, that are both modern and popular. "Traditional" musical modes, in the words of the Nigerian composer Akin Euba, "not only flourish, but are the main musical fare of most Africans." This is probably true of Africa as a whole, though less so perhaps of East, East Central, and Southern Africa than of the West and the Congo-Angola region.

Most discussions of modern African pop music have concentrated on one or another of the main forms, but despite sharp contrasts in styles between one area and another, it is clear that certain processes have taken place in much the same way everywhere. These are, not necessarily in chronological order:

1. The increasing accessibility to Africans of music from other parts of the world, through the radio and phonograph records
2. The introduction and, more important, the availability of Western instruments, in particular very cheap guitars
3. The invention of new forms of popular music by young people

Basically, and obviously, (3) was influenced by (1) and (2). This did not happen in the same way everywhere, nor at the same time. Apparently random happenings came together in one place and stayed separate in others. A widespread, dynamic, and confusing situation was complicated by several factors. First, what was taking place was usually disapproved of by people who might have been in a position to analyze it. Second, it was only partially documented in some of its phases by commercial phonograph records. Third, most anthropologists and musicologists regarded it until recently as a disaster rather than an interesting phenomenon of social change. As a result, the evidence, which consists mainly of people's often inaccurate memories of something to which they did not pay much mind at the time, is only just beginning to be sifted.

Roughly speaking, African *traditional* popular music can be divided into two kinds: group or communal music—made, at least in West Africa, by the basic complement of three drummers plus other percussion, and produced for an audience of dancer-singers —and more personal music, in which one or maybe two people play largely for their own self-expression and amusement. An example of the more private music might be a man singing about his troubles with his wife to an audience of two or three fellow-husbands and accompanying himself on a hand-piano. One of his listeners might be tapping a couple of sticks, and another clapping gently. These categories shade into each other at times, but mostly they produced different types of music.

The appearance of modern African pop music involved both forms. The change was symbolized, when it was not actually precipitated, by the guitar. There has been dispute about when the European guitar—that is to say, either the modern six-stringed, so-called Spanish guitar or any of the variants that existed before it became standardized—reached Africa. The most likely date would seem to lie between the sixteenth and twentieth centuries, and I do not mean that facetiously. It is inconceivable that the Portuguese should not have introduced the guitar into Mozambique and Angola early on, and yet in Ghana (formerly Gold Coast) good guitarists were rare enough in the 1930's to attract a good deal of admiration. Besides, there is a good deal of difference between the presence of a few instruments and the use of the guitar by Africans in any numbers. There is no evidence of the *customary* use of the European guitar, or any version of it, before the twentieth century, with the possible exception of the *ramkie,* a guitar-like instrument found in the Cape area of South Africa. There are a few examples of West African instruments influenced by European guitars, such as a hybrid form of guitar-fiddle photographed in the Congo. But there is no sign that the European details on these (mainly a matter of guitar-like tuning pegs and a flat finger-board, as opposed to the normal African stick-like finger-board and tuning rings) are old.

The adoption of the guitar by musicians all over Africa led to one of two main generic styles of modern pop music. The first was typically played by a group consisting of one or two guitars and some sort of percussion, almost always a bottle tapped with a knife to give a high chinking note, which filled the role of the *gankogui* in Ewe music or the *claves* in Cuban; by a single guitar; or by a guitar with another instrument, usually African, with or without percussion. The second style came about through the addition of European instruments (usually, at first, guitar) to a traditional percussion dance ensemble. In so far as such categories have any significance in African music, the first was a "song" or "listening" style, in which the words were important, and the second a dance style.

The music played by the small guitar-based groups varied widely. The essential factor for change at first was that the European guitar gave an African string-player a much larger number of notes than he had had before. The big Guinean *seron* has nineteen strings, and the Senegalese *kora* twenty-one. Most African stringed instruments have far fewer: The Luya *lidungu,* from Kenya, has six, for example. The important factor is not the number of strings, however, but the fact that very few African plucked instruments are stopped. That is to say, each string produces only one note, like a traditional European harp string. In most parts, stringed instruments have played a semi-rhythmic role, in which a small choice of notes is not a limitation. But music suitable for an instrument with half a dozen notes or so and no fretting system clearly wastes much of the capability of the guitar, which can produce more than a hundred notes. Therefore, one important factor in the development of the new music was the greater range of the guitar.

Some African musicians who took up the guitar began by playing on it patterns much like the ones they had played on whatever stringed instruments were traditional for them. It is reasonable to assume that this was, in fact, the first step for most musicians. As a result, there are recordings from all over Africa of tribal songs accompanied by guitar, and often bottle-and-knife, of an extremely traditional kind. Many Africans (who, like most people anywhere, tend to notice the song rather than the style) appear to regard this type of music as traditional, though of course it is really only partly so. A good example is a recording made in Sierra Leone of a Mandingo song to Sumailia, accompanied by a guitar and a traditional *kora* and sung by two women in a traditional style.

A version of guitar music that is less obviously traditional but is still not particularly "Westernized" stems from the beggars frequently found in West Africa, musicians who often have highly individual styles. They are a species of *griot* but lack the courtly and dynastic associations of the more exalted *griots.* Being professionals, they have tended to show personal characteristics. A Nigerian famous in the streets of Lagos in the early 1950's, Benjamin "Kokoro" Aderounmu, was an example. Kokoro developed an intensely personal style, accompanying himself with a talking drum. Kokoro's music did not sound "traditional," because he created it out of a blend of traditional and personal elements. But it *was* traditional, in that the creation of individual styles using traditional material has always existed in parts of Africa. A new form of guitar music grew up when musicians began using the guitar to do what Kokoro had done with a traditional instrument. This procedure has been most common in the regions where strolling musicians are still numerous.

The same process in a different form was spectacularly illustrated by a Congolese guitarist who became popular for a short time throughout East Africa. A clerk called Mwenda Jean Bosco was recorded by Hugh Tracey in 1951, and his best-known song, "Masanga," is still popular some twenty years later. Consciously or not, Bosco transferred certain characteristic elements of his own tribe's traditional music onto the new instrument.

Specifically, he took rhythms and melodic patterns used on hand-pianos and played them on the guitar. The short, repeated, tumbling, rather bell-like phrases and the trick of using a phrase early as a secondary theme, then making it the major theme later on, are typical of the hand-piano music of the Sanga tribe, to which Bosco belongs. Just how close his guitar was to the hand-piano playing of his area can only be grasped by comparison. Fortunately, there are examples of Sanga hand-piano in Hugh Tracey's immense series of records of African music, *Sounds of Africa,* and "Masanga" was issued on the Decca *Music of Africa* series, also overseen by Tracey.

Besides the guitar–hand-piano links, "Masanga" showed some interesting features in the singing. The general quality of the vocal line was indigenous, with short phrases, a descending tune, and a fairly straightforward rhythm against which the complications of the guitar rhythm were set off, somewhat as if the voice were accompanying the guitar rather than the other way around (a common tendency in earlier African music). But Bosco departed from local tradition by singing in a kind of semi-Swahili, apparently to explore the freedoms offered by melodies unrestricted by tonal considerations.

A vital factor in African music from the 1930's on (and "Masanga" was recorded in 1951) was the availability of foreign records. Naturally, many African musicians copied what they liked from these. At the opposite end of the scale from the semi-tribal "folk" songs were many recordings that were almost straight translations of foreign styles. I have on tape an old 78 rpm record in Venda, a South African language, that is a lift from Jimmy Rodgers, the white American singer of the 1920's and 1930's. The language is Venda, but the vocal tune and the guitar style are pure Rodgers. I also have a Kenya disc of *circa* 1952 that gives a highly lugubrious version of the Inkspots' style.

Much the greater part of African guitar music, wherever it came from, falls between the two extremes of imitation Western and traditional-on-a-new-instrument. At the same time that Bosco was recording "Masanga," Nono Ngoi and Anastase Kabongo, also Congolese, were recording equally semitribal music in a very different style, one more reminiscent of East African lute-playing. Also at the same time another couple, Patrice Ilunga and Victor Misomba, were recording music based on imported Cuban records, with all the various Cuban characteristics transposed for guitar, which was the acoustic-guitar ancestor of the Congolese dance music we shall be discussing later. Mozambique examples of this acoustic style, which the Kenyans call "dry" guitar, show slight (never strong) Portuguese elements. More particularly, there are traits that are apparently Brazilian, whereas the common Latin influence (direct or indirect) in other areas is practically always Cuban, except in the early days in the Congo, where there was some biguine influence (the Congo being Belgian, and thus French-language, administered).

One contribution to dry guitar music was local and traditional. The other was not simply "Western," but Afro-American. In the Congo, and in West Africa to a lesser extent, it was Cuban, while in South Africa it was jazz. There is no mystery about why different Afro-American styles were influential in different parts of Africa. In West Africa and the Congo, Cuban music was returning with interest something that had largely come from there anyway, and so there was the most natural of affinities. South African traditional music is quite different from West African and Congo-Angolan. As a generalization, it tends toward rhythmic complexity of singing voices over a regular beat; its polyrhythms come from the voices, which vary their accentuation relative to the basic rhythm. This is remarkably like jazz, especially the 1930's and 1940's music of Count Basie and others, who riffed and soloed against a rock-solid four-four beat. Another important influence was inter-African. Kenya, for example, has an extremely strong tradition of dry guitar-playing and singing, which appears to owe a good deal to imported records of the early Congolese musicians. But the plain fact is that a wide range of unmistakably African guitar musics exists, and although foreign influences can be discerned—some strong, some weak—the national styles are overriding: One can never mistake a Kenyan record for a Congolese, let alone a Nigerian.

As I have said, there were popular percussion bands in all parts of Africa where drums were a salient factor in local music. They were mostly cooperative enterprises, sharing expenses and earnings, much like the semiprofessional musicians who have supplied the bulk of rural dance music in most parts of the world at all times. Some, like the bands of the Gogo people of Tanzania, which performed complex forms called *nindo*, were connected with musical associations. The associations provide musicians, dancers, club atmosphere, and nonreligious ritual and inculcate local pride by competition with nearby similar groups. A highly developed version is the Malawian chiwoda, a modern dance form influenced by the European-style military marching and counter-marching of the old King's African Rifles. Chiwoda, a women's dance (there is a men's equivalent), involves a total commitment, including heavy rehearsal, submission to the discipline of leaders, and obedience to rules. It is curiously and significantly reminiscent of certain "nation" and post-"nation" dancing groups of the New World, which tended to develop—as with the Brazilian marchas—around a joint military-carnival spirit involving dance and parade. The Chiwoda allows for intense competition, both group against group and between individual dancers; but chiwoda groups also act like many Afro-American organizations with musical connections, including, significantly, a definite role played by chiwoda members at the death of a companion or a companion's relative. A particular chiwoda group may also be hired for communal work.

Chiwoda had something of a parallel in the Gold Coast. A form of the dance called concoma, developed in the Kumasi district in the early 1940's, entailed a sort of semimilitary parading, with well-drilled squads of dancing-marching teen-agers in special uniforms. B. Casely-Hayford, of Ghana Television, has collected a large number of oral reports about early developments in modern Ghanaian dance music. They give evidence that the word "concoma" was in fact applied to several different dances, rather as happened with the samba in Brazil. At all events, there are a number of explanations for its origin, varying according to region. Casely-Hayford sees concoma as adding an element to highlife, that is, as a parallel or subsidiary form. On the other hand, Edna Smith reported in *African Music* in 1962 that most Ghanaians considered concoma a forerunner of highlife. One writer claimed that highlife was concoma instrumentalized.

Nketia thought highlife grew up as a street dance, whereas Casely-Hayford seems to feel that, in accordance with its name, it started among the African middle class. Nketia, in another article in *African Music,* put the beginning of highlife in the 1890's, while Casely-Hayford estimates the second decade of the twentieth century.

It is clear that European influence existed in the Gold Coast in the nineteenth century. The Basel Mission is said to have introduced brass band instruments there in mid-century. Casely-Hayford also suggests that the presence of the West India Regiment in the 1860's may have introduced West Indian forms to the Gold Coast. But the underlying suggestion (also made elsewhere) that calypso had much to do with highlife at that stage is unlikely: As we have seen, calypso was only beginning its own development in the 1860's. There *was* a major calypso influence in West Africa, but it came much later.

The theory that highlife originated with the West Indian garrisons of the late nineteenth century seems to be part of a Sierra Leonean claim to parentage of the style. Some Sierra Leoneans believe that the large West Indian garrison in Freetown brought the style to Africa and that all the Ghanaians did was get it on record first. This kind of argument almost certainly results from the fact that there was no single original "highlife," only a wide range of dances of differing names and similar natures, for which highlife was always—or rapidly became—a vague generic label.

This is not to deny that Krio Sierra Leoneans, being the descendants of freed slaves, may have had some Afro-Americanisms in their music. But the historical circumstances make it more likely that the gathering together of freedmen of a number of tribes in an African enclave produced a generalized "neo-African" music, through a process similar to what happened in the New World. It is believed that the maningo music of Sierra Leone was brought there from America, but the Congolese maringa form has been associated with maningo, causing a confusion of names and styles that makes this difficult to verify. Besides, the fact that the Mandingo people live partly in Sierra Leone suggests that the dance may be derived from something of theirs. Another form, the gumbay, has been attributed to the

West Indians (though Caribbean writers trace their versions back to Africa!). Such attributions are shaky because: (1) African music is powerful and quite capable of creating its own blends; (2) the West Indians were in West Africa for a short time long ago; (3) other transitory influences have rapidly been absorbed by African music; and (4) the various European elements were present over a continuous period before, during, and after the emergence of modern West African dance music.

In the light of all this, in fact, there seems to be no good reason for accepting a West Indian effect on highlife of any significance at all, except for the much later calypso craze beginning in the 1940's. It is more logical to assume that the encounter of similar factors from two musical cultures—West African and British—in the West Indies and in West Africa produced somewhat similar results independently.

By the late 1940's highlife had become a highly developed form or group of forms. In Ghana its basic structure is the guitar band, consisting usually of two guitars, often with a bass or bass guitar, percussion instruments, and of course vocal. The style-setting band of this type in Ghana was formed by E. K. Nyama, a self-taught musician who went professional in 1953. E. K.'s Band, as it was called, was more venturesome than most guitar bands, which were apt to copy each other inordinately.

Highlife in Ghana tended to divide between the guitar bands, which are still the most typical, and groups that added front-line instruments. It is the latter groups that have shown the most "Western" influence, often brought in to supply ingredients where Ghanaian tradition was lacking in precedents. Thus, Ghanaian highlife still shows signs of the borrowed arranging styles of popular British sweet dance bands, such as that of Joe Loss. The band of E. T. Mensah, and particularly Mensah's trumpet playing, owes something to another sweet British musician, Eddie Calvert, whose muted version of "Cherry Pink and Apple Blossom White" is echoed frequently on Mensah's records from the 1950's to the 1970's. The other main foreign influences on Ghanaian highlife are Afro-American—and logical. Trumpeters and trombonists are affected by jazz, and flutists by Afro-Cuban flute-playing of the sort found in Johnny Pacheco's first bands.

Different styles of jazz have been favored at different times. In the late 1950's one heard little that was particularly modern, because the local radio did not feature it. But a record put out in 1966, "Awere How Be Kumi," has trombone solos whose stylistic original was obviously J. J. Johnson.

Various subforms of highlife have been popular from time to time, including the slow highlife, also called the blues at one time (it bore no relation to black U.S. music). But by far the longest lasting "foreign" music, played in both Ghana and Nigeria for at least fifteen years, was calypso. There are any number of examples of African calypsos, ranging from professional imitations to very localized versions. On the whole, they tend to modify the rhythm in the direction of highlife, to simplify the lyrics, and to make them more repetitive (that is, re-Africanize them).

A minor form, which falls between calypso and highlife, is the pidgin highlife, sung in a local English-based language. It is freed from the melodic restrictions that the tonal African languages tend to place on music, but otherwise it resembles highlife.

Highlife lyrics, like all African pop lyrics, deal with—besides love—subjects similar to those of traditional music. There are songs of praise and insult, topical songs, and a very popular formula, especially in Nigeria, that makes use of traditional proverbs to weave new lyrics.

Stylistically, highlife is characterized by a low degree of interest in harmony and a high rhythmic interest. It is quite experimental and at the same time tradition-based. One of the earlier postwar groups, the West African Rhythm Brothers (formed in 1946) chose its personnel from traditional musicians and trained them in Western instruments, so that traditional or at least indigenous elements remained strong. Highlife is also intertribal, at least to the degree permitted by the multiplicity of languages. A Nigerian band, Victor Ola-Iya's Cool Cats, in 1962 had Yoruba, Ibo, Hausa, and other tribes represented among its musicians, and E. K.'s Band at one time or another employed players from most Ghanaian tribes. The same was true of nearly all, if not all, highlife bands from Nigeria as well as Ghana. Indeed, one of the points about highlife is that the groups contrived to combine constant renewal of contact with traditional material, "modern" trends in pop music, and intertribalism. Thus, Sir Victor Uwaifo's band is highly polished, with a good deal of soul-type showmanship, yet Uwaifo introduced the Calabari *akwete* rhythm into highlife and uses a traditional xylophone in his lineup.

A huge vogue for James Brown recently developed in West Africa, and it is said that soul is killing highlife. However, I was told in 1966 that Congo music had already killed highlife. What appears to happen in all musical fields is that a new fashion will emerge, apparently sweep the field, then give way to another new fad, leaving only a few useful stylistic traits behind. Meanwhile, the local music goes on, at every moment seemingly about to be swept aside, but always surviving.

The soul phenomenon, which is common to most parts of Africa, has produced some slightly odd results in places, just as did all the other imported elements before becoming acclimated. But the digestion process is under way. A Gambian band, the Super Eagles, plays versions of James Brown and Aretha Franklin hits in a manner audiences often prefer to the originals, which indicates re-Africanization rather than incompetence in the variations. The same can be said of any number of soul pieces by African bands. A most striking, and rather unexpected, example occurs on a tape made by a BBC staffer in Ethiopia of an Ethiopian soul group, with the typical electric bass line but a strongly Ethiopian singing style.

It will be seen that the modern dance music of Nigeria and Ghana presents a picture of broad similarity with considerable local variations. One such variation was the Yoruba juju, a guitar music with rather more obvious traditional content than Ghanaian guitar music. The intensely individual sound of juju stems less from the guitar work—which falls into the general highlife-like pattern of simple chording and single-string-picking—than from the use of Yoruba percussion, such as talking drums, and from a singing style akin to the highly distinctive traditional Yoruba style. Many Nigerians date the beginning of juju in the early

1960's, when the bandleader I. K. Dairo became famous. But it would be more accurate to say that Dairo altered and perhaps "modernized" juju, and widened its appeal. A less famous juju musician, Tunde Nightingale, appears to have started playing a very similar music in 1944–45, though paradoxically it was the later man, Dairo, who introduced the traditional percussion and *gbedu* rhythm. Tunde Nightingale claims that juju is tradition-ally a Yoruba party music. Again, there seem to be problems of naming. Whether Nightingale was juju or pre-juju depends largely on what is meant by juju.

Dairo turned juju into a music that went beyond the Yoruba tribe, and yet he also incorporated more Yoruba traditional ma-terial. This is less of a paradox than it seems, because his changes made a rich music out of a rather thin one. He did so in two ways. First, he made his music reflect its own tradition more truly by a bit of research: "Many older people have come to ask me for the meanings of some of the words I use in my songs and the majority of my Yoruba listeners are baffled at some of the incantations, verses and expressions I use. . . . I have to travel around, talking to old men who know a lot about such things: I then go back home to turn them into modern music." And sec-ond, he designed his modern music to appeal to non-Yoruba: "What I usually do is to concentrate more on the rhythm, the time and, most of all, the beat. . . . To make my music appeal, I have introduced various beats and tempos to suit the different tribes." Dairo's procedure in fact reflects an abiding dualism in African music of all kinds. He has produced music that is new but that asserts its newness in a framework of the past, thus sup-plying both novelty and continuity to a people who value both.

It has been claimed that juju evolved from a music called *kokoma*, which was played in the Lagos region in the early 1950's, using a basis of vocals, three drums, and the simple Yoruba hand-piano. The talking drum is said to have been in-troduced into *kokoma* in the mid-1950's. These events are shrouded in confusion, which appears to result from the use of different names in different areas for similar developments. Two things are certain: Dairo was a major figure in juju (he introduced the accordion into it); and recent juju groups, like that of Ebenezer Obey, have been heavily influenced by modern Congolese guitar styles.

Congo music, in fact, has affected to some extent every other African pop style in the last ten years. Indeed, its pan-African influence goes back almost to its own beginnings. Congolese modern modes of music, like those of other countries in Africa, can be divided into the guitar-song and dance-band forms. The most immediately noticeable fact about Congo dance music since the late 1950's is its heavy debt to Afro-Cuban music, specifically its rhythm, derived from various versions of the rumba. In an article in *Africa Report*, Pierre Kazadi states that what he calls the "rumba" style began in the early 1950's with a dance called the maringa, which used traditional or "folk" tunes backed by a rectangular drum, a hand-piano, and a bottle playing the *claves* part. Soon new instruments began to be added, and a period of great musical adventurousness set in, when lineups such as fiddle, guitar, drum, and two hand-pianos, or even kazoos, were recorded. In 1953, a group was recorded in Stanleyville that played biguines using two clarinets, but in general wind instruments seem to have been rare in that period. There was even then a clear preference for foreign elements that corresponded in some way to local ones. A purported biguine, for instance, might in fact be played with a basic rhythm of fast triplets. On the other hand, some groups were as imitative as they could manage to be of the biguines they copied. A feature that seems to have become standardized from Cuban music at the time, in Congo pop and in East Africa as well, was the use of parallel thirds for most vocals. Wherever found in modern pop music, it appears to be a sign of Congolese influence.

By the late 1950's, a period of consolidation was under way. The biguines had dropped out, and the definitive foreign ingredient was Cuban, or at least Afro-Cuban (the early discs of Congo music using fiddles may well be a response to such groups as the Orquesta Aragón and the Cuban charanga ensembles). Another influence—inferred from the jazz-style entries to solos that soon evolved—may have been Cab Calloway, whose records were very popular with Belgians in the Congo of the 1940's.

Perhaps the most crucial event in Congo pop music, possibly even more crucial than in highlife, was the adoption of electric guitars. Until about 1958, Congo bands were playing in a fairly skilled Cuban-derived style, in which elements of an original guitar technique (going back to the music of Patrice Ilunga and others in the early 1950's) and an Africanization of melody lines were offset by fairly Cuban rhythm lines and sax or clarinet influence. The electrification of the guitar brought into prominence the Congolese guitar style, which had already shown its originality (and power to modify other African styles). This style, of immense force and flexibility, at first sounds somewhat Latin American, but there is actually nothing like it in the New World. It seems to have grown partly from localizing techniques like Bosco's, and partly from the playing on guitar of lines that, in Cuban music, were brass or sax lines. Certainly Congolese records from the early 1960's, like "Afrika Mokili Mobimba," suggest this essentially Afro-Cuban brass sound in their guitar work.

The choice of the rumba, a strongly neo-African form in its Cuban version, had several important results. First, the rumba has built-in possibilities for improvisation in its second section, or *montuno*. This gave Congo lead guitarists a chance to develop their music and to shine when they did so. Moreover, the use of a rhythm that was basically generalized African but was not associated with any one part of Africa, as was highlife, accounted to some degree at least for the remarkable spread of Congo music. Highlife never caught on in East Africa, because it was too *West* African. The rumba—at least as reinterpreted by Central Africans—was, paradoxically, less foreign to East Africans.

Stylistically, Congo music shows a number of interesting features (apart, that is, from the development of a highly original and influential guitar style). One of them is its way of getting around the melodically limiting factor of a tonal language without disrupting a two-voice vocal using basically parallel-third harmony. The first voice follows the speech-tone pattern, while the second voice departs from it. This resolved a problem faced by earlier Congolese musicians, who had either to ignore the tone-patterns, with often peculiar results, or allow themselves to be restricted by them (though "restricted" could be the wrong word; the tone patterns may well have helped Congolese groups to break away quickly from overly Cuban-style melodies).

The social background of modern African pop musicians is interesting. They spring neither from the elite (though they may become members of the elite if successful) nor, on the whole, from the peasantry. The famous Congolese musician Rochereau was a minor civil servant in education, and Jacques Kibembe, who founded the Orchestre Sinza, was a bicycle repairman. Docteur Nico, another prominent figure in music, was a technical college teacher.

Before dealing with the last of the major modern style-areas of Africa—South Africa—it is worth returning to East Africa for a look at two countries that have been deeply affected by Congo music while retaining an individuality of manner not achieved by the rest of French-speaking Africa (with the possible exception of Cameroun).

Tanzanian dance music in the early 1960's, as represented by groups like the Cuban Marimba Band with Salim Abdulla, showed strong Congolese influence, but with an Arab element due to the Islamic civilization of the coast. Certain pop discs were almost purely Afro-Arab in singing style, and Salim Abdulla once brought off the stylistic *coup* of using an Arab-style bridge between one Congo-type section and another. Later, the Arab content seemed to vanish, except perhaps for a certain quality in Tanzanian vocal tone, a gentle but not sloppy sadness. The Tanzanian bands continued to evolve under the influence of Congo music—any rhythm fashionable in Kinshasa would be fashionable in Dar es Salaam a couple of months later—yet with unquantifiable differences that make a Tanzanian record instantly distinguishable from a Congolese. Even the Tanzanian guitar styles, though it is impossible to analyze how they differ from Congolese, are unmistakable. Certain groups, such as the Western Jazz, experimented with such things as trumpet solos, but this was rare. The most obvious variant, the use of Swahili, is the least important, and besides, the Congo groups out of Kisangani use Swahili also, though they are not the most-recorded bands.

Kenya's pop music is most noteworthy for its charm and its

large degree of non-Kenyan components, despite which it contrives to sound entirely underivative. There were, until about 1966, two fundamental Kenyan beats. One, vaguely Latin, was introduced via the Congo but was given idiosyncrasy by the Kenyan two-voice, two-guitar formula and by the use of a form consisting of three verses, each of a couplet repeated, and then the whole thing repeated. The other beat, the so-called African twist, was a version of the South African kwela, which a European producer who had worked in South Africa introduced to certain bands in Kenya at the time of the twist craze. It caught on despite its origin, and it returns from time to time in various guises. The Kenyan style is song-oriented, rhythmically simple, and very jaunty. Since around 1966, the hipper bands have all gone Congo. At the same time, the old "dry" guitar style is still popular, though scorned in Nairobi, and is in fact perhaps the least derivative type of Kenyan music. Though some of its rhythms appear to stem from very early Congo discs, there are also precedents for the peculiar phrasing and instrumental interplay of the guitars in Luya and Luo traditional string techniques.

A noteworthy feature of pop songs (usually sung in the intertribal language, Swahili) is the insight their lyrics give into the life of ordinary Kenyans. Though the general subject-range is much the same as that of all modern African pop, the Kenyan songs perhaps reflect the thought and concerns of their public more plainly because they are mostly "listening songs" rather than lyrics to accompany dancing. They cover most of the broad categories of human interest, including politics of a fairly simple order—usually either praise songs for political leaders or a form of abstract praise song for politically popular themes, like (at one time) East African Federation or (at the time of independence) *uhuru* (freedom). These songs tend to optimism and are less doctrine-exposition than sloganizing. They are not, however, government-inspired.

Education, especially the effects of not having it, is the subject for a significant number of songs. Some exhort poverty-stricken parents to resist the temptation to take their children out of school. Others offer rueful comment: A man remarks that education is fine if you have it but makes life hard if you don't; in the old days you could at least join the police, but now even *they* have to be able to read and write.

Another "social problem" category covered by Kenya pop songs is unemployment, which bulks large among the preoccupations of any African nation. One song puts the problem subtly: The singer has been accosted by a beggar who claims to be just out of jail but who, it turns out, is simply out of work. The point is that joblessness is so common as to raise less sympathy than being an ex-con.

A large number of lyrics deal with more private social ills—or a little less public, anyway. One song reprimands car thieves (Nairobi singers rather like rebuking their erring brethren), another is about old men who get drunk, and a third concerns swearing off liquor. Several songs reflect local stresses on the marital front, such as the bride-price (lack of) or "Nairobi marriages," semipermanent liaisons between working-class towns-women and men who may have wives in the country.

One amiable category of records simply exploits local color and local identification. For example, a song that is largely a list of low-income housing projects in the order in which they were built has this as a chorus: "Then we began to move again, belongings on our backs." One song addresses a bus conductor: "Conductor, give me a ticket, so I can go to Jericho [a neighborhood of Nairobi] to see my baby." Another, by a man from the Taita district, is a piece of pure tourist-bureau puffery, but to a charming tune.

Money trouble in lyrics takes second place only to man trouble and woman trouble. There are songs that warn women about wicked men, who typically "wear a suit" (that is, put on airs) but "don't even have a bed at their place" (that is, are broke), and even more songs that lament the ways of women. My favorite of these, both for its content and its music, is "Kerena," which takes a fatherly tone to a girl who is always sick when it is her turn to go to the fields for food, but never when there is a dance on hand. Otherwise, most of the woman trouble is pretty standard, though Nairobi songs, like the blues, have a way of slipping in convincing little local details.

If both Kenya and Tanzania have strongly derivative elements in their music, Uganda has a pop style that lies entirely in a set of vocal-line characteristics, including melodies modified by Luganda speech-patterns and a cool vocal tone stemming, I think, from widespread mission-school education. This singing is backed by one or two foreign styles, Congolese or Kenyan, and the reasons for this reflect economic realities in the African music business, as well as a dash of past politics. Partly owing to the Congolese political crises of the early 1960's, Uganda was full of Congolese musicians looking for peace and quiet and a job. As a result, the Congo band style swamped Kampala's night clubs early and thoroughly. On the other hand, the recording industry was in Nairobi. The Ugandan singer therefore found himself backed by a Congo sound in club dates, but when he made a record he had to go to Nairobi to do it, and Nairobi record companies were not about to pay session men's fares when they had their own resident groups.

So far, all the regions I have been discussing have been tied together in one way or another. South Africa is something else again. South African traditional music is quite dissimilar in many respects from that of the areas considered so far. Most important, from the point of view of the evolution of South African modern pop music, its rhythmic approach is different. Instead of instrumental polyrhythms, with the vocal line simply supplying another rhythmic layer, South African music, which is short on instruments, partly because the South African ecology is on the whole short on materials out of which to make them, tends toward a pattern of complex sung rhythms set off against a steady beat, whether from handclaps, drum, or rattle. (This is, of course, a tendency, not a universal rule.) The effect of this on South African pop music is twofold: First, it has supplied a local element very different from those of other African pop forms; and second, Afro-Cuban music has meant relatively little to South Africans, and certainly very little to the development of their pop music. Jazz, on the other hand, has meant a good deal.

Jazz has become a part of South Africa's modern urban music because it blends in a number of ways with certain inclinations in the indigenous traditional music. The kwela beat of the mid-1950's was rather like a solid, Count Basie–type, four-four rhythm, but not quite. Kwela had a shuffle to it, caused by a light, lifting beat between the main beats—an eight-to-the-bar effect, but quite distinct from the barrelhouse eight-to-the-bar. It owed its existence to the fact that many traditional rhythms also had a pattern of firm beats with light, lifting beats in between. Again, many Zulu women often sing with a less sharp voice quality than is common to most of the rest of Africa, especially in the more private forms of music.

A big increase in the foreign records available to black South Africans, either to buy or to hear on the radio, occurred in the late 1930's and early 1940's, when big-band sounds with a steady, driving beat and the singing of Ella Fitzgerald and her imitators were the best-selling black American music. The mark of Ella Fitzgerald cannot be doubted if you listen to a very early recording, made in South Africa, of Miriam Makeba singing "Rocking in Rhythm" or, reissued on the same album, a singer called Toko Tomo singing "Zulu Boy Kwela." Many of the turns of the highly distinctive group-singing style of "township jazz" of the 1950's were vocalizations of U.S. big-band arrangers' tricks.

In the mid-1950's the Americanization of South African pop music was such that some of the penny-whistle kwela tunes of the time used twelve-bar blues patterns, and some singers were backed not by the kwela beat, with its lilting shuffle, but by a straight four-four beat. This gives the game away, showing the importance of an apparently small traditional element, for while the kwela beat was incredibly lilting and swinging, the examples of straight jazz rhythms plodded.

But the idea that the South African township jazz is simply an imitation of American jazz would be just as false as the notion that Congo pop is merely pseudo-Cuban. The basic instruments of this style, like all the others, are human voice and guitar. The singing, when it is not solo, is almost always call-and-response, a root Africanism in this area as everywhere else. But more significant, the very characteristic relationship of leader and chorus —with its interweaving of voices in the choral part and more overlapping of solo and group than is common in other parts of Africa—is not a foreign feature. It is a version, "urbanized" and probably generalized slightly, of a choral singing style common to most of the big South African ethnic groups, though it varies a good deal in detail from one to another. It happens that some techniques of big-band jazz, with the soloist riding a pattern of riffs, fuse with this South African vocal pattern. All this means that there are some components that resemble each other in jazz and South African music, seen in very general terms. It does not, however, mean that there was a direct link in the past between the two, as there was between Cuban music and West African and Congo-Angolan styles.

The jazz–South African pop connections had some ongoing results, including a greater emphasis on instrumental music (despite the fundamental guitar-voice complex). The instrumental sector, naturally enough, tended to show slightly stronger jazz characteristics than the vocal, as there was inordinately little South African traditional instrumental technique to carry over. There are striking similarities of phrasing between some traditional South African flute-playing and the penny-whistle mode of the mid-1950's, but there is a good deal of reinterpreted jazz in the successive South African instrumental fashions, especially at the beginning of any one of them. And fashions there were, the vogue for penny whistle being just one of them. Others included mouth organ, accordion (apparently an Afrikaner influence), and more recently sax. The fairly new sax sound, generically called "sax-jive," is a pop phenomenon not to be confused with the use of saxes for backing or section work by the bigger and more "sophisticated" groups, or their use by the South Africans (of whom there were quite a few) who played "pure jazz." The jazz influence on "township jazz" is slight. It is typical that a record called "Charlie the Bird" had no detectable trace of the Parker touch.

The successive pop styles went beyond mere fashions in instruments to reflect more fundamental crazes in dance rhythms. Kwela and phatha-phatha are two that, it so happens, have been heard of outside South Africa. But there were, and are, plenty of others, two of the most recent being monkey-jive and 'smodern. All these rhythms, of course, differed from each other noticeably or there would not have been much point in them, but the overall stylistic continuity of South African popular music overrides the variations. Obvious Africanisms abound even in the instrumental pop, such as versions of call-and-response, a proneness to extreme repetition (deliberate and functional, as we have seen), and the direction of all musical endeavor toward polyrhythmic rather than melodic ends.

In all the main areas we have been examining, the concept of "Westernized" pop music is a vague phrase covering a more significant reality: The root of all African pop styles is a blend of reinterpreted traditional—or at least local—elements with any foreign ingredients that may enhance them (besides, of course, impressing people as desirably "sophisticated").

In practice, these foreign elements are almost all Afro-American—even many of the apparently non-Afro-American influences have themselves been influenced by black music. Therefore, modern African pop music is a good deal more than a simply "Westernized"—hence presumably neocolonialist—music would be. In fact, it contains a high degree of Africanism, direct and indirect, and completes a very satisfactory black-music circle binding together the Old World and the New.

SELECTED
BIBLIOGRAPHY

(In all categories, see also accompanying notes to Folkways and Library of Congress records listed in Discography.)

GENERAL

NETTL, BRUNO. *Folk and Traditional Music of the Western Continents.* Englewood Cliffs, N.J.: Prentice-Hall, 1965.

AFRICAN

BASCOM, W. R., and M. J. HERSKOVITS, eds. *Continuity and Change in African Cultures.* Chicago: University of Chicago Press, 1959.

BEATTIE, JOHN, and JOHN MIDDLETON, eds. *Spirit Mediumship and Society in Africa.* New York: Africana, 1969.

BEBEY, FRANCIS. *Musique de l'Afrique.* Paris: Horizons de France, 1969.

CARRINGTON, J. F. *Talking Drums of Africa.* Westport, Conn.: Negro Universities Press, 1969.

CHILIVUMBO, ALIFEYO. "Malawi's Lively Art Form," *Africa Report,* October, 1971.

Colloquium on Negro Art. Présence Africaine, 1968.

Drum magazine, 1964–70, *passim.*

EDET, E. M. "Music of Nigeria," *African Music,* Vol. 3, No. 3, 1964.

EUBA, AKIN. "Music Adapts to a Changed World," *Africa Report,* November, 1970.

JONES, A. M. *Studies in African Music.* London and New York: Oxford University Press, 1961.

———. Article on Indonesia/Africa in *African Music,* Vol. 2 (1964), No. 3 (and rebuttal by Jeffreys, *African Music,* Vol. 2, No. 4.)

KAZADI, PIERRE. "Congo Music: Africa's Favorite Beat," *Africa Report,* April, 1971.

MENSAH, ATTA ANNAN. "Music Education in Modern Ghana," *East African Journal,* 1971.

MERRIAM, ALAN P. *African Music on LP: An Annotated Discography.* Evanston, Ill.: Northwestern University Press, 1970.

————. "Music" columns in *Africa Report*, 1962–69.

NIKIPROWETZKY, TOLIA, ed. *La Musique dans la Vie*. Vol. 1, OCORA, 1967; Vol. 2, ORTF, 1969.

NKETIA, J. H. KWABENA. "Modern Trends in Ghana Music," *African Music*, Vol. 1 (1957), No. 4.

————. *Our Drums and Drummers*. Accra: Ghana Publishing House, 1968.

Papers in African Studies, 3. Legon: Ghana Publishing Corporation, for Institute of African Studies.

ROBERTS, JOHN STORM. "Songs to Live By," *Africa Report*, August, 1965.

RYCROFT, DAVID. "The Guitar Improvisations of Mwenda Jean Bosco," parts I and II, *African Music*, Vol. 2 (1961), No. 4, and Vol. 3 (1962), No. 1.

SMITH, EDNA M. "Popular Music in West Africa," *African Music*, Vol. 3 (1962), No. 1.

TRACEY, HUGH. *Chopi Musicians*. London and New York: Oxford University Press, 1970.

VANSINA, JAN. Kingdoms of the Savanna. Madison: University of Wisconsin Press, 1968.

EUROPEAN AND ARABIC

ANGLÉS, HIGINI. "Hispanic Musical Culture from the 6th to the 14th Century," *Musical Quarterly*, 1940.

BOUALI, SID-AHMED. *Petite Introduction à la Musique Classique Algérienne*. Algiers: SNED, 1968.

CHASE, GILBERT. *The Music of Spain*. New York: Dover, 1959.

Encyclopédie de la Musique et Dictionnaire du Conservatoire, Vol. 4: *Music of Spain and Portugal*.

KNOSP, GASTON. *Encyclopédie de la Musique et Dictionnaire du Conservatoire*, Vol. 5: *Canary Isles*.

LAMBERTINI, MICHEL'ANGELO. *Encyclopédie de la Musique et Dictionnaire du Conservatoire*, Vol. 4: *Popular Music of Portugal*.

LLOYD, A. L. *Folk Song in England*. New York: International Publishers, 1967.

ROUARET, JULES. *Encyclopédie de la Musique et Dictionnaire du Conservatoire: Arab Music of the Maghreb*.

VAUGHAN WILLIAMS, RALPH, and A. L. LLOYD, eds. *The Penguin Book of English Folk Songs*. Baltimore: Penguin, 1959.

AFRO-AMERICAN GENERAL

BASTIDE, ROGER. *Les Amériques Noires*. Paris: Payot, 1967.

CURTIN, PHILIP D. *The Atlantic Slave Trade: A Census*. Madison: University of Wisconsin Press, 1970.

HAMMOND, PETER B. "West Africa and the Afro-Americans," in *The African Experience*, ed. by JOHN N. PADEN and EDWARD W. SOJA. Evanston, Ill.: Northwestern University Press, 1970.

HERSKOVITS, MELVILLE J. *The Myth of the Negro Past*. Boston: Beacon Press, 1941.

————. *The New World Negro*. Ed. by FRANCES S. HERSKOVITS. Bloomington: Indiana University Press, 1966.

HOWARD, JOSEPH H. *Drums in the Americas*. New York: Oak Publications, 1967.

WHITTEN, NORMAN E., JR., and JOHN F. SZWED, eds. *Afro-American Anthropology*. New York: The Free Press, 1970.

SOUTH AMERICA

ALVARENGA, ONEYDA. *Música Popular Brasileña*. Mexico City: Fondo de Cultura Económica, 1947.

Cancionero Noble de Colombia record liner notes (see Discography).

FREYRE, GILBERTO. *The Mansions and the Shanties: The Making of Modern Brazil*. New York: Knopf, 1963.

GARAY, NARCISCO. *Tradiciones y Cantares de Panama*. Panama City: n.p. 1930.

HAGUE, ELEANOR. *Latin American Music*. Fine Arts Press, 1934.

HARRIS, MARVIN. *Town and Country in Brazil*. New York: Norton, 1971 (reprint of 1956 ed.).

HERSKOVITS, MELVILLE J. *Surinam Folklore*. New York: Columbia University Press, 1936.

ORTIZ ODERIGO, NESTOR R. "Negro Rhythm in the Americas," *African Music*, Vol. 1 (1956), No. 3.

PERDOMO ESCOBAR, J. I. *Historia de la Música en Colombia*. Bogotá: Biblioteca Popular de Cultura Colombiana, 1945.

RAMON Y RIVERA, L. *Música Folklórica y Popular de Venezuela*. Caracas: Ministry of Education, 1963.

————. "Rhythm and Melodic Elements in Negro Music of Venezuela," in *J-IFMC*, 1962.

SLONIMSKY, NICHOLAS. *Music of Latin America*. New York: Crowell, 1945.

CARIBBEAN AND CENTRAL AMERICAN

BELTRÁN, GONZALO A. *Cuijla: Esbozo Etnográfico de un Pueblo Negro*. Mexico City: Fondo de Cultura Económica, 1958.

BOWLES, PAUL. "Calypso—Music of the Antilles," *Modern Music*, March–April, 1940.

BRATHWAITE, EDWARD. *Folk Culture of the Slaves in Jamaica*. Boston: New Beacon Books, 1970.

COURLANDER, HAROLD. *The Drum and the Hoe*. Berkeley and Los Angeles: University of California Press, 1939.

————. "Musical Instruments of Cuba," *Musical Quarterly*, April, 1942.

————. "Musical Instruments of Haiti," *Musical Quarterly*, July, 1941.

CROWLEY, DANIEL J. "Towards a Definition of 'Calypso,'" *Ethnomusicology*, Vol. 3 (1959), Nos. 2 and 3.

CRUZ, FRANCISCO LOPEZ. *La Música Folklórica en Puerto Rico*. Sharon, Conn.: Troutman Press, 1967.

DEMORIZI, EMILIO R. *Música y Baile en Santo Domingo*. Santo Domingo: Librería Hispaniola, 1971.

EDWARDS, PAUL, ed. *Equiano's Travels*. New York: Praeger, 1967 (reprint, first published in 1789).

ESPINET, CHARLES S., and HARRY PITTS. *Land of the Calypso*. Port of Spain: n.p., 1944.

HERNANDEZ, JULIO ALBERTO. *Música Tradicional Dominicana*. Santo Domingo: Julio D. Postigo, 1969.

JEKYLL, WALTER, ed. *Jamaican Song and Story*. New York: Dover, 1966.

KNIGHT, FRANKLIN W. *Slave Society in Cuba During the Nineteenth Century*. Madison: University of Wisconsin Press, 1970.

LABAT, R. P. *Voyage aux Îles de l'Amérique*. Paris: Lacharte, 1931 (reprint).

LEON, ARGILIERS. *Música Folklórica Cubana*. Havana: Biblioteca Nacional José Martí, 1964.

LIGON, RICHARD. *A True and Exact History of the Island of Barbadoes*. London, 1673; Facsimile edition, London: Frank Cass, 1970.

MÉTRAUX, ALFRED. *Haiti: Black Peasants and Their Religion*. London: Harrap, 1960.

MUÑOZ, MARIA LUISA. *La Música en Puerto Rico*. Sharon, Conn.: Troutman Press, 1966.

ORTIZ, F. *La Africanía de la Música Folklórica de Cuba*. Havana: Cardenas, n.d.

PEARSE, ANDREW. "Aspects of Change in Caribbean Folk Music," *J-IFMC*, 1955.

QUEVEDO, RAYMOND, ed. *Victory Calypsos*. Port of Spain: n.p., n.d.

ROBERTS, HELEN H. "Possible Survivals of African Song in Jamaica," *Musical Quarterly*, July, 1926.

SALDÍVAR, GABRIEL. *Historia de la Música en México*. Mexico City: SEP, 1934.

SEABROOK, W. B. *The Magic Island*. New York: Harcourt, Brace, 1929.

SERRA, OTTO MAYER. *Panorama de la Música Mexicana*. Mexico City: Colegio de México, 1941.

THOMSON, KELVIN. *Background of Trinidad's Carnival and Calypso*. Port of Spain: n.p., n.d.

VAN DAM, THEODORE. "Influence of the West African Songs of Derision in the New World," *African Music*, Vol. 1, No. 1.

UNITED STATES

ALLEN, W. F.; C. P. WARE; and L. M. GARRISON. *Slave Songs of the United States*. New York: Oak Publications, 1965.

BLESH, RUDI. *Shining Trumpets*. New York: Knopf, 1946.

BLESH, RUDI, and HARRIET JANIS. *They All Played Ragtime*. New York: Grove Press, 1970.

BORNEMANN, ERNEST. *A Critic Looks at Jazz.* London: Workers' Music Association, n.d.

BRADFORD, PERRY. *Born with the Blues.* New York: Oak Publications, 1965.

BROONZY, WILLIAM, as told to YANNICK BRUYNOGHE. *Big Bill Blues.* London: Cassell, 1955.

CHAPMAN, ABRAHAM, ed. *Steal Away: Stories of the Runaway Slaves.* New York: Praeger, 1971.

CHARTERS, SAMUEL. *The Bluesmen.* New York: Oak Publications, 1967.

————. *The Poetry of the Blues.* New York: Oak Publications, 1963.

CHASE, GILBERT. *America's Music from the Pilgrims to the Present.* New York: McGraw-Hill, 1966.

COURLANDER, HAROLD. *Negro Folk Music, U.S.A.* New York: Columbia University Press, 1963.

DUBOIS, W. E. B. *Souls of Black Folk.* Reprint of 1903 ed., New York: Johnson Reprints, 1969.

DUCAS, GEORGE, ed. *Great Documents in Black American History.* New York: Praeger, 1970.

FEATHER, LEONARD. *The Book of Jazz.* New York: Horizon Press, 1965.

FRAZIER, E. FRANKLIN. *The Negro Church in America.* Liverpool: Liverpool University Press, 1964.

GARLAND, PHYL. *The Sound of Soul.* New York: Regnery, 1969.

GILLETT, CHARLIE. *The Sound of the City.* New York: Outerbridge & Dienstfrey, 1970.

Gospel Music Jubilee magazine, *passim.*

HANDY, W. C. *Father of the Blues.* New York: Collier Paperbacks, 1970.

JOHNSON, J. WELDON, ed. *The Books of American Negro Spirituals.* New York: Viking Press, 1964.

JONES, LEROI. *Black Music.* New York: William Morrow, 1968.

————. *Blues People.* New York: William Morrow, 1963.

JONES, MAX, and JOHN CHILTON. *Louis: The Louis Armstrong Story, 1900–1971.* Boston and Toronto: Little, Brown, 1971.

KEIL, CHARLES. *Urban Blues.* Chicago: University of Chicago Press, 1966.

KIRKEBY, ED. *Ain't Misbehavin': The Story of Fats Waller.* London: Peter Davies, 1966.

KMEN, HENRY A. *Music in New Orleans: The Formative Years, 1791–1841.* Baton Rouge: Louisiana State University Press, 1966.

KOFSKY, FRANK. "Ornette Coleman: Jazz Musician," *Jazz and Pop,* November, 1970.

KREHBIEL, HENRY EDWARD. *Afro-American Folksongs.* New York: Ungar, 1962.

LINCOLN, C. ERIC, and MILTON MELTZER. *A Pictorial History of the Negro in America.* 3d ed. New York: Crown, 1968.

LOMAX, ALAN. *Folk Song Style and Culture*. Washington, D.C.: American Association for the Advancement of Science, n.d.

————. *Mister Jelly Roll*. New York: Duell, 1950.

LOMAX, JOHN A. *Adventures of a Ballad Hunter*. New York: Macmillan, 1947.

McCARTHY, ALBERT, et al. *Jazz on Record: The First Fifty Years, 1917 to 1967*. New York: Oak Publications, 1969.

MALONE, BILL. *Country Music U.S.A.* Austin: University of Texas Press, 1968.

MORGAN, ALUN, and RAYMOND HORRICKS. *Modern Jazz*. London: Gollancz, 1956.

MURRAY, ALBERT. *The Omni-Americans*. New York: Outerbridge & Dienstfrey, 1969.

ODUM, HOWARD W., and GUY B. JOHNSON. *The Negro and His Songs*. New York: New American Library, 1969.

OLIVER, PAUL. *The Blues Tradition*. New York: Oak Publications, 1970.

————. *Savannah Syncopators: African Retentions in the Blues*. New York: Stein & Day, 1970.

————. *The Story of the Blues*. Philadelphia: Chilton, 1969.

PARRISH, LYDIA. *Slave Songs of the Georgia Sea Islands*. New York: Creative Age, 1942.

ROSENBERG, BRUCE A. *The Art of the American Folk Preacher*. London and New York: Oxford University Press, 1970.

RUSSELL, ROSS. *Jazz Style in Kansas City and the South-West*. Berkeley and Los Angeles: University of California Press, 1971.

RUSSELL, TONY. *Blacks Whites and Blues*. New York: Stein & Day, 1970.

SALAZAR, MAX. "The History of the Up-Tempo Latin American Music in New York City" (unpublished study).

SARGEANT, WINTHROP. *Jazz: Hot and Hybrid*. New York: Dutton, 1946.

SCHULLER, GUNTHER. *Early Jazz*. New York: Oxford University Press, 1968.

SHAPIRO, NAT, and NAT HENTOFF, eds. *Hear Me Talkin' to Ya*. New York: Rinehart, 1955.

SPELLMAN, A. B. *Four Lives in the Bebop Business*. New York: Pantheon, 1966.

STEARNS, MARSHALL, W. *The Story of Jazz*. London and New York: Oxford University Press, 1970.

ULANOV, BARRY. *A History of Jazz in America*. New York: Da Capo Press, 1971.

WILLIAMS, MARTIN T., ed. *The Art of Jazz*. London and New York: Oxford University Press, 1959.

WORK, JOHN W. *American Negro Songs and Spirituals*. New York: Bonanza Books, 1940.

SELECTED
DISCOGRAPHY

EUROPEAN

Britain

Folk Song Today, Peter Kennedy, HMV DLP 1143 (Eng.)
Row Bullies Row and *The Blackball Line,* A. L. Lloyd, Ewan Mac-
    Coll, Topic T7 and T8 (Eng.)
A Song for Every Season, the Copper Family, Leader LEA 4046–9
    (Eng.)

Portugal

Anthology of Portuguese Music, Ethnic Folkways FE 4538 A/B
Sempre que Lisboa Canta, Columbia 33CS 7 (Eng.)
Fados from Coimbra, Philips 631 206 PL

Spain

Antología del Folclor Musical de España, Hispavox 10–107 to 110
    (Sp.)
La Niña de los Peines, Everest FS 256

AFRICAN TRADITIONAL

The outstanding single collection is Hugh Tracey's immense *Sound of
Africa* series. I have listed only a handful of its records (under their
prefix, AMA), and my reference is to tracks or styles I have mentioned
in this book. Details of the others can be had by writing to:

> The Librarian
> International Library of African Music
> P.O. Box 138
> Roodepoort
> Transvaal, South Africa

Regional

Africa South of the Sahara, Folkways FE 4503
Music of Equatorial Africa, Folkways FE 4402

Musique d'Afrique du Nord: Maroc, Algérie, Tunisie, Vogue Contre-point MC 20.016 (Fr.)
Musique d'Afrique Occidentale, Contrepoint MC 20.045 (Fr.)

By Countries

Algérie, Philips 844 925 BY (Fr.)
Danses et Chants Bamoun: Musique de la République Fédérale du Cameroun, Ocora SCR 3 (Fr.)
Musiques du Cameroun, Ocora OCR 25 (Fr.)
Nord Cameroun: Musique Fali, Ocora (no number) (Fr.)
Musique Centrafricaine, Ocora OCR 43 (Fr.)
Anthologie de la Musique du Tchad, Ocora OCR 36–38 (Fr.)
Congolese xylophone-playing on AMA 035
Musique Kongo, Ocora OCR 35 (Fr.)
Music of the Princes of Dahomey, Counterpoint Esoteric 537
Musiques Dahoméennes, Ocora OCR 17 (Fr.)
Ogun: God of Iron (mainly Yoruba liturgical music from Dahomey), Vogue Contrepoint MC 20 159 (Fr.)
Musiques du Gabon, Ocora OCR 41 (Fr.)
Ewe Music of Ghana, Asch AHM 4222
Musique Baoulé Kodè, Ocora OCR 34 (Fr.)
Folk Music of Liberia, Folkways FE 4465
Les Dogon (Mali), Ocora OCR 33 (Fr.)
Maroc, Philips 844 926 BY (Fr.)
Musique Andalouse (Morocco), Koutoubiaphone KTP 33–003 (Mor.)
Musique Maure: République Islamique de Mauritanie, Ocora OCR 28 (Fr.)
Niger: La Musique des Griots, Ocora OCR 20 (Fr.)
Nomades du Niger: Musique des Touareg et des Bororo, Ocora OCR 29 (Fr.)
Drums of the Yoruba of Nigeria, Ethnic Folkways FE 4441
Unesco Collection: *An Anthology of African Music 6, Nigeria: Hausa Music I,* Bärenreiter-Musicaphon BM 30 L 2306
Music of Africa, No. 19: Songs from the Roadside, No. 2: Rhodesia (rec. Hugh Tracey), Gallotone GALP 1113 (S.A.R.)
Wolof Music of Senegal and the Gambia, Folkways FE 4462
South Africa Traditional, AMA 010 (S.A.R.)
Musique Kabrè du Nord-Togo, Ocora OCR 16 (Fr.)
Tunisie, Philips 844 924 BY (Fr.)

SOUTH AMERICAN

General

Black Music of South America (rec. David Lewiston), Nonesuch H-72036
South America, Philips BL 7777

By Country

Black Orpheus, Epic LN 3672

Bola Sete: Bossa Nova, Fantasy 8349

1° Festival Nacional de Musica Popular Brasileira, Odeon MOFB 3549 (Brazil)

Folk Music of Brazil: Afro-Bahian Religious Songs (ed. M. J. Herskovits and F. S. Herskovits), Library of Congress AFS L13

Music from Bahia, Vogue Contrepoint 20.138 (Fr.)

Songs and Dances of Brazil (rec. Oneyda Alvarenga), Folkways FW 6953

Afro-Hispanic Music from Western Colombia and Ecuador (rec. Norman E. Whitten), Ethnic Folkways FE 4376

Cancionero Noble de Colombia, Universidad de los Andes LP 501–3 (Col.)

Musique de Guyane (rec. Francis Mazière), Boite à Musique LP 308 (M) (Fr.)

Cumbias et Tamboritos du Panama, Vogue CLVLX 373 (Fr.)

Folk Music of Venezuela (ed. J. Liscano and C. Seeger), Library of Congress AFS L15

CARIBBEAN

Bomba! (mainly Puerto Rican), Monitor MFS 355

Caribbean Dances (rec. Walter and Lisa Lekis), Folkways FW 6840

Caribbean Folk Music, Folkways FA 4533 (4 sides)

Caribbean Islands Music: Haiti, the Dominican Republic, Jamaica, Nevis. (rec. John Storm Roberts), Nonesuch H-72047

Bahamas

The Real Bahamas (rec. P. K. Siegel and J. Stecher), Nonesuch H-72013

Religious Songs and Drums in the Bahamas (rec. Marshall Stearns), Ethnic Folkways FE 4440

Various tracks from Library of Congress AAFS L5

Cuba

Celia Cruz with the Sonora Matancera, Seeco SLCP 9067; SLCP 9271

Cult Music of Cuba (rec. Harold Courlander), Ethnic Folkways FE 4410

Décimas Guajiras, Rumba LPR 55516

Música de Cuba Pre-Castro (rec. Sam Eskin), Cook 1083

Orquesta Aragón, Deskite 6947

Quarteto Machin, Legitimo LPL 001; Esquivel LP 001

Septeto Habanero, Originales LP 010; Amir-Oasi LP 514

Septeto Nacional, Ignacio Piñeiro, Patty LPP 127; Seeco SCLP 9278; Esquivel 004

Dominican Republic

A Bailar la Mangulina, Rafael Solano, Kubaney 422 (Dom.)

Guandulito y su Conjunto Tipico, Patty LPP 135

Dutch Antilles

ABC of the Antilles, Philips PHI 444

Haiti

Calypso—Méringues (rec. Harold Courlander), Folkways FW 6808
Drums of Haiti (rec. Harold Courlander), Ethnic Folkways FE 4403
Folk Music of Haiti (rec. Harold Courlander), Ethnic Folkways FE 4407
Haitian Piano, Fabre Duroseau, Folkways FW 6837
Méringue!, Nemours Jean-Baptiste, Cook 1186
Réminiscence, Nemours Jean-Baptiste, Ibo ILP 145
Songs and Dances of Haiti (rec. Harold Courlander), Ethnic Folkways FE 4432
Super Jazz des Jeunes, Ibo ILP 113

Honduras

The Black Caribs of Honduras, Ethnic Folkways FE 4435

Jamaica

Folk Music of Jamaica (rec. Edward Seaga), Ethnic Folkways FE 4453
From the Grass Roots of Jamaica (rec. Olive Lewin), Dynamic 3305 (Jam.)
Jamaican Cult Music (rec. George Eaton Simpson), Ethnic Folkways FE 4461
"Cherry Oh Baby," Eric Donaldson, Jaguar J 08 (45 rpm) (Jam.)
"Free the People," Bruce Ruffin, Beverley S. R. 157 (45 rpm) (Jam.)
"Jordon River," Maxie and Glen, Hit (no number; 45 rpm) (Jam.)
"No Man Is an Island," Derrick Harriott, Crystal 1076 (45 rpm) (Jam.)
"Satta Amasa Gana," The Abysinians, Clinch (no number; 45 rpm) (Jam.)
"Selah," The Ethiopians, Sir J. J. (no number; 45 rpm) (Jam.)

Martinique

Hommage à Stellio, Alphonso et son Orchestre, BAM EX 283 (E.P.) (Fr.)
Martinique (rec. Carter Harman), Cook 1021

Mexico

Folk Music of Mexico (rec. Henrietta Yurchenco), Library of Congress AAFS L19
The Real Mexico (rec. Henrietta Yurchenco), Nonesuch H-72009
Various tracks on Library of Congress AAFS L5

Puerto Rico

Canario y su Grupo (plenas), Ansonia ALP 1232
El Conjunto Tipico Ladi, Ladi Martinez, Alegre LPA 806
Cortijo y su Conjunto, Tropical TRLP 5098; TRLP 5107
Folk Music of Puerto Rico (ed. R. A. Waterman), Library of Congress

AFS L18
Ismael Santiago y sus Pleneros, Ansonia ALP 1444
Melodias de Ayer (danzas, valses), Alberto ALP 1002
Plenas Criollas, Lucy LP 104

Saint Lucia
Music of St. Lucia (B.W.I.) (rec. D. J. Crowley), Cook E 103

San Andres
Caribbean Rhythms, Folkways FW 8811

Trinidad
Bamboo-Tamboo, Bongo and the Belair, Cook 5017
Calypso Kings and Pink Gin, Cook 1185
Calypso—Méringues (rec. Harold Courlander), Folkways FW 6808
Cult Music of Trinidad (rec. George Eaton Simpson), Folkways FE 4478
Epilogue to the String Band Tradition, Grand Curucaye String Orchestra of Trinidad, Road Runner 5020
Jump Up Carnival, Cook 1072
Nancy Stories—West Indies (rec. Emory Cook), Cook E 105
The Sound of the Sun, Westland Steel Band, Nonesuch H-72016

UNITED STATES VOCAL

Calls, Work Songs, Hollers, etc.

Afro-American Spirituals, Work Songs, and Ballads (ed. Alan Lomax), Library of Congress AAFS L3
Negro Blues and Hollers (ed. Marshall W. Stearns), Library of Congress AFS L59
Negro Folklore from Texas State Prisons, Elektra EKS 7296
Negro Prison Camp Worksongs, Ethnic Folkways FE 4475
Negro Prison Songs (rec. Alan Lomax), Tradition TLP 1020
Negro Work Songs and Calls, Library of Congress AAFS L8
Play and Dance Songs and Tunes, Library of Congress AAFS L9

Religious: Collections

Many tracks in *Anthology of American Folk Music,* Vol. 2: *Social Music,* Folkways FA 2952
Christ Was Born on Christmas Morn, Historical HLP 34
An Introduction to Gospel Song, RBF Records RF 5
Negro Church Music (rec. Alan Lomax), Atlantic 1351
Negro Religious Songs and Services, Library of Congress AAFS L10
The Revealing Book of Life, Vol. 2, Song Bird SBLP 220
Sanctified Singers, Parts I and II, Blues Classics LP 17–18
Swinging Preachers and Their Congregations, Blues Classics 19
Ten Years of Black Country Religion, 1926–1936, Yazoo L 1022

Religious: Groups and Singers

Elder Charles D. Beck, *Urban Holiness Service*, Folkways FR 8901
The Caravans, Everest GS 61
James Cleveland and the Angelic Choir, Vol. 3, Savoy MG 14076
Dorothy Love Coates and the Gospel Harmonettes, Nashboro 7065
The Consolers, "May the Work I've Done Speak for Me," Nashboro 950 (45 rpm)
Rev. W. Leo Daniels, "Quit Talking to Yourself" (sermon), Peacock PLP 161
Rev. Gary Davis 1935–1949, Yazoo L 1023
Mahalia Jackson, *Inédits*, Vol. 1, Vogue CLVLXGI 427
Blind Willie Johnson, Folkways FG 3585
Rev. Cleophus Robinson, *A Better Place Somewhere*, Nashboro 7086
Rev. Cleophus Robinson and Sister Josephine James, "Sweet Home," Peacock 5 1854 (45 rpm)

Blues: Collections

Blues from the Deep South, Kent KST 9004
The Blues Roll On, Atlantic 1352
The Country Blues, Vols. 1 and 2, RBF Records RF 1 and RBF 9
I'm Wild about My Lovin' (1928–30), Historical HLP 32
Memphis Blues, Kent KST 9002
Mississippi Delta Blues, Vols. 1 and 2, Arhoolie 1041–2
Out Came the Blues, Ace of Hearts AH 72 (Eng.)
Rare Blues of the Twenties, No. 2, Historical ASC 2
Southern Prison Blues, Tradition 2066
Sweet Home Chicago, Delmark DS 618

Blues: Individuals

Juke Boy Bonner, Arhoolie F 1036
Leroy Carr, *Blues Before Sunrise*, Columbia CL 1799
The Legend of Sleepy John Estes, Delmark DS 603
John Lee Hooker, *Moanin' and Stompin' Blues*, King KS 1085
Lightnin' Hopkins, Tradition TLP 1035; Kent KST 9008; Arhoolie 2010
The Legend of Elmore James, Kent KST 9001
Blind Lemon Jefferson, Milestone MLP 2013; Biograph BLP 12000
Robert Johnson, *King of the Delta Blues Singers*, Columbia CL 1654
B. B. King, Kent KST 9011; ABC ABCS 713
Leadbelly's Early Recordings, Folkways 2024
Leadbelly, Library of Congress Recordings, Elektra EKL 301/2
Mance Lipscomb, Arhoolie F 1001; Reprise RS 6404
Mississippi Fred McDowell, "I Do Not Play No Rock 'n' Roll," Capitol ST 409
Memphis Minnie, Vols. 1 and 2, Blues Classics 1 and 13
Ma Rainey, *Blues the World Forgot*, Biograph BLP 12001
Bessie Smith, Columbia CL 855–8; G 30450
Sonny Terry and Brownie McGhee, *Where the Blues Begin*, Fontana

SRF 67599

Willard "Ramblin" Thomas and Blind Lemon Jefferson, *Early Jazz Classics*, EJC 1200 (Eng.)

T-Bone Walker, *Stormy Monday Blues*, Blues Way BLS 6008

Muddy Waters, *Sail On*, Chess 1539

Bukka White, *Parchman Farm*, Columbia C 30036

Big Joe Williams, *Tough Times*, Arhoolie F1002

Sonny Boy Williamson, Blues Classics 3

Rhythm and Blues, Rock, Soul, etc.

Bobby Bland, *Two Steps from the Blues*, Duke DLPS 74

James Brown, King 1022; King S 1047

Ray Charles, Showcase SSH 102 (2)

Earth Wind and Fire, Warner WS 1905

Aretha Franklin, *Spirit in the Dark*, Atlantic SD 8265

Wynonie Harris, *Good Rockin' Blues*, King KS 1086

History of Rhythm & Blues, Vols. 1–5, Atlantic SD 8161–64 and 8193

Junior Parker, *Honey-Drippin' Blues*, Mercury SRB 64004

Otis Redding, *Love Man*, ATCO SD 33 289

Martha Reeves and The Vandellas, *Natural Resources*, Gordy GS 952

Santana, Columbia CS 9781

Sara Vaughan, *Images*, Oriole MG 26005

Eddie Vinson, King KS 1087; Blues Time BTS 9007

Jimmy Witherspoon, *There's Good Rockin' Tonight*, Fontana 688 005 ZL

Zydeco

Les Blues du Bayou, Melodeon IVILP 7330

Clifton Chenier, *Louisiana Blues and Zydeco*, Arhoolie F 1024

UNITED STATES INSTRUMENTAL

Collections

Chicago South Side, Vol. 2, Historical HLP 30

Country Brass Bands, Folkways FA 2650

Jazz from New York, 1928–1932, Historical HLP–33

The Jug, Jook, and Washboard Bands, Blues Classics BC 2

Jugs, Washboards and Kazoos, RCA Victor LPV–540

New Orleans: The Music of the Streets, the Music of Mardi Gras, Folkways FA 2461

Parlor Piano 1917–27, Biograph BLP 1001Q

Ragtime: 1. The City; 2. The Country, RBF 17 and 18

The Sound of Chicago (3 records), Columbia C3L 32

The Sound of New Orleans (3 records), Columbia C3L 30

Territory Bands, Vols. I and II, Historical HLP 24 and 26

Groups and Musicians

Cannonball Adderley Quintet, *Accent on Africa,* Capitol ST 2987

The Louis Armstrong Story, Columbia CL 851–4

Count Basie in Kansas City, RCA Victor LPV 514

Sidney Bechet, RCA Victor LPV 510; Blue Note BST 81201–2

Big Black, *Elements of Now!,* Universal City 7308

Art Blakey, *Holiday for Skins,* Blue Note BST 84004

Art Blakey and the Afro-Drum Ensemble, *The African Beat,* Blue Note BLP 84097

Clarence "Gatemouth" Brown, "Just Before Dawn," Peacock 5 1692 (45 rpm)

Blind James Campbell and His Nashville Street Band, Arhoolie F 1015

Cannonball and Coltrane, Limelight LS 86009

Charlie Christian with Benny Goodman Sextet and Orchestra, Columbia CL 652

Ornette Coleman, *Friends and Neighbors,* Flying Dutchman FDS 123

Miles Davis, *Bitches Brew,* Columbia GP 26

Miles Davis, *Seven Steps to Heaven,* CBS BPG 62170

Johnny Dodds, RCA Victor LPV 558

Johnny Dodds and Tommy Ladnier 1923–28, Biograph 12024

Eric Dolphy, *Last Date,* Limelight LS 86013

Eureka Brass Band, Atlantic SD 1408; Folkways FA 2462

Ella Fitzgerald Sings the Duke Ellington Song Book, HMV CLP 1213–14

Erroll Garner, *Feeling Is Believing,* Mercury SR 61308

Stan Getz with Laurindo Almeida, Verve SVLP 9150

Dizzy Gillespie, RCA Victor LPV 530; Everest FS 237

Lionel Hampton, Showcase SSH 102 7

Herbie Hancock, *Mwandishi,* Warner WS 1898

Freddie Hubbard, *Backlash,* Atlantic SD 1477

Scott Joplin—1916, Biograph BLP 1006Q

Piano Rags by Scott Joplin (pl. by Joshua Rifkin), Nonesuch H–71248

Freddie Keppard and Tommy Ladnier, *New Orleans Horns,* Milestone MLP 2014

Roland Kirk, *I Talk with the Spirits,* Limelight LS 66008

Hugh Masekela, *Reconstruction,* Chisa CS 803

Charlie Mingus, Fantasy 86017; Limelight LS 86015

Thelonious Monk with John Coltrane, Jazzland JLP 46

Jelly Roll Morton (piano solos), Jazz Trip JT–1

Jelly Roll Morton, *I Thought I Heard Buddy Bolden Say,* RCA Victor LPV 559

Jelly Roll Morton and His Red Hot Peppers, RCA RD 27113

New Orleans Ragtime Orchestra, *Instrumental Rags,* Arhoolie 1058

King Oliver in New York, RCA Victor LPV 529

King Oliver's Creole Jazz Band, 1923, Riverside RLP 8805

Charlie Parker, Allegro ALL 798; Vogue LDE 016 (Eng.)

Don Redman—Master of the Big Band, RCA Victor LPV 520
Robert Shaw, *Texas Barrelhouse Piano*, Arhoolie F 1010
Jabbo Smith, Vols. 1 and 2, Melodeon MLP 7326–27
Sun Ra, *Nothing Is . . .*, ESP–DISK 1045
The Leon Thomas Album, Flying Dutchman FDS 132
Wali and the Afro-Caravan, *Home Lost and Found*, Solid State SS 18065
Ben Webster, *King of the Tenors*, Verve MGV 8020
Lester Young and Teddy Wilson Quartet, *Pres and Teddy*, Verve MG V 8205

Latin Jazz

Alegre All-Stars, Vol. 4: *Way Out*, Alegre SLPA 8440
Joe Bataan, *Poor Boy*, Fania SLP 371
Pete Bonet and Louie Ramirez, *Pete and Louie*, Fania SLP 390
Willie Colon, Fania LP 337; Fania SLP 00406
Joe Cuba Sextet, Tico LP 1146
New Swing Sextet, Cotique DB/003
Orquesta Flamboyán, *Different Directions*, Cotique C/CS 1052
Johnny Pacheco y su Charanga, Alegre LPA 801; Alegre SLPA 8050
Johnny Pacheco with Pete Rodriguez, *La Perfecta Combinación*, Fania SLP 380
Pacheco and El Conde, *Los Compadres*, Fania SLP 00400
Charlie Palmieri, *Latin Bugalu*, Atlantic SD 8166
On the Scene with Ricardo Ray, Fonseca SLP 1107
Ricardo Ray, Kent Gomez, and Willie Rodrigues, *Estamos en Algo*, Fonseca LP 1119
Roy Roman, *The Youthful Mind*, Cotique C/CS 1051
Sabu's Jazz Espagnole, Alegre LPA 802
Mongo Santamaria Orchestra, *Mongo's Greatest Hits*, Fantasy 8373
Monguito Santamaria, Fania SLP 382; Fania LP 386; Fania LP 338

Anglo-American

Anglo-American Ballads, Library of Congress AAFS L7
Anglo-American Shanties, Lyric Songs, Dance Tunes and Spirituals (ed. Alan Lomax), Library of Congress AAFS L2
Anglo-American Songs and Ballads, Library of Congress AAFS L12, L14, and L20
Anthology of American Folk Music, Vols. 1 (*Ballads*) and 2 (*Social Music*), Folkways FA 2951–52
Ballads and Breakdowns of the Golden Era, Columbia CS 9660
Cajun Songs from Louisiana, Ethnic Folkways FE 4438
Cowboy Songs, Ballads, and Cattle Calls from Texas, Library of Congress AAFS L28
Early Rural String Bands, RCA Victor LPV 552
Folksongs of the Louisiana Acadians, Arhoolie 5009
Instrumental Music of the Southern Appalachians, Tradition TLP 1007

Play and Dance Songs and Tunes, Library of Congress AAFS L9
Sacred Harp Singing, Library of Congress AAFS L11
Smoky Mountain Ballads, RCA Victor LPV 507
White Spirituals, Atlantic LP 1349

AFRICAN POP

Music of Africa: No. 5, *The Guitars of Africa* (rec. Hugh Tracey)
London LB 829
Du Sénégal au Congo, Pathé Marconi STX 224 (Fr.)

Congo

"Africa Mokili Mobimba," Kale-Roger, Rochereau, and l'O.K. Jazz,
ASL 7 1542 (45 rpm) (E.A.)
Cha Cha with l'O.K. Jazz, Vol. 2, New Sound NSL 1014 (E.A.)
Congo early "dry" guitar music on AMA 024, 025, 124 (S.A.R.)
Franco et l'O.K. Jazz à Paris, Pathé Marconi STX 229 (Fr.)
Kasongo (early Congo pops), Capital 10005
"Kiri Kiri Mabina ya Sika," Dr. Nico and l'Orchestre African Fiesta,
ASL 7 1841 (45 rpm) (E.A.)
"Merengue Fafa," Dr. Nico and l'Orchestre African Jazz, ASL 7 1647
(45 rpm) (E.A.)
Les Merveilles du Passé, No. 1, Franco and l'O.K. Jazz, African 360
010 (Fr.)

Ghana

"Akesesem," The Brigade Swingers, Philips PF 383284 (45 rpm)
(W.A.)
"Broadway Special," Broadway Dance Band, Philips PF 383293 (45
rpm) (W.A.)
"Ma Yeyie Ni," E.K.'s Band No. 1, Philips PF 383305 (45 rpm)
(W.A.)
"Obi Mfre No Name," Royal Brothers Band, Decca GWA 4164 (45
rpm) (W.A.)
"Wiase Amanehunu," Authentic Workers Brigade Band No. 1, Philips
PF 383283 (45 rpm) (W.A.)
"Wo Begyae Me," Ahamano's Guitar Band, Philips PF 383276 (45
rpm) (W.A.)

Kenya

The Ashantis, Vol. 2, Lamore LRM 502 (E.P.) (E.A.)
"Kondakta," Nashil and Peter, Equator EU 7 114 (45 rpm) (E.A.)
"Kula Ajae na Shari," Yaseen Mohamed, Mzuri HL 7-7 (45 rpm)
(E.A.)
"Nimeacha Ulevi Catherine," Isaya Mwinamo, Philips PK 7 9003 (45
rpm) (E.A.)

Top 1, Quality LTJ 204 (E.A.)
"Usimalize Mali," Williamu Osale, CMS 7 2007 (45 rpm) (E.A.)
"Western Shilo," Daudi Kabaka and George Agade, Equator 7 EU 195 (45 rpm) (E.A.)

Mozambique

"Dry" guitar styles on AMA 007, 008, 011 (S.A.R.)

Nigeria

"Ade Ori Mi," I. K. Dairo and His Blue Spots, Decca NWA 5309 (45 rpm) (W.A.)
"Duduke," Sir Victor Uwaifo and His Melody Maestroes, Philips PF 383315 (45 rpm) (W.A.)
Ebenezer Obey and His International Brothers in London, Decca WAPS 28 (W.A.)
"Ijo Palongo," Ligali Muikaba and His Group, Decca NWA 5271 (45 rpm) (W.A.)
"Look Look Look," Godwin Omobuwa and His Sound Makers, Decca NWA 5054 (45 rpm) (W.A.)

Sierra Leone

"Toomus Meremereh Nor Good," S. E. Rogers, Rogie R 14 (45 rpm) (S.L.)

South Africa

Malompo Jazz (avant-garde jazz), Gallotone GALP 1464 (S.A.R.)
Miriam Makeba, *Appel à l'Afrique,* Syliphone SLP22 (Guinea)
Something New from Africa, Decca LK 4292 (Eng.)
Spokes of Africa, Spokes Mashiyane, Gallotone GALP 1049 (S.A.R.)
Star Time, Vol. 2, Dark City Sisters and Flying Jazz Queens, HMV JCLP 69 (S.A.R.)

Tanzania

"Lipa Kodi ya Nyumba," Western Jazz Band, Philips PK 7 9006 (45 rpm) (E.A.)
"Mpenzi Zaina," Njohole Jazz Band, African Beat AB 7 5064 (45 rpm) (E.A.)
"Napenda Nipate Uhakika," Nuta Jazz, African Beat AB 7 5065 (45 rpm) (E.A.)
"Ngoma Iko Huku," Salim Abdulla and Cuban Marimba Band, Mzuri HL 7 28 (45 rpm) (E.A.)
"Nimeona Uwa," Kiko Kids Jazz, Mzuri HL 7 15 (45 rpm) (E.A.)

Uganda

"Ekkomera," Fred Masagazi, Equator 7 EU 243 (45 rpm) (E.A.)
"Gwenasobya," Frida Sonko, Equator EU 7 163 (45 rpm) (E.A.)

INDEX